Siren Song

Also by Quinn Fawcett

Against the Brotherhood
Death to Spies
Embassy Row
The Flying Scotsman
The Scottish Ploy

A Tom Doherty Associates Book FORGE® New York

Siren Song

QUINN FAWCETT

This is a work of fiction. All the characters and events portrayed in this novel are either fictitious or are used fictitiously.

SIREN SONG

This book is printed on acid-free paper.

A Forge Book
Published by Tom Doherty Associates, LLC
175 Fifth Avenue
New York, NY 10010

www.tor.com

Forge® is a registered trademark of Tom Doherty Associates, LLC.

ISBN: 0-312-86928-2

First Edition: July 2003

Printed in the United States of America

0 9 8 7 6 5 4 3 2 1

*To Messrs. Connery, Niven, Lazenby,
Moore, Dalton, and Brosnan*

Siren Song

Chapter 1

THE JAUNTY notes that Noël Coward was coaxing from the piano on the dais seemed appropriate to a more intimate soiree, Ian Fleming judged with some amusement. But the formality of the evening's gathering had decidedly declined, and most of the prominent guests had vacated the hall and were by now snugly home to their lavish city estates or suburban manors. Fleming eyed the large Roman numerals of the clock above the hall's arched entryway. It was growing late.

He had enjoyed himself tonight, this which was to be his last night in his homeland, at least until the winter was safely past. He was booked on a flight to Kingston at quarter of ten that morning. Jamaica would be a welcome change from the sharp January chill of London. Still more welcome would be his return to the private tropical Eden of his house on the island's coast.

This first week of January had seemed one successive string of galas, as the Christian world celebrated the dawning of the new year. Fleming couldn't recall what this evening's event had allegedly been in honor of; it certainly seemed merely a continuation of the social festivities that had been raging since New Year's Eve.

The world might be nearly nineteen and a half centuries old, but Fleming remained relatively young—nearing forty, agile, fit, handsome, mannerly, well-educated and charming. He appeared quite elegant in his tailored evening clothes. He betrayed virtually no signs of age, either outwardly or inwardly. He had found himself caught up in a few pleasant flirtations tonight with the party's female guests. He enjoyed this sort of harmless trifling. It would be some months before he saw England again, and it was nice to think that he would be remembered in his absence.

He lit a Players with his gold cigarette lighter and took a last sip from his gin-and-tonic. One more drink, he decided, and then he would take his leave. His luggage was already packed, and he had no worries beyond getting himself to the airport in time for his flight.

He had hoped for a private word or two with his friend Coward, but Noël had already drawn a sizable crowd around the piano and was plainly relishing the attention. Where Fleming was quietly debonair, Noël Coward was a showman. Fleming decided he would airmail his friend from Jamaica. It certainly wouldn't do to barge in on his performance to get in a few words of good-bye.

Fleming crossed the varnished mahogany squares of the wide floor toward one of the three full-service bars. The hundred or so guests that remained made small chattering clumps here and there. The bar Fleming approached had gathered its own group. He had to wait a moment to get the red-uniformed bartender's attention.

"Gin, please. A splash of tonic. No ice."

The drink was placed on a cork-topped coaster. Fleming set down his empty glass and picked up the fresh one, taking a final puff from his cigarette and snubbing it out in a nearby ashtray. As he turned from the bar-top to wander the floor once more, his elbow was jostled.

"Dreadfully sorry—" he began automatically, though it was he who had been bumped.

"Might I trouble you for a light? I seem to be out of fluid."

He was reaching reflexively for his lighter before he even took note of who had addressed him. When he did, he squelched the urge to stop and gawk, something which would not have been in keeping with his usual manner.

The object of his sudden attention was a woman he judged to be no older than thirty-three. Her hair was a vast cascade of shimmering red ringlets held in perfect place by a number of ornamental clips. Her features were startlingly narrow, though by no means gaunt. High angled cheekbones and a tapering chin formed the outline for a genuine vision of loveliness. She had fine rouged lips and limpid blue eyes beneath arching brows. The face might have appeared delicate, like a china doll's, were it not for the ruddiness of her tan and the sly self-possessed smile that curled the corners of her mouth.

She held a cigarette lighter of dull metal in one hand and now gave it a flick with her thumb. It sparked, but no flame followed. It was one of those lighters American GIs carried, Fleming noted distantly. Zippos, weren't they called?

Then he realized he had after all stopped unceremoniously in the act of lighting her cigarette and now hastened to do so. Her gloved fingers touched his knuckles as she dipped her head slightly to touch her cigarette tip to the flame. It was some dark filtered cigarette.

"Thank you so."

"Indeed," he said.

She wore a very becoming gown of printed silk and a decorative lace scarf. Careful not to ogle, Fleming nonetheless realized her figure was as striking as her face—generously youthful and apparently well-kept.

"Would you care for a cocktail?" he asked.

The defunct lighter disappeared into a tiny handbag with silver clasps.

"That would be lovely. But wine, I should think. Something red. Perhaps you might choose . . . ?" The sly smile brightened a few effective degrees.

Fleming employed a bit of insistent elbowing to reach the bar-top again. He quizzed the same bartender as to available stock, picking from the list of merlots a prewar French that seemed suitable. He delivered the glass to the young lady.

"You're most kind," she said, lifting the drink in a chipper salute.

"Chin-chin," replied Fleming.

Though she constructed her sentences in an English manner, the accent was American, and she was taking no pains to disguise the fact. Fleming correlated his observations—accent, her obvious grasp of English dialect, her suntanned complexion—and concluded that this woman was well-traveled. An ambassador's daughter perhaps? The wife of a career American military man?

"I am horrid and rude," she pronounced abruptly. Fleming blinked. "I have imposed upon a stranger to light my cigarette and fetch me a drink. Shame on me. My name is Nora Blair DeYoung. You must forgive me."

"Nothing to forgive," he returned suavely. She was far and away the most attractive woman he had met this evening. "I'm Ian Fleming. It's a pleasure to meet—"

"Ian Fleming?" One brow arched even higher. "Not the journalist?"

"Why, yes," he said, a bit surprised by her reaction and more than a little gratified. It was no sin for one to take pride in one's livelihood.

"Dear heavens, what a treat! I'm happy to say I've admired your work for some time."

"Thank you, Mrs. DeYoung."

"Miss, actually," she said offhandedly. "Never have found the time for a husband. But you"—returning eagerly to the previous topic—"you're the first person I've met at this tedious affair I can honestly say I know—or at least know *of.* I can't tell you what a relief that is."

"I'm pleased to be of service, then. I'm sorry you've found the evening disagreeable."

"Oh, only up to now. Really, I should like to hear of your work. That is, of course, if you don't have to dash. . . . Do you?" She smiled even brighter this time.

Fleming's gaze started to shift toward the clock again, then he caught himself and leveled his eyes with her limpid blue ones. In the elegant heels she wore she was only a hand shorter than he.

"Nothing urgent," he reassured her smoothly. "Perhaps you'd care to sit?"

"I would."

Her gloved hand wound over his elbow as he ushered her across the hall to an unoccupied lounge upholstered in rich velvet with lacquered arms. He felt a few curious stares following them and wondered if among them was whoever had escorted this young lady to this event. He waited while she sat, then settled himself onto the neighboring cushion.

A waiter bearing a tray with perfect poise glided up and offered Miss DeYoung a sampling of hors d'oeuvres. Dinner had been held some hours ago in the hotel's adjoining banquet hall, and Fleming had eaten well of the steamed mussels and game hen and broiled beef, even indulging in a slice of cheesecake topped with a hot rum sauce. He'd felt a prickling of his conscience, thinking that much of England was still suffering heavily from the shortages which were part of the war's legacy. He had also noted that the food, though undeniably tasty, lacked the exotic tangs of spices which he would soon be enjoying in Jamaica.

He saw with some surprise that Miss DeYoung had gobbled several of the morsels from the waiter's tray in rapid order. They appeared to be sautéed mushrooms stuffed with a thick blend of cheese and crab meat. Fleming declined when the tray was presented to him.

"Ah," she said with some relish. "Famished. That's much better."

Fleming's brow furrowed. "Did you find the dinner unappealing?"

"Missed it, I'm afraid. I only arrived a short while ago."

Which explained, thought Fleming, why he hadn't noticed her earlier, an oversight that up till now he'd been unable to fathom.

She sipped at her wine, and he took a swallow of his gin.

"Now, really, might I ask you about your work?" she pressed with a kind of irresistible merriment.

"I can't imagine that the life of a journalist would be of any real interest. It consists, I tell you truthfully, of mostly sitting around in chilly airports waiting for planes, making phone calls and quarreling with editors. If you think it's a romantic style of living, I'm terribly afraid I must disappoint you."

She gave a fine musical laugh. "Oh, Mr. Fleming, it's too late to disillusion me."

"You've met other journalists, I take it?"

"Certainly."

"Is one of my professional fellows perhaps your escort this evening?" he asked casually, casting among the guests strewn about the hall. Noël Coward was drawing in even more numbers as he regaled his audience with snippets from old and new theatrical productions, probably weaving in a few of his own wry spirited ditties.

Miss DeYoung laughed afresh. "Mr. Fleming, are you attempting to be subtle? Let me settle accounts and say that I've come unescorted."

Fleming felt a mild flush of embarrassment which he hoped didn't show above his collar.

"I'm terribly sorry to pry—"

"Nonsense. Don't think of it. Or—you can make it up to me by divulging. Give"—which was a decidedly American expression—"tell me about your work."

"Very well. But I've warned you in advance, Miss DeYoung. Journalism is not to be confused with anything exotic."

"And I say, Mr. Fleming, that I'm perfectly enlightened as to the day-to-day trivialities of the profession. In fact, I am *intimately* familiar with them. I too belong to the fourth estate." Her smile this time was droll but no less bright. "Perhaps you've even heard of me. I write under the name of Blake Young."

Chapter 2

IN FAIRLY short order Fleming found himself addressing the lovely young lady, at her insistence, as "Nora." He had also quickly dismissed any ungentlemanly thoughts that she was duping him. This person was indeed, amazingly, the noted journalist Blake Young—or the individual *behind* that evidently fictitious persona.

Fleming had read Blake Young's feature stories during and after the war. Young had a gripping prose style that realized in fine detail any event or locale. The features had appeared regularly in a number of high-profile newspapers and magazines, both in the States and abroad. Much of the journalism during the war years had, naturally, consisted of coverage of that awesome conflict. Some of the accounts had been frankly harrowing—reports of air raids and artillery attacks that lent the reader an awful sense of immediacy to the events.

Following the war Blake Young had started popping up in still more exotic and remote locations—Rhodesia, Chile, Bombay and once, Fleming recalled with some astonishment, Antarctica. These features remained as engrossing as Young's war correspondence, which was a feat unto itself. The stories had a way of transporting the reader across oceans and continents. Whenever Fleming had found himself visiting for the first time a place that Blake Young had written of, he was always startled by the feeling of déjà vu that overcame him. The accounts were just that evocative and precise.

Fleming had for many years respected and rather envied the great Blake Young and so was astounded to be sitting here conversing intimately with Nora Blair DeYoung, who was in fact "he." Young's rousing prose had always struck Fleming as quite virile and manly. The unexpected reversal of genders was still difficult to absorb.

Nora was quite insistent, however, about hearing of Fleming's own work. Despite being pleased by this attention, he took pains to point out that his career rather paled alongside her accomplishments.

"Oh, tish-tosh, Ian," she said, having also adopted the familiar address.

"Really, Nora, that any individual could raise journalism to the level you've managed, elevating it nearly to an art form, is quite exceptional enough. But to do so being a *woman*—" He thought belatedly that this compliment might be misconstrued as a slight and winced inwardly. He certainly had no desire to offend this remarkable lady.

She gave her now familiar musical laugh. "Truthfully I think being a woman gave me advantages—unfair ones at that. Oh, there were many things that were barred from me, to be sure. But in some cases being overlooked aided me immensely. A dainty female isn't expected, for instance, to bribe a tank commander to take her into the middle of a skirmish with the Nazis. There were also many times when gentlemen in the field, who'd not set eyes on a woman for months, found themselves incapable of refusing me any request. My press credentials weren't always taken seriously, but chivalry is a higher authority."

"Amazing," Fleming said sincerely.

"But I believe you're still being evasive, Ian. I do want to hear of your work."

"Very well."

They talked at some length about Fleming's career as a journalist, from his joining Reuters in the early 1930s. Nora seemed particularly interested in the *Times* assignment that had taken him to Moscow in '33 to report on the Metropolitan-Vickers trial. Despite his self-effacing minimizing of his career, he recalled this period of his life with fondness. He omitted much of his personal history that took in his years when he had tried his hand at being a stockbroker; instead he jumped ahead to when he had reentered the journalistic profession. He offered only those details that gave no hint of the life he had led in Whitehall. He hardly needed to remind himself that the National Securities Act forbade him to divulge such activities.

"Amazing," it was now Nora's turn to say.

Fleming shrugged. "If you insist. I would be a churl to disagree with a lady." A thought suddenly occurred, and he leaned toward her with an earnest expression. "I should like to make clear, Nora, that I have no intention of revealing your identity—or, I should say, that of Blake Young. If the world at large discovers that Blake Young is Nora Blair DeYoung, it shan't be from me. Rest assured."

"I never doubted your discretion." Her smile this time was quietly sincere. "We're just two professionals letting our hair down."

Returning her smile at the quaint expression, Fleming finally did raise his eyes to the clock above the hall's arched entrance. Before, the hour had been late; now it was *indeed* late.

"Time for you to dash, I see," Nora said with a mild tone of disappointment.

"I'm afraid so. I have a flight in the morning." Likely he would find himself sleeping on the plane.

"Off on an assignment?"

"No, actually. To Jamaica. I've a house there. It's where I spend my winters."

She nodded. "Yes. There's nothing quite like sitting out the Northern Hemisphere's chill in a tropical clime. I find I envy you."

Being envied by Blake Young, Fleming wondered. How extraordinary.

"I do hope you enjoy the rest of the party," he said. "What remains of it." Half the guests who had been here an hour ago were now gone. Noël Coward had even managed to slip away without Fleming noticing. He realized he'd been quite engaged with Nora.

"Oh, I think I'll simply wander back up to my room," she said.

"You're a guest of the hotel?"

"Indeed."

He wondered why, then, she hadn't arrived in time for the dinner.

Nora seemed to pluck the thought from his head. "A guest of the hotel's . . . not a guest of this affair. I'm afraid I crashed the gate. It's an old habit. Scandalous of me, isn't it? Worse, I suppose, admitting it to you."

Fleming couldn't help but chuckle. "You are an uncommon woman, Miss DeYoung," he said formally.

"And you are charming company, Mr. Fleming. I thank you for a delightful evening."

He stood, offering his hand. When she was on her feet, he bent, kissed her gloved fingers and said into her clear blue eyes, "My pleasure entirely."

Her final smile was radiant.

Turning to leave, he found himself unable to resist adding, "I do hope to see you again."

"I also."

Then Fleming did turn and cross the emptying hall. Once again he felt a few curious stares following. He wondered what the party's gossips would make of his prolonged tête-à-tête with Miss DeYoung. Nothing as outrageous as if the two of them were departing together, he judged. There had certainly seemed to be a covert invitation veiled in that statement she'd made about going back up to her room in the hotel. Though the thought, imagined or not, was frankly enchanting, practicality had to win out. Fleming did not want to miss his flight. He had made all the arrangements to have his house in Jamaica opened, and spoiling his plans at the last moment wasn't sensible.

Still, the thought dogged him as he walked down toward the lobby.

FLEMING HAD GOOD reason to think himself watched, though not exclusively by the gala's remaining guests.

As he was exiting the cavernous hall through the archway, one of the red-uniformed attendants set down his tray and ducked quickly through a service door. Around a bend in the low corridor beyond, he picked up the receiver of a wall-mounted phone and waited through a single ring before the other end was picked up.

"He's heading down to the lobby," the attendant said and immediately hung up. He smiled to himself in the service corridor's dimness. Keeping an eye on Fleming's movements at the party and placing this brief call hardly seemed worth the ten pounds he'd been paid earlier that afternoon. Still, the money was more than welcome.

He returned to the dwindling party, hiding the smile.

IN THE HOTEL'S broad lobby Fleming retrieved his worsted overcoat from the check room and ordered a taxi. The fatigue of the long evening was finally catching up with him. He stifled a yawn and stepped out through the thickly paned doors. The night was quite brisk, though not windy. The sky above was a nearly uniform grey, the dull melancholic slate of England's winters. There was no taste of snow in the air, for which he was grateful. He wanted nothing to interfere with his travel arrangements.

He lit a Players and waited at the kerb.

Headlights turned the corner a block from the hotel's main entrance, and Fleming squinted to see if it was his cab. Instead, a large dark sedan glided up to the sidewalk's edge and stopped, engine purring. The thing looked as heavy as an armored car, with long sides and a broad bonnet, upon which perched an elaborate chrome ornament.

Fleming stepped aside as the rear door opened, glancing in either direction along the otherwise vacant avenue. He only peripherally took note of the short middle-aged man in the dark suit who stepped out onto the sidewalk.

That was, until he heard himself addressed: "Mr. Fleming."

It wasn't a question. The man was staring at him with small colorless eyes and a hard expression. He held an accordion-file under one arm. Fleming returned his flat stare wordlessly.

"We require you to accompany us," the dark-suited man said stonily. Fleming now noticed the official stamp decorating the file's outer face. "Get in the car, Fleming."

Chapter 3

THE REAR compartment of the spacious sedan was partitioned from the front and lit by a tiny anemic overhead light. Beyond a slab of murky glass Fleming made out the chauffeur behind the wheel. The short man in the dark suit had ushered Fleming into the auto ahead of him and taken the adjacent seat on the back bench. Facing the seats was another bench of the same supple leather upholstery, upon which sat a man in a grey suit, features younger than the first man's and pasted with a rather cordial smile. He had a firm jaw that was smudged with a hint of burgeoning stubble. Threads of silver marked the temples of his mousy brown hair, which was neatly cut. His eyes were mild.

"Mr. Fleming, it's a pleasure to meet you," he said amiably, then casually lifted a hand to rap the glass partition twice. The sedan pulled away from the front of the West End hotel and onto the empty avenue.

Fleming thought of the many responses he might make to the overture and finally chose among the least tactful.

"We've not met yet," he said with false mildness.

The grey-suited man chortled quietly. "Indeed. My manners—where have they gone? My name is Davenport, Francis Davenport. I think you may already have divined who and what I work for. The man beside you is named Stahl. He's my aide."

"You'll forgive me if I don't accept your claims blindly," Fleming said dryly. It hadn't, after all, been so long ago that he'd been duped into believing he was dealing with an official representative of the British Secret Service; the truth, much to his chagrin, had turned out to be something quite different. That had been that whole foul business with Sir William Potter. "Your identifications, gentlemen," Fleming continued. "If you would."

Davenport produced his good-naturedly enough, but Stahl handed his over with marked hostility. Fleming studied the identifications thoroughly, though it seemed plain at first glance they were authentic. He returned them.

"Marvelous. Now that the pleasantries have been seen to, I trust you gentlemen are here to transport me to my home. I have an early flight."

"Which you will be aboard, no fear," said Davenport. "Perhaps you'd like a cocktail? We have gin, brandy, a passable Scotch."

"Thank you, no," Fleming said. "I never drink when I'm being kidnapped."

Davenport smiled easily. Alongside Fleming the short middle-aged man was tapping his thumb impatiently against the official government seal on his folder.

"But we're making our Mr. Stahl anxious, I see," said Davenport, unruffled by Fleming's comment. "Let's get to the business at hand, shall we?"

Fleming, annoyed by this strange turn, was unwilling yet to give any semblance of cooperation.

"I am a private citizen, Mr. Davenport. Unless you can furnish a reason for detaining me in my private affairs, I strongly suggest—"

"There are citizens, and then there are citizens of a different stripe, Mr. Fleming. Especially those who have, shall we say, so interesting a history as yours."

"I'm a journalist."

"And you once worked for DNI," Davenport countered. "That's a mark that never really fades. A distinguished mark, of course."

Fleming sighed. It was useless, he knew, to try to evade this situation. One way or the other he would have to hear this Davenport out; and the sooner done, the sooner home he would be. He thought peevishly of the scant hours of sleep he might manage to scratch out tonight before he would have to rise and make for the airport in the morning.

"Yes," Fleming said, somewhat grudgingly. "I once worked for the Department of Naval Intelligence. I retired. I'm no longer in the game. It was all a very nasty business, and I have no desire to reenter that community, in any capacity. Do I make myself clear?"

Davenport nodded. "Perfectly. Curious you should say so, though, since no one's made an invitation to you." He leaned toward a small varnished chest nestled beneath the seats, flipped open its door and extracted a glass and a bottle of Scotch, which Fleming judged to be only marginally passable. "If you don't mind, I'll drink without you. The night is a bit bracing." He poured two fingers, drank and refilled the glass.

Fleming waited silently through the delay.

"Your journalistic career, Mr. Fleming—do you enjoy it?" Davenport asked with measured congeniality, as if they were conversing relaxedly in some drawing room.

"I make my living at it," Fleming said neutrally. "A sufficient one."

Beside him Stahl gave a muted *hurrumph* of impatience. Fleming found himself furtively eyeing the door handle and lock on his other side, briefly and vaguely entertaining a fantasy of hurling himself out of the moving auto.

Davenport gave another chuckle, apparently noting his

glance. "You really do fancy you're being kidnapped, don't you, Mr. Fleming? I suppose I should assure you that we mean you no harm. In fact, we are at this moment ferrying you home, just as you wished. It does, however, leave us the opportunity to talk a bit. Is that so disagreeable?"

"Then what, pray tell, is it you wish to talk about?" Fleming asked, finally willing to broach the heart of this matter, the sooner to finish it. "My time with DNI or my current career as a journalist?"

"Both," said Davenport levelly. "Surprisingly there's a connection between the two. A beneficial one at that. You have a unique chance, Mr. Fleming, to serve your nation."

"I would've thought I'd served her well enough already."

"Indeed. Your record makes fine reading. I look forward one day to poring over your memoirs."

Fleming thought ruefully it would be some many decades before he could even begin to make a factual accounting of his activities for the British government, something he had little desire to do. Davenport hadn't made mention of "Churchill's Boys," speaking only of the DNI. Fleming was thankful. Churchill's Boys had been just that—handpicked agents who'd manned a postwar operation according to secret directives of the PM, ferreting out and dispatching former Nazis who, in Churchill's opinion, had gotten off far too lightly. The task had been a grim one . . . and perhaps the primary reason Fleming had subsequently retired from the spy game. It was good that Davenport didn't know every detail of his past.

"My memoirs would make for rather implausible fiction," he finally said.

"It's the combination of your record and your present situation," Davenport continued, "which single you out as peculiarly qualified to take on this appointment."

"I am no longer a member of the Secret Service, Mr. Davenport. You're in no position to think you can dole out any assignment to me."

"You're not being asked to rejoin the ranks." Davenport finished his second drink and poured a third. The Scotch jiggled in the glass as the sedan turned a corner. "Actually, what I am authorized to offer you would only benefit your journalistic pursuit."

Fleming frowned, perplexed. "How is that?"

For the first time since entering the auto, Stahl spoke, words clipped with irascibility: "We're offering you an exclusive story, Fleming. In the parlance of your profession, a *scoop*."

The sedan's engine purred on a moment uninterrupted, while Fleming frowned deeper, trying and failing to digest this bit of information.

"How is that?" he asked again.

"We'd like you to break a story," said Davenport. "It's a hot one. It'll grab headlines. Isn't that the sort of renown you newspapermen seek—to be first on the scene, as it were?"

"My name as a journalist is already credible." Fleming thought somewhat proudly of the interest Nora, aka Blake Young, had expressed in his career at the party.

"Now, Mr. Fleming, a satisfactory reputation is one thing." Davenport pinched a particle of black lint from the lapel of his grey suit. "But to make a splash, a big one—that's worth at least considering."

"Speaking in abstracts as you are, Mr. Davenport, it's worth a thought. However, I've heard no specifics."

Davenport's smile warmed, as though he had been waiting for Fleming to express some direct interest. Fleming had been his personal choice for the assignment. The many hours he'd spent studying this man's impressive dossier, reading it carefully between the lines so as to glean a sense of the person behind the deeds, were paying off.

Davenport tilted his chin toward Stahl, who immediately opened the accordion-file and began rummaging within.

"There is a man named Oscar Winterberg who we would very much like to expose publicly," he said, sipping contentedly at his third Scotch. "He's currently residing in the States. San Francisco, to be precise. He's making waves there and gaining a good amount of support, both from the public sector and the clandestine political structure there—namely, the labor unions. He's gathering influence by geometric bounds. He's a very effective leader and organizer. Quite intelligent. It's estimated that by now he has some direct leverage over the government of California itself."

"I take it his influence is negative," Fleming commented cautiously, leery of letting himself appear too interested.

"Not as the public sees it. Oscar Winterberg advocates workers' rights. Financial benefits. Compensation for laborers injured on their jobs. Safety standards. A crackdown on the use of child labor. The abolition of sweatshops. Really, his crusade is quite extensive—and impressive. When he appears at rallies, he has the power to whip his audiences into veritable froths. He speaks for the common man. The needy, the struggling, the disenfranchised. He has his finger squarely on the pulse of a particular breed of American—the persecuted laborer."

"Yet there's more than meets the eye, I'll wager," said Fleming, his fatigue momentarily retreating before his mounting curiosity. He knew full well Davenport was skillfully baiting the hook; but just because he, Fleming, was showing signs of interest, didn't by any stretch mean he would bite. "What has this Winterberg done that you gentlemen should be so concerned about his activities an ocean and a continent away?"

"Oscar Winterberg is not what he seems," Davenport pronounced with a kind of leering somberness. Fleming wondered if the man's rapid intake of Scotch was already affecting him.

"Who among us is?" asked Fleming, thinking of Nora Blair DeYoung's startling revelation.

"Hurrumph," Stahl repeated, at last extracting a sheaf of densely typeset paper from his folder. He pursed his lips quarrelsomely a moment, then tossed the blue sheets unceremoniously into Fleming's lap.

"There you'll find the *real* Oscar Winterberg," Davenport said. "And it is that man we wish the public to know about—to topple him before he causes irrevocable damage."

Chapter 4

DAVENPORT, OF course, absolutely refused to allow Fleming to take the dossier away with him. Fleming was to read it here, now, in the car, or not at all.

"I would be able to give this much better attention after a good rest."

"Mr. Fleming," Davenport chided pleasantly, "it would be reckless of me to let these papers out of my sight, much less out of the country. You are bound for Jamaica in the morning, are you not?"

Fleming immediately checked his automatic annoyance that his travel plans should be known by this man. Those plans, after all, were hardly secretive. He had made the conditions of his employment—that yearly he be allowed to spend these winter months in Jamaica—quite clear to Kemsley Newspapers. Any Secret Service agent worth a fig could have learned this with minimal effort.

Fleming warred with himself, the blue sheets still lying enticingly in his lap. This Oscar Winterberg certainly sounded intriguing enough, and his journalistic instincts and natural curiosity begged him to take a look. Yet his predisposition against reinvolving himself in any way with government work made him almost recoil from the pages. Giving in to any of these impulses, then, would not satisfy him. Logic would have to decide.

Plainly this was some sort of great opportunity. A scoop, as Stahl had pointed out, would do his career no harm. Revealing Oscar Winterberg to be whomever or whatever he truly was would boost his reputation, so Davenport was insistently hinting. Perhaps not to the levels of eminence Blake Young or Fleming's globe-hopping wordsmith brother Peter had achieved, but advancement of some measurable sort seemed to be in the offing. Fleming took his career as a journalist seriously. It was, after all, his present livelihood. That his previous work for the DNI had been more dramatic didn't matter; journalism was in its way a quite fulfilling profession. Categorically ignoring a chance to better himself made little sense. His reporting of the '33 Metropolitan-Vickers trial in Moscow had been his first real stepping-stone into the field.

Fleming, erasing all emotion from the equation, asked himself if being a pawn of the Secret Service really mattered in this instance. Was it truly significant where a lead came from if it led to headline-grabbing notoriety? Could he rightfully object to being put on the scent by this Davenport character?

Fleming calmly juggled these serious questions as the dark London streets slid by beyond the sedan's windows. One could almost feel the deprivation out there behind the stony house fronts, England's long-suffering citizenry hoarding their scraps of food and rationed goods. The war had changed this nation, perhaps irreversibly.

Stahl was now tapping the toe of his shoe on the floor. Davenport was eyeing Fleming patiently.

"If I were to take a look at these pages," Fleming said measuredly, "it must be understood that I am not committing myself to anything."

"As you've pointed out, we're hardly in a position to constrain you, you being a private citizen." Davenport put a droll spin on the words that made the statement sound like sly mockery.

Fleming returned him a cool gaze. His conditions met, he at last nodded.

Davenport rapped the partitioning glass once again, and the auto slid neatly to a kerb. The engine cut off, and London was quiet and cold around them.

"I believe I will take you up on that drink now," Fleming said.

"I thought you might." Davenport reached again to the chest beneath the seats.

"Gin. Neat."

Davenport set down his Scotch and poured Fleming a more generous glass than he wanted. Despite the inconvenience of this whole strange episode, he retained enough manners to say, "Thank you." Then, experiencing an odd sense of great moment, he lifted the first of the dozen or so sheets from his lap where Stahl had dumped them.

The file was worded in typically crisp terse official fashion. The rudimentary facts of Oscar Herbert Winterberg were first presented. Born 1917, Munich, the youngest of five sons, father and mother both employed by a ceramics manufactory. Humble childhood. Excellent marks in school; but young Oscar was evidently a disciplinary problem, finally being expelled at the age of fifteen for beating a fellow student. Suggestions of radical political leanings, specifically anti-Nazi. Left home at seventeen and did not resurface until 1937 in Nice, where he was organizing a small fanatical bloc of socialists. His movements during the war were sketchy, but several effective guerrilla-style raids on Nazi occupation forces in France were attributed to his group, which apparently dissolved or was annihilated sometime in 1944, shortly after D-day.

Meanwhile, Winterberg's estranged father and mother had both passed away, and three of his elder brothers were enlisted in the German army. The fourth sibling was arrested as a homosexual and interned at Mauthausen-Gusen, where he was eventually shot.

In the spring of 1945 Winterberg materialized in England, living under the false identity of Charlie Winters. He circulated socialist pamphlets that called for the end of parliamentary government. During the waning months of the war he learned that two more of his brothers had been killed, these in combat, leaving him only one other surviving family member, Carl Winterberg, who was a lieutenant in the Luftwaffe.

Fleming sipped at the gin, wincing slightly at the cheap acrid aftertaste. The Winterbergs were hardly the only family torn asunder by the war, he mused. Oscar's life seemed beset with misfortune but was hardly the stuff of Shakespearean tragedy. He read onward.

After the war Winterberg, still passing himself off as Charlie Winters, secured passage to Canada and sometime during 1946 entered the United States. He met and quickly married June Rogers, a widow residing in St. Paul, Minnesota, evidently to obtain legal citizenship. He reclaimed his birth name and relocated with his bride to San Francisco.

There followed a fairly detailed account of his rise in labor union politics. His organizational talents came sharply to bear, and he swiftly made himself an indispensable component of that machinery. It was strongly suggested, though not verified, that some of his tactics were of a criminal nature—e.g., using vandalism and coercion to bend business leaders' opinions about workers' rights. There was mention of a popular rumor among Winterberg's detractors (heads of business mostly) that he had been instrumental in the kidnapping of a plant owner's twelve year old son.

The boy's ransom had been the upgrading of the factory's safety standards. The story that the boy had been returned with his head shaved and his left middle finger missing was wholly undocumented and sounded more the stuff of modern campfire tales.

Fleming, having read more than half the file by now, lifted his eyes toward Davenport, his expression nonplussed. Oscar Winterberg's background might seem exotic by some standards, but Fleming couldn't see what threat he evidently constituted. It was certainly unclear why the British government should be taking any interest in this character.

"Read on, Mr. Fleming," Davenport said reassuringly. "It gets rather lurid."

Fleming turned more pages, and the real story of Oscar Winterberg unfolded.

Over the past four months British intelligence had intercepted two encrypted communiqués passing through England, evidently en route to Soviet agents operating in Europe. The code had as yet proven unbreakable, but the two couriers had both, under intense interrogation, divulged a name: Charles Winstead. Winstead was the name—or the code name—of their agent in the United States. The couriers relaying these communiqués through England were both British nationals with strong ties to the socialist community. Neither knew if this Charles Winstead was the originator of the encoded messages or merely a link in a long message chain. The communiqués were received via airmail from a post office box in San Francisco.

"I presume this Winstead is suspected of being your Oscar Winterberg," Fleming said, glancing up from the dossier once more.

Davenport nodded. "And the couriers, naturally, are contacts he made while circulating his seditious pamphlets in England."

"What sort of information is he suspected of smuggling out of the United States?"

"There's the rub. We don't know. The code is at least as diabolical as the Germans' Enigma."

"Which we broke," Fleming observed.

"Yes. And we'll break this one as well. Meantime, however, there is a semi-secure line of communication between subversive agents in the United States and Russia."

"It sounds like a problem for the Americans."

"It is their problem. We've alerted Hoover's lads to the situation. Yet they've declined to take any overt action. They feel the evidence is too thin. The leap of faith in identifying Charles Winstead as Oscar Winterberg is too great. Also they're unwilling to harass a figure of so popular public opinion. They've made efforts to keep Winterberg under observation, but security around him is extraordinarily tight, considering he's ostensibly merely a *private citizen*." Davenport strongly emphasized the phrase this time, making the mockery unmistakable.

Fleming scanned the remainder of the file. The closely set type and the lateness of the hour were making his eyes smart. Most of the last few pages were conjecture. There was no hard evidence that Winterberg, despite his history of socialist leanings, had ever been recruited by the Soviet intelligence apparatus.

A glossy was clipped to the final page. It was no grainy surveillance snapshot but more probably a blow-up of some official photograph, such as from a driver's license. Oscar Winterberg was ruggedly handsome, with deep penetrating eyes and thick dark hair. A wry smile seemed to tug at an edge of his firm mouth. He exuded confidence and a paradoxically coarse brand of savoir faire.

Fleming spent a moment neatly realigning the blue sheets, then handed them back to Stahl, who returned them to the accordion-file. Finally he set his gaze levelly on Davenport.

"What nugget of information has been omitted from that report?"

Davenport frowned. He swallowed the last finger of his third Scotch. "What makes you think that report is less than complete?"

"Enough, Mr. Davenport," Fleming said sharply. "If you've gone to the FBI with this kettle of supposition, it's no wonder they're taking so little action. There's an intelligence leak coming out of the United States. Very well. You've got two of the couriers, presumably still under lock and key. You've got hold of the coded messages. Your fixation on Oscar Winterberg as the ultimate culprit in this affair is a bit murkier. What makes even less sense to me, after having read that report, is what you expect me to do as a journalist. Expose him? Expose him as what? Charles Winstead might well be a variation on Winterberg's former alias of Charlie Winters. Yet that doesn't remotely necessitate that the three identities belong to the same man. For all you know you're being led a merry chase." Fleming shook his head. "I'm forced to agree with the Americans. The evidence is far too thin . . . unless you're withholding some damning piece of information."

The calm amiability with which Davenport had been treating him abruptly evaporated.

He's been bluffing me, Fleming thought with some satisfaction.

Stahl cleared his throat sharply, probably sending some signal to his boss. Davenport ignored his aide, returning Fleming's stare coolly. The standoff stretched for long seconds.

Fleming decided to break it. If he spoke first, it would save Davenport some face. He could see no sense in prolonging this night.

"Do you or do you not have some firmer evidence against Winterberg?" he asked.

Eventually Davenport shook his head. "No. Winterberg is our chief suspect. You've read our evidence, speculative though it might be. This matter is urgent, however, for different reasons." He fell into brooding silence, plainly unhappy with the turn this conversation had taken.

"They being?" Fleming prompted before another wordless impasse could occur.

Davenport gathered a deep breath. "One of the British couriers we captured, in November, is the nephew of Lord Hemmingford."

It was a name Fleming immediately recognized. Lord Dale Hemmingford was well placed in the upper echelons of British society. Fleming recalled he had met the man once briefly on some social occasion, an elderly but formidable white-maned figure. Hemmingford had interests in banking, oil and merchant vessels. He was moneyed, powerful, worldly.

"It's Lord Hemmingford, who predictably has a wide influence, who wants this resolved. He wants the source of the intelligence leak plugged. More than that, he wants the source neutralized. He seems to feel that if the root of the problem is torn out, the culpability of his nephew in the matter will be diminished. He fears a scandal."

Fleming sighed, a vague sense of disgust creeping through him.

"It's no small matter, Mr. Fleming," Davenport said reproachfully. "Lord Hemmingford's industries are vital to the British economy. The word from my superiors is that he is to be . . . indulged. At any rate, it's to the benefit of our—and the Americans'—intelligence community at large to break this corridor of subversive communication. Surely you can see that."

"What I see, Mr. Davenport," Fleming said coolly, "is that you are attempting to recruit me to do your dirty work. You want me to go to San Francisco and denounce Oscar Winterberg in the press. I don't imagine that you're feeling too scrupulous about how I would accomplish this. If I had to resort to yellow journalism, I doubt you'd bat an eye. Oscar Winterberg is to be brought down at any cost—whether he's guilty in this affair or not."

Fleming handed his empty gin glass back to Davenport.

"If that's all, gentlemen, I'd appreciate it if you'd finish transporting me home."

It was a good night for surveillance. At least, it must have been since twice tonight Fleming had been watched covertly. The second time, though, it wasn't the retired English spy who was the central target of curiosity. Instead, it was Francis Davenport, and it was the Scimitar who was interested in him.

Granted, "Scimitar" was a burdensome code name, but one accepted what one received. The Scimitar possessed a decidedly non-Slavic face—lean, soft-lipped, with no pronounced ridges, a downy blondish moustache riding above a mouth that rested naturally in a neutral sort of smile. He was of average build and only slightly above medium height. His command of English was exceptional, outstripping even his proficiency in French, Turkish and German. English somehow was a restful tongue, and its endless idioms seemed to come effortlessly to him, so unlike the others in the Russian language academy where he'd trained.

It had been chancy enough following Davenport to that West End hotel. There was too little traffic this late. The Scimitar had picked up the MI5 official a short distance from his Whitehall office, staying at least a block behind the entire way. When Davenport's dark sedan had pulled up to the hotel's entrance, the Scimitar had eased his similarly dark roadster to the kerb and extinguished its lights.

With a practiced hand he'd aimed his camera and waited to see if Davenport and his aide meant to disembark here or take on another passenger.

It turned out to be the latter, and the Scimitar had snapped three good shots of the long-legged man in the evening clothes through his sharpshooter's camera lens. The man had then, apparently reluctantly, entered the sedan, to be ferried away to some unknown destination.

Too risky to follow further. Davenport, so intelligence was certain, was heading the operation to trace the English couriers, who'd been captured smuggling communiqués into Russia, back to their original source in the United States. This was of serious interest to the Scimitar's superiors; and when those faceless men expressed interest in something, action *had* to be taken. And so it had fallen to him, he who had been almost enjoying this rather mild English winter, he who had blended seamlessly with this isle's inhabitants for over a month now. His vacation was now over. But he had been planted in this capitalist country to do just this sort of work, and he wouldn't shirk his duty.

Presently he was guiding his black auto—such a luxury a private car was!—back to his lodgings. The first order of business would be to develop tonight's film. Then he would determine the identity of the man who'd climbed into Francis Davenport's sedan. Perhaps this man was the beginning of a trail. And if he were told to follow that trail, he would. The Scimitar knew an order was an order.

Chapter 5

A MIGRAINE was coming over him. Shafts of pain knifed into Fleming's skull from the bridge of his nose, where a metal plate had been put after a sporting mishap in his youth.

The quadruple propellers of the Boeing B-314 seemed to be buzzing somewhere between his ears throughout the long crossing of the Atlantic. The Yankee Clipper's interior trappings were composed of wood and burnished brass, like a lounge that had been launched into the sky. He found himself sitting next to a jolly portly American man who naturally wanted to strike up a prolonged conversation. Was it an inbred trait of Americans that compelled them to make the acquaintance of their seatmates? To worsen matters, the man—Archibald Havens, his name—sold insurance for a living and apparently couldn't resist illustrating the wonders of his trade to Fleming.

Mercifully Fleming fell asleep during a long-winded cheerful exposition by "Archie," as he liked to be called; and when he woke sometime later, the American had changed seats.

He came in and out of consciousness in fits and starts, at one point waking long enough to accept a pillow and a bland cup of tea from the stewardess. The hot beverage, nonetheless, managed to soothe him somewhat. He felt exhausted. The escapades of the previous evening had taken their toll. The precious few hours of sleep he managed to get had left him in a daze when he'd had to rise to make for the airport this morning.

The layover in New York was brief, but Fleming had booked himself into a hotel nonetheless. He ate a meal of steak and gravy in the rather dreary hotel restaurant and retired to his room. As he lay in the bed, memories of Nora Blair DeYoung dribbled away into the photographed face of Oscar Winterberg. Fleming dreamt of Davenport insistently offering him glass after glass of cheap gin, while Stahl *hurrumphed* impatiently. It seemed only minutes after he'd closed his eyes that his wake up call jangled him out of sleep. Again he made for the airport in the thinly sunlit morning hours.

The second leg of his journey was as wretched as the first, this aboard a less crowded, southward bound twenty-seater. He was treated to the tireless crying of an infant from the rear of the plane, punctuated by its mother's increasingly desperate efforts to shush the creature. His headache had cruelly reasserted itself by the time they touched down briefly in Baltimore to refuel.

He had done the sensible thing in categorically rejecting Davenport. Under different circumstances Fleming would have followed up on the story. It certainly had elements of intrigue, some of them newsworthy. It was when he learned that Lord Dale Hemmingford was pulling strings to move this project forward that Fleming had decided to deal himself out. The ethics of the situation were unsound. Perhaps even more than that, the evidence against Oscar Winterberg simply didn't hold water. It was a flimsy bit of intelligence work that Davenport had tried to sell him, not at all the sort of thing Fleming would have given credit to during his own career in that community.

Logic, then, had made his decision for him after all, which pleased him. He was no longer young enough to act solely on intuition and caprice.

However, purely as a journalist, he felt somewhat needled that this intriguing story had been dangled before him in the first place. If it weren't for the strings attached to it, he would surely have leapt upon it. Being more or less forced to pass on it was irritating. He was in the news business, after all, and an exposé of Oscar Winterberg would have been something of a feather in his cap.

During the final hour or so of the flight, Fleming at last fell into deep untroubled sleep. When the comely stewardess gently nudged his shoulder to advise him to buckle up, he blinked awake to find his vicious headache had vanished. He rubbed at his nose and yawned, thinking for the first time that day of food. There had been no time for breakfast during his hurried morning.

Lush white clouds swelled beyond the aircraft's windows. Here and there through them Fleming caught glimpses of the sea—not the metallic grey iciness of the Atlantic which surrounded England, but the soft blues and greens of the Caribbean. These waters promised warmth and gently rolling tides. He could almost feel those waves breaking about his unshod feet as he strolled the white sands of his beach front.

He had dressed himself for his arrival on his beloved tropical island—white linen pants, a striped cotton shirt of blue pastel and a light jacket—but already the clothes felt lived in. He would change when he reached his house.

Jamaica spread itself below, a flourishing carpet of greenery and rock, virtually prehistoric in its abundance of organic sparkle, despite the visible signs of modern human habitation. Foam bordered the great island, where the festive pastels of the sea broke against its beaches.

The twin-engine put down at Kingston in as smooth a landing as one could wish for. The wheels kissed the pavement, and the craft settled and taxied for the terminal. Fleming's interlude with the customs officials passed as peacefully. In short order he was strolling out of the airfield's terminal into the bathing sunlight and humidity of Jamaica. The kinks of having slept so erratically on the plane seemed to melt from his muscles with every step.

He shaded his eyes against the late-afternoon light and focused immediately on the welcome sight of his 1935 Lagonda Rapier, parked at the kerb. The sports car's polished blue-green body gleamed like an enormous jewel.

Someone interposed himself between Fleming and the object of his adoration. He was another welcome sight: Isaiah Hines, Fleming's houseman. Isaiah had been hired after the unfortunate death of Cesar Holiday. Cesar's murder—for murder it had been—was one for which Fleming would always take at least his share of blame. Cesar had been in the wrong place at the wrong time, namely in Fleming's company when his house had come under sniper fire. It was impossible not to remember Cesar fondly. The man had been a superb cook and butler and, more so, a fine honest individual.

It had been difficult for Fleming to replace him, difficult in the sense that placing someone else in Cesar's post felt something like betrayal. But practicality had to carry the day. Fleming simply couldn't do without a minimal staff to maintain his house. Cesar Holiday certainly wouldn't expect him to live in discomfort as a misguided show of respect.

"Mistah Fleming, sah. Welcome. I trust your journey was pleasant."

Fleming's face broke into a broad grin. "Nothing of the sort, Isaiah. A genuinely miserable flight. Which makes arriving here all the sweeter."

Isaiah Hines was a tall figure of a man, perhaps half a decade Fleming's junior. His Negro skin was muted by some European ancestry, giving his flesh the appearance of heavily creamed coffee. His body, beneath a red short-sleeved shirt and tan trousers, was deceptively lean. Isaiah's muscles were hard and corded, and he seemed to carry not an iota of fat on him.

"I've collected the rest of your baggage, sah. May I take that one?"

Fleming slipped the small black bag he'd carried onto the plane off his shoulder. Isaiah put it in the Rapier's boot. Fleming found himself meditatively studying his surroundings, the easy flow of traffic around the airport, the clucking commotion of a passing van-load of chickens, the fluid melodic beats of a steel drum being played somewhere nearby. The tempo of the island itself seemed gently paced, so different from the urgency of London. He had chosen well when he'd selected Jamaica as his wintertime retreat.

"If you'd like to get in the car, sah, I'll drive you home," Isaiah nudged.

"I think I'll take the wheel, Isaiah." Fleming removed his light jacket and settled into the driver's seat. When Isaiah had climbed in, he turned the key in the ignition and smiled as the motor fired. The mechanical pitch was perfect and soothing. His auto had been well kept in his absence.

He pulled away into the sluggish traffic, which quickly thinned as they reached the road out of Kingston. Fleming passed a large swaying lorry, pressing harder on the accelerator, thrilling to the sensation of mounting speed. He kept masterful control over the automobile as he whipped along the road, sliding through its curves and darting along its straightaways.

Jamaica! More and more it was feeling like home, a haven where he could withdraw from the world at large. Perhaps he had seen too much of that world. Perhaps the complacency of age was settling over him. At the moment Fleming felt no need to examine the feeling closely. He was merely delighted to be here.

"What will you be requiring, sah, when we reach home?" asked Isaiah above the giddy rush of the wind. "Are you hungry?"

"Famished." With his headache and the accompanying mild nausea gone, Fleming now felt ravenous. He thought wistfully of Cesar Holiday's wonderful chowder.

"Very good. Dinner, then? Or something lighter?"

"I believe I could do with a full meal, thank you, Isaiah." As filling—if rather prosaic—as last night's dinner had been in that miserable New York hotel, he was keenly looking forward to some local cuisine, something elaborate and spicy.

"The kitchen is fully stocked. If you have any preferences, please let me know."

"I'll leave it to you, Isaiah."

"Very good, sah."

Isaiah Hines had come well recommended to Fleming. He was a bachelor and a native of the island, though he'd spent some years in Europe. He had a fine grasp of both English and French and seemed more educated than the average Jamaican. He had been attached for some while to a ranking officer in HM's military mission in Kingston—a Captain Bertrand, if Fleming recalled correctly. Bertrand had shipped out back to England at roughly the same time the position of houseman had come available in Fleming's home. The timing had been fortunate.

Fleming had also hired Isaiah's elder sister, Ruth, as laundress. Cesar Holiday's widow and nephew—Bathsheba and Joshua—had both quietly resigned from Fleming's service after Cesar's tragic death. Fleming couldn't blame either of them. As vividly as he remembered Cesar, surely his ghost was even more animated to his surviving family members.

Fleming lit a Players as he followed the road. The drive seemed timeless. He fell into a pleasant trance of movement. When the journey eventually came to an end, though, he felt no disappointment. His home was nestled along the water a short distance outside of the small township of Oracabessa.

He nosed the Rapier into his driveway and cut the engine, watching as dust settled around the car. A warm breeze shook the branches of the surrounding trees. There was a gentle buzz of insect life in the air. He gazed a moment at the retreat of his house. It had been some years since he'd first dreamt of settling into a home like this. He had used to make fanciful blueprint doodles for its construction. Now here it was, though even now it was still a work in progress.

Isaiah retrieved Fleming's bags and preceded him inside, showing no sign of strain as he hefted the unwieldy load. Fleming entered, casting about the ground level rooms for a pleasant moment while Isaiah delivered his luggage to the upstairs bedroom. All looked in order.

"I think I shall have a bath, Isaiah," he called as he climbed the stairs. "Would you lay on some hot water?"

"Yes, sah. Then I'll see to dinner."

"Thank you, Isaiah."

When his houseman had retreated downstairs, Fleming stripped away his clothing, dumping the articles into the silent valet in the bedroom's corner.

He scoured himself with a cake of scented soap, then spent some while just luxuriating in the warm water of the tub. The sense of perfect relaxation was mesmerizing. Here he had no deadlines, no urgent obligations which had to be met. He sighed contentedly.

Eventually, before he found himself dozing in the water, he roused himself. Toweling dry, his scrubbed flesh tingled. In the bedroom he selected a pair of airy khaki trousers and a short-sleeved shirt of neutral green. Slipping his feet into a pair of sandals, he strolled back downstairs. He would see to his unpacking later or have Isaiah take care of it.

He followed the savory aromas which were emanating from the direction of the kitchen. There he found Isaiah efficiently dicing a small bowl of peppers on the surface of the butcher block island. Pots and pans hung above him. Something mouth-watering was cooking in the oven.

"That smells splendid," Fleming said, leaning in the door-frame.

"Saltfish, sah." Isaiah looked up from his chopping. "I am also preparing soup—tomato, garlic, okra—"

Fleming lifted a hand to bring the recitation to a halt. "No need, Isaiah. I've put myself in your hands. I've no doubt the menu will be superb."

"Thank you, sah. Perhaps you'd care for a drink before the meal?"

"My word, yes. A cognac, I should think."

"Very good. Shall I bring it to the lounge?"

"Yes."

Fleming took a slow tour of the rear verandah, breathing in the organic air. How different the atmosphere was from London's. No tinge of industry in this air, just the soft scents of growing. He paused to gaze down the pathway toward the arcing line of the cove's beach. Evening had come while he'd indulged himself in the bath. Golden light buttered the undulating emerald carpet of the sea. In it swam fragile gold angelfish and thicker rainbow parrot fish, not to mention lobster, octopi and the occasional barracuda. The motion of the waves was delicate and unhurried.

The bell sounded from the lounge, and Fleming reentered the house. In the lounge he found the pear-shaped glass of cognac. The libation was refreshing, wiping away memories of Davenport's inferior gin. Jamaica's nightly outgoing Undertaker's Wind was blowing through the slatted wood louvres of the unglassed windows. Isaiah had lit the house's lamps. The light was as soft as the setting sun's. Fleming's home was without electricity.

It wasn't long before dinner was served. As the cooking aromas had promised, the meal was excellent. The hints and outright abundances of the food's varying spices woke dormant pleasures on Fleming's tongue. Too long he'd been eating stern British food, he thought amusedly. These flavors were lively.

Isaiah performed his duties efficiently. Fleming eyed his houseman as the tall Negro cleared dishes from the table. With Cesar Holiday the Englishman had enjoyed a kind of lax banter, their relationship less formal than most which took place between blacks and whites on this island. Isaiah, instead, kept a respectful emotional distance from his employer. His manner was always scrupulously impartial. He served in this house, and that was all. Whatever else occupied his life, Fleming didn't know. Isaiah seemed like a reader. He wondered for the first time if the man played chess, a game Fleming had enjoyed with Joshua, Cesar's nephew.

Well, he mused, he had hired Isaiah as a butler and cook, not to serve as a personal companion. If they eventually developed a similarly liberal relationship to what he'd had with Cesar, it would have to occur naturally. For the present Isaiah Hines was fulfilling his duties faultlessly. That was more than sufficient. Fleming was paying Isaiah and his sister Ruth relatively decent wages.

As he nibbled at a dish of steaming pudding, Fleming felt sleep washing over him. It was barely eight o'clock, but the flight and the change of time were now taking their toll dramatically. He ate another spoonful of the rich dessert, savoring the taste of raisins and brandy, then pushed the dish aside.

"May I bring you something more to drink, sah?"

Fleming stood from the table, shaking his head. "I'm afraid I'm to bed, Isaiah. The last few nights were a bit too adventurous, and I feel the need to catch up on my sleep. Be sure to lock up when you leave."

"Of course, sah. Good night then to you, Mistah Fleming."

"Good night."

His steps were sluggish as he mounted the stairs. In the distance he could hear the faint murmur of the sea. Nearer was the steady croaking of frogs. The sounds were comforting as he undressed and laid himself in his bed.

Memories of last night intruded once more into his thoughts as sleep began settling firmly over him. Davenport. Stahl. Nora Blair DeYoung. The faces blurred in his mind. They were all far away now, and, Fleming judged with his last dwindling shred of consciousness, it was quite likely he would never see any one of them again.

Chapter 6

IT ENDED up taking some several days to fully adjust himself. Jamaica's healing climate helped matters along, thawing out the durable chill that seeped into one's bones during England's winter. His bodily tempos, disrupted by the brusque change of time and locale, righted themselves. The easy tropical rhythms of the island soon infused themselves into Fleming's very being.

He ate well of the meals which Isaiah deftly prepared. Already Fleming's new houseman was learning the idiosyncracies of his employer's appetite. Breakfast was light, consisting of eggs, toast, perhaps a few strips of bacon. Dinners were more exotic, as Fleming happily reacquainted himself with Jamaica's tangy fare.

Isaiah's older sister, Ruth, saw to the laundry. She was easily two decades Isaiah's senior. Her manner was polite and taciturn. When she spoke in the melodious patois of the island, Fleming sensed, as he did with Isaiah, undercurrents of formal education.

Fleming was hardly the only Englishman to have digs in Jamaica. After those first few days of unwinding and acclimation he paid a select casual call or two on his nearest neighbors. He had purpose in this; it was to announce to the social circles of the island that Ian Fleming was officially in residence once more.

An invitation appeared dutifully the following day, before noon. Isaiah presented it on a tray as Fleming sat with a fat volume of Dickens open on his lap in his lounge's plush armchair. He tapped the ash from the tip of his Players into the brass ashtray atop a nearby three-legged stand. He picked up the stiff white envelope with a smile. It was one thing to ensconce oneself in a tropical retreat. It was something less seemly to cut oneself off entirely from society. Here on Jamaica, however, it was easier to select one's company.

He pulled free the note. He recognized the telltale red ink of Lionel Brew-Fox's fountain pen before he had even read the first word. Brew-Fox—"B.F." as he categorically insisted on being called—had been a resident of the island almost since the day of his retirement as a high-placed executive of a Continental branch of a large British banking concern. B.F. had resigned at the tender age of sixty-two, a decade ago, and often delighted in telling the guests of his soirees that he'd fully expected to die a few scant months after withdrawing to Jamaica. His health, he claimed, had never been good. Also the stress and strain of his longtime position had seemed on the verge of taking its final fatal toll.

But this island, B.F. further asserted, had quite simply rejuvenated him. Jamaica had breathed life back into his weary soul. There seemed some substantiation to this avowal. B.F., now in his seventies, looked to be as near in the pink as a man of his years could hope to be.

It would be pleasant to see him again, Fleming mused as he briefly scanned the invitation which called for his appearance at eight o'clock that evening. As were all of B.F.'s parties, this was to be an informal gathering. Socializing on the island was often unceremonious, though Fleming had of course brought along evening clothes for those more formal affairs which occasionally cropped up.

More than seeing the robust retired banker, Fleming

was anticipating reacquainting himself with B.F.'s only daughter, one Margot Brew-Fox, twenty-seven years of age, unmarried and rather vivacious.

Though his romantic pursuits might have been called reckless by some, he had in truth been quite cautious in his liaisons. He couldn't deny that some of his amorous entanglements had, on occasion, gotten him into a certain amount of hot water. A particular incident during his school days came readily to mind. But all in all he had played a canny game. He steadfastly avoided those romantic snarls that had snared many a man before him.

This attitude did not make him a cad. He was merely a pragmatist, recognizing the stark reality of things. What, after all, could he offer a woman beyond the pleasures of his company? To delude any of his past paramours would have been a much crueler act. Besides, he could see no purpose in turning away from this reasoning now at this relatively late stage of his life.

He stayed with his Dickens, reading of Pip and Miss Havisham, until quite unexpectedly the light was dimming beyond the lounge's unglassed louvres. Isaiah entered the large, tastefully furnished chamber to ignite the lamps.

"Good Lord, Isaiah," he said, finally shutting the volume, feeling now the crick that had worked itself into his neck muscles. "What have I done with this day?" He chuckled.

"It is easy to lose oneself in a good book," the houseman observed, completing his rounds. The lounge now glowed with soft, almost buttery lamplight.

"I agree. Do you read much?" Fleming stood from the armchair, stretching luxuriously, noting that he'd nearly filled the brass ashtray with the ends of his Players.

"When I find the time, sah. It's most diverting."

Illiteracy was hardly uncommon among the island's residents. Fleming was pleased that his houseman wasn't included among those masses. His suspicions about Isaiah's formal education would likely prove out under questioning, but he had no desire at the moment to grill the man.

"I shall be attending Mr. Brew-Fox's affair this evening. Eight o'clock. That gives me a bit of time."

"Would you care for dinner beforehand, sah?"

"Something light, I should think. B.F. always lays a nice buffet, and it would be tactless not to eat something while I am there. Still, I imagine fortifying myself with a small meal wouldn't be out of order. Soup, I believe."

"I can prepare a bowl of something hearty, sah. It won't take long."

"Very good." Isaiah exited the lounge. Fleming went upstairs, idly rubbing the mild cramp from his neck. He had nearly forgotten how easy it was for the hours, even the days, to slip past on the island. It was very much as if Jamaica cast an enchantment over its inhabitants, even its non-permanent ones. Time lost its rigidity here.

Informal or not, Fleming hardly intended to attend Brew-Fox's soiree in his present attire, which consisted of a rather bright red shirt, short cotton trousers and sandals. He selected his wardrobe leisurely, laying out a white linen suit for himself. He went downstairs when Isaiah rang the bell and fairly devoured the thick savory soup that had been prepared. There were chunks of crab meat, along with grains of wild rice and assorted tangy vegetables, all of it stewing in a rich spiced broth. He also ate several of the steaming doughy rolls the houseman had baked, dipping them into the soup and chewing them hurriedly before they crumbled.

Following the meal, he returned upstairs to his bedroom

and dressed. He added a pastel blue short-sleeved shirt to his ensemble and permitted himself an indulgent moment before the mirror.

There was time enough for a libation before he headed out. Isaiah brought his gin-and-tonic to the lounge. The cocktail was in its own way fortifying as well, preparing him for the night's festivities which would doubtlessly include a fair amount of drinking. Though Fleming regularly indulged this habit, he was quite vigilant about it, never allowing himself to actually become intoxicated. There were few sorrier sights in this world than a drunk staggering about a party making a perfect ass of himself. He had a reputation to defend, that of the mannerly, worldly man. He had rightfully earned that status and would allow nothing to detract from it.

He lit out at ten minutes of eight, figuring to arrive fashionably late at the Brew-Foxes. B.F. was a widower, but his daughter lived permanently with him. His two sons, both employed by the same British banking concern where B.F. had spent the bulk of his life, visited sporadically. Neither, so far as Fleming knew, were presently on the island. This was fortunate, as the brothers were annoyingly protective of their sister.

Lionel Brew-Fox also had a home along the beach. Fleming guided the Lagonda Rapier along the coast road, encountering no traffic beyond the darting of the occasional insect that smudged his windscreen.

Overhead, against the broad starry veldt of the sky, the moon hung nearly full, beaming through a few errant whispers of cloud cover. It was some few miles to B.F.'s abode.

The domicile came into view. It was a larger affair than Fleming's home, fronted by an elaborate rock garden that was almost Japanese in its precise layout. B.F., unlike

Fleming, evidently could not make do without the modern conveniences. Toward this end he had installed a generator in a shed to one side of the sprawling dwelling. The house fairly radiated with electrical light. However, the buzzing of that generator was rather horrid. Fleming was glad, as always, that he was a relatively distant neighbor. How awful it would be to find oneself continually assaulted by the sounds of that machinery.

He parked the polished blue-green Rapier off to one side of the front of the house. Other vehicles had already accumulated. If this was anything like B.F.'s normal gatherings, there would be no more than two dozen guests, enough people to properly dress the scene without creating unwanted crowding.

He rang the bell, wincing slightly at the nearby clamor of the generator. When B.F.'s young Negro serving maid opened the door and he was safely inside, the mechanical drone was less severe. Brew-Fox came immediately to greet him, breaking away from his early guests and raising quite a fuss over Fleming's appearance. B.F.'s flesh was a permanent hardy bronze. His eyes were bright in a balding skull whose remaining ring of white hair was nonetheless dense and healthy-looking. His movements suggested the vitality—physical and spiritual—of a man who had found something akin to true happiness.

"Back in the land of the Stone Age, are you then?" B.F. crowed merrily, pumping Fleming's hand enthusiastically. That was another of the man's quirks; he evidently relished referring to his adopted island home as primitive, despite the blaring electric light illuminating his residence.

"Yes," Fleming said amiably. "I've secured another reprieve from yet one more of England's winters."

"Fine thing too, old man. But you're without a drink.

Come, we must remedy this unfortunate turn. Perhaps in the process we'll even manage to introduce you to a few of the others in attendance." He guided Fleming deeper into the expansive house, through an open archway into an enormous parlor. One wall was made up of carefully mortared stone, the others laid over with dense wood paneling.

Naturally he was already acquainted with most of the other guests. The same faces routinely appeared on these social circuits. It was a pleasant outlet for these transplanted Britons and those of other European nationalities. These affairs could, of course, become monotonous if one overindulged. Fleming was careful to appear rarely enough on the scene that when he did, it was virtually guaranteed that he would be a refreshingly welcome sight.

These being among his first days back on Jamaica after his usual prolonged absence, however, made him the natural center of attention for some while. B.F.'s maid supplied him with a cocktail while the guests peppered him with eager questions. The Newtons were there; along with Irving Harlowe, retired from an investment firm; Godfrey and Ethel Ridges, who had emigrated following the loss of their only son, a bombardier, during the war; Louis Cook, who fancied himself something of a poet; Brook Jones; Kirby Matthews and escort; Richard Miles and so on and so forth.

Fleming dutifully engaged all in conversation, punctuating the exchanges with a witty bon mot now and then to keep his audience amused. He was decidedly deft in handling himself in these social situations, a skill that one either possessed or blatantly lacked. During the course of these dialogues he had spotted B.F.'s daughter, Margot, nearby the broad bay windows that overlooked the Brew-Foxes' private stretch of beach front. The effervescent

Margot was being accosted by Louis Cook, who appeared to have gotten himself inebriated in record time. Likely the wild-haired poet was reciting verses to her. Margot was holding her own, chuckling with undisguised amusement at the young bohemian's antics. Fleming had no worries that she could manage herself.

Margot caught his eye and offered a small winsome smile, which Fleming returned.

It took several more rounds of conversation and another cocktail before Fleming could hope to break free from the center of things. Other guests had appeared while he'd been holding forth on a variety of subjects, and these fresh visitors helpfully drew away some of the attention that had been heaped upon him since his arrival. As much as he enjoyed such socializing, it was pleasant to escape the heart of the fray.

He looked again for Margot, but she had vanished. He wondered if Louis Cook, by now playing the role of drunken buffoon to a tee, had finally frightened her off. Ah well, mused Fleming good-naturedly. Whatever he privately thought of his own urbanity, he couldn't expect every woman in the world to be drawn to him like iron to a magnet.

A fresh drink in hand, he stole through B.F.'s kitchens, where a quite portly cook paid him no mind whatsoever, and slipped out the house's rear door. A walk along the tranquil beach would brace him for another round of socializing. Then perhaps he would call it an early night. This being his first social affair of the year on the island, he didn't wish to overdo it.

The generator's buzz again assailed the air. Really, were Edison's bulbs so dashedly important to Brew-Fox that he was willing to keep a whole district of the island awake?

Fleming shrugged. To each his own. He took a leisurely sip of his cocktail, scouting the rear verandah, finding it empty and stepping down onto the swath of pruned greenery that spilled in a gentle slope downward to the rolling moonlit sea.

His crepe-soled shoes crackled softly over fallen bits of twig and leaf as he made his way toward the gently swelling foam.

"Ian!" came the stage whisper from his left.

He had actually sensed her human presence a heartbeat before she'd spoken. The blip had appeared on the automatic radar of his senses. If this were another time and place, he would be primed for combat, he would have a weapon drawn, he would—

The past, he reminded himself, instantly at ease again. He was no longer in that business.

The surf crashed sedately a short distance away. Frogs croaked among themselves. The moon cast fluid shadows from the surrounding trees, creating a murky kind of ambience that was at once mysterious and alluring. Margot detached herself from one of these liquid shadows and eased out into a pool of spectral moonlight. She had left her shoes somewhere and now stepped barefoot toward him. She was wearing a flowing, almost diaphanous gown of purple and pink that dipped daringly toward her impressive cleavage. Her figure was taut and youthful. Her hair was a lustrous shade of blond that appeared to glow with an inner light when the moon brushed it. Her features were not beautiful, though she was far from homely and possessed a winning buoyancy of spirit. Evidently she had inherited a measurable portion of her father's vigor. Margot smiled engagingly at him once more.

Fleming, as much as he genuinely liked B.F., was glad

the older man wasn't present at the moment as he moved forward to meet his daughter.

"Margot," he said. "This is an unexpected—"

Margot apparently had little interest in conversation. She stepped up to him and slid her arms forthrightly about his waist.

Nearly nose to nose he spoke again. "Would you care to join me for a stroll along the water?"

Evidently not. At that their mouths met. Fleming's arms wrapped about her, his cocktail tumbling to the sand.

Sometimes fate was kind. He didn't imagine for an instant that she had any romantic illusions about the two of them. It was all well and good. This was then, ultimately, mere friendly sport.

And that, he thought, was how he wanted things.

THE PARTY WAS not a rendezvous point—at least not one for intelligence agents. Yet "rendezvous," the Scimitar knew from his familiarity with English, was an apt term, although "tryst" fit the bill even better.

He had watched with a strange mixture of amusement and repulsion the doings of his target and the blond woman. His amusement came naturally as he observed the pair commingling. (How carefree were these Westerners!) His distaste was a learned thing, the Party line. (Look at the decadent sex-crazed capitalists!)

The Scimitar had no fear of forgetting the duties of maintaining a proper mind set. He had been thoroughly screened during his long training. His loyalties were firm. He would not be corrupted by the enemy . . . but it was his ability to adapt so deftly to these foreign ways that had assured him his place in the Russian intelligence community. If it wasn't a paradox, it was near to one.

Ian Fleming had been identified from the surveillance photos he had taken in London. He was listed as inactive, retired, at least as far as could be ascertained. The Scimitar didn't know how his superiors could even begin to access the top secret information in Whitehall's files. That wasn't his field. His job was to blend, to shadow, to observe unseen. Which was just what he had been doing since securing a flight from England to this near-equatorial island.

He presumed that this Englishman—retired or not—was suspected by his superiors of being involved in that business of the couriers. Likely they thought this man had been charged with backtracking those communiqués to their original source in the United States. If so, he had chosen a quite roundabout route.

It was also safe to presume that other Russian operatives were attached to this assignment, keeping an eye on other English Secret Service agents that Francis Davenport might have enlisted. Safe to presume? In truth, presumption was a dangerous pastime, and the Scimitar didn't indulge in it with any regularity. He trusted his superiors, trusted the entire infrastructure of the community to which he belonged, trusted the Party and the Motherland. And he was content in this all-consuming trust.

Presently he crouched atop a brief sandy ridge that overlooked the stretch of moonlit beach. The fronds of native greenery brushed his cheeks as he continued to peer through the lenses of his compact binoculars. Fleming's activity with the blond woman appeared to have come to an end. The Scimitar readied himself to move. He would circle back toward the road to observe the front of the house, some distance from where he had secreted his newly rented auto in a field. Obviously he couldn't enter the bustling house, but Fleming would not leave undetected.

He suppressed a grunt as he rose silently from his crouch. He was forty-one, not young any longer, though still quite able. The beige linen suit he had purchased to blend him into the local scenery was rather weighted with equipment: a pouch for the binoculars, a fourteen inch jemmy (for the event of a break-in), a small torch, a money belt. Also on his person, in an adapted rucksack that hung beneath his linen coat under his left arm, was the bomb, spigot and fuse that had required some clever concealment when he had passed through customs with his forged identification.

The Scimitar didn't speculate what his next orders would be. Communicating with his superiors at this distance was laborious but hardly impossible. Whatever he was called upon to do, he would perform with the same unswerving dedication and efficiency that had made him an active member of his community for better than ten years.

Silently he moved toward the road, keeping an eye on his target as Fleming strolled back toward the house.

Chapter 7

ALL IN all it felt splendid to be back on the island.

On his fourth morning back Fleming opened his eyes at precisely five minutes before he'd ordered Isaiah to wake him. It was his habit to rise early, a tendency left over from his military days. He smiled contentedly as he stretched and slipped out of bed. Yes, his internal clock had certainly adjusted. He dressed himself in casual attire. Isaiah would hear his movements and not intrude.

Fleming shaved leisurely, then spent an extra moment contemplating his reflection. Faced with an open agenda, he decided then how he would fill the day.

He would visit the water.

He smoked a cigarette before breakfast. Isaiah delivered the meal to the table with the poise of a lifelong waiter in the finest of restaurants. The food was perfect, the poached eggs delicate and seasoned with a dash of paprika. Fleming sipped a glass of cool pineapple juice and fixed his houseman with an easygoing smile.

"I believe I shall spend a few hours beneath the water."

Isaiah's large eyes lifted from beneath dusky brows. "I trust you will exercise caution, sah. Not all that swims in the sea is hospitable."

"I've acquainted myself well with our aquatic neighbors, Isaiah, but thank you for your concern."

"I'll fetch your mask then, sah. Will you require the spear as well?"

"Why not?" said Fleming, now having voiced his plan

warming to it even more. "Perhaps I'll skewer us a lobster for dinner."

"Very good, sah."

He followed the pathway down to his cove's beach. The early morning sunlight lit the scene magnificently. The lush greenery fluttered in the tepid breeze, and the white sands seemed to positively glow. Passing birds threw fleeting shadows across the land and water. Fleming had changed into a pair of snug swimming trunks. He stood a moment at the water's edge. The lazy waves broke over his ankles. Then he started forward.

The silt beneath the rolling water gave under the soles of his bare feet as he trudged outward. When the water had wrapped him about his waist, he dove forward.

Once, some years ago in Canada, Fleming had briefly undergone some formal underwater training. He had enjoyed the experience. This, however, was much more pleasant—a casual dip into the Caribbean waters that rolled against his shore.

The sea was warm. Sparkling sunlight brightened the shallow depths, falling over stones and kaleidoscopic coral and illuminating the radiant carpet of silt that was the bottom of this cove. Fleming's toned body flexed as he swam in random directions, turning this way and that, quickly adapting himself to the alien gravity of the water.

Sea life bustled around him. Bright tropical fish, swimming in their tiny herds, scattered in marvelously coordinated patterns as his movements disturbed them. He breathed easily through his mask. He held his spear in a loose but controlled grip, ready to bring it to bear at any moment. He wasn't only on the lookout for a dinner lobster. Isaiah had been quite correct when he'd warned Fleming of the inhospitality of some of the sea's creatures.

A darting barracuda could tear away a man's limb with its razor-sharp teeth.

He thought back on the previous night. His clandestine tryst with Margot Brew-Fox had been gratifying—but only in the most elemental sense. They had parted as they had once or twice before, with friendly words that carried no untoward overtones. Today the incident was merely filed in the storehouse of his memory.

He patrolled the cove, falling into the splendid trance of this underwater world. The sounds of his kicking limbs were muffled in his ears. How peaceful it all seemed. Yet, of course, it was not. The sea, like the land, had its predators and prey, its strong and weak. This was a world of minute by minute survival. The untold variety of sea creatures hunted each other mercilessly. Here, in the water, there wasn't even the tempering of human ethics to stave off the ongoing slaughter. Here it was a free-for-all.

Yet the water teemed with life. The cycle of renewal was inexorable. No matter how ruthlessly these creatures hunted and devoured one another, there were always more, an endless assortment of colors and shapes.

Fleming happily nurtured these meandering philosophical thoughts as he swam. His body was fit, and this exercise was surely doing him good.

He paused for a moment to watch the cove's bottom as a vibrantly colored octopus curled its way along. Its multilimbed movements were so strange, yet so natural. A little further along he thought he caught the briefest glimpse of a barracuda, a dark cloak of a shape flitting by some distance ahead. He lingered a while, eyeing the waters cautiously. When all seemed safe, he continued onward.

Eventually he did spear a lobster. A group of four or five of the creatures was lumbering blithely past. Fleming dawdled a moment over his choices, as if he were selecting one from a tank in a restaurant. Then, moving swiftly and ably, his impaled his prize.

He rose from the water, realizing he'd spent some two hours beneath the surface. He located the large towel he'd dropped on the sand and dried himself. He felt invigorated and at ease. He imagined for a moment taking a similar dip into the January waters of the Thames and laughed aloud. Such a swim would have brought on a case of hypothermia.

He carried the lobster, spear, mask and towel back up to the house, eager to show off his catch to Isaiah.

Dutifully impressed, Isaiah remarked, "It will make a fine meal, sah."

"Yes, I should think," Fleming said proudly. He turned toward the stairs. He would change out of his swimming trunks and figure out what to do with the rest of the day, perhaps deciding over a cool libation.

"Sah?"

Fleming turned back with a questioning glance.

"A message arrived while you were out."

"Another invitation?" asked Fleming.

"I don't know, sah. Hand-delivered by a young man on a motorcycle. From Kingston."

Fleming frowned mildly.

"I have it here." Isaiah took a plain envelope from his shirt pocket.

Fleming noted it had no postage and no address beyond his name written in florid script. He opened it and found a sheet of creamy white hotel stationary. The same elegant hand had written the message. Fleming's gaze traveled over the words, eyes widening as he read.

He returned the letter to the envelope and tapped it pensively against his thigh a moment.

"Bad news, sah?" Isaiah asked neutrally. Not out of mere curiosity, Fleming judged; merely to ascertain if he could be of service in the matter. Yes, Isaiah was shaping up to be a fine houseman.

"No," Fleming said. "Not bad news at all. You'll want to put that lobster in cold storage, though. Isaiah, I'll be taking the car into the city in a short while."

Chapter 8

FLEMING TUCKED the canvas hood over the seats and steering wheel of the Lagonda Rapier, then climbed the few bleached stone steps to the entrance of the Chabrol Arms. The edifice was fronted by tall supporting columns, and a red-and-green striped awning lay a long cooling shadow over the entryway. The noon sun shone directly downward.

The drive into Kingston had been as stimulating as the one he'd taken from the airport to his home on the day of his arrival. He had gunned the Rapier along the road, slipping nimbly among the plodding lorries and saloon cars and donkey-driven carts. Once again the sensation of speed had stirred his nerves. That, mixed with the keen anticipation he only half admitted to feeling, had worked him into an eager state.

He removed the dark-lensed glasses he had worn to cut the glare of the sun, slipping them into the pocket of his stylishly cut tan jacket. He cast about the hotel lobby. It was furnished with tasteful European flair. The floor appeared to be black marble, its gleaming surface veined with squiggles of gold. Wall-mounted faux gas lamps, which were in fact electrical, spread a rich amber glow about the scene.

This was probably the most expensive hotel on the island. It catered to moneyed travelers—tourists, artists, writers, dignitaries from abroad.

Fleming accosted a passing bellhop in a tight-fitting

scarlet uniform, complete with golden epaulets and shiny brass buttons.

"I'm looking for a Miss DeYoung. Nora Blair DeYoung. Would you locate her for me? My name is Ian Fleming."

The Negro boy, no older than thirteen, bowed his head and said enthusiastically, "Yassah! Right away!"

Fleming watched him scamper off. He lit a Players and waited. He had left Nora's letter at home. Its contents had been simple enough: an invitation to come to the hotel at his leisure. She would be on the island a few days, stopping over on her way to the States. *It would be delightful to see you again, Ian, even though our last brief meeting was so recent.* So she had written.

Fleming had smiled at the familiar address. A solicitation from the vivacious and attractive Nora Blair DeYoung, alias Blake Young, to stop by her hotel. How could he pass that up? He smiled again now as the bellhop returned.

"Mistah Fleming! Please if you come dis way, sah." The boy's teeth gleamed as he offered a solicitous smile.

He followed the bellhop out of the lobby. Fleming had washed himself of all the scents and grit of the sea. In addition to the light tan coat, he had donned a white collared shirt, dun-colored trousers that Ruth had neatly pressed for him and a pair of gleaming soft-soled shoes. He looked at once casual and cosmopolitan, the urbane transplanted European lollygagging in the tropics, which, he supposed, was a rather fair assessment.

He didn't imagine that Nora's appearance on Jamaica was any sort of mere coincidence. The odds that the island had originally been on her itinerary were unlikely. Fleming supposed she possessed a certain amount of leverage with her editors and had altered her route to the States of her own accord. It seemed glaringly obvious that she had come here specifically to see *him.*

It was impossible not to be flattered. Fleming had entertained few thoughts of the woman since his arrival, but that was only because he'd figured he would likely never meet her again.

Now, coming into a broad red-carpeted lounge on the heels of the bellhop, he saw her . . . and wondered how she'd ever slipped his mind.

She was sitting in a club chair of supple leather, one knee crossed over the other, showing off the better part of a shapely calf. Her attire, like his, was nonchalantly elegant. She wore open-toed shoes with mildly sloping heels and a breezy-looking dress patterned in white and ocher. It looked like something she'd just thrown on indiscriminately; yet the dress was quite flattering, tucked here and there to accentuate her curves. Her smoldering red hair was let down, and the lush ringlets draped her finely molded shoulders, which the dress left bare. She had attired herself strategically, either for the weather or for Fleming's benefit or both.

"Madam," enunciated the bellhop with great decorum as Fleming privately smirked at the misplaced appellation, "Mistah Ian Fleming to see you!"

Nora's limpid blue eyes lifted from the rather tattered book—a Jane Austen novel—which lay in her lap. A dark filtered cigarette hovered over an ashtray which rested on the club chair's broad arm. A fine pleased smile spread over her lips. Her sculpted features brightened as her eyes met Fleming's.

"I would ask you for another light, Ian, but I'm afraid I've got plenty of fluid this time. Besides, one should never repeat a gambit. Thank you, Jules. Here, something for your pocket."

She passed a coin to the bellhop, who grinned avidly, bowed deeply and dashed out of the lounge. The broad room was occupied by only a few other guests, a typical assortment of the type of European travelers this hotel seemed to attract. There was a light relaxed buzz of conversation, in several languages and numerous dialects.

Fleming's attention, however, was quite naturally taken up with Nora. He decided he hadn't enhanced her appearance in hindsight one jot. She was as comely as she had appeared in London.

"It's quite an unexpected pleasure to see you again, Nora."

"Unexpected?" Her smile grew droll. "Then you didn't get my letter after all and only happened to chance upon this hotel. How marvelous! Such flukes of fate are rare and fanciful."

Fleming laughed, warming to the moment. "Of course I received your letter, Nora. How did you know where to deliver it?"

She set aside her book, then lifted her hand, turned down at the wrist. Fleming took it in his fingers and set his lips to it, letting them linger an instant longer than he might have. He glanced up to see her reaction. She smiled winsomely.

"Why don't you sit down first?" she said. "We'll have a nice little chat. Then perhaps some lunch, if you haven't yet eaten. Oh, but let's not get too far ahead of ourselves. The day will plan itself."

Fleming settled into a facing club chair. The leather was soft, and the low back and solid sides seemed to cradle him.

"When did you arrive on the island?" Fleming asked.

"Yesterday."

"I hope your flight here was more pleasant than mine."

"I spend so much time in the air, Ian, it's a wonder I haven't sprouted wings. I've flown in all sorts of conditions. Did you encounter rough weather on your way here then?"

Fleming told her of his mildly unpleasant journey from London to Kingston, of Archie Havens the insurance salesman and the caterwauling infant, making a harmless amusing anecdote of the story. How easily they had fallen into the rhythms of pleasant conversation, he noted. It was as if they were already longtime acquaintances.

They chatted easily at some length before Fleming again asked his question: "How did you know where to deliver your letter?"

"Oh, that." She tittered. "Of course I had no idea where you might be staying since I'd neglected to wile any specifics from you last time we met. Jamaica looks small on the map, but finding a lone individual on this island proved daunting. I finally paid a call at the Government House. A Mr. Stowe was very helpful. Having secured your location, I thought it would be a bit . . . forward . . . to go traipsing out to your home unannounced and uninvited. You had no phone, and I didn't want to wait around for my letter to reach you through normal postal channels. So I hired a young man with a motorcycle to deliver it. I paid him five pounds for the favor. Do you suppose that was too much?"

Fleming tried to imagine Stowe, the dour secretary at the Government House with whom he'd dealt before, being helpful. Friendliness didn't seem to be a part of the man's natural character. Yet it was no difficult matter to imagine Stowe bending over backwards to accommodate Nora.

Another uniformed hotel staffer—this a black man in his sixties—made the rounds through the lounge, seeing if any of the guests would care for a beverage. Nora and Fleming both ordered brandies.

Sipping at their drinks, relaxing into each other's company even further, Fleming said, "It's quite convenient that your flight to America included this particular stopover. Speaking of rare and fanciful flukes of fate." He added an ironic spin to these last words.

"Oh, dear," Nora said in mock-horror. "I do believe you've seen through my ruse. How dreadful. I suppose I should flee to my room and lock the door."

Fleming chuckled.

Nora went on, "The success of my career—if I may toot my own horn—allows me a good deal of latitude when making my travel arrangements. I can tell my editors I need to be flown here or there in order to follow up some lead or conduct some interview. They never give me much static about it because I always deliver."

Which was essentially what Fleming had guessed. He nodded. "And your journalistic career is quite extraordinary, if I may say so."

Nora smirked. "You may."

"Perhaps you'd allow me to ask you a few questions. . . ."

"Oh, Ian. This isn't going to degenerate into a Q and A about the grand and glorious exploits of Blake Young, is it? As you pointed out, journalism consists in great part of long waits in drafty airports and arguments with editorial staffs."

"Yet your accomplishments are legendary in the field."

"Ah, now flattery." She tittered again. "It would be frankly immodest of me, I suppose, to deny that some of my adventures have been . . . oh . . . quite adventuresome.

But one doesn't cultivate friendships with fellow journalists for the specific reason of talking shop, does one?"

Fleming shrugged. "I suppose not."

"I've only a few days on your island, Ian." She leaned a few degrees forward in her club chair. Her limpid blue eyes fixed him steadily. "I should like to enjoy myself—and, if at all possible, forget for these few days my responsibilities."

"Very well," said Fleming, standing. He gave her his most charming smile. "Perhaps, Miss DeYoung, you'd like to get out of this hotel and permit me to show you some of my island."

She lifted her hand again to allow him to help her to her feet. "Why, Mr. Fleming, I thought you'd never ask."

Chapter 9

In the end it was an easy matter to mentally separate Nora Blair DeYoung from her counterpart Blake Young.

Blake Young, by dint of "his" heroic journalistic exploits, particularly during the war, conjured up images of gruff masculinity. If Fleming had ever conceived a mental image of the correspondent, it would have been of a mid-forties, square-jawed, coarsely handsome fellow, cheeks dusted with raspy stubble, eyes hard and narrow, dark hair greying at the temples. Blake Young would also be broad-shouldered and tall, at least six foot two. He would drink heavily and cuss like a sailor. Pushing the fantasy even further, Fleming speculated he would also be a notorious womanizer, bedding the wives of high-placed diplomats and narrowly escaping scandal at every turn. Blake would have scarred knuckles from barroom brawls and a slight limp from an automobile smashup that occurred in his twenties. He would smoke like a furnace and tell ribald tales of exotic lands and women.

Nora, obviously, did not fit this speculative profile. It was therefore simple for Fleming to set aside his natural awe of the renowned journalist and enjoy Nora as *Nora*.

She was proving to be, now that several hours had elapsed, perfectly marvelous company. She was enthusiastic and boundlessly energetic. Fleming had been deeply gratified by her first reaction to the sight of his automobile.

"Lagonda Rapier!" She clapped her hands, her tanned features lit almost as brightly as when she'd first laid eyes on him in the hotel's lounge. "19 . . . oh . . . 1935, I daresay! Am I right?"

"You are indeed," Fleming confirmed, beaming. He had peeled away and stowed the canvas hood, then held open the passenger's door for her.

When Fleming had fired the engine, giving it a little extra gas before putting it in gear, she positively squealed her delight. "My God, Ian! Listen to it purr and roar! You must keep it in excellent shape. Who looks after this treasure when you're away?"

"I have a houseman." Fleming had pulled them away from the front of the hotel, swinging into Kingston's colorful afternoon streets.

What had followed were several hours of winding travel. First Fleming took them through Kingston in haphazard fashion, taking streets arbitrarily, pointing out whatever sight of interest happened to appear beyond the windscreen. Kingston was a diverse city, its local color vibrant and only mildly diluted—at least on the surface—by long European influence.

Nora kept up a steady stream of counterpointing commentary. She had visited the island some years ago, just before the war, but had only dim recollections. She would ask after this or that business or restaurant, piecing together her hazy memories. Fleming tried to confirm or deny the existence of these establishments but, as often as not, had to merely shrug. Most of his time on Jamaica was naturally spent at the private preserve of his house, which was the entire point of owning a home on the island. He didn't know Kingston like the back of his hand and admitted so.

"No bother," Nora said cheerfully. "For all I know I'm thinking of some restaurant in Bonn or Rio. Oh, Ian, this is wonderful!" Her hair streamed behind her in flattering fashion.

He took her up into the Blue Mountains, revving the Rapier to speeds that were exhilarating, though not outright dangerous. The high roads wound lazily, offering startling views at every turn, which Nora dutifully soaked up.

"It's rather paradisiacal, isn't it?" she said with a fetching grin.

"I like to think so, yes."

Eventually they slipped down toward the coast once again.

"Would you like to see Montego Bay next?" he asked.

"Perhaps we could get a bite to eat first. You know, we've completely forgotten about lunch."

"So we have." Fleming slowed the Rapier, which he'd certainly put through its paces today. He glanced up at the sky. The first tinges of creamy pink were coloring it. "It seems supper might be more appropriate. Where has the time gone?"

Nora patted his hand where it rested on the steering wheel. As when he had kissed her hand earlier, her touch lingered a prolonged moment. Fleming enjoyed the sensation of the contact.

"We've been squandering it on unproductive sightseeing," Nora said impishly. "Really, I can't recall the last time I felt like a genuine tourist. Always when I land somewhere, I've got something to do. Something that must be seen to immediately. An assignment. An interview. A bit of research for a story. It's pleasant in the extreme to be wayfaring all about the place like this. Thank you for going to the trouble of ferrying me around."

"No trouble whatsoever," Fleming said truthfully. "As to dinner . . . ? That is, if you're not yet bored with my companionship." It was a silly flirtatious ploy, forcing her to express her desire to remain in his company. But Fleming wasn't entirely above such machinations. It was how the game was played.

"Ian, you might be a great many things I don't know about, but boring is unlikely to make the list."

"Did you want to eat at the hotel?" he asked.

"My word, no." Nora wrinkled her nose in mild distaste. "Stuffy Britons—pardon me—and sour-faced Belgians beleaguering the staff? *Exotic* European cuisine? Hah! I've had my fill of it these last weeks. I should very much like to try something local, something intrinsically Jamaican. Would that suit you?"

He smiled appreciatively. "It would, yes."

"I haven't even asked. Did you have any other plans? Am I upsetting your personal agenda?"

"I warned my houseman, Isaiah, I might not be returning for dinner." He lifted an eyebrow. "Do you suppose that was presumptuous of me?" It was the same flirtatious tactic.

"Not in the least," she reassured. Then added coyly, "What harm could come of dinner between a man and a woman?"

"THAT'S THE UNDERTAKER'S Wind," Fleming said as it blew the branches of the open-air restaurant's overhanging trees. The twilit court was further illuminated by standing torches. The tablecloths were vibrantly red linen.

"It blows at six every evening," he continued. "It goes out to sea, taking all the stale air of the island with it. At nine every morning the Doctor's Wind blows new air ashore. These winds keep the island fresh."

"It certainly smells different from the cities. I think the whole of America could use a good airing out at this point."

Nora lifted a generous glass of red wine. Fleming tapped his glass against hers.

"Chin-chin," he said.

Fleming had eaten only once before at the restaurant, but the experience had been favorable. It seemed just the right place to take Nora to introduce her to Jamaica's native fare.

Most of the other diners were whites, but they didn't seem to be tourists. The atmosphere was low-key and the staff efficient. A violin was being played somewhere beyond the moss-ridden stone walls of this rear courtyard, a soft, almost romantic melody. Fleming decided he couldn't have asked for a better venue for entertaining this lovely lady.

The waiter came to clear their plates. The meal had been fine—artichoke hearts and boiled spicy cabbage, soft rolls and marmalade, the entrée consisting of slabs of broiled suckling pig which had glistened and crackled with hot juices. Fleming felt a bit overfed, in fact. He lit a cigarette and settled back in the cushioned wire-framed chair and sipped leisurely at his wine. They had ordered a second bottle, at Nora's insistence. Fleming thought it unlikely either of them would become intoxicated, considering the amount of food they had just consumed.

With evening settling over the semi-idyllic scene, the normally breezy pace of the island seemed even more nonchalant.

"So, is this how you typically spend your winter days?" Nora asked above the brim of her wine glass.

"The charm of your company makes this particular day something of a rarity," Fleming returned.

"You spar well, Ian. I admire that. From another man those words might sound only rakish."

Fleming smiled. "And yourself, Nora? Walking in the footsteps of Blake Young, so to speak, do you often find yourself dining with strangers in faraway locales?"

"Strangers?" She gave a *hurrumph* that for a moment sounded remarkably like one of Stahl's grunts. "Yes, I dine with countless strangers—as a part of my doing business. I do not, however, consider this one of those occasions. I find it difficult to think of you as a stranger, Ian. A new acquaintance, yes. But . . . I think a distinct kinship has already sprung up between us. Do you agree?"

He nodded a bit solemnly. "I do."

"Surely merely founded on the mutual respect of two professionals working in their chosen field." There was no mistaking the wry tone.

"Oh, surely."

Her familiar musical laugh was by now rather endearing.

There was a wide and varied range of possible conclusions for this evening, Fleming knew. Under other circumstances he might try to steer events determinedly toward one specific culmination. But Nora's company seemed too precious to risk spoiling anything. Even if things remained at this initial flirtatious stage and went no further, he would not feel cheated.

Nagging at the back of his mind, however, was still a tenacious curiosity regarding Blake Young. Fleming had been exposed to any number of celebrities in his lifetime. Yet Blake Young was among the most intriguing, specifically because there *was* no Blake Young. Only Nora. This extraordinary, feisty woman who had probably broken down more gender-based barricades than the most militant suffragette.

In the end he couldn't resist asking the question . . . though he would have genuine reason to regret it.

"So"—he leaned forward to snub out his Players in a white ceramic ashtray—"what new assignment is taking you to the States?"

Nora gave her red-ringletted head a tilt. "We're going to talk a little shop after all, are we?"

"Not if you're averse to it," he said, already retreating from his impulse.

"No. It's fine, Ian." She set down her glass, and Fleming moved automatically to pour her another drink. "I'm off to the West Coast. San Francisco, in particular. There's some juicy scandalous story brewing there. Just the sort of thing I find myself delving more and more often. Sensation grabs headlines, and this promises to go the distance. Sometimes I miss the war, you know. I'm sure that's a horrid thing to say, but in those days a correspondent could tackle the meatiest of stories."

Fleming slowly set the wine bottle back on the red tablecloth.

"San Francisco?"

She gave him another head-tilt, this one accompanied by a somewhat perplexed expression. "Yes. I trust you've heard of the city—"

"Would it be too forward of me to ask who the subject of your assignment might be?" Despite the genteel phrasing of the question, it sounded rather brusque, even to Fleming's ears. He studied her with steady eyes.

Abruptly the casual scene had taken on a cast of subtle tension. Nora, alert to the shift, narrowed her blue eyes slightly.

"Well . . . it's a bit of telling tales out of school," she said somewhat ambivalently, "but the party is one Oscar Winterberg, evidently something of a rising star among the labor union people. He—"

Again Fleming rather churlishly cut her off, unable to help himself. "Oscar Winterberg," he pronounced with quiet fatalism. Coincidences happen, he told himself. Even wild coincidences. Rare and fanciful flukes of fate. But these self-assurances were all in vain. Doubt did not so much creep over him as it did knife through his breast. She had indeed come to Jamaica to see him specifically . . . though not, it seemed now, because she had been so taken with him in London. Winterberg. That must be the reason. That was their mutual affiliation.

By now Nora was returning his fixed gaze with growing puzzlement. "Yes. Oscar Winterberg. Do you know of him? Ian, is something wrong?"

"As one professional to another, Nora," he said with false ease, "I'd be curious as to what sort of story you're planning and why you chose this Winterberg in the first place. You needn't provide details if you fear I mean to scoop you"—he conjured up an easy smile to soften this—"though I assure you I don't intend to steal your assignment."

Nora nodded. "Very well. It's a profile of Winterberg, but it may well lead to something more—the scandal I mentioned, which in fact I'd rather not elaborate on. As to why I've taken this particular assignment . . . one must earn a living, mustn't one?"

He drummed his fingers on the tablecloth. His thoughts of only a minute ago, about where this evening might lead to, scattered into the coming night.

"Tell me, Nora," he said softly but evenly. "Do you know a man named Davenport? A man named Stahl?"

Chapter 10

THE EVENING was spinning on a new axis now, shifting the pleasant climate to one subtly threaded with tension, apprehension and, quite possibly, mistrust. Fleming tried to tell himself he was overreacting. But despite all efforts, it was no small feat to link Nora Blair DeYoung to her current assignment of investigating Oscar Winterberg without tossing Davenport into the equation.

"Davenport?" She blinked her limpid blue eyes. "Do you mean Stanley Davenport, on the staff of the Secretary of Commerce?"

"No," said Fleming. "A Mr. Francis Davenport. Stahl is his aide."

Nora was frowning. "I don't know anyone named Stahl. Your Davenport doesn't ring any bells either."

"Perhaps the names have merely slipped your mind," he said, maintaining an even tone. "They are connected with MI5. Does that sound more familiar?"

He kept his manner from becoming confrontational, even as he felt his backbone trying to stiffen and shoulders hunch.

Nonetheless, Nora appeared to sense something of the sudden shift in his mood. "Ian, what on earth is this all about?"

It was a moment of crux. He could pursue the matter. He could confront her with the suspicions now churning through him, which were these: that Nora might be in some sort of cahoots with Davenport or perhaps—though this might indeed be stretching—that she was an agent of MI5 herself. He could go so far as to browbeat her, to interrogate, even to threaten her. These, he knew, were the instincts of his military days. Dilemmas then had been resolved quickly, even lethally. One effectively solved a problem by seizing the jugular. Yes. Indeed. And he recalled those days now, vividly . . . and the ruthless predator such necessary tendencies had made of him. He hadn't liked what he'd become. He didn't now wish to revert to that old self. He had, after all, quit the spy business before that became his permanent condition.

To pursue the matter, however, he would have to tell her about being waylaid by the two Whitehall minions. It was a conundrum. Fleming stalled.

"I apologize, Nora," he said, trying to restore the amiable ambience of the previous moment before it was irrevocably lost. "I had thought for a moment that I recognized the name Winterberg in connection with Davenport, a man I know slightly. Rethinking the matter, I believe I've confused my facts. I'm frightfully sorry." He offered her a disarming smile, mildly regretful at the modest lie he'd just told. He forcibly relaxed his posture.

Nora, however, didn't appear to be "buying it," as the Americans would say.

"Do you regularly mix with MI5 agents?" she asked a bit pointedly.

"Davenport, you mean? No. As I said, I know him only slightly. Met him in passing." Which, at least, was relatively true.

"But when I mentioned Oscar Winterberg," she persisted, "your reaction was one of sure recognition, Ian. Are you going to try to deny it?"

Whenever one was caught in a lie, however small, matters grew geometrically complicated as one tried to extricate oneself. Fleming thought again of divulging all he knew. But that wouldn't be proper, he admonished himself. Davenport, whatever Fleming might think of the man and his aide, had trusted him with classified information. Not the sort of facts he was at liberty to be gossiping about with a high-profile member of the press. Whatever else Nora might or might not be, she *was* a correspondent, he reminded himself.

"Please, Nora," he said. "My apology is, I assure you, most sincere. The mental files I—as does any journalist, I think you'll agree—carry about in my head sometimes get a bit disorganized, owing to the clutter. The name Winterberg, umm, *rang a bell.* I believe that was the colorful term you used. As it happens, it was a false alarm." Again he ventured a winning smile.

The violinist beyond the courtyard's stone walls abruptly ceased scratching his bow across his strings. Into the lull came the grumbles of Kingston's evening traffic.

It was Nora's turn to drum her fingers on the red tablecloth.

"Ian," she pronounced, making two distinct syllables of his name. "I've interviewed quite literally hundreds of people before. One of the reasons for my success in this game is that I can sniff out a falsehood or an omission or a dodge like nobody's business. Now, I realize that this isn't an interview, and you're not my subject, but habits die hard. You've piqued my curiosity. You know something about Oscar Winterberg, and you've decided not to tell me. That's perfectly fine. But, say it direct. Tell me to drop it. Tell me you can't talk about it. Don't lead me around the bush."

Her frankness was discomfiting. But, Fleming reflected,

she was perhaps within her rights. Remotely, at some safe mental distance from this somewhat strained conversation, he felt a deep admiration for her talents in ferreting out deception, however minor. As Blake Young, those skills must be frequently effective.

"Drop it, Nora," Fleming said. "I can't talk about it."

He had been half expecting a negative reaction, imagining her demand for honesty might be some feminine wile. Instead, Nora only brightened, her fetching smile returning to her face. "There. Much better. Let's have a last glass of wine."

THE INCIDENT, IT seemed, hadn't marred their evening. Even so, Fleming didn't like the awkward position he'd been put in, withholding information from this woman, all because the file he'd read on Oscar Winterberg was confidential. He also resented the suspicions that had been planted in him concerning Nora. He found himself growing peeved, in hindsight, at Davenport. If Davenport hadn't snatched him from in front of that London hotel and tempted him with the Winterberg file, he wouldn't now be troubled with these thoughts. Damn the man, he thought. Damn both Davenport *and* Winterberg, he added for good measure.

Nora bubbled on blithely into the onsetting night. Fleming had taken her to a club. It was a windowless dugout of a place, the floors, walls and low roof composed of slats of dark timber. The furnishings were made of sturdy wood, evidently handcrafted. Rich local music was being played by a talented combo of Negro musicians. Steel drums twanged and banged a furious tattoo. It all smelled of sweat, the sweet sawdust-scent of lumber, cigarette smoke and alcohol. It tasted of frenetic revelry, that peculiar brand of Jamaican merrymaking that celebrated life's most primal beauties. Here in this club it did not matter, at least for these hours, that many of these people were relatively impoverished, that their individual existences were made of drudgery and menial repetition. Here they were freed by the music, the atmosphere, by their amassed animated energies.

Fleming and Nora ensconced themselves in a booth near the rear wall. The cushions were crosshatched in a vivid mix of colored threads. They were sitting away from the dancing space in front of the spotlit stage. There young men and women in colorful local dress gyrated and cavorted, twisting their nimble bodies about in the low-ceilinged club's smoky haze. Their energetic movements were at once almost lewd and ceremonial, as if this were some voodoo rite.

Nora stayed with wine, while Fleming switched to gin, his thoughts deepening with every drink, even as he carefully maintained a casual front. Still, vague tension rode his back, closing fingers about his neck.

"This is marvelous, Ian. So lively!"

"I'm glad you're enjoying yourself," he said, trying to match the giddy tone of her voice. His happy guise seemed to be fooling her, or at least she wasn't letting on this time that she was wise to the deception. Fleming didn't need to be reminded how perceptive this woman was.

Davenport. Nora. Winterberg. The same names that had haunted him during his flight from England. Here they were again, troubling him anew. Only now the three identities seemed more tightly tied to each other—into a complex puzzling bundle, in fact.

Was it possible that Nora had gotten the scent of Oscar

Winterberg from some source other than Davenport? Of course it was. It was *possible.* But the happenstance of her suddenly flying off to San Francisco to investigate Winterberg, so soon after Davenport had tried to recruit Fleming to do the same task, stretched all probability.

On the other hand, Nora might have picked up this investigative assignment days or weeks before Fleming had been approached by Davenport. Nora was a professional journalist, well known for plumbing stories others in the field couldn't hope to scratch. She doubtlessly had numerous sources, feeding her Lord knew how many leads, to say nothing of the editorial staffs that surely were constantly tossing choice assignments to their star correspondent.

On the other *other* hand, Davenport might have approached Nora—perhaps the same night Fleming had met her—under some other guise. Davenport, with or without Stahl in tow, could have assumed any convenient identity, concocting whatever front seemed suitable. He was, after all, in the spy business. How difficult would it have been to tempt Nora with Oscar Winterberg's story? The socialist German expatriate's tale was certainly intriguing enough to kindle a journalist's curiosity. Fleming's own inquisitiveness had been keenly aroused, he reminded himself.

That scenario would explain why Nora had disavowed knowing Francis Davenport. Fleming found he simply didn't want to believe that Nora would deceive him on that matter, which sharpened the guilty pang he already felt over his own small lies.

Not knowing how many removes he was from the original thought, he wondered again if Nora were actually working for MI5, sent down here to tempt him into doing Davenport's—and Lord Hemmingford's—bidding. That was the simplest and least appealing explanation.

It was complex indeed. Fleming realized he was only adding to that complexity by brooding over the situation. More than likely there was some pat innocuous accounting for it all.

It simply wouldn't do, however, to broach the subject again, not after he'd been so brusque and closemouthed about the matter. He would simply have to let it go. He could enjoy these next few days with Nora here on the island, then see her off when she left for the States. Whether or not she was doing Davenport's bidding, intentionally or unwittingly, she would no doubt break the story. Oscar Winterberg's past would be exposed to the national and international media. Nora would probably even dig up some further fascinating facts about the man, facts even the British intelligence apparatus had missed. She was just that good an investigative journalist. As a fellow newsman, he admired that.

"Shall we have another, Ian?"

A waiter in a white dinner jacket was hovering deferentially over their rear booth, evidently seeing if they wanted refills. He was in his twenties, kinky hair cut short. A pale scar bisected the outer extremity of his left eyebrow.

"Why not?" Fleming smiled at Nora. Her good looks and charming manner were almost enough to turn his thoughts completely away from his inward meditations. She was something more than a static object of beauty, though. The dynamic atmosphere of the club seemed to be affecting her, perhaps *in*fecting her. A distinct sexuality charged the air. Her brow wore a light shine of perspiration. Her vibrant eyes were now a-glimmer, promising depths of passion beneath them. Her finely molded shoulders moved to the spirited tribal rhythms of the band. Her breasts rocked slightly—and alluringly—to her movements. He had folded his arm across the back of their seat, and her hip and thigh pressed him repeatedly. Her flesh felt soft through the breezy material of her dress.

"You're not getting tired, are you, my dear?"

"Not in the least," she said effervescently. "This is a wonderful place. I could spend hours."

"Another round, then, my good fellow," Fleming said to the waiter, who gathered their glasses. Nora beamed.

No, Fleming decided. He definitely would not reopen the subject of Oscar Winterberg or Davenport with Nora. The topic was too fraught with tension. If he felt the need to probe the matter, in order to scratch his nagging itch of curiosity, he would have to pursue other avenues.

The waiter delivered their fresh drinks. As the music built toward an awesome thundering climax, the dancers whipping about wildly now as though possessed by spirits, Nora's soft fingers closed over Fleming's hand, her touch stimulating and cool even in the hot smoky grotto of the club.

"We don't necessarily have to spend *hours* here, you understand," she purred, lips now close to his ear. "If you have some other location in mind. . . ."

Chapter 11

FLEMING RETREATED at the last moment. It was a mental, emotional—not to mention physical—wrench.

They had left the ripe atmosphere of the club. He had guided the Rapier to her hotel. The mood was one of allure and promise, though neither of them had specified in words what that promise entailed.

The familiar telltales would be obvious to a blind man. Nora's sultry glances were coming with increasing regularity. Her speech was peppered with tasteful but still suggestive double-entendres.

Under almost any other circumstances Fleming would have followed through. He knew the motions well. Nora was certainly attractive, disarmingly so. He silently admitted that some of the thoughts he'd entertained earlier in the evening concerning this woman had been less than gentlemanly.

Yet, now, parked before the Chabrol Arms' fronting columns with moonlight spread about the quiet street, he shied from the moment. The hotel loomed above, the green cupola five stories up a blocky silhouette. The stars over Kingston stood out sharply, even against the contesting moonlight, individual jeweled points in the black tropical sky. The Rapier's motor was still running.

He found himself saying, "Nora, I am afraid the day is overtaking me. I feel rather fatigued. May I drop you here?"

Her blue eyes blinked in sharp surprise. A ripple of disappointment crossed her features. Nonetheless, she held a steady smile on her face, for which Fleming was grateful. His intention hadn't been to put her out. "Why, of course, Ian. I apologize for wearing you out so."

"Nonsense," he said. "Your company has been most invigorating."

"Evidently too much so," Nora noted wryly.

"I should like to see you tomorrow, if I may."

"Delightful. Six-ish, let's say."

"I'll collect you here."

He stepped out and circled around the rear of the auto, somewhat aghast at himself for this withdrawal from the night's favorable proceedings. He eyed Nora a moment from behind, lingering over her rich cascade of red hair and bare shoulders. A pang of regret pinched him. But he was, quite simply, too distracted by all this Winterberg folderol. He wanted to satisfy himself thoroughly on at least one matter before he saw Nora again. He would require tomorrow morning to set things in motion. Until then he simply had to beg off.

"I'll see you into the lobby," he said, extending a hand to lift her out of her seat.

Nora came to her feet, giving his fingers only a good-natured squeeze this time. "There there, Ian. I think I'm capable of covering the distance alone. Really, it's been a wonderful time."

Before he could speak, she had pecked a brief kiss on his cheek and was moving away. Moths trembled frantically through the light of his headlamps as he watched her sashay toward the striped awning. Each sensual motion of her body was a piercing reminder of what he had elected to forgo. She strolled through the hotel's doors, the hem of her white and ocher dress swirling elegantly as she vanished.

He drummed his fingers a moment on the steering wheel, thinking somewhat mournfully of the road not taken, then turned the car about and headed home.

GENUINE FATIGUE DID overtake him as he cruised homeward, careful of the nighttime road, keeping his speed at a modest level. He guided the Rapier down his drive and into his front yard and cut the engine. And heard—saw? sensed?—something. Something to make him immediately alert, though he couldn't determine what had tripped his internal alarms.

Fleming gave no especial credence to those extrasensory gifts some claimed to possess. That a few people *sensed* things beyond accepted human scope seemed easily enough explained: an individual might not always be aware of his senses, but they functioned nonetheless; sometimes sensory information bypassed the otherwise engaged—or lax—consciousness and entered the subconscious. So it was that one *felt* someone staring at him, when he had only been notified of this by one or another sense to which he was currently paying no attention.

He sat a moment in the Rapier, in the sudden hush. Here there was no generator buzzing through the night, and only the voices of crickets and frogs were to be heard.

Making as if to check something in his pockets, he stalled a moment, ears now deliberately tuned to his surroundings, his eyes furtively combing the darkened greenery that encircled his home. There were endless places to hide amidst that foliage. Was he being watched from those trees and bushes? It certainly *felt* so.

Isaiah would be long gone by this late hour. A single lamp still burned within the house, the one customarily glowing in the entryway beyond the front door and seeping about its edges.

In the surrounding bushes Fleming saw and heard nothing. He climbed from the auto, his fatigue already dissipated by his suddenly heightened vigilance. It was more than likely that nothing was out of the ordinary, that he was in no danger whatever, but ingrained habits were not easily shaken.

Inside the house he had a pistol, an Enfield Mk II .38. He would not have felt comfortable being entirely without access to a weapon but had never felt the need to carry it about with him on the island. Of a sudden, though, he wished he had it now on his person—

Snap.

A twig. A twig stepped upon and snapped by a human foot trying to move with stealth. These were, perhaps, extreme conclusions to jump to, but Fleming's alerted senses told him what he had heard. He showed no outward response to the sound. Keeping a cool head was second nature to him. He felt no especial fear, merely caution. He was in a potentially perilous situation, and he would handle it.

The sound had been real enough, whatever its source. It had originated to his left, behind a screen of trees, no more distant than twenty yards. He moved toward his front door, steps even. It would have been a fine thing to dash inside and retrieve his .38, but now seemed the more appropriate time for action, if he meant to take any.

Three strides from the door he abruptly ducked and darted. He pivoted and used his shoulder to cut through the bushes abutting the front of his house, swiftly running its length. Seconds later he was diving through the line of trees, knowing each chink where a man might slip past.

Here he paused, listening intently. And heard unmistakably the noises of someone else scrambling away through the greenery. *There*—cutting away from the house!

Fleming burst after, seeing still some distance ahead the whipping limbs of foliage in the moonlight. Someone *had* been spying on him! He didn't spare any thought to who it might be. Such niggling details could wait. Instead, he leapt through the undergrowth beneath the trees, his nimble body making good headway through what was a challenging obstacle course in this light.

The shapeless figure ahead was zigzagging madly but making better speed than he. Fleming had no way of knowing if this individual was armed but naturally presumed so; and so he exercised more caution than his pursuer, who was free to sprint as best he could.

A jagged branch caught the sleeve of Fleming's stylishly cut tan jacket and wouldn't let go. He lost several seconds yanking the fabric free, not even wincing when he heard the cloth tear.

Turning once more to resume his pursuit, however, he saw nothing moving ahead of him.

Blast! His prey may have simply dropped to the ground, either lying still or creeping away on his belly, careful not to disturb any bushes. Or perhaps during the brief distraction he had made for the road or the beach, beyond Fleming's sight. And each second of inaction meant his quarry was getting that much further away.

Fleming had come this far. He ran for the road, moving even slower now so that he wouldn't simply step past his pursuee if indeed he was trying to conceal himself on the ground. Reaching the road, he found nothing. No traffic. Not even the fading sound of an engine.

Doggedly he recrossed the patch of bushes, finding no one and nothing hidden amongst them, and came out on the far rocky crescent of his cove. There was nothing to see but the calmly lapping waves and a tract of undisturbed sand glowing mutely in the moonlight.

He spent ten more minutes searching the immediate vicinity, certain he would find nothing and not being disappointed.

The likeliest explanation was, of course, that he had interrupted a burglar meaning to break into his home. That would account for the speed with which the man had fled. Someone meaning him personal harm wouldn't have been frightened off so easily. Perhaps he should alert the police, let them know a prowler was about. But not tonight, no; surely it could wait. Once more he was tired, his fatigue creeping back over him now that the minor crisis had passed.

Fleming walked back to his house, pausing to button the canvas hood over the Rapier's interior, then letting himself into his front door. He examined his torn sleeve, sighing mildly. Likely Ruth, his laundress, could mend it.

A short while later, as he prepared to retire, he retrieved his Enfield Mk II from its hiding place and set it atop his bedside table.

Chapter 12

HE DIDN'T stir until Isaiah's hand gently nudged his shoulder. He slitted open his eyes to the rosy glow of sunrise in his bedroom. Despite the late hours he often kept, he remained determined to keep this his customary time of awakening, military habit or not. The morning smelled fresh, as crisp as the laundered sheets cocooning his body. Birds were celebrating the daybreak with a chorus of trilling song.

He recalled instantly the late events of last night—the prowler he'd surprised and chased through the bushes. In the daylight they seemed more minor than before.

"Good morning, sah."

"Good morning, Isaiah." He pinched at the corners of his eyes. "Be a good fellow, won't you, and lay on some hot water. Afterward, some strong coffee, then breakfast. I'll be going into Kingston again today. I'll stop in at Henry Long's. Does the house require any supplies?"

Fleming washed and dressed. Ruth had delivered a load of freshly laundered clothing, and he chose a few casual items. He pinned a note to the lapel of his tan jacket with the torn sleeve and left it atop his silent valet. She could collect it on her next visit. Then he made his way downstairs.

Isaiah had indeed brewed strong coffee. The hot liquid sent stimulating tendrils through his body, awakening his last nerve endings. He realized belatedly that he had, after all, had a fair amount to drink last night with Nora. The alcohol, though, he decided, hadn't been a contributing factor to his worries over Davenport and Oscar Winterberg.

A simple, though savory, breakfast followed. Isaiah produced a slip of paper that was a brief list of items for the household.

"Very good, Isaiah. I'll include these in my errands. I shan't be long. I'll return for lunch."

Isaiah opened the front door for Fleming. "Mistah Fleming?"

"Yes?" Fleming lingered on the threshold. The day outside was bright and already heating.

Isaiah's lips pursed themselves pensively a moment. "Sah, was it bad news after all?"

Fleming frowned mildly, puzzled by the non sequitur. "What do you mean?"

Isaiah hesitated another moment, as though leery of committing a breach of protocol. Finally he said, "Yesterday, sah. When that message was delivered and you went into Kingston. I asked if it were bad news, and you said it wasn't."

"Yes?" Fleming pressed, eager to get under way but also curious as to what his houseman was getting at. Plainly the man was ill at ease.

"I . . ." Isaiah lowered his large eyes, his brows creasing above them. "I wondered if perhaps the news had been bad after all. If it's not too impertinent to ask."

Fleming by now was thoroughly perplexed. Was Isaiah trolling for gossip? That seemed rather out of character for the man, who so far had comported himself quite professionally while in Fleming's employ.

"And why on earth would you ask?" Fleming asked somewhat pointedly.

In a gentle deferential tone Isaiah said, "As I came in

to wake you this morning, sah, you seemed to be having an . . . unpleasant dream. Thrashing about. I feared something might be troubling you."

Fleming blinked, startled. He recalled no dreams, but evidently he had dreamt quite violently, if it had caused Isaiah to remark on it. He wondered why he'd been unable to remember the nightmare on waking and wondered further what his subconsciousness had been wrestling with—though if he had to, he might make a fair guess. Apparently this Winterberg business was troubling him on some deep level.

He smiled easily and reassuringly at his houseman. "Nothing to fear, Isaiah. No bad news. We all have unpleasant dreams from time to time."

"Very good, sah. I beg your pardon for bringing up the matter." He made a shallow bow as Fleming stepped out into the day. The morning was striped with a few bone-white clouds that offered, at best, minimal relief from the full weight of the sunlight. The sultry heat cloaked his body.

The display of concern had been rather touching, Fleming decided as he followed the road into the city. It was nice to think of Isaiah Hines as something more than an indifferent hired man. Fleming reminded himself to ask him if he played chess. A game now and then would be a pleasant way to help pass the coming months.

He parked and buttoned up the Rapier. The shaped canvas hood fastened to the body of the car and the upper edge of the windscreen with a series of metal snaps, completely tenting the interior which otherwise would lie exposed.

He entered the nondescript grey building outside which he had parked. The blinds drawn over the windows hid what Fleming knew to be an almost tireless buzz of activity. News offices were rarely idle, and this branch of the Kemsley newspaper empire remained in virtually constant motion. Fleming had taken a job with the enterprise following his retirement from the spy game. He had worked as a correspondent in his younger days, and returning to a familiar trade—one that didn't involve murder and cloak-and-daggery—had frankly been a relief.

He made casual greetings as he threaded his way through the pool of news desks. The office was indeed bustling with its usual—and only tenuously controlled—flurry. Staff members scuttled to and fro. Voices barked into phones. The rapid-fire *tap-tip-tap* of multiple typewriters overlapped to create a hive-like clamor. Fleming crossed to the door of Merlin Powell, his editor, and rapped his knuckles on the glass.

"Come in," he heard from within and entered.

The office was large but nonetheless exuded a sense of immediate claustrophobia, owing to the tall columns of metal filing cabinets that stood along every available inch of wall space.

Powell's great square body was wedged behind a desk that was a riot of clutter. An electrical ceiling fan twirled its vanes overhead, hard enough to shiver the corners of a few stray papers on the desk top. Powell, however, still appeared to be suffering heroically in the heat. A phone, which he was currently speaking into, was lodged against his neck. Both his hands were busy, one making rapid notations on a pad of yellow lined paper, the other furiously waving what looked like a geisha's fan in his face.

The editor eyed Fleming with surprise and curiosity as he finished his phone call, then laid the mouth- and earpiece contraption back in its cradle.

"Fleming," he said, the brightly printed fan still waving violently. "Good Lord, what brings you out into this cauldron? Don't tell me you're reporting for work." Powell's expression turned droll.

Fleming returned him a wry smile. "Just out enjoying the day. Marvelous weather today, wouldn't you say?"

"A more beastly climate I can't recall since Bombay," Powell grumbled.

Fleming took a facing hardback chair. "After being subjected to the start of another English winter, I find this quite refreshing."

"Fleming," Powell said, leaning forward, "you might be out on a lark today, but I am conducting business as usual. If this is merely a social call, please get on with it and then begone."

The island's sultry clime was evidently grating heavily on Powell's nerves. The editor's large body oozed with irritability. The blue short-sleeved shirt he wore was damp beneath the arms. Fleming eased back in his chair, exuding a deliberate air of aplomb. "Very well. To business. I should like to ask a favor."

"Indeed?"

"Yes. Information. A verification actually. How good are your contacts in Whitehall?"

Powell's brows came immediately together. "What are you up to?"

There was no mistaking the note of suspicion in his editor's voice. Fleming said, "Nothing disreputable, I assure you. I merely want to confirm—or disprove—that a particular MI5 agent is indeed just that. I saw the man's credentials"—and false credentials were the spy game's stock in trade—"but I should be more satisfied on the matter if I had some more significant substantiation."

"Why?" Powell asked flatly. His rounded shoulders hunched as he leaned slightly forward, as though his general annoyance at the island's torrid weather were finding focus.

"Is that of any real importance?" Fleming countered. "Do you imagine that I'm launching myself into a new career as a double agent?" Powell knew something of his past, though not to the extent that he was privy to Fleming's ultra-secret postwar activities as one of "Churchill's Boys." Powell had served as an administrator in the RAF during the war.

"No. I don't imagine that."

"Very well. Can you aid me?"

"I don't especially like this." Powell's Oriental fan kept a steady cadence, hopelessly trying to beat back the humid air. "Are you working on a story?"

"No."

"No," Powell grumbled. "I didn't imagine that either." He heaved a heavy sigh. "Very well, Fleming. You've done adequate work for me in the past. But if this leads to anything newsworthy, I will expect you to let me know."

Fleming smiled suavely. "Naturally." A news story was the farthest thing from his mind, but Powell didn't need to know that. If misleading his editor helped Fleming gather the information he desired, so be it.

Powell turned his paper pad to a fresh sheet and picked up a pen. "Name?"

"Francis Davenport. He has an aide, name of Stahl." Fleming spelled the name, recalling it from when he'd seen the agent's identification. "First name, Norbert. They're agents of MI5—or at least they're supposed to be. As I said, I only wish to know one way or the other. Allow me to thank you in advance for your gracious assistance."

"Check in here in an hour," Powell said as Fleming stood. "If I don't have the information, the wheels at least should be turning by then."

"Most kind of you." Fleming stepped out of the office, leaving Powell to agonize in the heat.

The hubbub in the main news room was even more tumultuous than when he had first entered. Clerks were now zinging among the desks, nearly crashing into one another in their haste. The babble of voices had risen to a level that made picking out individual words impossible. Likely some new story was breaking, something important by the looks. Fleming, ignoring his reflexive journalistic curiosity, maneuvered rapidly through the chaos and out the door. Whatever was happening didn't immediately concern him, and he still had an errand to run.

His next stop was Henry Long's. The distance from the newspaper office was not far, and on impulse Fleming decided to walk the half mile.

He followed a series of cluttered side streets, passing walls of flimsy wood and cheap corrugated metal that had been painted in gentle pastels. Dark colors absorbed too great an amount of heat; whites threw back blinding glares from the sun. The sky remained scudded only by those same wisps of cloud from earlier. Barely dressed dark-skinned children scampered about, hollering and laughing in the unaffected exuberance of youth, while mothers clucked over them and gossiped.

The side streets eventually emptied onto a broad busy marketplace, the flow of commerce undaunted by the heat of the day. Carts and stalls were strewn about the scene. Fruits and vegetables were being hawked and haggled over enthusiastically. Fleming's sandals slapped the pavement in a steady rhythm as his long legs carried him through the bustle. At some nebulous distance he detected the wail of a siren. He was pleased that Merlin Powell had been cooperative. He had no doubt that the man could ferret out, with no great effort, the information that would ease—or increase—some part of Fleming's present worries.

And if it turned out that Davenport and Stahl *weren't* legitimate members of the British Secret Service, what then? He didn't know. It would, however, certainly put a new spin on things.

Henry Long's chandlery was a large affair, its interior dimly lit and its shelves crammed with every imaginable piece of automotive and nautical equipment. Fleming approached the empty counter.

"Ah, Mr. Fleming," Henry said, emerging an instant later from a curtained back room. "Always a pleasure, sah." Henry was large and dark, like his cluttered establishment. His poor eyes peered at Fleming from behind tiny-lensed spectacles that sat atop the bridge of an ample nose.

"Henry, how is business?" It was a broad question, one that might be answered in a number of different ways. Henry Long did a fine lawful trade in his goods. He was also the man who knew *everything* that happened on the island, a human switchboard of dubious gossip and reliable information. It was a pity, Fleming thought, that his sphere of influence was limited solely to Jamaica. Otherwise he could have delved into this Davenport business himself. Fleming had made use of Henry as a source of information in the past.

"Business is business, sah," Henry said enigmatically in his low voice. He was drawing meditatively on a pipe filled with pungent tobacco. "What business would you like to conduct today?"

Fleming extracted Isaiah's brief list of household supplies and laid it on the countertop. "A few items, Henry. Nothing more. The two-gallon tin of kerosene is the most important."

Henry's crocodile eyes squinted through his preposterously tiny lenses and the intervening cloud of pipe smoke. "Yes, sah. These shall be no trouble."

While Henry shuffled his ample figure around the chandlery collecting goods, Fleming idly wandered the aisles, lighting a Players. Again in the distance, but louder now, he thought he heard the keening of a siren—or sirens. Fire trucks?

When Henry returned to his counter, wrapping up the items, Fleming asked, "Do you hear those sirens?"

"Yes, sah. It is my eyesight that is poor, as you enjoy pointing out, not my hearing."

Instead of retorting with some similar item of banter, Fleming, beginning to frown now, asked, "Is something burning in the city?" He could not recall seeing any tinge of smoke in the morning sky.

"I believe it was a small fire. And it is already contained."

"How do you know that?" asked Fleming as Henry presented the bill. He counted money onto the counter.

"I endeavor to be informed," Henry said with a small, almost private smile.

"Where then was the fire?"

"It was a bomb, sah."

"A *bomb*?" Fleming said sharply, startled. Did this have to do with that commotion that had been erupting as he exited the newspaper office? Yes, surely.

"Yes, sah," Henry replied, unperturbed. "It exploded in a room at the Chabrol Arms a short while ago."

A hard wave of shock and dread went through Fleming's

body, and he found himself gaping dumbly for several hammering heartbeats.

An instant later he was in motion, racing for the chandlery's door. "Hold my goods, Henry! I'll return for them later!" Then he was sprinting into the street.

Chapter 13

He made far better time sprinting the distance than he would have if he'd backtracked to retrieve the Lagonda Rapier from in front of the newspaper office. Fleming dashed in a headlong rush, his long athletic legs carrying him through pedestrian and vehicular traffic. He met with cries of surprise and anger as he nearly bowled over others walking in the streets or cut off a cart or automobile.

At the moment he cared nothing about niceties. It was of the utmost urgency that he reach the hotel.

He saw the fire trucks and milling policemen. A few uniformed officers from the Government House were directing the chaotic movements of the firefighters and members of the local constabulary, who wore uniforms of crisp white against their dark skins. The police were attempting to push back the crowd which had inevitably gathered about the commotion.

Fleming, pulling up and heaving deep breaths, silently cursed the mob. It would make gaining access to the hotel or even information about what had occurred that much more difficult.

He edged through the curious jostling locals, being none too gentle about elbowing his way toward the wavering cordon the police were laboring to set up. Agitated guests of the stately hotel were pouring from beneath the red-and-green striped awning, demanding in loud indignant voices to know what was happening. Men clad in firefighting gear were entering and leaving the building, booted feet clomping heavily on the bleached stone steps that led up to the entrance. The sirens of the trucks cut out as Fleming neared the blockade, and the confused babble of voices rose louder.

He still saw no smoke in the sky. The tall windows of the hotel, rising five imposing levels to an elegant green cupola, all appeared to be intact. The front supporting columns stood as firm as ever. Perhaps the bomb had detonated in a rear room . . . if indeed there had been a bomb after all. Henry Long's information was often reliable, but he was not omniscient.

"Officer!" he called, pressing past a stout black woman wearing a colorful head scarf.

The man from the military mission turned his head, eyes narrowing until he saw Fleming. He was young and had yet to truly grow into his sharp patrician features, including a striking hawk-like nose. Nonetheless, he exuded a precise military bearing, a proud representative of Her Majesty's government in Kingston. On seeing Fleming, obviously a fellow countryman, he stepped forward.

"Yes, sir?"

Fleming, immediately adopting the cool stoicism of a to-the-manor-born Englishman, asked, "What, pray tell, has happened here?"

"Just a bit of bother, sir. Nothing to trouble yourself over."

Fleming quietly clenched his fists. The tumult of the scene belied the officer's cool assurances.

"Perhaps if I might trouble you for a few specifics? I've a . . . friend, you see, staying at this establishment. I should like to assure myself that she is unharmed. It certainly appears there's been some excitement this morning." He gave the officer a winning smile, maintaining his composure.

"Oh, I see, sir. May I inquire as to the name of this party?"

"A Miss Nora Blair DeYoung. I fear I don't know her room number."

"And your name?"

"Ian Fleming."

The officer nodded. "One moment, sir." He moved off through the stirring mob.

Fleming craned his neck to scan the crowd, searching for Nora among the milling guests. He did not see her. He felt a coldness closing about his innards, a prescience that surely had no basis in reality. Evidently *something* had occurred here today. But what, in the end, was the likelihood of a bomb actually exploding in one of these rooms? Jamaica might have its moments of unrest, but it was hardly a war zone. And what reason did he have to think that Nora might be involved in the incident, that something untoward might have happened to her?

It was foolishness, but of course Fleming would not be satisfied until he set eyes on her.

It was several more minutes before the officer returned. The throng of onlookers meanwhile continued to ogle and stir. One of the fire trucks, bleating its horn, pulled away from the scene. Evidently whatever immediate danger there had been was past.

"Mr. Fleming?" The officer, having crept up unseen through the milling bodies, was now standing at Fleming's elbow. "Would you please come this way, sir."

Simple rationality had told him to expect the officer to return with word that Miss DeYoung was unharmed in her room or had been out shopping in one of the marketplaces when the incident occurred. A darker, less logical part of his mind told him that the officer would return with the sad news that Nora had been injured . . . or killed. Though Fleming was a cool-headed individual, he wasn't impervious to all irrationality.

Fleming followed the poised strides of the young officer as he cleared a path toward the hotel's entrance.

The black-floored lobby was almost as fraught with activity as the outside of the hotel. The guests here were raising an even louder and more furious hullabaloo, demanding explanations of the staff, who were themselves scurrying about frantically. Several were being questioned by local policemen. Firefighters tramped about the scene, pointedly ignoring the outraged outcries of the guests. They didn't, after all, work here and didn't have to answer to these pompous Europeans.

Now finally Fleming did smell a tinge of smoke, a harsh scent of burning that weaved subtle threads through the air. There appeared to be no signs of damage, however, at least in this lobby.

He caught sight suddenly of Colonel Robert Vanderbrook, the official who'd assumed leadership of the military mission when Lord Peter Broxton had been quietly packed off back to England, following a rather ignoble scandal. Vanderbrook was a hard leathery figure in his forties, his iron-grey hair cropped short, his shoulders broad. The insignia marking the collar of his military shirt were brightly polished. He stood like a statue in the middle of the turbulent foyer, bronze-bodied and unmoving, only his keen eyes shifting beneath dark brows. Fleming realized the young officer was leading him directly toward this figure.

"Colonel." The officer saluted. "Mr. Ian Fleming. He claims to know—"

Vanderbrook's returning salute turned into a curt gesture of dismissal as his eyes focused on Fleming. The officer scuttled away somewhat sheepishly.

"Mr. Fleming. A pleasure." Vanderbrook's hard-edged voice matched his general demeanor. "I've heard mention of you."

Fleming was unable to tell from this brusque comment if what Vanderbrook had heard was favorable or otherwise. "Colonel, at last we meet. I knew Lord Broxton—"

"No need to bring Broxton's name into the picture," Vanderbrook said with frank distaste. "I'm afraid I must ask you about your whereabouts during the past hour. Anyone with any connection to Miss DeYoung is being questioned. I'd rather you were questioned directly by me rather than the police or one of my junior officers." In a softer—or at least quieter—tone he added, "I know something of your accomplishments during the war. Fine work. If you'd like to step in here?" Vanderbrook gestured toward a nearby door marked MANAGEMENT.

Fleming didn't move. "Colonel," he said rather sharply, "I can account for my whereabouts and will be happy to do so. But—*please*—I would like to know if Miss DeYoung is unharmed or not."

Vanderbrook seemed to take no offense at his tone. "She's uninjured, Mr. Fleming. She was not in the room when the device exploded."

Relief thawed the coldness in his midsection. "Then there was a bomb?"

"Indeed. It's all being thoroughly investigated, I assure you. The men in our bomb detail are quite professional.

They handled explosives during the war. Are you a . . . close friend of Miss DeYoung?" The sly hesitation caused Fleming to wonder if Vanderbrook knew something about him beyond the general facts of his military service record.

He decided that adding to the exaggerated gossip surrounding his amorous reputation could do no harm. "She's a recent acquaintance. But—we've become rather close in a short period."

The colonel nodded. "Very well. Once we've finished, I'll take you in to see her. She's already provided all the information she can."

Fleming's interrogation took place in the small office marked MANAGEMENT. It was an austere sort of cubbyhole, containing a well-ordered desk and a pair of filing cabinets. The cone of light from the gooseneck desk lamp lit the room's center in a perfect white circle. Taking the two chairs before the desk, Vanderbrook and Fleming turned to face each other within that circle.

It was a familiar sort of squaring off, familiar in a discomfiting sense, harkening back to Fleming's military days. He had, more than once, sat in the interrogator's chair, grimly determined to extract whatever information was necessary to the moment from the individual he was facing. The means he used had varied. At their extremes those means had occasionally been . . . extreme.

It was all part of a past he had shut off from himself. But the instincts remained, embedded on a mental level below that of the conscious. And he could see no good reason for not drawing on those abilities now—as a means of defense.

"Will you please retrace for me your movements of this morning?" Vanderbrook asked.

That presented no difficulties. Fleming recited his

morning's itinerary—leaving home, stopping in at the newspaper office to see Merlin Powell, then at Henry Long's. It was a small matter to omit his reasons for visiting Powell. Vanderbrook listened to each detail with a curt nod.

"I've no reason to disbelieve you. . . ." Vanderbrook said hesitantly, possibly mildly uncomfortable questioning a fellow Englishman, particularly one with a war record he admired.

"But if you want to corroborate my account," Fleming finished, sparing him the bother, "you will find no trouble doing so."

Vanderbrook nodded. He seemed to silently appreciate Fleming's good sportsmanship. Nonetheless, he pressed on with his inquiries, a man with a job to do.

"Where did you first meet Miss Nora Blair DeYoung?"

Fleming's guard went up immediately, though his features betrayed nothing. In an eye blink he had sorted through the possible avenues of deception and half-falsehood he might use, then decided to start with the simple truth.

"In London."

"I see. Yet you say she is a recent acquaintance?"

"She is. We met at a sort of belated New Year's Eve celebration. I was leaving for Jamaica the following morning." He was still on safe ground but wary of the potential pits of mire surrounding him. There were things he would not reveal to Vanderbrook. His first impulse was to protect Nora from being unnecessarily grilled by this man. His second was to hold back any mention of Davenport or Winterberg until he could satisfy himself as to Nora's involvement in that tangled matter.

"Curious she should appear on our island only a few

days later, wouldn't you think?" Vanderbrook's tone was now perfectly neutral. "Or perhaps you two made plans to rendezvous?"

"Actually we made no plans," Fleming said smoothly. "However, as I mentioned, we became . . . close . . . in a brief period." Vanderbrook hopefully would draw his own conclusions, knowing the embellished rumors concerning Fleming's reputation as a Lothario.

"So Miss DeYoung took the initiative to call on you here on the island?"

"Yes. And I'm quite pleased she did. Our time in London was all too brief."

"I see." Vanderbrook's dark brows rippled as a thought passed behind them. "Tell me, Mr. Fleming, are you able to think of any person or persons who would wish to visit harm on Miss DeYoung?"

Fleming's face grew quietly grave. In a flicker of thought he recalled the prowler in his bushes last night, but what bearing could that have? He had even forgotten that he meant to inform the police of the incident. "No one, Colonel," he said firmly. "No one whatsoever. I must confess, this matter has me desperately concerned."

"And I also, Mr. Fleming," said Vanderbrook as solemnly from the far edge of the circle of light. He nodded once more, this gesture apparently indicating that the questioning was done.

Despite Fleming's urgent desire to see Nora as soon as possible, his professional instincts forced him to ask, "May I know the details of the bombing?" It would be best to acquire the facts while he could, and Vanderbrook seemed the surest source.

It was a good indicator that the colonel was satisfied as to Fleming's innocence in the incident when he answered readily, "The package was delivered to Miss DeYoung's room at approximately nine thirty-five, by a bellhop. She had made arrangements to have any letters or deliveries brought up to her room immediately."

Which made sense for a journalist, Fleming thought. If an editor sent something to a correspondent, it was a foregone conclusion that he wanted it read at once.

"Surely the bellhop has been questioned?" he asked.

"Of course. A uniformed courier dropped the package—a medium-sized papered box wrapped in twine, addressed to Miss DeYoung's room number—at the desk. We're looking for that courier now."

"Was her name on the parcel as well?"

"The desk clerk says not. The package was then given to the bellhop, who brought it up to her room on the third floor. He knocked several times, then opened the door with a passkey and left it on a small table in the entryway. Miss DeYoung had gone out just before nine."

"What sort of bomb was it?"

Vanderbrook hesitated a moment, perhaps belatedly reconsidering giving out so detailed an amount of information. Then with a decisive nod he continued.

"Apparently a rather simple device," the colonel said. "Inside the box was a coffee canister. The can was filled with what the investigators believe to be buckshot, the sort from shotgun shells. In fact, they are already supposing that several boxes' worth of shells were used to make the bomb. The shot filled the coffee can. Buried in the middle of the can was a small glass jar, and this was crammed with the shells' gunpowder."

"How did the device activate?" Fleming noted silently that the sort of explosive device he was describing had a single purpose: to eliminate *one* specific individual, without doing serious damage to anyone or anything else. Whoever had planted the bomb had meant only to target the occupant of Nora's room. "Was it a timer?" he asked.

"Evidently a hollow steel rod was drilled through the coffee can's lid and down into the smaller gunpowder-filled jar. The tube was stuffed with match heads. The tube was connected in some fashion to a hand-sized alarm clock, which had probably had its bells removed. After that it was simple enough. It was apparently set for quarter to ten. At least, that's when it detonated."

"Did the desk clerk or bellhop not hear the ticking?" Fleming asked with a mild frown.

"They both said no."

"Perhaps they might not have," Fleming mused. "The parcel was likely only in either's possession for a very few minutes. Perhaps not enough time to detect a sound as soft as a small clock's ticking from inside a package. Still . . ."

"I understand your doubts, and we of course are acting on these same suspicions. It is the courier we suspect, though. A white fellow. Nondescript. He wore a cap pulled low over his eyes. He dropped the package, then disappeared. No one had a good look at him."

"You said he wore a uniform."

"Yes. A simple grey workingman's coveralls and the cap. However, his courier company's name wasn't printed on the uniform. He didn't identify himself in any way. In fact, the desk clerk says all he said was the word *delivery* and then set down the box."

"Asking for no signature?" asked Fleming.

"No."

"Curious. Was the room badly damaged?"

"No. It wasn't much of a bomb, the lads in the bomb

squad say. A loud bang, a good deal of smoke and some buckshot in the walls was mostly the extent of it. The windows didn't even break. The fire was small, and the staff was in the room before it could take hold. Still, it obviously caused quite a stir."

Vanderbrook at last stood, apparently at the limit of what he intended to divulge.

Fleming stood as well. "You have my deepest thanks, Colonel."

"Fine, Mr. Fleming. And I appreciate your cooperation. I'll take you to Miss DeYoung now."

Chapter 14

NORA WAS in the same broad red-carpeted lounge where Fleming had called on her yesterday—in the same club chair, in fact. The spacious room was this morning, however, in a tumult. Policemen, firefighters, guests of the hotel and staff members made an unintentional and maddening barrier between Fleming and Nora, who hadn't yet seen him enter the room. It was Vanderbrook who parted the waters, clearing aside the bodies seemingly by using only his forceful presence. He snapped orders to his officers to remove anyone without official business from the lounge.

Fleming caught glimpses of Nora above the bobbing heads and shoulders. She was dressed in quite casual fashion—hiking boots, dungarees, a soft-colored man's cotton shirt. She was fanning her face with a wide-brimmed straw hat, stirring stray ringlets of her hair which was tied back into a simple knot. She appeared composed, but a leery watchfulness about her blue eyes betrayed some degree of disquiet. Her gaze darted among the bodies, wary and suspicious . . . and frightened.

Her eyes lit upon Fleming as Vanderbrook broke through the last of the crowd. Her well-tanned features, which at the moment looked decidedly pale, lit abruptly with emotion, and she dropped the hat carelessly to the floor and launched herself out of the deep chair. Before Fleming could speak, she had tied her arms around his neck and buried her head against his chest. He lifted his arms around her shoulders, inhaling the floral scent of her hair. Her body was trembling, a deep-rooted shivering that seemed to come from her bones.

Vanderbrook excused himself with a wordless nod and set about hastening the clearing of the lounge. Nora pressed herself tightly to Fleming.

"Nora—" Fleming began, seeking words of comfort.

"Oh, Ian," she murmured against his chest. "It's been a harrowing morning."

She started to sag, as though her knees were now going limp with relief. Fleming eased her carefully back toward her chair, then dropped to one knee on the carpet. She took both his hands in hers, gripping with some desperation. Her composure was fragmenting rapidly, and her limpid blue eyes were growing glassy with tears that had yet to spill down her cheeks. Her trembling worsened.

"Nora," he tried again, "they told me you were unharmed. Is that true?"

"Unharmed?" She considered the word, as if it were unfamiliar to her. After a moment she nodded. "Yes. Yes, Ian. I'm unharmed. At least as far as that I wasn't in my room when that . . . bomb . . . exploded."

"I was dreadfully worried," he said, somewhat inanely.

"Thank you. Thank you for being here—Wait." Nora's gaze abruptly sharpened. She blinked away her gathering tears. "Ian, what *are* you doing here? Our plans were for later in the day."

They had made those plans last night. He had been scheduled to meet her at the hotel at around six, and they would go out from here to dinner. He had been determined that the evening wouldn't be intruded upon again by the specter of Oscar Winterberg.

He explained that he had come into the city to pick up

supplies from Henry Long's, omitting his other errand of stopping in at the newspaper office. He wondered in a distant corner of his mind if Powell was already ferreting out the information about Davenport and Stahl that Fleming had requested. The matter seemed strangely unimportant now, upstaged as it was by Nora's near-tragedy.

"I'm so very glad you're here," she said, squeezing his hands even tighter.

"I'm glad you weren't in your room during the . . . incident," he said with heavy sincerity.

"Yes. Lucky, that. I've always had good luck. I went out to the shops, sometime around nine, I think. Imagine if I'd slept late. . . ." And now a single tear did spill, winding down her angled cheekbone.

She fished a dark filtered cigarette out of her cotton shirt's pocket, her hand still quivering slightly as she put it to her lips. Fleming lit it for her with his gold lighter.

"There there. The danger's past. You're safe." He wondered silently what right he had making such assurances.

"Who would want to murder me?" she asked in a sudden choked whisper. It was decidedly unnerving, he thought, seeing this strong-willed woman reduced to this state—though having one's hotel room blown up would surely distress the most staunch individual.

"I can't imagine."

"Neither can I," she said, sniffling. "There are precious few people who even know I'm on this island. Do you think the bomb was placed in my room by mistake?"

"I really haven't any idea."

Nora wiped her eyes, hanging onto Fleming's fingers with one hand as she drooped back into the club chair's deep cushions, drawing deeply on her cigarette. Fleming remained kneeling, only vaguely aware of the lounge emptying around them of the bulk of its occupants.

"When I returned from the shops, before that colonel—Vander-something—accosted me, I had no idea what had happened. There were people running. I smelled smoke."

"Were your things damaged?" Fleming winced a bit at this, his second inanity. But keeping her talking seemed best. Color was returning to her face.

A tiny smile curled one corner of her mouth. "Only a few items. Fortunately old habits saw me through. I keep a full suitcase beneath my bed whenever I travel, in case of the need of a quick getaway. The fire didn't reach under the bed." She ground out her cigarette, half-smoked, in the ashtray, sighing. "The management, of course, has been falling all over itself apologizing and trying to make amends. They made a great show of tearing up my bill. I will say, Ian, this has been a hell of a way to get a free room." The small laugh she snorted was rueful but seemed to signal that the initial shock had passed.

"So," Fleming said after a moment of silence, "it remains to discover if this really was an attack on yourself personally. Or if, as you mentioned earlier, this bomb was delivered to your room mistakenly."

"Yes. The colonel assures me the matter is under very serious investigation. There's a manhunt on for that courier—Do you know the details of what happened?"

"I do."

"They're still scouring my room for clues. What also remains to be seen is where I'm going to spend tonight."

"Where?" he asked, perplexed.

"Well, you don't think I'm staying here, do you? If I presume the worst—and one has to in a situation like this, doesn't one?—then I must assume that my life is in jeopardy. Colonel Vander-whatever-his-name-is has promised that I will be protected. He's offered to put me up at the Government House for my next three days on the island, where I'll surely be surrounded day and night by men in uniform—"

"I've a better idea," Fleming said suddenly, the thought taking a fierce grip on him.

Nora tilted her head quizzically. "What's that?"

"Come out and stay at my house." He leaned forward as he said it. Distantly he realized that only a short time ago he had been nursing vague but serious suspicions about this woman, going so far as to wonder if she herself were connected to MI5. All that seemed suddenly absurd, overwhelmed by the crisis she had just undergone. Whatever else she was, she was currently a woman in need; and Fleming, being a gentleman . . .

Nora's arched brows raised themselves. She smiled after a few seconds, lips twisting into something near to a smirk. "Well, now that's a thought," she said with some coyness.

Fleming smiled back. "It's your safety I have in mind, you understand. If we slip you away, tell no one but Vanderbrook, then your assailant, if indeed it is you he is after, will have no way of tracing you. You'll be some distance from Kingston—"

"—and much closer to you." Her smile warmed. "Ian, that is the single most delightful invitation I've received in some time. I accept."

He helped her out of the chair. They would retrieve whatever salvageable goods were in her room, then he would inform Vanderbrook of their plans. He would collect his supplies from Henry Long, bypass his appointment back at the newspaper office (all that could wait) and spirit Nora to his home. His heart beat happily at that thought.

THERE WERE FEWER places better to conceal oneself than at the scene of the crime, thought the American man, particularly a scene as chaotic as this. It was not difficult to loiter unseen among the other onlookers, watching along with the rest of the curious crowd as the last of the firefighters departed. The police that remained on the scene didn't give him a second glance, and why should they? The courier's uniform had been immediately disposed of, and the anonymity of his appearance virtually guaranteed that even if he were brought before that idiot at the front desk, he would go unrecognized.

Reflexively he scanned the crowd as well as the hotel. The onlookers were a hodgepodge of local brown types and imported Europeans. Everyone was gawking excitedly at the spectacle. Furtively picking through the faces, his eyes settled briefly on a particular individual—a white male, about forty years old, average build, blondish moustache, wearing a beige linen suit. This one was standing quietly, hands in pockets, observing the scene with a peculiar air about him. He wasn't ogling or gaping. He was watching with what looked to be calm purpose.

The American man studied this figure, some thirty yards distant among the jostling bodies, for a moment, then finally turned away. He had other things to attend to.

He quietly circled the hotel, having earlier identified all its entrances and exits. It was from a utility door nearby the kitchens that he noted—without appearing to note—that Fleming twerp and the good-looking girl emerge. He was carrying two pieces of her luggage. They looked like a pair of nitwit elopers.

Fleming too was an idiot. That the Brit had detected and chased him through those bushes last night didn't diminish the fact. A moment of carelessness, that was all it had been. And he hadn't gotten caught, had he?

They walked off, and he did not follow. He knew where they were going.

A short while later he listened through the buzzes and whirs of the overseas telephone connection. Once it was engaged, the line rang once. He spoke shortly, and a moment later a new voice came on.

"Monsieur H.," the American man said in a flavorful French accent. "The operation is *succès*—a success."

"Marvelous!" cried the heavy British voice. "I'll wire the second half of your payment immediately—"

He dropped the telephone onto its cradle and lit a pungent cigarillo, slouching in the wicker chair and putting his feet up on the rickety table. The room was small but functional, and he had little need of it beyond its phone and bed. Soon he would be off this detestable nigger-ridden island.

He thought of his payment, his ordinary features breaking into an eerie feral grin around the stump of his cigar. Of course that hoity-toity old bastard would wire him his second half. He probably had some idea of what might happen to him if he tried to welsh.

Chapter 15

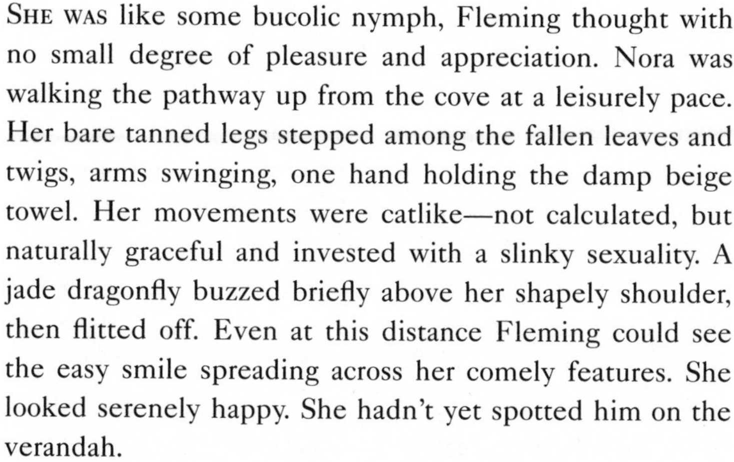

She was like some bucolic nymph, Fleming thought with no small degree of pleasure and appreciation. Nora was walking the pathway up from the cove at a leisurely pace. Her bare tanned legs stepped among the fallen leaves and twigs, arms swinging, one hand holding the damp beige towel. Her movements were catlike—not calculated, but naturally graceful and invested with a slinky sexuality. A jade dragonfly buzzed briefly above her shapely shoulder, then flitted off. Even at this distance Fleming could see the easy smile spreading across her comely features. She looked serenely happy. She hadn't yet spotted him on the verandah.

It was her second swim of the day, and it wasn't yet even one o'clock. He had eagerly joined her for that first morning dip but had struck his left knee against a stone on the cove's bottom, and so had begged off this second escapade. The very minor injury had been entirely his own fault, though it had certainly smarted at the time and would likely bruise. He had been diving from a rocky outcrop and miscalculated the depth of the water below. He had been showing off for Nora, pure and simple, like an infatuated schoolboy eager to impress.

In truth, it was something like an adolescent schoolboy that Fleming was feeling—happy, excitable—though he was making some efforts to hide such feelings from Nora. And from himself.

Nora was hardly the first female company he'd had to

his home. Women did periodically make brief appearances in his life. Not to belabor the point, but his romantic career was a fairly distinguished one. This, however, was the first time he'd had to inform the head of the military mission that he was taking in a guest. Colonel Vanderbrook hadn't been especially sanguine about the idea, but he was hardly in a position to take Nora into protective custody. Fleming had assured the colonel that Nora would be in safe hands. Vanderbrook had lifted a dark brow at that comment. Fleming hastened to add that he had a gun at his house and was quite capable of using it should any hint of danger toward Nora materialize. In the end Vanderbrook sanctioned the plan. He said that Miss DeYoung would receive any updates in the progress of the manhunt for the bogus courier. He had also asked that she check in at the Government House before leaving the island.

Fleming had only realized when they had reached his home that he'd neglected to inform the police in Oracabessa about that prowler in his bushes. Ah, well. What did it matter?

He was lolling happily on the verandah, feet up on a wicker footstool. He was still wearing his swimsuit from his earlier dip, to which he'd added a short-sleeved floral-printed shirt. He had a fine view of Nora's progress up the path. Her wet hair was plastered about her head and shoulders, the red darkened to a chestnut hue, the ringlets in delightful disarray. The white swimsuit she wore was molded to her most excellent figure, leaving bare her thighs and offering a provocative glimpse of cleavage. The tropical setting seemed idyllic for her, as though she were meant to dwell in this lush scene.

Leaving the island. Two more days and she would be

gone. The thought was more wrenching than he cared to admit.

Nora finally saw him on the verandah, lifted her free arm and waved. Fleming toasted her with his cocktail and smiled.

"Chin-chin," he said as she climbed the steps and strolled toward him, draping the towel over the railing.

"You don't suppose I might have one of those?" she asked sweetly, trailing her fingertips along his bare forearm where it rested on the lounge's arm.

Fleming smiled. "Of course. Here at Goldeneye our guests' needs are our paramount concern. Isaiah!"

Isaiah, however, had already assembled the cocktail inside the house and now swept out onto the verandah with it, neatly draping a large fresh towel over the cushions of the empty adjacent lounge before Nora could settle herself into it. A tiny smile on Isaiah's face betrayed the pleasure he was feeling at his own efficiency. Fleming eyed Nora's body, so becomingly encased in its damp swimsuit.

"That's such a curious name for a house. Though, being an American I must admit I find the naming of one's home a rather quaint custom. Still, Goldeneye? What does it mean?"

"It was the name of a dog I had as a boy," he said casually.

He had awarded his home the title after a wartime operation of the same name against the Germans in Spain. But passing such information on to Nora would reveal more of his personal history than he was willing to. It was best to let her think of him only as a journalist and not a retired member of the British Secret Service.

Isaiah delivered Fleming a fresh drink as well. His manner hadn't changed since Nora's arrival late yesterday morning. He had accepted her presence at the house with the unflappable aplomb of the first-rate houseman he was proving himself to be. His sister, Ruth, had also encountered the house's new guest yesterday. She had been putting in one of her brief appearances to deliver cleaned washing and take away the soiled laundry. She had voiced no complaint about the heavier load, made so by the articles that Nora added to the basket.

They chatted with companionable ease as they sipped their drinks. They didn't speak of the bombing of Nora's hotel room nor of her imminent departure from the island. Neither did Oscar Winterberg's name surface. It was merely breezy conversation, the sort that lovers engaged in.

He had installed her in the neatly furnished guest bedroom yesterday. But even as she slid her suitcase beneath the bed, according to her old habit, they had both known she wouldn't be sleeping the night in that room. And that night had proven to be a glorious one.

Was his attraction to this woman merely physical? It seemed not. Decidedly not. No, Nora's rather exquisite female physique would not be enough to hold his attention so. It was her forceful spirit, which was almost masculine in its intensity, that had cast a spell over him. And that was it, wasn't it? He *was* under her spell.

Another aspect of his attraction to her was, curiously, her professional credentials—the fact that she *was* a consummate professional in the same field as he, a woman of the world in fact, with a keen intellect and an impressive store of worldly wisdom. She was her own person, confident, capable. She was quite unlike the other women in his past.

"Penny for your thoughts," cooed Nora from the adjacent lounge.

He blinked, only now realizing their airy exchange had lapsed into silence. Recovering, he smiled. "What's that in pence, my dear? You'll have to refurbish my memory on the exchange rates."

She snickered softly and let the matter drop.

Moments later, rising in the still moist air, there came the sound of an approaching engine, clearly heard even from here at the rear of the house.

"I believe we have company," he said, finishing his drink and levering himself out of the chair. "Perhaps its one of Vanderbrook's minions with news of your mad bomber." He instantly regretted the light tone of his voice. It was, of course, no laughing matter. And Nora was well within her rights to be sensitive about the subject.

She only smiled, shrugged and stood. "Shall we go see?"

Arm in arm they entered the house, reaching the front door behind Isaiah, who opened it, revealing the heavily breathing bulk of Merlin Powell.

Fleming stopped short. He had neglected to return to the newspaper offices to collect the information he'd requested on Davenport and Stahl. The pertinence of that information had waned dramatically in the face of the bombing at the Chabrol Arms. He had relegated the whole affair to a place of secondary importance in his mind.

"Fleming . . . oh, and—Miss?" Powell removed his straw fedora.

"Miss Nora Blair DeYoung," Fleming filled in automatically. "And this is Merlin Powell, my editor at the newspaper."

"How do you do?" they said simultaneously. Powell was

making a valorous effort not to ogle, but Nora's curve-hugging swimsuit would likely test the manners of a monk. Powell took two lumbering steps inside the house. Isaiah closed the door behind him. If Powell had journeyed all the way out here, Fleming thought, it wouldn't do for Nora to know that he had been clandestinely delving for information about Davenport and Stahl. He would need to separate the two.

"Shall I serve drinks in the lounge, sah?" Isaiah piped up in the nick of time.

Fleming said casually, "Yes, that would be capital." To Powell he said, "Is this more nonsense about that feature assignment you've been trying to lure me into taking on?" He threw a subtly pointed look at his editor. Nora, still hanging on his arm, glanced between the men.

Powell, divining instantly the role he was supposed to play, said, "It's not good for a man to be idle, Fleming. There've been some . . . developments I think you should be apprised of."

Turning, Fleming said, "Nora, dear, would you excuse us? This is going to be a brief tedious visit while I explain to this gentleman that I'm presently not interested in his assignment."

She smiled. "Certainly, Ian. I believe I'll make use of your beach once again. Mr. Powell? A pleasure to meet you."

"And you, Miss DeYoung," he replied. His eyes followed her helplessly as she disappeared back into the house. A moment later her padding footsteps could be heard on the verandah.

"Thank you," Fleming said, breathing easier. Before Powell could respond, he quickly added, "Into the lounge with you. You know the way. Isaiah will fix you something."

Fleming went upstairs, wincing slightly as he put too much weight on his mildly injured left knee. He peeked from a window, saw that Nora was indeed heading again to the cove and went to his bedroom to change. Powell was hardly formal company, but he stripped off his swimsuit and the rather heinously floral short-sleeved shirt nonetheless. Then he changed into more dignified attire to receive his guest.

Padding downstairs in sandals, white slacks and a decorous ash-colored shirt that was much less of an eyesore, he entered the lounge. The room was large and comfortable, with a good deal of breathing space between the furnishings. It was carpeted in an earthen-toned nap that nearly matched the rich wood of the wainscotting. Powell had planted himself on the settee and was dabbing his brow with a kerchief and fanning himself with his fedora. He set aside both items to attack the large tropical-looking drink Isaiah had concocted. The tall glass was beaded with moisture. Powell heaved a sigh.

Before the conversation could again degenerate into grumblings about the weather, Fleming, still standing in the doorway, said, "I do appreciate that bit of footwork. You take your cues quite astutely."

"A man must think on his feet." Powell rocked his weight forward on the settee. "So . . . who's the young lady?"

Fleming moved forward and took an armchair that faced the settee across a swath of the carpet. "Precisely who I told you. Miss Nora Blair DeYoung."

"That wasn't what I was asking," the editor said somewhat tartly.

Fleming did understand the intent of the question. He lit a Players and tapped the ash into a hammered brass ashtray set atop a nearby three-legged stand. "She's in the journalism game," he finally said, though he naturally had no intention of revealing Nora's alternate—and more renowned—identity of Blake Young.

"Really? And what's she doing here?" One could almost hear the leer in his voice.

"Being a most courteous guest for the time being."

"I see."

"Did you come all the way out here to be snide?"

Powell looked momentarily wounded. "I've come to deliver the information you requested, Fleming. Since you didn't see fit to come get it yourself."

Fleming now leaned forward in his seat. "You've had word from your spies in Whitehall?"

"Spies? A harsh word, don't you think? Conjures images of cloaked desperados plunging knives into the backs of kings."

"Nonetheless," pressed Fleming. "Have you information regarding Davenport and Stahl?"

Powell picked a folded sheet of lined yellow paper from his shirt pocket. "Francis Nathanial Davenport and Norbert Stahl, no middle name, to be precise. And, yes, they are both legitimate members of the Secret Service. Their names appear in the personnel files. I can't tell you what their exact positions are within the branch—and can't find out without causing more of a stir than I'm willing to merely on your say-so. Stahl is, however, Davenport's subordinate. That much I learned." Powell took another generous swallow of his drink. "You said you wanted only a yea or a nay, so there you have it."

"I appreciate your efforts." That matter, at least, was now thoroughly settled. Only Oscar Winterberg remained enigmatic. Although there were also Lord Dale Hemmingford's machinations to consider. And Nora . . . did she have some part in this curious matter, beyond what she claimed? He especially didn't like these last doubts, particularly now that Nora and he had . . . had—what? "Bonded" might be the word.

"I would still like to know what all this is about," Powell said quietly, interrupting these thoughts.

"I may have misled you somewhat," Fleming said carefully.

"I thought as much." Powell's tone was smug.

"I *may* have. I truly cannot say with certainty. However . . . I may investigate the matter further."

"What matter?"

"I am considering flying to the States in a few days," Fleming said, the present tense of his statement absolutely accurate; he hadn't, not until this moment, consciously considered the move.

"To follow a story?" Powell now appeared keenly interested.

He hesitated only an instant, then said, "Yes."

"A story which I will receive at your earliest conven— No. Allow me to rephrase. Which I will receive *immediately* upon completion. Not to mention that you'll keep me notified of its progress at every stage. That is, if you expect the newspaper to pay your airfare and expenses, as I imagine you do."

Fleming could not suppress the admiring smile which twisted the corners of his mouth. "Your terms are reasonable."

"More than that, I might venture to say." Powell cleared his throat. "Now, then. It remains for me to know what this story concerns."

Again he was hesitant. Again he divulged. What choice did he have? "A man named Oscar Winterberg. Resides in San Francisco. A champion in the labor union movement there. You might turn your attentions toward him. He's the object of my . . . curiosity."

Powell had instantly produced a pencil and was scribbling on the same sheet of folded yellow paper. He lifted his gaze. "I would like a bit more to go on."

"Whatever other clues I might have would be irrelevant to the story I have in mind. Cast your net, Powell. Whatever data you can retrieve regarding Winterberg will aid me immensely in bringing home a feature . . . one the readership will surely devour."

The editor eyed Fleming greedily, then picked up his straw fedora and stood with some effort. Fleming rose as well.

"One thing, Fleming. You shooed that charming young lady out of here rather abruptly. She's a journalist, did you say? Tell me, are you keeping secrets from each other? Perhaps you're both chasing down this same story." Powell offered one of his rare grins, revealing large teeth that were not unlike a barracuda's.

He thought of making some sharp retort to that statement. Instead, his words sounding suddenly hollow and far-off even to him, Fleming found himself saying, "Nora Blair DeYoung might be another name you would want to investigate. I would be curious about her journalistic credentials." Nora's Blake Young identity had been kept secret from the world at large for some years now, but so far as Fleming knew, that secret had never been tested.

He would rather have Powell's spies in Whitehall once more delving the personnel files, seeing if Nora's name appeared anywhere. But he could see no way of requesting this without sending Powell into a paroxysm of suspicion.

But what if, despite her claims, Nora actually did work for the British Secret Service and had been put on Oscar Winterberg's scent by Davenport? If such were the case—and this was a worse thought—then she had doubtlessly been sent here to tempt him, Fleming, into participating in this absurd operation to discredit and defame Winterberg. He knew there was a certain logic to this theory. Yet he turned from the thought. All this warred enormously with his burgeoning feelings for Nora.

He hastened his editor out of the house, then set out from the verandah toward the beach.

HE FELT CADDISH. Adding Nora's name to Oscar Winterberg's for Powell to look into was not the act of a gentleman. Yet, Fleming could justify his actions. Davenport and Stahl were settled. They were members of MI5, and thereby the Winterberg file and their attempt to recruit him into the affair were both legitimate. Other factors were still in question, however. And like it or not, Nora was one of those factors.

He kicked off his sandals when he reached the white-sanded crescent of the beach. Nora hadn't returned to the water after all but was crouched and picking curiously among fragmented bits of washed-ashore sea shells.

She stood, hearing his footsteps. She smiled warmly. "Did you tell your editor to bugger off?"

He was only briefly startled by her use of language. He returned the smile as Nora crossed to him. He took hold of her hand.

"Not entirely." He gazed into her limpid blue eyes. "Actually I managed to engineer a favor."

"And what's that?"

"I've negotiated the price of an aeroplane ticket."

"Really?"

"I'll be leaving in two days."

"Two—?" Nora's head tilted quizzically.

"I'm bound for San Francisco," he said nonchalantly. "That is, of course, assuming you're not averse to my company by that time."

She let out what could only be described as a joyous whoop, then threw both arms about his neck. Fleming caught hold of her hips, lifting her feet from the sand and turning her luscious body in a full circle. When he returned her to earth, she mashed her lips tightly against his. It was blissful.

That bliss carried through the following day, despite the preparations for travel they both had to make. Only in brief introspective moments did Fleming nurture his uneasy thoughts about the whole affair. Davenport, Winterberg, that damned bomb someone had set in her hotel room. Had Winterberg been behind it? That was difficult to imagine, even stretching probability to its limit. Nonetheless, Fleming's instincts were to protect this woman. That night, without Nora's knowledge, he again placed his pistol—his Enfield .38—in the night table next to the bed, within easy reach.

Chapter 16

NORA CINCHED tight her seat belt and draped herself back into the aeroplane seat's gaudy teal and scarlet upholstery. She appeared as at ease in this reclining posture as she had lounging on Fleming's verandah.

The flight aboard this twin-prop Douglas DC-3 would ferry them to Florida, where they would transfer to a larger craft which would take them across the considerable span of the United States, stopping to refuel in Dallas, Texas. The airport in California was actually somewhere outside the limits of San Francisco. Nora had arranged for a rented automobile to be waiting for them.

It was a curious thing to be winging away from his island paradise so shortly after his much anticipated arrival. But this trip was important. Fleming meant to watch over this woman as she pursued Oscar Winterberg. He was also unwilling to part from her company so soon.

"I really don't care much for takeoffs and landings," Nora said, her tone oddly nonchalant. "That's when most accidents occur, statistically. I get this icy sensation beneath my ribs. Even after the many, many miles I've logged in the air."

"You don't appear particularly ill at ease."

"Ian, once you've experienced the very same fear innumerable times, even it—no matter if it's your worst phobia—becomes monotonous and easy to control."

She took his hand nonetheless where it rested on their joined armrest. His fingers twined with hers.

Their final full day together on Jamaica had been a flurry of preparation that interrupted their tranquil interlude. They had both packed for the journey. Then Fleming had been forced to make yet another run into Kingston, finding himself for the first time growing quite bored with the drive. They had visited the newspaper office together, where Merlin Powell handed over Fleming's plane ticket and an envelope containing money for expenses with a meaningful glower. His expression changed instantly to one of delighted cooperativeness when Nora asked if she might use his phone. She spoke briefly to one of her New York editors, finalizing some aspect of her current arrangements; then, despite Powell's fawningly indignant protests, she insisted on paying for the call.

From there they had gone to the Government House, which had a grand whitewashed Georgian facade and towering wrought-iron gates. The mixed look of horror and lechery on Stowe's face when she had entered the edifice on Fleming's arm was quite precious. The distraught secretary had fallen over himself ushering them into Vanderbrook's office, which was a stuffy mahogany and carved oak affair once occupied by the equally pontifical Lord Broxton. To Vanderbrook's credit he'd removed the oppressive velvet draperies and enlivened the interior somewhat by laying down fresh, brightly woven carpet.

The colonel's manner toward Nora was deferential and apologetic, with none of the furtive ogling Fleming was growing used to seeing following her about. He had seemed not entirely pleased with Fleming's presence in the room but didn't voice an objection. He told Nora candidly and contritely that he had no news for her—or news only in the negative. No further findings from the investigation of her former hotel room, no scent of the phony courier, no auxiliary leads on the case whatsoever. Vanderbrook assured her that every effort had been made, and that his men had enjoyed the full cooperation of the local authorities, under orders from the Chief Constable. They had investigated the staffs of every courier company on the island. No likeness of the bomb-delivering courier had been circulated, since no meaningful description of the man could be obtained from the desk clerk at the Chabrol Arms.

"I am appallingly sorry, Miss DeYoung," Vanderbrook said with perfect sincerity, standing at parade rest behind his desk. He hadn't sat during the interview. "We pride ourselves that Jamaica is a safer place for our presence. It's a miserable bit of ill fortune that your stay was not untroubled."

When Nora stood, Fleming did as well. "Your efforts are appreciated, Colonel," she said, offering her hand. Vanderbrook took it across the desk top, did not stoop to kiss it but only squeezed it briefly. Then they had departed.

Fleming had put petrol into the Rapier, and they returned to the house. At one point on the road the car had uncharacteristically backfired, and he saw her start sharply and fearfully. He had thought her fully recovered from the bombing incident; evidently some normal anxiety lingered. This was understandable.

That night, after Isaiah prepared another sumptuous feast of local cuisine and departed, was one of unbridled delight, a hedonistic indulgence in all the pleasures he and Nora could draw from each other. The joy of their commingling was intense enough to push away Fleming's lingering worries . . . even the doubts about Nora he would now scarcely admit to himself. Those doubts had been nearly eclipsed by his growing feelings for her.

The plane's PA suddenly crackled with the captain's voice, advising the passengers that they were ready to taxi. A pair of shapely stewardesses pranced down the aisle, seeing that all occupants were firmly secured. Then the craft was in motion, the whine of the propellers escalating in pitch, and minutes later the velocity of the DC-3 was pressing Fleming back into his seat. They lifted and climbed. He bade a silent farewell to the island through the porthole-like window, though he knew fully he would have felt much worse had he now been standing below in the terminal, watching with shaded eyes as Nora rose away from him.

He shrugged with a small movement of one shoulder. No need for the dramatics, man, he told himself. Jamaica was a steadfast mistress—loyal, constant, abiding. She would be waiting tolerantly on his return, without tears or recriminations.

Nora, on the other hand, was a woman of flesh and blood. Had he let her slip away, there would have been no saying when next he might have seen her, if ever. They had encountered each other in London—good Lord, a little more than a *week* ago—purely by chance (so he still insisted on thinking); and her reappearance on Jamaica had been almost as improbable. If fate were going to go so far off its natural orbit, then how could he justify letting her escape him now?

He had to admit there was a certain relief to be leaving his beloved island. With any luck they were also leaving behind the bomber who had delivered that lethal package to Nora's hotel room. With a further increment of luck that unknown assailant would be apprehended by the authorities in their absence or suffer some equally poetic fate. Nonetheless, before and during boarding Fleming had kept a watchful eye on their fellow passengers. Even now he remained alert to movements in the aeroplane's aisle . . . though what good this vigilance would do if a bomb had been planted on the plane he couldn't say. There seemed little he could do if such were the case.

He glanced at her alongside. She gave him her winsome smile.

"Do you like avocados?" she asked, apropos of nothing.

"Pardon?" He blinked, then said, "Why, yes. Delightful little things." Cesar Holiday had prepared many a fine salad using the pulpy fruit. He could not recall at the moment if they had ever turned up in any of Isaiah Hines' dishes. "Why, if I may, such a curious question?"

"Do you enjoy the flickers?" she went on, still smiling. "The picture shows. Cinema."

"I see them when I'm able. They're diverting."

"Did you serve during the war?"

His corresponding smile abruptly hitched. He had been willing to humor Nora along, to play whatever word game this was that she'd concocted. But his war record . . . that wasn't a seemly subject for casual badinage.

"I did serve."

"Branch?"

"Naval," he said shortly.

"Do you have parents?" she asked, again switching tacks. Then she sniffed a laugh at her own wording. "Sorry. Are your parents still alive?"

This topic, for different reasons, was nearly as delicate as the previous. "My mother survives. My father lost his life during the Great War."

"Ah. My condolences," she said with brief level sincerity. "For me it's the reverse. Mother's dead. Father is still very much a living spirit."

"Nora," Fleming said, perplexed, "what is this about?"

"I'm asking you questions," she said guilelessly.

"Without rhyme nor reason, so it seems."

She placed her fingertips together, her angled cheekbones rising a degree as she squinted at the forward seat. She seemed momentarily at sea in her thoughts. Beyond the rounded window there were now only the aquamarine waters of the Caribbean.

At last she spoke, measuring out her thoughts with more care than before. "It has occurred to me, Ian, that, when all is said and done, I really know very little about you. Oh, you're a journalist and a fine one. You enjoy swimming and your home and the tropics and fast cars. You're an encyclopedia of knowledge when it comes to fine wines. You're debonair, and you know it, though not to the point of being a pest about it. But . . . it's the filler, as we newspaper folk would say, which is lacking. The trivialities. The little things. The passing opinions, the casual biases, the random bits of personal history. I find, having spent the time together that we have, that I'm curious about these things. I'd like to truly know you. And not just in the Biblical sense."

This final bit of clever verbiage brought a guffaw from Fleming's chest. When he recovered himself, he considered what she'd said. It was a legitimate point. He was, after all, nurturing a decided curiosity about this woman, so much so that he had put Powell on her scent. He was still having some difficulty absolving himself of the guilt of that act. Still, it was entirely fair that she should be curious of him.

"Very well, Nora."

So it was that a good deal of the first leg of their journey to San Francisco was consumed by a haphazard but frank exchange about the multitudinous facets of their personalities. Much of this was, as she'd said, filler. "Avocado" facts he came to think of them. So it was that at the end of this give and take, his sketchy portrait of Nora Blair DeYoung hadn't been substantially enlarged.

He was content to leave it at that, but Nora surprised him—not for the first time—by leveling her eyes at him and saying, "Well, so much for small talk. Want to hear the story of my life?"

This piqued his interest immediately. "If you'd care to tell it, you will find me an attentive audience."

"Good," she said.

She had been born, he was surprised to learn, a rather impoverished farm girl. She grew up in a township, whose picturesque name he immediately forgot, in the state of Oklahoma.

"You don't speak with that peculiar twang, though," Fleming observed.

"That I had to unlearn," said Nora. "It's hard to be taken seriously as a journalist while throwing *y'alls* all over the place."

The 1930s were evidently a luckless time to be an inhabitant of this particular American region. A relentless drought created the great Dust Bowl, which in turn forced the DeYoung clan—Nora, her widower father and six siblings—to become migrant workers, picking crops here and there, as constantly on the move as a band of Gypsies. Her father, a Mr. Wilford Devon DeYoung, was possessed of an unstoppable will when it came to sustaining his family.

Nora's life as a migrant "Okie"—the term crude and quaint at the same time—ended in her seventeenth year. Her father abruptly found himself the sole heir of his great uncle's not inconsiderable fortune. Mr. DeYoung had known "Uncle Tommy" only as a remote glowering old miser, who had amassed his riches by opening a chain of lucrative automotive supply houses. Thomas DeYoung disapproved of every member—living or dead—in his bloodline and made no bones about his opinions. When the DeYoung clan traveled to Los Angeles, California, to collect the fruits of Uncle Tommy's estate, the will gave no clue as to why the gruff tycoon had singled out Wilford as his solitary beneficiary. Perhaps the man had gone mad in his final days. Or had repented his ways, choosing Wilford arbitrarily as the object of his belated contrition.

Mr. DeYoung settled the family in Los Angeles and saw, as always, to their needs. He placed the older children into jobs and Nora's younger siblings into school. When Nora asked breathlessly if she too might have a formal education, Mr. DeYoung acquiesced. Nora was enrolled in a New York university.

Nora had learned to read at an impressively young age and gobbled information voraciously. School seemed a place to apply her natural talents. That she chose to study journalism had been more whim than a deliberate career goal. Nora admitted to Fleming that she might as easily have set a course toward being a novelist or legal researcher or accountant. Her instructors were initially ambivalent about training a young lady in the journalistic field, but her unyielding drive, apparently inherited from her father, flattened all resistance.

That same tenacity got her introduced into the circle of national journalists. She recounted meeting H. L. Mencken at a cocktail party, where the great caustic American wit had told her ribald jokes and anecdotes that left her sides aching.

Entering the field was inevitable. The creation of Blake

Young too, perhaps, was predetermined. When she'd first been allowed a byline, she picked the name, which swiftly developed into something of an alter ego. Blake became Hyde to Nora's Dr. Jekyll. Blake Young wrote with a punchy masculine strength, and it was only a few short years before he gained a respected notoriety as a journalist who could plumb the depths of newsworthy features others in the profession could not. Of course, it was Nora's charm—and doubtlessly her good looks—which allowed her to unravel stories her male counterparts couldn't begin to untie. Nora admitted freely the advantages she had, but Fleming suspected she was downplaying her natural journalist ability. The benefit of a pretty face could not account for the noteworthy career she had created from grit and determination.

By the time the twin-engine alighted in Miami, they each had a clearer impression of the other as a rounded individual. They produced their passports for the customs officials, Fleming pausing at the currency exchange kiosk, and boarded the larger Boeing 307 Stratoliner which would convey them across the length of the States. By then Fleming felt himself on sure enough footing that he brought up, once again, the topic of Oscar Winterberg.

Chapter 17

"IT SEEMS more than a little negligent," said Nora, "letting a fellow journalist peek at the notes of a story I've yet to write."

She had retrieved a valise from an overhead compartment and sifted within it until she produced a file, which she passed to Fleming. He made a cursory examination of the contents—clips from newspapers, scraps of mismatched note paper, some typewritten, some scrawled upon.

"You needn't worry about me rushing out an exclusive, Nora. I may have, inadvertently, given Merlin Powell the impression that I'm working on a feature. But the truth remains that I am on holiday."

"Pulled a fast one on your editor, did you?" She smirked.

"It seemed an uncomplicated means to obtain a plane ticket." He narrowed his eyes at the disorganized pages.

"You may find some of that difficult to decipher. My penmanship is the bane of my editors' lives."

"I think I shall manage," Fleming said, not entirely sure of his statement. Softer he said, "Thank you for letting me see this, Nora."

She shrugged, then lit one of her dark filtered cigarettes with her dull-metaled Zippo. "Well, Oscar Winterberg obviously interests you, Ian. No, I don't want to have that same roundabout conversation again about how you don't know the man or can't talk about him. I accept that you're unwilling to divulge whatever you might know. But, if this information is of concern to you, then by all means take a look. I'll sit here quietly."

She opened the tattered Jane Austen paperback she'd been reading in the lounge of the Chabrol Arms several days ago and buried her nose in it.

The aeroplane, a much larger affair than the twin-prop that had seen them to Florida, was well out over the Gulf of Mexico by now. Fleming lit a Players and set about examining the file.

It was decidedly less ordered than the Winterberg file Davenport had shown him. He first read the news clippings, most of them from San Francisco papers. These were blurbs on Oscar Winterberg's rise within the ranks of the local labor unions. The facts matched those in the MI5 dossier, but here they were more colorful. One column, reporting on a mayoral luncheon, was headed by a grainy photograph. There were several men in business suits posing for the shot. Winterberg was the farthest left.

He was smiling into the camera, his expression confident, his features gruffly handsome. His penetrating eyes seemed full of a kind of unsettling mirth. He appeared slightly older than he had in the glossy Fleming had seen in Davenport's file. His thick dark hair was flecked with grey, though that might only be a trick of the lighting. Still, the flesh about his piercing eyes was lined. The caption beneath the photo read: LABOR BIGWIGS LUNCH WITH MAYOR.

There were other articles—Winterberg leading an outdoor rally of the plumbers' union, Winterberg calling for a hotel strike until conditions for employees were improved, Winterberg cutting the ribbon of a newly built charity clinic. The press seemed to have nothing but praise for the man. He was painted in dramatic prose as the people's champion, a staunch defender of workers' rights, charismatic, outspoken, righteous. It was hardly the dispassionate officialese of the MI5 file, but it was perhaps more illuminating.

There was no mention in these clippings, however, of Winterberg's past. The only reference to his personal life was that his wife June was expecting a child in April. Winterberg had married the Widow Rogers, late of St. Paul, Minnesota, to obtain citizenship, Fleming recalled. How much did she know of her husband's past?

He set about reading Nora's notes, expecting to find data on Oscar Winterberg's beginnings. What he discovered was something else entirely.

Nora's penmanship was indeed atrocious, decidedly unlike the florid script of the letter she'd first sent from her hotel to his house on Jamaica. She seemed to have developed a confusing amalgam of cursive and block lettering, so that her written words moved in fits and starts, like a clogged pipe. That and her apparent habit of omitting vowels and verbs at random made the going difficult. She also seemed fond of abbreviations, so that a typical sentence read: *W. pblc image spotles, pet of th pres, never saw a pblc figure so revered, partic'ly somone in unions. Dirty dealings somwhr.*

W. of course meant Winterberg. Decoding the rest was just a matter of concentration, Fleming realized. Nora doubtlessly could unravel her own cryptography at a glance, but he didn't want to disturb her. She had been generous in offering him this look at her research. Also he wished to keep his reactions private.

Slogging onward, he found mention of that apparently popular rumor that Winterberg had been involved in the kidnapping of a plant owner's twelve year old son, just as he had read in Davenport's file. The boy had been ransomed, and that ransom was an upgrading of the factory's safety standards, thereby assuring that fewer workers would be injured on the job. Nora mentioned that the owner's son was returned to his father's custody with a shaved head and a missing finger; but this information was not recorded as verified. In fact, the entire section was circled in red ink, bearing a large question mark atop it. Rumor, then. But could it have at least a bit of truth about it? Was this, then, what Nora was investigating?

He examined the few typewritten sheets among the hand-scrawled ones. These too were in Nora's personal shorthand but were at least easier to make out. They contained more information about Winterberg's ascension in the unions, an apparent meteoric rise to power. Again the facts corresponded to what he'd already learned from Davenport's file. Winterberg was a relative newcomer to the scene but had already created for himself an eminent position within the power structure. Enough so that he was being invited to lunch with the mayor, Fleming mused.

Exhausting these items, he turned once more to Nora's hand-drawn notes, resigning himself to a laborious untangling. Squinting at the sheets for several minutes, he felt the first stirrings of a headache, the throbbing of the bridge of his nose its harbinger. He flagged down a stewardess and asked for a gin, neat.

Fortifying himself with a few swallows, he delved Nora's notes. Soon enough the process became less effortful, as he learned the parameters of her code. He read several pages in reasonably short order and frowned. He had anticipated information on Winterberg's past—his youth in Germany, his socialist leanings, his guerrilla actions during the war. There was none of this. Not even mention of

Winterberg's postwar activities in England or his escape through Canada into the United States.

Instead there were multiple references to a *D.B.* Fleming had to cross-reference several sections of scrawled text to come up with the name that matched these initials.

Deborah Byrd.

Evidently this woman held a good deal of interest for Nora. D.B. was a stenographer in a prestigious San Francisco law firm. She was twenty-four years old. She had no family. She had spoken to someone named Minter two weeks ago. Fleming scanned the texts seeking a clue to this man's identity. Finally he concluded, reading between the garbled lines, that Mr. Minter was employed in some capacity by the New York newspaper syndicate. He had passed along certain claims from Deborah Byrd which had forcefully grabbed the attention of Nora's editorial staff.

It took some meticulous rereading for Fleming to uncover just what those claims were.

It was Deborah Byrd's contention that she was the wife of Oscar Winterberg. That he had met her in the course of legal doings involving the unions and seduced her in September of the previous year. Miss Byrd—or Mrs. Winterberg, was it?—asserted that she and Winterberg had had an intense liaison and that she had become pregnant by him in late October. Winterberg had then taken her to Nevada, where they had married.

A secret marriage, Fleming thought with some awe. No stranger to affairs himself, he was still astonished by this Winterberg's brazenness. If Deborah Byrd's claims were factual, what had possessed him to *marry* the apparent object of his affections? Had D.B. cast such a clouding spell over him that he'd felt compelled to break the laws of God and man by taking a second wife?

It was staggering. Oscar Winterberg was a bigamist.

This Minter character was currently in Nevada, quietly investigating marriage records. Meanwhile Nora would meet with Winterberg in San Francisco, ostensibly to do a profile on the celebrated labor leader. The facts were another matter. It would be under Blake Young's well-known byline that news of Winterberg's second secret wife would be revealed to the world. There would be uproar. There would be enormous scandal. There would be headlines.

Did MI5 know anything of this matter? No, he decided. They wouldn't have attempted to recruit Fleming if they had. He realized as he tried to outguess the British Secret Service that he was thinking like a spy once more. Old habits were difficult to entirely erase.

Fleming read Nora's notes to the last. Then, finishing his gin with a final grim swallow, he returned the pages to the file.

Nora turned down the corner of the page she was reading and set aside her book. She gazed at Fleming levelly.

"So, Ian, what do you think?"

"Remarkable," he said honestly. "If it bears out."

"Well, that's for our intrepid Mr. Minter to uncover. I've only waited this long to meet face to face with Oscar Winterberg so that the truth could be confirmed or denied. New York will send word shortly after we arrive in San Francisco."

"Bigamy," Fleming murmured. "It seems something out of the Dark Ages."

"Oh, not quite that far back. Mr. Winterberg would hardly be the first practitioner uncovered in our modern world. But rarely does one find so public a figure—and so venerated a one—caught with his hand in this particular cookie jar."

He gave a quiet chuckle at this bit of vernacular.

"And you will note, Ian," Nora continued evenly, sliding the file back into her valise. "There's no mention in there of your Mr. Davenport, the MI5 agent, or Mr.—what was his name?—Stahl. No mention at all."

How utterly in error he had been. How foolish of him to have nurtured suspicions over this woman who was only doing her job. She was no MI5 agent.

"I . . ." he started, hesitated, then began again, "I'm profoundly sorry about all that rubbish. I was indeed mistaken about certain matters. I hope you might find it in your heart to forgive me . . . at your leisure, of course." He added a smile to this.

Nora returned it, lifting her hand to brush her fingers across his cheek. "Ian, there's ample room in my heart. Enough for forgiveness . . . enough for you."

He didn't know which of them initiated the kiss, but it lasted long enough that several nearby heads turned, their fellow passengers smiling at the happy couple. From the intensity of their passion, Fleming thought, most probably assumed the two were newlyweds.

Chapter 18

THEY MADE a night landing in San Francisco—or rather one of the famous city's outlying municipalities. Oakland, Nora said was its name, though Fleming saw no signs of oaks as their large Stratoliner skimmed down onto the runway. Absent, of course, was any hint of the lush tropical greenery that festooned Jamaica. The clouds they had descended through were also not the same innocuous puffs that hung above his island getaway; instead the atmosphere was thickly grey and decidedly cold-looking, underlit by Oakland's lights. Fleming sighed inwardly. He had only just recently escaped England's winter. Now he seemed to be arriving in a similar climate. He resigned himself to his fate.

Normally a flight like this landed at the larger airport just a few miles southward along the peninsula, the tip of which was capped by San Francisco. Owing to some vagary about refueling for this airship's ensuing jaunt across the Pacific, they were instead landing here.

Nora had cautioned him to dress warmly for their arrival.

Nonplussed, he had asked, "I understood that California's winters are mild."

"They are. But we are going to San Francisco, dear Ian. And San Francisco is only technically a part of that temperate state. Trust me. Bundle up."

He did trust her. He'd had to rummage about his closets to find warmer wear, unearthing a knee-length wool greatcoat that he had no memory of bringing to Jamaica. He donned it now as the stair-and-platform affair was rolled up to the aeroplane's hatchway. He felt cramped from the flight.

The stewardesses, as bright and fresh as ever even after their long hours in the air, ushered the passengers out with gleaming smiles. As Fleming followed Nora from the craft, blinking at the runway's dazzling lights, he felt the first blast of the air. A sturdy wind raked the field, and tendrils of cold wormed their way through the open front of his coat. He hastily buttoned up. Despite Nora's warnings, he had still half expected to find the climate like that of Florida—clement, a touch balmy, blind to the calendar which insisted it was indeed winter. Instead, the temperature was scarcely warmer than what he'd gladly left behind in London. More than anything he felt irritated by this.

Uniformed airport officials were on hand to guide them toward the gate. A taxiing twin-engine drowned out all other noise as it passed nearby.

After retrieving their baggage Nora, dressed as warmly as Fleming in an overcoat and snug checkered scarf, led him to a kiosk inside the small terminal building. Here, she had told him, they would retrieve the keys for the rented auto for which her editors had arranged. She presented her identification to the young blond crewcut man behind the counter. The man—*boy,* Fleming decided, not a day above eighteen—fumbled through a number of drawers, leering nervously again and again at the lovely lady at his counter. Eventually he produced a set of car keys and a form for Nora to sign.

"Thank you, Miss De-De-DeYoung," he fairly sputtered. "Enjoy your drive!"

Impishly she patted his hand where it lay on the counter top. "Thank you, you dear thing," she said sweetly.

Fleming chuckled as they exited the terminal. "I think you'll be much in that poor lad's thoughts when he lays himself down to sleep tonight."

"Not jealous, are you, Ian?" She smirked.

"Not in the least. When we stop flirting, my dear, we begin to die a little."

"How profound."

They came out onto a small dirt-packed parking lot, which held a scattering of automobiles. A few tall light poles cast wide pools of glaring electric light. So much different from the gentle romantic glow of the kerosene lanterns of his island home. Fleming shrugged. He would simply have to get used to "civilization" all over again.

They walked briefly through the chill. Nora consulted the carbon copy of the form she had signed. At last she cried triumphantly, "Ah! Found it. Let's get in and turn the heater on full!"

He found himself standing a moment in the frosty wind, gazing wide-eyed at the automobile. Its color appeared to be a sunburned bronze.

"My word, Nora. Did you order a car or a boat?"

"Splendid, isn't it?" She grinned merrily as she tried one key, then the next on the driver's side lock.

"It's monstrous," he said with a matching grin. "I mean that in complimentary fashion."

"Of course you do, my sweet. It's a Cadillac. Every year they get bigger. I like bigger. Come now, get inside." She had unlocked her door and now slipped within the metal behemoth, reaching across the broad front seats to release the lock on the passenger door.

Fleming lingered a moment longer, taking in the auto's impressive length and bulk, a size totally unsuited to Europe's narrow roads, to say nothing of the expensive petrol it would take to move this thing. It had large wheel guards over its radiant whitewalls, a bonnet that seemed to stretch out forever and an overall mass that made Davenport's armored-car-like sedan look puny by comparison. His likening the monstrosity to a boat suddenly seemed not so farfetched. Its shape was curiously nautical. All it would require would be heavy-duty inflatable canvas pouches beneath those oversized wheel guards, which would spread a buoyant apron underneath the craft. They would be activated with the throwing of a switch inside the auto. At the same time the pilot would trigger the drive system. Propulsion could be generated by a number of means beneath the belly of the "boat-car". Why, given the size of the engine that must be underneath that bonnet, moving this craft across water would be . . .

The revving of the motor woke him from this fanciful reverie. He tugged open his door, set his and Nora's suitcases across the wide rear seats and pulled shut the door against the night's chill.

"You didn't exaggerate about the weather," he said, rubbing his hands together and wishing he had packed gloves.

"You were warned." Nora pressed a switch on the Cadillac's complex-looking dashboard panel, and warming air, smelling vaguely of insulating materials, washed out of the vents. It was, of course, curious to be sitting in the passenger seat on the *right* of the automobile. There were other differences to European cars: dissimilarities in the shapes of the side windows, the expansiveness of the interior, details among the mechanisms that operated the headlamps and other controls. Still, it was hardly an occasion for culture shock. Fleming had after all visited the States a number of times previously, though never this far west.

"I suppose California's mild winters are just a beloved myth."

"Winter has little to do with it, Ian. At least as far as San Francisco's concerned. It's chilly over here, in Oakland, because it's January. Where we're going, across the bay, it's cold because it's always cold—or at least crisp. San Francisco has roughly the same temperature year-round. Fifty-five degrees, windy, foggy, with a good chance that it'll get cooler before it gets warmer. It's being at the mouth of the Golden Gate that does it, you see. Those chilly Pacific winds. San Francisco gets its summer in late September, and it lasts about five weeks. Sunny days, pleasant nights. The rest of the time it's as Twain described it. That *coldest winter I ever spent was a summer in San Francisco* quote. Although I've heard it's been wrongly ascribed to him or at least misquoted. I forget which."

"You seem familiar with this locale," Fleming observed as the engine and the Cadillac's interior continued to warm. The idling motor made a confident growling, like a straining beast under reins. It was almost as though this engine had a particular voice, a trait he had found all fine automobiles possessed. *Chugga-mugga-chugga-mugga* went this one. He shook his head to clear away these nonsensical thoughts. He must indeed be feeling the effects of the long flight. "Do you spend much time here?"

Nora lit a filtered cigarette with the dashboard's lighter. "As much as I can, whenever I can. It's a convenient stopover to many places. I adore the city. I can't wait to show it to you."

"We shall be crossing that grand Golden Gate Bridge, then?"

"No, my dear. That span connects San Francisco to Marin County. It's that way." She waved a gloved hand over her right shoulder, though Fleming had no idea which direction was being indicated. She, at least, had been wise enough to bring along her gloves, he noted.

They glided out of the lot, the Cadillac's assured growl barely rising in pitch as they moved. Nora handled the steering wheel with a light efficient touch of her fingertips. They slipped across several empty lanes, then wound through Oakland's impersonal streets. As always on visiting the States, there was that initial vertigo in finding himself driving on the *wrong* side of the street; but this passed quickly. Large darkened commercial buildings alternated with weedy empty lots. Fleming had seen photographs of San Francisco and knew its avenues possessed more character than these.

"There's our bridge," said Nora cheerily. "It's called the Bay Bridge. We'll be crossing a segment of the largest natural harbor in the world."

"I see you're going to be my native guide for this safari," he observed dryly.

"Not native, bwana," she countered easily. "Remember, I'm just an innocent farm girl from Oklahoma. I hope you're not expecting me to beat the bushes for game."

"I shall be perfectly satisfied if you can take us to shelter. Where is this St. Francis Hotel that we've booked into?"

"Over there, Ian. Over there." She waved ahead now as they rose up onto the Bay Bridge. Its scope was impressive, a colossal construction of girders, concrete and massive pilings. At its far end, twinkling through a jacket of fog, were what could only be the lights of San Francisco. Even at this distance they seemed to have an ethereal, almost enchanted quality.

The bay's dark waters spread widely below them now.

Fleming noted the drifting lights of ships. This was a hub of much oceangoing commerce, he knew. This had also been an important location for the United States Navy during the war. Only Hawaii and a few other American protectorates out in the Pacific stood between here and Japan. How exposed these people—the civilians of this city—must have felt in the weeks, months and years following Pearl Harbor.

Not that these people had endured the horrors of the Blitz, he thought with that peculiar pride the English took in their own suffering.

Nora pointed out the sights as they approached across the wide swath of the bridge's roadway. She rattled off place names at an alarming rate, singling out this cluster of lights or that hilly mound of buildings faster than he could absorb. He decided to leave her to her monologue. They would be at the hotel soon enough, surely. They had dined on the aeroplane just an hour ago. Now would be the time for a proper drink, once they were settled and stationary.

As the Cadillac came off the bridge in a seamless glide, onto San Francisco's lively nighttime streets, Fleming was struck immediately by the famous hills that rippled the landscape. Rome had been built on seven; San Francisco looked to have at least that number. These weren't barren knolls of land either. No, each mound had been built upon, layered over by the city surface, as though its architects had simply thumbed their noses at these interruptions to the terrain. It was, at least in this respect, like no city England could boast.

"That's Market," she said, evidently enjoying her role as guide, indicating an amazingly broad city artery as they passed across its foot. He counted four sets of trolley tracks laid along it and dozens of lighted coaches creeping along the street's length, which stretched off into the fog and went, as far as he knew, all the way to the boundary of the Pacific Ocean.

Winding the giant automobile a short distance up one of the city's hills, Nora still chattering away, they eventually reached the hotel's front. That was Union Square across Powell Street, she informed him, pointing to the quaint lighted plaza just across the way. The hotel was a towering regal affair, making the Chabrol Arms in faraway Jamaica appear almost shoddy by contrast. A valet accepted the car's keys with a mannerly bow, and uniformed bellhops wrestled out the luggage.

Nora, after Merlin Powell had agreed to pay Fleming's travel and accommodation expenses, had been kind enough to make his room arrangements at the hotel herself. She had assured him, with a suggestive sultry smile, that they would find a connecting suite waiting for them.

Voices and footfalls echoed in the high-ceilinged, almost cathedral-like lobby they found at the top of a long flight of broad exterior steps. It was richly appointed, every decorative square inch of mahogany and oak varnished to a high gloss. The fronds of giant ferns spilled elegantly from massive ceramic urns.

At the marble-topped front desk the clerk—a diminutive bespectacled figure who greeted them with gracious warmth—handed over the keys to that promised suite. The lobby was bustling. San Francisco was, after all, an international city, bringing in visitors from all corners of the globe.

"And Miss DeYoung?" The clerk lifted a sheet of paper. "A telegram arrived for you. Not twenty minutes ago."

Nora took the paper, her blue eyes suddenly especially

bright. Fleming was following the bellhops as they headed toward the lifts. Now he paused, glanced back and cocked a questioning eyebrow as Nora read the message.

She lowered the paper from her face, revealing glimmering eyes, then a mouth twisted into a profoundly satisfied smirk.

She gazed silently at him a moment, apparently relishing the moment. Then she said, “It’s word from our diligent Mr. Minter, currently passing time in Reno, Nevada. He’s uncovered a particular marriage certificate.” She folded the sheet deliberately, fine white teeth now appearing in that gratified smile. “We’ve got him, Ian. We’ve *got* him!”

Chapter 19

IT TURNED into a night of quite giddy merrymaking. Nora, before Fleming's eyes, transformed into a capricious, almost flighty adolescent girl. She seemed to giggle happily with nearly every breath, reading and rereading the telegram, quoting it to Fleming time and again, as if it were fresh news. He was swept along in the wake of her blissful state, amused and perhaps a touch overwhelmed by the intensity of her delight.

He had never known a journalist to be so elated by a story.

"So, now that the facts are confirmed," he said as they rubbed shoulders with the other patrons of the jammed ritzy cocktail lounge, "what expressly do you intend to do with them?"

Her limpid blue eyes were positively radiant. "Why, expose our Mr. W. naturally!" She had adopted the habit of speaking of Oscar Winterberg as "Mr. W." while in public, explaining that bandying the popular labor leader's name about might not be wise. Fleming agreed with the tactic.

"Will you first confront him with what you know when you interview him?"

Nora paused, tapping her fingernails against the brim of her highball. They were seated toward the red-carpeted lounge's curtained front windows. The atmosphere was rife with cigarette smoke and perfume. Voices babbled all about.

Finally she said, "That interview isn't for three more

days. I haven't decided if I should present him with the facts and thereby force him to try to deny them—that would be juicy, wouldn't it? Or conduct the interview above board and have it printed alongside the news of our Mr. W.'s illegal second marriage. Either way it'll make for a sensational feature. Don't you think?" She tittered, high and loud.

"Yes." He nodded. "Sensational, in every respect."

Her eyes darted across the small round table, one of several dozen, where the press of the lounge's well-to-do patrons had forced them to huddle. "Do you disapprove?"

Fleming shifted on the velvet-seated stool. He had showered at the suite—and a sumptuous set of rooms it was—and changed into evening clothes, but still he felt vaguely aslant of his bearings from the long flight. Nora, however, had insisted on celebrating, and so here they were. This lounge, located somewhere in the large hilly downtown district, was the second stop on what promised to be a protracted night of tavern-hopping.

She was still eyeing him carefully, a crease beginning to show itself between her plucked brows.

"Disapprove?" he said lightly. "Not in the least, Nora. This story obviously has some meaning for you. Perhaps I've simply never seen you in . . . such a froth before." He capped this with a flattering smile.

She took a swallow from her glass. It would take some effort for Fleming to battle his way back to the bar to refill it. He hoped they would be leaving after this round, to find quieter surroundings.

"It is something of an anticlimax, I suppose," she said thoughtfully. "Being made to report on stories that certainly lack the substance of the work I did during the war. Still, Blake Young is nearly as widely read as he ever was.

His name still carries weight. If I have to settle for airy and commercial features above those of true significance, I put it down to the times we live in. Without the war to galvanize people's feelings we, as journalists, must reach them however we can."

"I quite agree, Nora," he said. "I had no intention of deflating your victory."

She squeezed his hand across the table, her dazzling giddy smile returning. "I know, Ian. Of course you didn't. And you haven't. Nothing could diminish the sweetness of *this* victory, rest assured."

They did push on when their glasses were empty, for which he was grateful. They had left the massive Cadillac at the hotel and were traveling San Francisco's night by taxi. A wide variety, fleet cabs and independents, prowled the streets. Fleming opened a fresh pack of Players and lit one as their taxi climbed an unthinkably steep hill. What kept the buildings from sliding to the bottom? It seemed a perilous feat of architecture, particularly when one considered the devastating earthquake that had nearly demolished this city early on in the century. It did demonstrate a certain degree of pluck on the part of these San Franciscans that they chose to make this place their home.

The taxi gunned through the sprinkling of traffic, swerving briefly into the oncoming lane—which Fleming thought automatically as the *proper* lane for them to be in. Why had these Colonists transposed the rules of the road so? They passed a canvas-covered freight lorry and slipped nimbly back into the right-hand flow. They turned two more corners, the taxi's tires making a perfunctory squeal of protest, then jerked to a halt.

"You'll adore this place, Ian," Nora said breathlessly as they climbed out. Momentarily resuming her role as tour guide, she explained, "It used to be a bona fide speakeasy. During Prohibition. The distillery was next door, in the basement"—she indicated the adjacent building of darkened offices—"and they'd tunneled through the walls. Back then it was all bathtub gin and secret knocks. The glory days of the Barbary Coast! Isn't that exciting?"

Fleming allowed that it was, unable and unwilling to divert Nora's high spirits. It was pleasurable, he admitted, to see her so electrified. Yet, if he were to be thoroughly honest with himself, he must concede that their intimate interlude on faraway Jamaica had been more . . . tranquil.

They entered the club beneath a lurid neon sign, the name spelled out in an intricate calligraphy that was impossible to decipher in a single glance. If this had been an underground saloon during the time of Prohibition, it certainly made no bones about its function now. The club's happy hour prices were posted clearly on its windows.

They stepped out of the fog-roofed chilly night into the warmth and muted light of the club. Fleming was struck immediately by the snug intimacy of the place. A piano hunched in the far corner was being softly and adroitly played by a white-haired Negro, while an equally elderly white gentleman plucked the thick strings of a upright bass. The music was instantly soothing. Flamboyant gas lamps threw golden shadows from the walls. The carpeting was thick, and the furnishings had a flair and symmetry that rivaled the elegance of their suite at the St. Francis.

Nora unbuttoned the swarthy fur-trimmed coat she'd traded for her more practical overcoat at the hotel. She had also swept up and fastened her red-ringletted hair into a becoming coiffure. Adding dangling gleaming earrings, a stylish dress of patterned purple and blue, gloves, dark stockings and a pair of towering heels, she was the picture of refinement. It was only her flushed features and irrepressible smile that betrayed that otherwise cool grace.

The clientele consisted of no more than twenty or so impeccably dressed figures, dispersed among the tables which fanned out in a widening semicircle from the piano and bass combo in the corner. Fleming noted curiously that there didn't seem to be any women on the premises other than Nora.

Evidently on familiar ground she led the way to the long bar-top of rich stained wood, behind which an array of fine liquors gleamed in their bottles on ranked shelves. A bartender, wearing a spotless white waistcoat and black bow tie, glided forward to meet them.

"Randolf!" Nora cried above the music and the faint murmur of the patrons' conversations, loud enough that several heads turned. "You dear, dear man!"

The bartender—Randolf—returned her a charming and seemingly sincere smile, bowing from the waist. He looked to be in his fifties, his slightly pruning features held in a cast of flawless poise.

"Miss DeYoung, it is, as always, a perfect pleasure to see you. How long are you in town this time?"

Fleming saw with something of a start that though the bartender's hairline had receded somewhere toward the crown of his skull, the rest of his silvery precisely groomed hair hung several inches past his ears, nearly brushing his starched shirt collar.

Nora rose up on her toes and kissed Randolf's cheek smartly across the bar, whispering something Fleming couldn't make out, then following it with a delighted giggle. The bartender murmured something in return.

She spun about. "Randolf, this is Mr. Ian Fleming—journalist and all around good fellow. He's proving to be wonderful company. Ian, meet Randolf. A more darling man you'd be hard pressed to find."

Fleming offered his hand. Nora had neglected to provide a last name, forcing Fleming to say, somewhat awkwardly, "A pleasure, sir."

"And mine as well, I must say, Mr. Fleming." Randolf's grip was mildly limp, but his manicured fingers wrapped Fleming's hand with an odd sense of possession. As he broke the handshake, he realized that Randolf's hands were lightly dusted with talcum powder. The bartender was eyeing him levelly. Returning the gaze reflexively, he thought he detected a trace of talc upon the man's cheeks as well.

They ordered their drinks. Fleming paid, having exchanged Merlin Powell's notes for American currency while they were still in Miami. He escorted Nora to a table, feeling Randolf's eyes following him with inexplicable intensity.

"Queer chap, isn't he?" Fleming said after he'd held out Nora's chair and settled into his own. He breathed a long easing sigh, feeling much less confined than he had at the crowded cocktail lounge.

She smirked across the candlelit table, which was draped with immaculately white linen. "How very perceptive of you, Ian."

"Pardon?"

"Why, your reference to Randolf, of course."

He backtracked toward his original comment. When he deduced Nora's meaning, his eyes widened slightly. "Do you mean to say . . . ?" Somehow he could not finish.

"Naturally. Look around you, Ian. There's a perfectly good reason why there are no females here."

He turned his head slowly, again assessing the club's

patrons—well-dressed men, most of advanced years, evidently affluent, engaged in muted conversations at their tables. Several sets of eyes were turned in his direction. Though the lighting was faint, he thought he detected something vaguely predatory about those gazes, much like the odd stare Randolf had leveled at him.

"*Ponces,*" he said. "Dear Lord, Nora, what sort of den of iniquity have you brought me to?"

She tittered. "Be calm, Ian. No one's going to bite you. That is, not unless you ask politely."

"The humor of this escapes me," he found himself saying.

"Tosh. England has its share of buggerers, as you well know. This is a quiet friendly place, and I adore coming here. Now, let's not dwell on the matter." She had laid her pocketbook atop the linened tabletop. Her gloved fingers were fidgeting busily with the polished silver clasps. In it she carried the folded and refolded sheet of the telegram.

Before she could withdraw it and read it yet again, Fleming spoke up, deciding his best action would be to ignore their surroundings. "Tell me, this Deborah Byrd that Osc—That Mr. W. has apparently taken as a bride. Do you have any idea why she took it into her head to contact your Mr. Minter and divulge her burning secret?"

Now Nora did snap open her handbag. But only to extract a dark filtered cigarette. He lit it for her.

"I imagine, like most mistresses, she grew tired of being the other woman."

"But Mr. W. married her."

"Oh, Ian. Deborah Byrd knew her beloved was already married. It must've taken a vast effort of self-delusion to convince herself that *her* marriage had any weight over Mr.

W.'s original state of wedlock to June Rogers, who, you'll recall, is also bearing his child."

He had nearly forgotten the fact, which he'd gleaned from the clippings in Nora's file on Oscar Winterberg. He didn't recall any accompanying photo of Mrs. Winterberg—June, that was. So, Winterberg had seeded *both* of his wives.

"Miss Byrd certainly seems to have changed her mind in short order," he said. "She and Mr. W. began their illicit affair in September. By late October she'd been made pregnant by him. Presumably it was November before he spirited her away to—where?—Nevada so they could wed. Now it's January, and the heartsick and penitent Deborah Byrd is betraying the father of her child by leaking this shocking account to the press."

"It's a woman's prerogative to change her mind without warning," Nora observed dryly.

"Yes. I had an inkling you might say something to that effect." Fleming took a liberal swallow of his gin-and-tonic, steadfastly disregarding the stares of the elderly men he still felt boring into him from all sides.

"I'm sorry to make light of the matter," said Nora. "I am in rather high spirits. However"—she hunched forward slightly in her seat—"Deborah Byrd has obviously committed a serious ethical breach. She's evidently repentant, doubtlessly crushed by guilt. She wants to set things right, and the only means of doing so is to expose this scandal. That she'll be martyred in the process has surely occurred to her. But her remorse apparently outweighs that fact."

The tinkling tones of the piano abruptly jumped into a livelier rhythm. The bass thumped alongside, creating a spirited melody.

"How did Miss Byrd know to contact this Mr. Minter you keep referring to?" Fleming asked.

"Ah." Nora sipped from her cocktail. "Mr. Minter is an invaluable asset to my editors. He's a sort of advance scout, reconnoitering stories to determine if they're truly newsworthy. He's been on the trail of Mr. W. for over a month now—researching the man, attending his labor rallies, delving subtly into the particulars of his life. Blake Young had already received the assignment to interview Mr. W. Minter went ahead to discover if there might be anything about the man we didn't know. He chanced upon Deborah Byrd in the course of his delicate investigations, and she presented him with this bombshell. After that it was a matter of confirming her contentions. And that, as you well know, has been accomplished." Again she reached into her handbag, caressing the telegram with one gloved finger. Thankfully she did not remove and unfold it.

Fleming pondered for a moment. The music's tempo mounted still further.

"It would be interesting to speak to this young lady," he murmured somewhat offhandedly.

Nora lifted her shapely shoulders in a breezy shrug. "Then come along tomorrow."

"Tomorrow?" He frowned.

"Yes," she said. "I've arranged to interview Miss Byrd, the wayward pregnant bride of our illustrious bigamist. Your presence would be welcome. That is, if you're interested in having a ringside seat of these rather intriguing proceedings."

Chapter 20

HIS HEAD felt a trifle large upon awakening, but it was nothing a spot of breakfast wouldn't relieve. Nora remained immersed in the ample bed, breathing deeply and evenly, an arm curled beneath her tapering chin.

Fleming gathered the nightclothes he'd packed for this trip, knotted the brocaded sash of his velveteen robe and slipped soundlessly into the parlor. The chamber was large, filled with tasteful furniture, including a dining table. The wallpaper above the creamy wood of the wainscoting was cheerfully rosy, if a touch bright to his eyes this early morning.

He spoke softly to room service via the parlor's telephone, advising that they should rap lightly on the door. He moved toward the windows. The connecting suite was on the eighth floor of the St. Francis Hotel. Actually the ninth, since Americans insisted on calling the ground level of their buildings the *first* floor. He pushed back a pleat of the drapery, the fabric a lush olive with gold thread creating patterns of blooms and stems.

The view was commanding. San Francisco was languishing under what he imagined to be its customary cloud cover, but here and there appeared patches of vibrant blue. Sunlight spotted the landscape. He looked down upon Union Square, noting the graceful maze of its hedges and the tracts of grass. Tiny bustling figures moved through the puzzle. He saw policemen, newspaper vendors, bootblacks, a veritable array of San Franciscans setting about on their day's duties.

Beyond the common he found a fine line of sight directly down to the water. The bay sparkled where the sun's rays struck it. Boats of every category were performing a sort of complex nautical ballet on the waters—sailboats, a Coast Guard cruiser, larger commercial ships. At the foot of Market Street lay what Nora had called the Ferry Building. It looked something like a warehouse, but from its long middle reared a small squared tower that for all the world resembled a miniaturized Big Ben.

He absorbed the view leisurely, allowing his senses to take proper hold of him, until a gentle deferential rapping on the suite's door announced that breakfast had arrived.

He ate at the dining table, pouring himself cup after cup of coffee from the steaming urn, as he made short work of the eggs, seasoned ham, toast and jam. As he refilled the china coffee cup once more, he felt himself quite settled, the detritus of last night's merrymaking washed from his system. He wadded the pale blue cloth napkin and stood from the table. There was a matter he must attend to.

He entered the opposite bed chamber. Ostensibly this one was his, but the only signs of residency were the unbuckled suitcase atop the mirrored dresser and the toiletry articles he'd left on the lavatory's sink. The pallid pink coverlet remained perfectly smoothed over the large bed.

There was another telephone on the oak night table. He took the heavy receiver off its cradle. The hotel switchboard attendant first advised Fleming—voice rather wooden and bored, as though she'd uttered the phrase a thousand times previously—that charges for the call would be attached to his suite's bill. When he was relayed to a proper operator, it took several minutes for the station-to-station call to be placed. He waited through a series of electrical clicks and clacks.

The ringing sounded quite distant. So did Merlin Powell's voice when the editor picked up his office phone.

"Fleming," he said when his caller had identified himself. "I trust you've rung to bring me thoroughly up to date on the progress of this mysterious story."

He sounded peevish. In Jamaica, Fleming reminded himself, it was of course just another sweltering day, manufactured for the express discomfort of Merlin Powell.

"I'm gathering material as we speak," Fleming replied.

"Good. I want to hear about every bit of it. And speak up, man. This connection is appalling."

It wouldn't do to raise his voice too loudly. He had slipped out of bed early for the explicit reason that he might have privacy from Nora during this call. Keeping secrets from her still did not sit especially well with him, particularly since she'd proven herself innocent of any association with Francis Davenport. But there was no need to trouble her with the details of this game he was playing with Powell.

"I don't have much time," he said, speaking louder and cupping the receiver.

"Fleming, you'll *make* time. You promised me information. The newspaper is, may I remind you, paying for this jaunt of—"

"Powell," he cut in, "every minute of my investigation is precious."

"And every note this paper has spent on this outing of yours is also precious. You handed me off a slippery kettle of goods, Fleming, when you cozened me into financing this venture. And I allowed you to do so because I know you have a craftiness that, while rather nontraditional, has produced a number of excellent feature stories from you. But"—and Fleming could almost see the editor raising a finger toward his office's twirling ceiling fan—"you will *not* trifle with me. I demand some information. If you are reluctant to provide it, take a moment to consider that I have some say in your continued employment with Kemsley Newspapers!"

This last came out in something of an indignant roar. Fleming realized that he had pushed his luck nearer its limits than was prudent. Powell was no fool. In hindsight the editor patently had permitted Fleming to "dupe" him. Now he was calling in his debt. Fleming would have to give him something.

"There's more to Oscar Winterberg than meets the eye," he finally said.

"What a fine headline that shall make," Powell said sardonically. "Now, what shall we put beneath it?"

"Have you done any research on the man?"

"Yes. Just as you recommended. An interesting fellow. He sounds, frankly, like a Communist, what with his vehement promotion of workers' rights. But you're stalling, aren't you? Make no mistake, Fleming. You shan't squirm your way out of this."

An idea suddenly struck Fleming, and it was Powell himself who had helped provide him with the avenue of escape.

"It's interesting you should use that word. Communist. Though I think socialist might be more precise."

"Interesting? Why?"

Here Fleming would have to walk a decidedly fine line. The contents of Davenport's Winterberg file were, after all, the property of Her Majesty's government.

"I suspect that Winterberg has socialist leanings."

"*Leanings?*" Powell spat a disdainful laugh. "The man's a revolutionary. It's plain as day merely from reading the transcripts of his speeches. He venerates the American worker. He's an idealist. I doubt he'd be personally satisfied before every Yank laborer had a medal pinned to his chest and a guaranteed pension for his grandchildren. Bah! As though the Americans were the only people who'd suffered unpleasant working conditions. When my father was a boy in Liverpool—But I'm deflecting myself. Do you have something more material beyond your canny insight that Winterberg is something of a socialist at heart?" Powell's tone suggested that he had better.

Fleming said, "I don't merely assert that Oscar Winterberg's politics are socialistic . . . I contend that he *is* a socialist. With possible links to Russia. So I suspect."

"*What?*" Powell's roar this time carried a note of keen interest.

Knowing full well how thin was the ice on which he stood, Fleming pushed on. "I cannot substantiate my claims. I am currently following a line of inquiry which may—*may,* I say—corroborate my suspicions."

"And that line of inquiry is?" the editor asked pointedly.

"I'm not at liberty to say."

"You've no choice in the matter, Fleming. I insist—"

"No, Powell. On this I shall have to insist." There came a strangled growl from the phone's earpiece. "Hear me out. My investigation is of a most delicate nature. If I can establish that Winterberg is linked, via a network of agents, to the Russians, I will of course need to contact the Foreign Office . . . if the matter appears even remotely to be one of international security. That is only right and ethical—

and, I might point out, the lawful thing to do."

Brooding silence for a moment, then Powell said grudgingly, "That is a difficult point to argue."

Fleming felt a glimmer of hope. "But I will still be in position to break the story, should it not threaten international security." A secret smile pulled at his lips. He added, baiting the hook, "Think of the splash such a feature would make."

"Yes," Powell said slowly. "Quite a boost for the paper, I must say. Very well, Fleming. Understand that I am allowing you, once again, to eel your way out of a full disclosure. I am intrigued. That is sufficient for the moment. But you will keep me posted on the degrees of your progress—even if you find yourself unable to delve into specifics. One way or the other I should like to hear the full breadth of this story someday over a brandy in your lounge." His laugh this time was more sincere. "Tell me, though. Who put you onto the scent of this Winterberg in the first place? Was it the young lady, the journalist?"

The truth of the matter was, of course, out of the question. Finding no convenient falsehood at hand, Fleming said, "No. Miss DeYoung was not involved. My source must presently remain anonymous."

"Very well. Nora Blair DeYoung. I have done some probing concerning her."

"Yes?" Fleming had nearly forgotten that he had asked his editor to investigate Nora. He had certainly by now discarded that dubious suspicion that she was an agent of MI5; she was obviously investigating Winterberg along her own lines.

"There may be more to her than meets the eye as well."

In a suddenly cold level voice he asked, "And what would that be?"

"I don't know. That is my point. She earned her credentials at the University of New York some years ago. Following that, she virtually disappears. I cannot confirm that any newspaper actually employs her."

Fleming breathed a silent relieved sigh. Naturally Powell's investigations had proven fruitless. Nora Blair DeYoung had doubtlessly vanished soon after Blake Young came into being. Her employers had plainly gone to great lengths to disguise Nora's secret.

"Well, no injury done. I think we can safely allow the matter to—"

"That's not all of it," Powell interrupted. "It seems she has a police record. Arrested—where is it?" Papers were being shuffled at the other end of the line. "Here. 1938. New York, the borough of Manhattan. She was a suspect in a murder inquiry, no less. Evidently a Mr. Marcus McCune died rather dramatically when a bomb was exploded in his apartment. Your Miss DeYoung was romantically involved with him. When the police attempted to detain her for questioning, she fled. She was apprehended two days later. She was cleared of any involvement in the bombing. The case, incidentally, remains unsolved. Is this information of any interest to you?"

Fleming found himself pressing the earpiece hard against his skull. He forced his grip on the receiver to relax.

"You're certain of your facts?"

"Of course."

"Thank you for informing me," he said tonelessly. "I'll contact you again in the next few days."

"Before you ring off . . ." Powell's voice was suddenly soft. "If this young lady is a journalist, is she aware of your suspicions concerning Winterberg? Are you collaborating on this project?"

"No. Rest assured. She's working on an entirely separate feature. No involvement with Winterberg whatsoever. We're merely . . . enjoying each other's company for the duration of our stays in San Francisco."

"Very well. I'm forced to presume you know what you're doing. Goodbye, Fleming."

He returned the receiver to its cradle and stood motionless in the bedroom, his thoughts turning.

Nora arose shortly thereafter. Fleming went into the parlor to meet her. She had a habit of appearing radiant from the moment of awakening. She smiled and kissed him soundly.

"Well," she said, "today we meet Deborah Byrd. Things are rather exciting, aren't they?"

Though his responding smile felt brittle, he knew it was convincing. "Indeed," he said.

THE SCIMITAR THOUGHT it somewhat sad that few Russians—even those as versed in English as he—would be able to appreciate the differences of these Western cities. To the untrained eye San Francisco would appear much the same as London. Even the obvious dissimilarities, such as the inverted flow of traffic, would have little impact. A typically stolid Russian would see only the *foreignness*. He would wince at the overt decadence of it all: the restaurants, the music halls patronized by degenerate members of the bourgeoisie, the careless wealth of the typical Western "worker"—hardly proper proletariats—juxtaposing so sharply with the grinding poverty of those who'd fallen through the cracks of capitalist society.

But San Francisco, here in these United States, was much different from London, in faraway England.

This city was decidedly livelier, with a palpable air of festiveness about it. The war shortages of England were much less evident, as though that awesome conflict had already passed into distant memory here. The citizens of this metropolis seemed to enjoy life as no Russian would think to do.

The Scimitar appreciated these things but was, of course, not beguiled by any of them. He was a man of duty. He obeyed his superiors, and those superiors had ordered him to follow Fleming from Jamaica. His forged identity had not been questioned by the American customs officials, though he had prudently left most of his tactical equipment behind, retaining only the pistol for which he had a false carrying permit.

It seemed this Fleming Englishman was involved in that business with the couriers after all. So his superiors thought, and so the Scimitar thought.

So here he sat in his rented two-door automobile, parked across from the imposing edifice of the hotel on Powell Street. He had already confirmed that his target had taken rooms here, in the company of that woman with whom he'd left Jamaica. Her name, he'd learned through his investigations, was Nora Blair DeYoung, an American journalist. Curious companionship for a supposedly retired English Secret Service agent to be keeping, but her identity might well be false.

The weather was cool but not as chilly as London and certainly nothing to compare to a proper winter in the Motherland. The Scimitar sat patiently. He did not smoke or otherwise indulge in nervous habits and required nothing with which to occupy himself while he waited.

Chapter 21

"THE DEVIL is an angel," said Deborah Byrd.

Stockton Street ran through San Francisco's Chinatown. The district was vibrant, animated, peopled by more Orientals than Fleming had ever seen in one place. Freshly killed ducks and chickens hung in front of the stores. Signs were printed in the ornate exotic script of foreign lands. Bicycles were pedaled through the busy streets, and everywhere was heard the lyrical piping of the languages of the Far East. The quarter was lively and charming.

Inside Deborah Byrd's Stockton Street apartment the atmosphere was something different.

"Lucifer was God's beloved," she went on in the same eerie near-monotone. "He was God's second-in-command. He presided, at our Lord's right hand, over paradise. Before mankind was even a glimmer. Then he was cast down. He became Satan, Beelzebub, the Prince of Darkness and Lies. And he took his revenge in the Garden, tempting Eve . . . tempting Eve. But the Devil is still an angel. Only a fallen one."

Deborah Byrd, Fleming remembered from Nora's notes, was twenty-four years old; but he would have judged her to be no more than twenty. Her hair was that shade some referred to as strawberry blond. The wavy locks spilled past her shoulders, brushing the upper hemispheres of her pert breasts which were held snugly inside a plain white blouse. She was small of stature, just a wisp of a girl really. Narrowly shouldered, wasp-waisted, hips flaring in becoming feminine fashion. Her features were decidedly youthful, still caught seemingly in the midst of adolescent development. Her dimpled cheeks were mildly chubby. Her eyes were large and colored a delicate olive, soft long lashes framing the orbs and producing a gaze of beatific young innocence. Her lips were full. Without any concerted effort she radiated an air of pristine virginity.

Which was quite distant from the truth of the matter, he thought as he reminded himself that this girl—*woman*—claimed to be carrying Oscar Winterberg's child.

"Are you likening Mr. Winterberg to Lucifer?" asked Nora. She sat at the end of the reupholstered sofa, hunched forward, her knee nearly brushing Deborah's where the young woman sat in an armless chair.

"Oh . . ."

"Before or after his fall from grace?" Nora asked. Her tone was quietly persistent, almost compelling. Fleming was at last seeing her in her element. She was a deft interviewer.

"Before or after," Deborah said, not as if considering the question, more as though repeating a curious phrase. Her large eyes settled on Nora. There was some sort of absence behind those eyes, some mental or emotional dearth.

The flat was small and, frankly, humble. The furnishings were evidently secondhand, the pieces in this cramped front room mismatched. The petite kitchen was separated from this space only by a counter, which was topped by shutters partially folded back and missing several slats. The apartment was, however, clean and quite orderly, nearly to the point of sterility.

Fleming sat at the far end of the sofa, detached from the dialogue, feeling several odd lumps in the cushion beneath him. Nora had introduced him as her assistant when they'd arrived. Deborah Byrd had eyed him with that same vacuous yet strangely intense gaze.

"I understand that you began your relationship with Oscar Winterberg in September of last year," said Nora. A small tablet of paper rested on her knee, a few lines drawn on it in her scrawling code. She had not written down anything since they had entered the flat.

"The fifth of September," Deborah said, the words coming in an uninflected staccato. "A warm day. Cloudy, but warm. I wore this blouse. The fabric is light. It breathes well."

Nora nodded, as though this were a relevant insight. Fleming could have done with a cup of tea or coffee, but their host had only offered them cloudy lemonade from a pitcher.

"Yes," Nora said. "September fifth. Oscar Winterberg came to the law offices where you're employed—Armstrong and Utley. You're a stenographer there. Is it interesting work?"

"I went to school," said Deborah, her olive eyes straying away. "A teacher in my high school said I had an aptitude. I can type fast. I don't make mistakes. I know shorthand. I can take dictation, and nobody ever has to repeat themselves. Mr. Pearse at work once called me a human tape recorder. It was a compliment. He squeezed my shoulder when he said it. He smiled. I can type fast."

Fleming realized with a kind of vague horror that her manner was nearly that of a victim of shell shock. He had seen his share of cases during the war—the vacant faces, the wandering listless speech, too stunned and horrified by the events they had survived to be able to confront reality any longer in any meaningful fashion. Some recovered from the state. Some did not.

"Oscar Winterberg's visit to your offices on September fifth . . ." said Nora. "Did he compliment you too? Did he smile?"

The stenographer's gaze sharpened on something hanging invisibly in the center of the room. The silence began to stretch.

"You're most kind," she said finally.

Fleming blinked. He felt like something of an eavesdropper and was starting to regret coming along on this visit. Then he realized that the young woman's seeming non sequitur had been a quote.

"Why did Mr. Winterberg tell you you were kind?" Nora asked, a beat before Fleming's insight had completed itself.

"I brought coffee into Mr. Armstrong's office."

"Did Mr. Winterberg smile at you?"

"He took cream in his coffee. Two spoonfuls of sugar."

"Did you see him again that day?" asked Nora. She smiled softly, as if the two women were sharing secrets.

"He came out of Mr. Armstrong's office thirty minutes later. I was in the corridor."

"And Mr. Winterberg approached you?"

"We made love on the last day of summer."

She was hardly giving direct answers to Nora's inquiries, but the gentle flow of the questions seemed to be unlocking bits and pieces of pertinent information. It was nearly as if Nora were interviewing someone under hypnosis.

"Some two weeks after you'd first met?" asked Nora.

"Another warm day. Clear, this one. No clouds. Just blue sky."

A pen appeared in Nora's fingers. She tapped the tip on her pad of paper. "You were aware at that time that Oscar Winterberg was a married man?"

"I laid down, and he removed my clothing. He placed himself on top of me. His body was so warm. I closed my eyes. I thought of the Virgin . . . of Mary . . . of the Immaculate Conception. The angel that came to her to place Christ in her womb." Deborah Byrd smiled then, for the first time since they had arrived. It was an unnerving expression, her full lips spreading widely, spots of wetness appearing at the corners of her mouth. The smile didn't reach her eyes. "He flooded me with his seed."

Fleming shifted at his end of the lumpy sofa, wincing slightly when a spring twanged beneath him.

"You saw a good deal of him at this time?" Nora went on, as if she were receiving rational answers to her straightforward questions. Her pen moved now on her tablet, making a brief notation.

"He came to me. Here. Nights mostly, but days sometimes. Warm days in October, when the weather turns."

"And late in that same month you discovered that you were pregnant." Nora didn't inflect the sentence into a question this time.

"His seed," Deborah said, that macabre smile still on her youthful dimpled face. "His hot fertile seed."

"You had no reason to suspect the pregnancy was the responsibility of any other man." Again, this was stated, not asked.

"No reason."

"You were a virgin when Oscar Winterberg first made love to you."

"Pure. He liked that. He told me often. A well from which no man had drunk before."

The poetic crudity of the words caused Fleming to wince once more. He wished suddenly for a cigarette but saw no nearby ashtray.

"Did Mr. Winterberg ask you to marry him?" asked Nora.

"Flowers. Orchids."

"He gave you flowers when he proposed?"

"I pressed one in my Bible."

"Yet you knew he was already married?" Nora asked again.

"There is nothing else in this world. There is nothing . . . only you and I. We are apart. We are above."

Another quotation, thought Fleming.

"You eloped to Reno, Nevada," Nora said.

"I'd never been on an airplane before. We soared, high, above everything. Like angels. Like I was holding myself to his warm body while his wings beat and carried us."

"He gave you that ring."

Fleming noticed for the first time the simple band of white gold around her left ring finger.

"I . . . do. . . ." The smile at last slipped from her lips, leaving her face again in a void.

"Why did you agree to speak to Mr. Minter?" Nora's pen moved. "He is the man who came to your law offices last month. He asked questions about Oscar Winterberg, but no one would speak to him. But you spoke to him."

"Minter," Deborah Byrd repeated.

"Yes," Nora prodded gently. Fleming could not imagine from where she was finding the patience to conduct this meandering interview. "You told him what had happened."

"A cold day. Foggy. Very foggy."

"Why did you speak to him?"

"To . . . confess."

"You feel repentance."

"Confess. Repent. Forgiveness." The young woman was shaking now in the armless chair.

Nora did not relent, though her tone remained as subdued as before. "You feel remorse for what you've done. You want to atone."

"Oh . . ." It came out in a stifled gasp. Deborah's trembling increased. Her arms folded across her chest, hands squeezing her narrow shoulders. Her firm breasts were pushed upward against the fabric of her white blouse. "*Oh!*" she now yelped.

Fleming nearly made to rise from his seat but stopped himself. He had no active role here, he reminded himself. This was Nora's interview.

"I have the Devil's child in me!" Deborah Byrd abruptly hollered. "I confess, I confess, I *confess*!"

Tears came then, oozing from her large long-lashed eyes. Her full mouth twisted into a melodramatic rictus as she doubled over. The emotional barrier had been breached, and the poisoned waters of her contrition now came flooding out.

They stayed at the apartment long enough for Nora to calm her down, taking the young woman in her arms, rocking her gently, stroking her wavy hair. When the tears ebbed, Nora promised that she would be in contact soon. Then they left, Fleming glad to be out of that terrible place.

"Do you suppose she was once sane, that girl?" he asked as they scaled the steep hill on which Nora had parked the Cadillac. The breeze was mild and only slightly chilly.

Nora was jotting furious notes as she climbed. "I imagine she was a different person before Mr. W. deflowered her," she said.

"All those Biblical references." Fleming shook his head

and lit a Players. "A religious childhood, I would venture."

"So would I." Her pen moved independently of her speech, the notations even more muddled than usual. "She was swept off her feet. Mr. W. initiated her into the wondrous mysteries of sexual intercourse. Then he quite irresponsibly impregnated her. He might've married her as some bizarre means of making amends to her. But the guilt of it all has overtaken her."

"I take it you believe her story," he said as they reached the car. In the daylight its color was more a gleaming gold than bronze. He had first thought its shape to be oddly nautical; now, eyeing the monstrous vehicle once more, he had the curious thought that it was perhaps more aerodynamic. Yes, despite its bulk it was rather sleek overall, the bonnet tapered to nose into the wind. Wings could unfold from the undercarriage, great ribbed airfoils. Given enough thrust—a flaming jet out of the automobile's rear—it could conceivably *lift* this beast, like a rocket—

"I believe," Nora said, returning him to the moment. She produced the keys and unlocked the driver's side door, pausing before climbing inside. "Everything she said matches what she told Minter. Her marriage to Mr. W. has been factualized. Why would you distrust her account?"

"Because she was carrying on like a bloody lunatic!" Fleming said more vehemently than he had intended.

"She has been through some traumatic events. We're not all strong and stoic like the English, Ian."

They climbed into the auto. It was parked straight into the kerb like the other vehicles on this ridiculously canted street. Fleming felt a brief flash of vertigo as Nora backed out, spun the wheel and started them hurtling downward.

They were not unobserved as the Cadillac pulled from its parking space. Eyes watched from an ordinary-looking face, into which an acrid cigar had been inserted. The American man had parked his nondescript rented car on the opposite side of the steep street, at the corner. He raised his right hand, index finger extended, thumb lifted to act as a sight.

"Bang," he said softly as the Cadillac started downhill toward Stockton Street, the profile of Fleming passing briefly through his pretended line of fire. San Francisco was an improvement over Jamaica, but he still didn't like the hilly burg, particularly this neighborhood that was so overrun with Chinamen. How simple it would have been to take out that limey fairy just now. Fleming never would have seen it coming.

As the Cadillac neared the bottom of the hill, another car—a small two-door—pulled quickly out of a space five slots up from where the Caddy had berthed. Hadn't that car parked only a few minutes after Fleming arrived? Again the American man saw the occupant clearly for a moment . . . and felt an unaccustomed jolt of surprise go through him.

Downy blondish moustache, distantly familiar features. He had seen this individual before. He—

It was the man he had observed in the crowd around the Chabrol Arms in Jamaica! The one who had been calmly watching, hands in his pockets. The two-door sped downhill, just as the Cadillac turned the corner at the bottom onto Stockton.

The American man bit down on the harsh-smelling cigar as a feral grin broke out across his mundane features. He turned the key in his ignition. Someone was trying to muscle in on his territory; and if there was one thing he didn't cotton to, it was having competitors.

Chapter 22

THERE WAS no practical means of asking Nora about the incident in 1938 in New York's Manhattan borough. Fleming simply could not reveal that he had persuaded Merlin Powell to investigate this woman to whom he was romantically linked. He rued the action silently. He would rather, he thought now, have not known that—what was the name?—Marcus McCune, her suitor at the time, had died in an explosion in his apartment. A bomb had been set. Had it been the same sort of bomb that had detonated in her room at the Chabrol Arms in Jamaica? And why had Nora attempted to flee in New York when the police came to make their inquiries?

He could not answer any of these questions, not without grilling Nora herself. He could find no easy link between the two events, but the ambiguity troubled him. She had not volunteered this information when they'd so lightly exchanged "avocado" facts about each other on the flight to Miami.

A rock and a hard place, he told himself, trying to find amusement in his plight. And I caught between.

He glanced sidelong at Nora as she eased the gigantic Cadillac through traffic. She had promised to take him to Fisherman's Wharf, which she described as gaudy—to the point of vulgarity—but a captivating and must-see sight nonetheless. He had agreed to the sightseeing venture. Yet, settled in the plush passenger seat, puffing idly on a cigarette, he felt quite literally merely along for the ride.

His decision to accompany Nora on this excursion to San Francisco had been impulsive. He had simply been unable to stomach the thought of her slipping so entirely out of his life after their blissful interval in Jamaica. But there were also deeper reasons.

He felt protective of this woman. He recalled vividly the icy dread that had gripped him when he'd learned that it was Nora's room where that bomb had exploded. He remembered his purpose in spiriting her away from the hotel, taking her to his home far outside of Kingston. He had wanted to guard her, to place himself heroically between her and whatever nebulous danger might be lying in wait.

He had, after all, assigned himself the role of bodyguard while she was here in this city to gather information on Oscar Winterberg. And also, as a journalist, he was professionally curious to see how her feature came out.

He stubbed out his Players in the dashboard ashtray.

Nora patted his outstretched hand. "We'll have some lunch on the wharf. Get some crab and wander along the piers and gawk, just like the tourists."

"That sounds enchanting," Fleming said and meant it. Being in her company was very nearly a narcotic stimulant. He was leery, out of old habits, from admitting what well might be the truth; but wasn't he coming to *need* Nora? He had so long been rather cavalier in his relationships with women. He simply did not want to consider, in the cool light of day, that the spell she'd cast over him was a potent one.

He turned his mind instead toward Winterberg. What a tangled web was *that*! He mentally reviewed the facts of the matter.

Fleming had turned aside from the task Davenport, at

Lord Hemmingford's instigation, tried to lay upon his shoulders, which was to use his journalistic talents to discredit and disgrace the union leader. Now, however, that mission was going to be adroitly accomplished by Nora. The scandal she intended to expose was of an entirely different order, but it would more than suffice. Oscar Winterberg was on the verge of being yanked violently from the pedestal of favorable public opinion. He would likely soon be facing criminal charges of bigamy. Davenport—or, more to the point, Lord Hemmingford—would be satisfied with the outcome.

That Nora had materialized in Fleming's life at just this particular juncture had proven to be a matter of coincidence. How had she once put it? That lyrical bit of alliteration . . . a fanciful fluke of fate.

Why then, he asked himself, were his instincts warning him that danger lay just beyond the next bend?

"Rot."

"What's that, my darling?"

"Ah . . . nothing, my dear," he said. "I am lost in the scenery."

"Exquisite, isn't it?" She smiled.

It was that. They were on Divisadero Street, a wide traffic corridor. Despite the Spanish-sounding name of the street there was little evidence of Spanish architecture. Instead, the styles of construction were peculiarly American; that was to say, a mélange of forms that somehow produced a different totality than the sum of its disparate parts.

Nora had taken them out of Chinatown and swung them about in a long leisurely detour. She seemed intent on making good her pledge to guide him through this city's apparently manifold spectacles. Her familiarity with the city was evident. She had said she booked as many possible layovers here en route to other locales, so to bask and frolic in these, her favorite stamping grounds.

Divisadero was rising up onto yet another of San Francisco's prodigious hills. The commercial establishments they had passed now surrendered to rather stately residences. Nora put the Cadillac into a lower gear and pressed hard on the accelerator, sending the great metal monstrosity climbing the final precipitous slope, beyond which there appeared to be only sky.

Gravity pushed Fleming back into his supple seat. He gazed about at the scenery, his eyes taking note of the side-view mirror as he had been doing for a number of blocks now. He had noted what appeared to be an accident involving two autos a few blocks behind.

The Cadillac crested the great peak, and they found themselves on a plateau that seemed to continue for only a short distance before plummeting off the far side. Nora crept the automobile toward that drop.

"I brought you around this way because I thought you'd appreciate the view," she said, braking.

It was a grand vista. This dizzying vantage permitted a sweeping view of the squared city blocks that led far down and off to the turbid blue waters of the bay. Those waters—so different from the Caribbean's sparkling aquamarine depths—were as jammed with ships and boats as when he'd viewed the eastward patch of bay early this morning from the hotel window. Here, however, looking to his left, he beheld for the first time the admittedly inspiring sight of the Golden Gate Bridge. It was a long majestic span, with its lofty towers and enormous pilings, its cables flowing in two vast dipping arches. It connected the two land masses that guarded the way into the Pacific. He understood why some had the audacity to call this modern engineering feat the Eighth Wonder of the World.

"Spectacular, isn't it!" Nora cried happily.

Fleming's eyes moved once more to the Cadillac's side-view mirror.

"I believe, my dear," he said evenly, "that we are being followed."

They continued to idle at the top of the hill.

"What makes you say that?" asked Nora. The question was not snide.

"That auto that's pulled in half a block behind us, the plain-looking grey one . . ."

Her eyes shifted toward the rear-view. She didn't crane her head around to look. "The Dodge."

"Yes. It's followed us for some while, through five different turns. There appears to be only the driver. It's remained as far back as a full block. But always in sight."

He expected her response to be one of incredulity. Instead, she tugged her seat belt from the cushion's folds and snapped the metal catch about her waist. "I recommend you buckle up, Ian." Her tone was businesslike.

He fastened his belt, saying even as he did so, "Perhaps, Nora, it might be best if I took the wheel—"

She had already shifted out of neutral. She depressed the accelerator, and the Cadillac leapt forward, hurtling itself off the vertiginous precipice of Divisadero Street. The auto didn't actually leave the pavement but very nearly so. Abruptly they were nosediving, the landscape rushing upward at them at a less than prudent velocity.

Nora braked at the next intersection. The car's whitewalls squealed sharply. Fleming braced himself with a hand on the dashboard. This junction was another small plateau.

Looking downward, he saw that the plummeting hill was built like a tiered garden, the steep slopes interrupted at regular intervals by flat crosscutting streets.

"There it is," she said coolly at the same instant he spied in the mirror the Dodge nosing past the hill's crest and downward. "Now for a test."

She twirled the steering wheel tightly, swinging right. Fleming missed the street sign, but the lane was pleasantly tree-lined. The Cadillac growled along at high speed past the silent homes of the fashionable residential district. They braked hard once more at the next intersection.

This time Fleming turned to look back. The grey Dodge turned onto the street behind them, taking the curve sharply and sliding out of its lane before righting itself. He peered but could see no details of the driver behind the windscreen, just a vague male shape.

"He wants to play," said Nora, teeth gritting together with grim determination that looked nonetheless high-spirited. Fleming found himself flung toward his door as they veered left, down another seemingly sheer drop-off.

He had been pleased with himself earlier that his old instincts had detected their pursuer. What he hadn't expected was that Nora would so forthrightly take matters into her own hands . . . though he had to admit she was quite a deft driver, keeping firm control of the immense speeding Cadillac.

"This may turn out to be nothing more than a prank, Ian," she said calmly.

He blinked, unfamiliar with being reassured by a woman, particularly since he was remaining quite clear-headed. He stayed turned about, holding tightly to his seat back, eyeing the Dodge as it too turned the previous corner, staying in pursuit—and pursuit this was, wasn't it?

Nora was quite correct, though. The pursuing Dodge had as yet done nothing that could indisputably be called hostile.

They swerved left again, going around the third side of the square block now. On this level ground Nora gunned the Cadillac, sliding nimbly around a small slow-moving coupé. The Dodge performed the same maneuver, picking up speed, gaining ground as they approached the stop sign at the intersection.

Instead of stopping, Nora shot the auto through the crossing with only the slightest tapping of the brake.

It was time for another test, thought Fleming. "Nora, stop this vehicle."

"Why?" she asked through her gritted teeth.

"To see what action our friend takes."

She jammed on the brakes, rising a few inches out of her seat in doing so, bringing the large car to a standstill midway along the block. Fleming continued to watch behind. The Dodge was still gaining distance, slowing it seemed, but not enough to—

"Brace yourself!" he shouted.

The collision was enough to jounce both of them violently against the restraints of their safety belts. Fleming pivoted to keep his still mildly bruised left knee from knocking the underside of the dashboard, but his right elbow banged smartly across the door handle. The Cadillac rocked wildly on its springs, then settled its bulk, evidently quite unruffled by the impact.

Behind, the grey Dodge's bonnet had crumpled noticeably, and an errant spew of steam was escaping from the grille. The driver's head was lolling against the steering wheel.

Fleming unbuckled his seat belt and grabbed for the

door handle. The doors and windows of curious residents were opening along the street.

"*Ian!*" Nora yelped.

He shoved open the passenger door, planting a foot on the pavement. He felt steady, despite the violence of the crash, but being collected in a crisis was one of his proudest traits. He turned back his head and asked, "What?"

"Take my gun!"

"Your what?"

She reached across and tore open the glove box. An instant later she slapped a pistol into his palm. He wondered when she had stowed it there—and what she was doing with the weapon in her possession. But there was no time for further questions.

He was still only halfway out of the car when the Dodge's rear door suddenly flung wide. A large male figure rose from below the level of the back seats, hopping into the street. He wore a black duster and black fedora which shaded his thick lumpy features. Fleming was still settling Nora's pistol into his grip, finger just curling around the trigger and thumb instinctively seeking the safety catch. The large man who'd emerged from the rear of the Dodge already had a pistol in hand—a blue-black automatic—and was leveling it.

He fired before Fleming could even raise, much less aim, his gun.

The report was loud and followed immediately by a heavy *thunk* as the bullet struck some part of the Cadillac's rear. The gunshot provoked frightened shouts and several womanly screams from the street's residents, many of whom had emerged by now from their houses. The shot also instantaneously catapulted Fleming back to his war days and memories of bygone moments of combat. All his old instincts, even those he had labored to mentally bury, resurged. He was ready to fight.

A hand, surprisingly strong, gripped the tail of his navy blue sport jacket and yanked. He had not yet settled both feet on the pavement and now felt himself tumbling back into the passenger seat.

"Forget it, Ian!" Nora barked. "*We're getting out of here!*"

With one leg still dangling out the opened door, the Cadillac leapt forward, fishtailing slightly as the whitewalls found traction. He yanked his foot inside just before the passenger door slammed itself shut. They were already a half block distant from the scene of the collision when he looked back.

The large man in black was scrambling around to the Dodge's driver's side, shoving aside the insensible shape behind the wheel. Housewives and other residents were still screaming and scattering. Fleming, looking hastily for any useful details, noted that the grey Dodge's somewhat crumpled front end bore no license plate.

Nora drove hunched forward, as though anticipating more gunfire. The Cadillac was now charging along at speeds that might only be safe on an open road. She cut the corner of the next intersection at a precarious angle, rocking the automobile again on its springs; then they were plunging down the steep grade of the hill once more. Fleming, heart beating heavily but nerves still steady, watched behind, but the grey Dodge did not reappear.

They reached Lombard Street at the bottom of the long hill. Nora paused halfheartedly for the stop sign, then raced them in random and elusive fashion through several more flat streets, finally slowing to something like a legal speed.

"We need a phone box," said Fleming. "We must call the police."

Nora nodded, her comely features still a mask of determination. "We will. But we'll phone from the hotel, where it's safe."

He thought that sound. He saw the pistol still in his hand and, with a last look at the empty street behind them, returned it to the glove box. The weapon was neat and small but had felt solid in his grip. It was a Beretta. He liked it.

"Your actions were quite swift and capable, Nora," he said as they made their way back to the St. Francis. The adrenaline surge of the incident had passed, leaving him in a curiously loosened state. "I must say, I was impressed."

"Thank you, my love." The tense cast of her face at last relaxed sufficiently to allow an imitation of her normal smile to show through. "We make a hell of a team, don't we?"

THE SCIMITAR HAD made a grievous mistake and was now paying for it.

He had tailed Fleming and the woman—that Nora Blair DeYoung—to the address on Stockton Street, then lain in wait for the pair to return to their auto. He had planned on later investigating who resided at that apartment building. When Fleming and the woman emerged and sped off, he had followed.

And *been* followed.

The Cadillac had cut across the city toward Divisadero Street, with the Scimitar keeping an eye on it from a reasonable distance. Between him and Fleming there was another auto—a Dodge, he knew from his studies of American makes and models—that was also following every turn the Cadillac made. Another tail? It was possible. He watched intently.

So intently, in fact, that he scarcely noticed the car that pulled alongside him, then gunned past on Divisadero's multilane thoroughfare. That car abruptly jogged sharply to the right, cutting immediately in front of him, tires squealing and smoking.

The Scimitar had applied the brakes frantically, and his rented two-door bucked, swerved dangerously but somehow avoided a collision. Unluckily the motor stalled, leaving him stranded in the middle of the wide street, his front fender inches from the side of the auto he'd nearly hit. Traffic flowed by on the left as he hurriedly tried to restart his car. The gold Cadillac and its Dodge pursuer were now climbing the hill some distance ahead, getting away.

He didn't see the plain-looking man who'd bounded out of the swerved auto until he was nearly at the driver's side window. The Scimitar glanced up into the almost formless features of the man, which were interrupted only by the stub of a cigar.

His hand twitched toward the handle that would roll down the window. His lips parted to speak.

The man outside the window was grinning. One hand was buried in the pocket of the long grey coat he wore with the collar turned up, and something tubular was in that pocket, and it was aimed—

Yes, a mistake, thought the Scimitar in those final seconds. He had failed. This Fleming was evidently popular game, and he had run afoul of a fellow hunter. Now he would not be able to complete his mission for his superiors, for the greater good of Mother Russia.

Nonetheless he made a game effort to wrest his revolver free of its shoulder holster. His fingers hadn't yet touched the butt when his side window exploded and the bullet entered his brain.

Chapter 23

THEY ATE lunch at the hotel, a haphazard meal of sandwiches and coffee that they nibbled at intermittently while the police took their statements. Fleming found himself rather disappointed that they had missed out on their planned outing to Fisherman's Wharf.

The detective's name was Casini, though he looked more Irish than Italian. He seemed roughly Fleming's age but had evidently been a willing accomplice in the middle-aged deterioration of his body. His soft midsection pressed loosely against the belt he was continually fidgeting with. His girth seemed somewhat out of place on a tall broad-shouldered frame that appeared to have once been rather athletic. His square-jawed face too seemed to have joined in the general physical decline. Flesh sagged from firm cheekbones, and the unseemly stubble along his jowls was more grey than the red of his severely cut hair. His loose features were lightly freckled.

"I saw Manchester once, during the war," he was saying, helping himself to another cup of heavily sugared coffee. Room service had had to bring in several fresh pots. "Never made it down to London but always wanted to. Guess I'll never get the chance now."

There were two other uniformed officers in the suite's large parlor. Fleming stood with Detective Casini as he eyed the rose-colored wallpaper as if it were of some interest. Nora was seated on the chamber's plush divan, methodically filling an ashtray with the dark stubs of cigarette filters. Her and Fleming's statements about the incident had both been duly recorded. The Cadillac, parked downstairs in the hotel's garage, had also been examined. The bullet had been carefully extracted from where it had only partially buried itself in the thick metal hull of the car's boot. The Cadillac's back fender had been only mildly bent out of shape during the collision with the Dodge.

"Which branch of the armed forces was yours?" Fleming asked, not out of any curiosity, merely because it seemed this detective wanted to make conversation.

"Marines," Casini said with what sounded like reflexive pride. He spoke in something of an unhealthy wheeze. "Yourself? That is, if you served."

"I did. Naval."

"Yeah, we all went into the meat grinder, didn't we?" Casini turned his meditative stare from the wallpaper to Fleming. "I had a buddy whose lungs were all scarred up from scarlet fever—from when he was a kid, y'know. Army drafted him anyway. They needed their cannon fodder. He got himself killed in Anzio. . . ."

"Detective," Fleming said as courteously as he could manage, growing suddenly tired of all this, "did any of your fellow officers assemble any germane information from the scene of the incident?"

Casini had made use of the parlor's phone several times, communicating with his colleagues in the San Francisco police department.

"*Germane?*" The detective cocked an eyebrow, evidently amused. "That's a fine two dollar word there. I always liked how you British guys talk. You never settle for plain speaking."

Fleming felt his impatience mounting.

"Anyway . . . your question. Well, eyewitnesses weren't

a whole lot of help. Nobody gave any better description of the gunman than I got from you, which isn't much to go on—and the description of the driver is pretty worthless. The shooter was a big fella, over six foot, late thirties to early forties, black coat, black hat. Hell, that could be me dressed up for Sunday." He made an asthmatic chortle at that. The two uniformed officers supplied a few supporting chuckles.

"I assure you, Detective, I took note of details as best I could under the—"

" 'S all right, buster," Casini said amiably. Fleming wondered with some annoyance why all such supposedly friendly American colloquialisms sounded so offensive. "You did good. Specially in the thick of it, like you were. Not everybody's so cool under fire. You did a swell job too, miss." He made a kind of clumsy bow in Nora's direction. "Fine driving. I just thank God nobody got hurt." Casini took a swallow of his coffee.

"Yes, there's much to be thankful for." Fleming crossed his arms. "Was anything helpful learned about the automobile those two men were driving?"

" '46 Dodge, grey," Casini recited as though reading from the notebook in which he'd been scribbling earlier. "Both plates removed. That wouldn't be much help either . . .'cept there was a car of that make that got stole last month out of an Oakland parking lot. We're talking to a Detective Blotner cross the bay. Maybe we'll get some sort of lead out of it. Maybe not."

Fleming didn't much care for the cavalier tone of this last statement and found himself saying so.

The amiability drained suddenly from Casini's face as he leveled his gaze. "Listen here, pal. The police are *very* concerned about this matter. A high-speed chase through the hills, thugs shooting off guns in the street . . . we don't like that sort of thing in our city. We don't like any trouble. Hel—"a glance toward Nora—"heck, we had a murder right in the middle of Divisadero Street right 'bout the time you two were zipping through the hills. Somebody plugged somebody else while they were sitting in their car. We don't like it. We're doing everything anybody could do to find these guys who hassled you. I got uniforms prowling the streets looking for this Dodge. I got people on the scene canvasing and still trying to milk details out of the witnesses. I want those two men that gave you both such a rough time. You don't see me wasting anybody's time by raising a stink about that pistol in the glove compartment."

"Miss DeYoung has a quite legal permit for it," Fleming said. Nora had showed him the papers.

"Didn't I just say I wasn't making a federal case about it?" Casini finished his coffee in one great swallow and set the cup on the parlor's dining table. "Besides, you were the one, chum, that had it in hand."

"I too have a carrying permit, Detective." It had been quite an oversight on his part, though, that he'd neglected to bring along his own pistol on this trip. But Nora's presence had been something of a distraction when he was packing—a very pleasant distraction.

"I'm happy for you. Now, look"—the detective raised a meaty hand—"don't let's go off on tangents. Neither of your actions are in question. What I'd like to know is if either of you folks got any—*any*—idea why those hoods came after you. You, miss, you said you were following up a newspaper story, right?"

"Correct," said Nora from the divan, lighting another cigarette with her Zippo.

"Well, what was the nature of that?" Casini produced

his notebook once more from a pocket of his rumpled coat.

"I went to interview someone."

"And that somebody was?" The detective's pen hovered over a fresh page.

"Anonymous," Nora said easily and evenly. "I received an anonymous tip about the story I'm currently assigned to. I went to meet this individual, but no one showed up."

Fleming's eyes widened only slightly as he turned them toward Nora.

"Where was the rendezvous?"

"Out in front of the Ferry Building."

Casini's pen scratched briefly. "What were you doing way out on Divisadero, then?"

Nora shrugged nonchalantly. "I said. My contact didn't show up. Mr. Fleming and I were heading for the wharf for lunch."

Casini nodded. "What's the story you're doing?"

"I'm helping on a profile of Oscar Winterberg."

The detective nodded again. "Good ol' Winterberg," he muttered, but from his tone Fleming couldn't glean Casini's sentiments. He pocketed the notebook. "Well, that's going to be it for now. Thanks to both of you for your cooperation."

"When can we hope to hear from you again about this matter?" Fleming asked as the two uniformed officers moved toward the suite's door.

"I'll be in touch tomorrow," said Casini, eyeing the parlor's furnishings as though they were again of interest. "Sooner if something breaks. It could happen. This is a really swell place here. I never knew you reporters traveled so swankily."

"Expense accounts can occasionally be wonderful things, Detective," Nora said affably from the divan.

Casini wheezed an appreciative chuckle. "I don't doubt it, Miss DeYoung. And thanks again for your help. Mr. Fleming"—he extended his hand—"sorry for any harsh words we might've had. Your cooperation's been appreciated."

The detective's grip was strong, almost unnecessarily so. He felt a twinge from his elbow where it had knocked the Cadillac's door handle.

The three policemen departed.

Fleming waited a full thirty seconds after the door had clicked shut before turning toward Nora.

"You lied to the police."

Her blue-eyed gaze was cool. "I did."

"Toward what end?"

"Ian . . ." Nora ground out yet another butt into the overflowing ashtray. "This story is important. Deborah Byrd's contribution to it is vital. Otherwise this will be just another publicity opportunity for Winterberg. I can't allow anything to interfere. And, believe me, the police would interfere."

"It will impede their investigation," he said, knowing in advance what Nora's view of the matter would be.

"There's more at stake here." Her tone, though soft, brooked no argument.

Standing before the divan, Fleming crossed his arms again and made an argument anyway. "Is it really so important, Nora, this Winterberg story? Yes, it shall be sensational. Yes, it will splash across the headlines. But . . . haven't you yet considered? Those two—*thugs* did that detective say?—yes, those two thugs attacked us shortly after we paid our call at Miss Byrd's apartment. Do you imagine that was mere coincidence? Another fanciful fluke of—"

"Of *course* I realize," she said, tone now more assuaging

than confrontational. "That's the whole point. Those goons belonged to Oscar Winterberg. I don't doubt it for a minute. They had to've had Deborah Byrd's place under watch. Probably had orders from their boss to, shall we say, detain any unexpected callers."

"Are you saying that Winterberg is a criminal—with hired strong-arm men—as well as being a bigamist?"

Nora squeezed one hand in her other, her expression growing intense. "Winterberg is a powerful man. Powerful men are not entirely constrained by the law. You think Winterberg's an exception? He's a leading figure in the labor unions. Some of the tactics those boys have used in the past are strong-arm ones indeed. Rioting against the police, making personal threats against heads of management. Winterberg himself is supposed to have been involved in the kidnapping and ransoming of a factory owner's twelve-year-old boy."

"Yes, I read of that in your notes." And in Davenport's file. "Do you imagine it's true?"

"Professionally, no. I can't confirm it. No one can. Personally, however, I have no trouble imagining Winterberg slicing off a child's little finger and delivering it to someone to make them see the light."

Fleming winced a bit at the image. If this single fact were true, it would build Winterberg into something much more fiendish than a bigamist.

Nora shook her head. "There are other . . . incidents . . . that he has supposedly been involved in. Unfortunately none can be strictly proven. Winterberg may have the popular support of the people, but there is an undercurrent of rumor surrounding him. The sabotaging of factories, reprisals against scabs—"

"Scabs?"

"Nonunion workers brought in to fill the slots of workers who've gone on strike. Some of those men—workers desperate enough to feed their families that they'll go against the unions—have turned up in hospitals . . . or morgues."

"I see," said Fleming.

"He doubtlessly wants Deborah Byrd to stay protected," she said, returning to the previous topic. "Maybe he's under the delusion that this situation with her will never come out, that he can have his cake and eat it too."

Fleming now eased down onto the seat next to her. He picked the hand she was wringing out of her lap and closed it between his own.

"Nora," he said gently, "this is dangerous. That man fired a gun at us. It's not, frankly, my safety that concerns me. Those men, if they are in fact Winterberg's hirelings, may now have an accurate description of you. Not to mention that Miss Byrd knows your name. Do you really think it's wise to pursue this further? I recommend strongly that you don't follow through with this interview of Oscar Winterberg." As he said this last, he felt Nora tense noticeably beside him.

She turned her gaze once more on him. Where before it had been cool, now it was positively icy.

After a prolonged silence she said, measuring out the words, "I will interview him, Ian. The dangers, the consequences are not relevant. Winterberg is mine, and I will have him."

This time he was afforded no opportunity to argue the point. Nora pulled her hand from his tender grip, crossed the parlor stiffly without glancing back and closed the bedroom door behind her.

Chapter 24

AT A loss, Fleming had retreated to the bedroom opposite the one he and Nora had been sharing. She did not emerge from that room. The expansive parlor seemed to lie between them like an unbridgeable gulf. He found himself lying down atop the bed's smooth pale pink coverlet, suddenly quite fatigued by the day's hectic events, and closing his eyes.

He awoke to soft lips pressing his cheek. He jerked upright, finding the light quite dim at the bedroom's window. He had evidently drowsed away the remainder of the afternoon.

"Hello, sleeping beauty," said Nora.

He blinked, swiftly gathering his faculties. He parted his lips to speak, but she laid a gentle finger across them.

"Before you say a word, Ian, I've got a peace offering for you. I also want to apologize. I don't like how I spoke to you earlier. I . . . I was upset over everything that had happened. You, unfortunately, just happened to be in the room with me. So. I went and got you something."

He unlimbered himself from the bed, realizing that he'd not even bothered to remove his shoes. Only a few years ago he would not have dozed off so.

Nora had apparently just returned from an errand. She was wearing her overcoat and checkered scarf. She kissed his other cheek, and he noted that her lips were cool from the outside temperature.

"Nora . . ." he began.

"Hush a moment, Ian. Please." She was holding an oblong box beneath one arm and now presented it to him with a hopeful smile. It was tied with a large bright red bow. "Here. Open this. Then you can call me any name in the book."

He accepted the box. It was fairly heavy. "Whatever this is, it's quite unnecessary, I assure—"

"Now, let's not start a sparring match of British manners. Just open the damn thing." Her smile was more forceful this time.

He returned her a small smile of his own and dutifully tugged at the ribbon. Inside, he pulled away filmy layers of tissue paper, then removed the box's contents. He unfolded the garment and held it up for perusal.

"I realize you're the last man on earth that needs fashion advice, but that bulky wool overcoat you've been tramping around in just doesn't become you. This, I think, will keep you both warm and stylish. I hope you agree."

"I do," Fleming said sincerely. The beige knee-length coat was made of fine silky fleece. Vicuña, he judged. It was cut quite elegantly and looked, at least at first glance, to be precisely his fit. The material was at least as warm as his wool greatcoat. "This is quite extravagant, Nora."

"It's a measure of my repentance, Ian." She was obviously waiting now for him to accept her apology.

He didn't leave her in suspense. "Thank you." He slipped on the coat. It lay nicely across his shoulders. He smoothed the sides, feeling as he did something in the deep right pocket. Curious, he probed within, his hand closing on a small metal object. Removing it, he found a sterling silver cigarette case, the face embossed with fine scrollwork. "Oh, dear Lord, Nora, now this really is too much."

"The finer things suit you." She laughed her familiar musical titter.

He moved to take her in his arms, but she stopped him with a gentle hand to his shoulder. "Open that as well," she said, nodding at the cigarette case.

He undid the catch. Inside, he found it stocked with a neat row of Players. On the underside of the lid words had been etched in the metal. *My dearest Ian . . . Eternally yours . . . Nora.*

When he looked back up, her limpid blue eyes were sparkling with unshed tears. Now he did embrace her, tightly, squeezing her to him, arms folding about her lovely body. He put his lips to hers for a long while, and that kiss sealed the peace between them better than any words he might have found.

THEY DINED THAT evening in North Beach, that district of the melting-pot city where Italian immigrants seemed to have settled heavily. The restaurant was marvelous, small but not at all humble, the staff consisting entirely of extended members of the same clan. They were a boisterous lot. There came raised voices and zestful laughing from the kitchen. Waiters and busboys—likely no more distant than second cousins—traded dialogue in barrages of their native tongue too swift for Fleming to pick out more than a few recognizable words. The family's patriarch, who also owned the establishment, was a mustachioed fellow in his sixties, whose barrel belly and florid features spoke of a vivaciousness of spirit, if not disciplined health. He meandered from table to table, greeting individual parties of guests with a cordiality that was almost intrusive, but not unwelcome.

The meal was as agreeable and authentic as one could hope to find in Naples. They ate delicate veal cutlets, mounds of linguine saturated in lemon butter, steamed baby clams in white wine, a steaming loaf of sourdough bread whose top was split and doused in a rich garlic sauce. The restaurant's wine assortment was admirable. Fleming ordered a bottle of fine Californian red.

He noted only distantly—and did not allow himself to brood upon the matter—that the variety of near-crippling postwar shortages still gripping England seemed markedly absent here in the States. Beyond the rationing stickers still adorning many an auto's windscreen, there were certainly no glaring reminders of that war not so long past. No battered ruins. No gaping wounds in the earth such as a German air raid might leave behind. . . .

He turned aside from the thoughts before they could take root. These people had assuredly done their part in that conflict. They had sacrificed untold lives, just as his nation had done. There was no rational purpose in comparing scars.

Afterwards they went out once again for cocktails. Nora swung the Magic Gold Cadillac, as he was coming to think of the auto, through San Francisco's abundant hills. He kept a reflexive eye on the side-view mirror, but no grey Dodge—nor any other make of car—pursued them.

It became another rather gay night. As before, they remained in no one place for any length of time; instead, they caromed about, using Nora's knowledge of the city to take them from one lively locale to the next. This American city evidently reveled in its night life.

Fleming was indeed kept quite snug and warm within the folds of his urbane vicuña coat. Nora remarked again and again how flattering it looked on him. Each time he thanked her for the gift and chided her with mock severity for the extravagance. She would respond to this with only delighted laughter.

"Do presents make you nervous, Ian?" she finally asked when they found themselves dancing in a basement jazz club on Montgomery Street a short distance off Market. The hour was growing late, but they were both reluctant to break away.

"It is perhaps more of a chore for a proper Englishman to receive rather than to give," he said, moving her nimble and cooperative body about the dance floor of red and white checkered tiles. The ceiling of the place was low enough that he was sure he could brush it with his fingertips were he to stand on his toes. Billows of cigarette smoke rolled through the circles of candlelight radiating from the crammed together tables circumscribing the dance floor. It was humid in here from the press of bodies, from the heated rhythms of the energetic jazz ensemble playing on the small bandstand. A sultry-looking Negro woman was dancing sinuously among the players, lending an air to the proceedings that was almost voodoo-like and vaguely reminiscent of Jamaica.

"Well, you have my thanks for withstanding the burden of accepting my gifts," Nora said teasingly as she spun about in perfect accord to Fleming's motions.

"One or the other would have sufficed, you realize," he said. "Either that marvelous coat or the engraved cigarette case."

Her movements flagged a moment. She leaned her head nearer his so that her hushed words could be heard.

"I have a confession to make, Ian."

He eyed her closely. Why was it that each time he imagined he had this woman pinned there always seemed to be some new fact about her ready to emerge? "And what could that be, Nora?"

"The cigarette case . . ." She shrugged her shapely shoulders, appearing for all the world like a young girl revealing a misdeed to a parent. "I had that engraved for you the night we arrived. I sent out a bellhop to do it while you were in the shower."

His gaze widened a bit. "Did you mean to say that inscription—"

"Yes. *Eternally yours.* That wasn't so much a peace offering, Ian. It . . . it's something I'm afraid I simply haven't—and might never have—had the nerve to actually say out loud. And . . . I've wanted to say it. For some time now."

He had taken the words embossed on that cigarette case to be something like friendly hyperbole. But evidently the message was sincere. *Eternally yours.* There was a great depth of emotion in that phrase. His instinctual response was to retreat.

He squelched the old impulse now, forcibly. Nora . . . Nora was different from other women who had come into his life. Perhaps it was time to admit to himself that he had never felt so strongly toward a female.

Again she was waiting, not for forgiveness this time, not even, it seemed, for some reciprocal declaration; she merely wanted his reaction, whatever it might be. She's waiting to see if I bolt or swoon at her feet, he thought with a welcome touch of drollery.

"Eternity is a long time, Nora," he said quietly. "But this present time together with you is, I should say, without compare."

The statement was decidedly more pragmatic than poetic, but it best expressed Fleming's feelings.

Nora absorbed his words with perfect aplomb. They had ceased dancing. She lifted gloved fingers and trailed them over his cheek tenderly.

"Thank you for that honesty, Ian," she said, her voice level and utterly sincere.

They returned to the hotel well past midnight. Nora snuggled against him as they mounted the stairs into the lobby. As late as the hour was, Fleming knew neither of them would be sleeping for some while. He smiled at the thought.

"Mr. Fleming? We have a message for you, sir."

The same diminutive bespectacled man from the night they'd arrived held out the slip of paper from behind the marble-topped front desk.

Fleming broke away from Nora, giving her hand a parting squeeze, and collected the message.

It was a simple one. *Must speak with you urgently. Will telephone your room at 9 tomorrow morning.* The message had been left at 8:05 that evening, while he and Nora were dining in North Beach. In the box identifying the caller was this name: Charles Winstead.

He pocketed the slip of paper as Nora came to tug on his arm, urging him toward the hotel's lifts. He moved with her in that direction.

"Anything interesting?" she asked as the lights above the elevator's doors lit.

"Just more twaddle from our dear Merlin Powell," he said casually enough that it was convincing to his own ears. "He's going to ring me tomorrow morning. I shall have to concoct something to keep him at bay."

They entered the lift, and the uniformed attendant closed the interior gate of the cage soundly behind them.

Chapter 25

FLEMING, HAVING mentally set his internal clock, woke once again before Nora. The act was purposeful. He slipped out of the bedroom, pausing only briefly for a backward glance. Nora's firm body was exquisitely outlined by the disarrayed bedclothes. She was sleeping at something of a tilt, toes and head pointing toward diagonally opposite corners of the bed. She was snoring lightly.

He crossed to the suite's second bedroom and quickly showered, shaved and dressed. In the parlor the clock showed it to be a few minutes past eight.

Picking Nora's car keys off the dining table where she had dropped them, he stepped quietly out of the rooms, taking the lift all the way down to the hotel's cavernous garage level. The broad concrete cave was filled with rank upon neat rank of autos and smelled of exhaust. No one accosted him as he located and unlocked the Magic Gold Cadillac. Really, it *was* an extraordinary-looking car. He opened the glove box and, with a swift furtive sleight-of-hand, transferred the Beretta from the compartment to the waistband of his charcoal grey trousers, sliding the pistol back until it rested invisibly at the small of his back. Its weight there felt comfortable and comforting.

On the elevator ride back up to the eighth floor Fleming contemplated the situation.

Someone calling himself Charles Winstead had left him a message yesterday, promising to ring him at the suite in a little less than an hour. He'd carefully betrayed none of the wariness the message had filled him with to Nora. "Charles Winstead" was, of course, the name which those English couriers—one of whom was Lord Hemmingford's nephew—had said belonged to their contact in the United States. He was the supposed individual sending coded communiqués into Russia from a San Francisco post office box.

Davenport had tried to convince Fleming back in London that Winstead was in fact Winterberg. The logic of that conclusion was flimsy. So Fleming had thought then and still judged now. But . . . what if Davenport were correct? And was it mere coincidence that this Charles Winstead would try to communicate with him on the same day that he and Nora had paid a call on Oscar Winterberg's secret second wife, Deborah Byrd?

Something was indeed rotten in the state of Denmark. Fleming had decided to err on the side of caution, to be prepared for any eventuality—which was his justification for borrowing Nora's pistol. He reprimanded himself silently again for not bringing his own gun from Jamaica. If he truly was Nora's self-appointed bodyguard for this excursion to San Francisco, he should have had more foresight.

The lift doors opened, and he stepped past the sleepy-eyed attendant into the empty carpeted corridor. The message he had received at the front desk last night might be a warning of some sort. The mysterious Charles Winstead had promised to telephone at nine o'clock this morning.

Fleming started to turn at the junction of the ninth floor's corridors, heading back to the suite, when abruptly and noiselessly he pulled back behind the corner.

The passage ahead was not empty. He had glimpsed a figure—male, short—standing nearby the suite's door.

Glancing at his watch, he saw it was quarter past eight. His right hand moved beneath the tails of his jacket and closed over the Beretta's grip. He edged warily toward the corner, cheek brushing the tasteful amber wallpaper, and spied the passageway again.

He was some ten yards from the loitering man. The figure had his back toward Fleming. He was wearing a dark blue overcoat over a dark blue suit. By his greying hair and posture Fleming judged him to be middle-aged.

Was this then another of Oscar Winterberg's—what was that blunt word Nora had used—*goons*? He thought suddenly and sharply of the bomb that had detonated inside Nora's room at the Chabrol Arms in Jamaica.

The loiterer lifted a hand from the pocket of his overcoat to knock on the door, then hesitated. He looked at his watch, looked to the door, wavering. Was he waiting for some particular, preset time? Was he a legitimate caller? Whatever, Nora was still asleep in the suite.

At that instant Fleming moved, gliding down the ten yards of carpeted corridor on virtually soundless feet. The man seemed to sense his approach nonetheless when Fleming was only a fast step away, but by then it was too late.

The man gave a sharp grunt as the back of his coat collar was seized and jerked upright. Fleming yanked the short man high, up onto his toes. In the same fluid motion he freed the Beretta and placed the bore firmly where the man's jawline met his right ear, his movements cool and professional.

"Fleming," said the man. The voice was familiar.

Fleming pulled him away from the suite door and, still dangling the short middle-aged man, pushed him firmly against the corridor wall, turning his head so that his face was visible in profile. Recognition came in a heartbeat.

"*Stahl*," he said in sharp surprise, not relaxing the pistol. "What the bloody hell are you doing here?"

"At the moment being manhandled and held at gunpoint," said the British Secret Service agent and Francis Davenport's aide. He appeared more annoyed than frightened. "I see your skills haven't entirely atrophied since the war." Though vaguely complimentary, the statement was phrased as a slight.

Fleming returned the Beretta to his waistband. He held Stahl's overcoat a few seconds longer, feeling an impulse to bang the man's skull soundly against the wallpaper, then released him.

Stahl took a moment to rearrange his clothing with peevish dignity. He shot Fleming an unpleasant look with his small colorless eyes.

"Explain yourself," said the retired spy to the active one, tone hard and uncompromising.

"I intend to." Stahl gave his overcoat sleeves a final irate tug. "And I expect you to do the same. I am on Her Majesty's official business."

"Don't bother trying to terrorize me with your incantations," Fleming said. "What in hell are you doing in San Francisco poking about my door? Can I presume *you* phoned me last night in the guise of Charles Winstead? And why—"

"Do you want to have this discussion here, Fleming? In the hallway? I would prefer a more private venue." He punctuated this with his familiar *hurrumph*.

A vulgar retort came to Fleming's lips, but he left it unsaid. Stahl, in this instance, was correct.

They could not speak in the suite. Nora could not know anything of this—whatever this might turn out to be. He nodded back down the corridor. "Come with me," he said.

A few moments later, in their new surroundings, Stahl remarked waspishly, "Well, this at least is private. I only hesitated to knock on your suite door because the hour is somewhat early."

"Your message said you meant to telephone."

"On reflection I thought a face-to-face encounter more apt."

They were sitting in the plush front seats of the Cadillac, the grotto of the hotel garage dim about them. From the outside they would be little more than shadows. Fleming had felt a territorial need to speak to this man on his own ground, and this auto would have to suffice. Besides, he didn't wish to be out in the open with Stahl. The man had been openly hostile toward him since they first met. He wondered at the root of that enmity. Perhaps Stahl—an aide, a not-so-glorified secretary—envied the more exotic career Fleming had carved for himself during his war years.

Fleming sat behind the steering wheel. He had yet to actually drive this monstrosity, though certainly he need only ask Nora's leave to do so. The intricate dashboard, with its many knobs and buttons, was enticing. He knew he was on the verge of yet another spate of capricious imagining, assigning fanciful functions to each of these controls. Instead, he focused his attention on Stahl in the passenger seat. The Beretta remained a succoring weight at the small of his back.

"What have you to say for yourself?"

The middle-aged Secret Service agent eyed him sourly—and rather tiredly, it seemed. If Stahl had just arrived in San Francisco from London, he must indeed be feeling the fatiguing effects of that long flight.

"Very well, Fleming. We've been keeping an eye on you. That is, Whitehall has. We were really only curious if you would make any move off Jamaica toward San Francisco. And, obviously, you did so. Tracing you to your rooms was merely a matter of telephoning hotels."

British intelligence must have enlisted Interpol's aid. When Fleming had flashed his passport in Miami, the alert must have sounded.

"Have I ceased to be a free citizen of the Crown, then? Is my travel restricted?"

"Don't play coy, Fleming. It's unbecoming on any male over the age of sixteen." Stahl seemed to make some superficial effort to rein in his irritation. He went on, "What my superior, Mr. Davenport, wishes to know is if you've decided to capitalize on the confidential information you were shown concerning Oscar Winterberg."

Fleming was hesitant to lie. Stahl, whatever he might think of the man, was an authentic member of the British Secret Service; that made the two of them, at least by generous definition, fellows in the same community, Fleming's retirement from that society notwithstanding.

Yet Fleming was rankled on another level, that of a journalist. He had effectively been cut off from this story when he'd declined to do Davenport's dirty work. There were fewer easier ways to pique a newsman's interest than by warning him off a potential story.

"I am traveling with a young lady," he finally said. "A Miss—"

"Nora Blair DeYoung," Stahl said flatly. "Yes. We know. A New York journalist. Tell me, she wouldn't be here in this city to investigate Winterberg?"

Again Fleming hesitated, then said levelly, "She is."

"How coincidental. Need I remind you of the strictures

of the National Securities Act, Fleming? Did you divulge any—*any*—information from our file on Winterberg to this woman? Perhaps to lure her into your clutches?"

Fleming very nearly cuffed Stahl at that instant. Instead, he drew a long breath. "I did not," he said evenly and truthfully.

"That's the word of an English gentleman?"

"It is."

Stahl nodded vaguely, as though the avowal had little or no meaning. "Very well. Then, pray, explain how this Miss DeYoung became so suddenly interested in Winterberg."

"You would have to ask her editors in New York. It is from them she received this assignment."

The short middle-aged agent *hurrumphed* again. "Then I shall ask you this. Does this newspaper story she is pursuing touch upon in any fashion the information which you saw in our Winterberg file?"

Fleming was once more on truthful ground. "It does not. The feature she is writing has no bearing on that balderdash about Winterberg smuggling coded secrets from the States to Russia. That, old boy, is a bundle of absurdity. And you know it."

To this Stahl sighed tiredly and lifted a hand to rub his eyes, the irascible expression leaving his features for the first time. In a rather resigned tone he said, "Yes, I suppose I do."

Fleming blinked. He hadn't expected to evoke such a response. Pressing, he said, "It's Lord Dale Hemmingford that is pushing this matter forward, no matter how preposterous, isn't it?"

"As you've ascertained." Stahl shook himself. "I have nothing further to ask you, Fleming. I shall report to Mr. Davenport that you've committed no breach."

"Do send him my love."

Stahl gave him a withering look, then reached for the passenger door handle. He hesitated. "There is one last thing. This Miss DeYoung, the newspaper correspondent. Is the feature she's writing . . . is it one that might damage Winterberg?"

Fleming let the older man wait a moment, then said, "You are asking if she's going to inadvertently aid you in your honorable cause of discrediting Winterberg? Freedom of the press is held sacred in the United States. You should be aware of that."

The fatigue was now heavy on Stahl's somewhat drooping features. "Damn—Please, Fleming," he said with some emotion. "This is important."

So it was, he acknowledged silently. Finally he said, "If the feature is published, it will not cast Oscar Winterberg in the most flattering of lights."

Stahl nodded slowly, apparently satisfied—or at least settling for this. He pulled the door handle and stepped from the Cadillac.

Fleming remained in the garage, alone, for some while. Then he returned to the suite to search for a telephone directory.

Chapter 26

THERE WAS little time for sightseeing that day. Nora's interview with Winterberg was slated for tomorrow afternoon, and she was in a flurry of preparation. Fleming had been keeping silent about his reservations of the meeting with the union leader, as it seemed evident she was not to be swayed from her course.

She had spread her jumbled notes all across the surface of the parlor's dining table, scribbling furiously on the mismatched sheets. She made multiple calls to her New York editors and received several in return. Fleming watched her ignite one cigarette from the glowing butt of another. Room service had delivered breakfast some hours ago, but she had shown interest only in the coffee, which she took with at least as many spoonfuls of sugar as Detective Casini had.

She was in a state of high nervous energy when he finally insisted that she eat something. She stood from the table, stretching what looked to be a painful crick from her back, and grinned.

"We'll go to Blum's. Let me freshen up a bit first."

She reappeared from the bedroom a moment later with her rich red hair bound back in a simple knot and wearing that boots, dungarees and man's shirt—this one flannel, instead of cotton—ensemble he had seen her in before. They left the St. Francis on foot, and Nora's apparel drew more than a few curious looks on the street. Today's chill was not too severe, though the scudding overcast and intermittently biting wind were sharp reminders of winter. The clouds were a charcoal grey, hinting at possibilities of rain. Snow, he knew, didn't fall in San Francisco.

Blum's turned out to be little more than a soda fountain, and a popular one at that. Bodies were pressed tightly along the counter. Nora ordered a crunchy-looking slab of coffee cake and an ice cream soda. Fleming declined to partake of any of the candied treats, watching in mild horror as she devoured her "lunch."

The sugar only intensified the manic energy buzzing through her. As he politely lit her cigarette when they were again on the sidewalk, it seemed as though her limpid blue eyes were vibrating in her skull.

"I'm just excited, Ian," she explained. "I get like this when I'm working, especially on something as important as this story is. I realize I must be acting strange to you, but don't worry. I just want this interview to go properly. I'm still deciding on my strategy." Her lungs swelled as she drew deeply on her dark filtered cigarette.

"Have you determined if you'll confront Mr. W. with what you know of Deborah Byrd?"

She shook her head sharply. "I'm on the horns of a dilemma there. Truly. I'm torn. I can't decide if it would be more fun to watch his expression when I drop that bomb or just let him babble away about workers' rights thinking his smug little secret is still safe."

Fleming eyed her curiously. "Fun?" he asked.

"Yes. *Fun.* I enjoy my work, Ian. Can that be difficult to understand?"

No, he silently decided, it wasn't. He himself took a definite professional pride in his work. He didn't think of it as drudgery; yet he wouldn't go so far as to call it "fun." Certainly it lacked much of the glamor of being a spy, but that was a career he had quite willingly left behind. Being a journalist, he finally judged, gave him a sort of necessary human intercourse with the world—to say nothing of supporting him financially. It was a career that suited him for the time being and for the immediately foreseeable future. If one day he found something else to do with his life, so be it.

They started moving along the bustling sidewalk. On the street taxis, lorries and autos jostled in their lanes.

"It almost seems, Nora, that you have something personal against Mr. W.," he said quietly.

He glanced sidelong when no immediate response was forthcoming. Nora was walking with sharp movements of her legs and arms. She finished inhaling her cigarette and stamped smartly on the smoldering filter.

"Mr. W.," she said tightly, eyes fixed ahead, "is a charlatan. He's an adulterer, a bigamist, quite possibly a kidnapper and even a murderer, and those thugs of his might well have killed us yesterday if we hadn't been lucky." Fleming didn't interrupt to point out that the two men in the grey Dodge hadn't been proven to belong to Winterberg. Nora went on as intensely, "Mr. W. passes himself off as a hero of the people, of the persecuted working class. And, yes, he's made significant strides for the greater good. But . . . *he* is not a good man. He's not worthy of the esteem and accolades which are being constantly heaped on him. His life is a masquerade, a false front, and behind his facade . . . there is evil."

Fleming found himself without any reply to this plainly heartfelt tirade. He walked along with Nora until they reached the hotel's entrance.

"Nora," he said, not taking the first step up toward the gleaming glass doors, "you're obviously going to be frightfully preoccupied for at least some while to come. I don't wish to be underfoot. Would you mind awfully if I excused myself and borrowed the car?"

"Darling, of course," she said, fishing keys from a pocket of her dungarees. "If you get lost, there's a map in the glove compartment."

As was her Beretta. He had replaced the pistol there before returning to their rooms from his meeting with Stahl in the garage.

She kissed him quite unabashedly on the lips, drawing a few more looks from passersby. "Well, I must get back to it," she said, her arms still wrapping his neck. "I've got a nemesis to topple."

Then she was bounding up the hotel's broad stairs.

Minutes later he was guiding the Cadillac carefully from the bowels of the sub-level parking garage. The machine handled marvelously, its bulk cornering with the grace of a fine stallion. He eased it onto the street, minding the inverted flow of traffic which in the midday of downtown was rather thick.

He liked the feel of the wheel beneath his hands, the assured growling of the engine. A feeling something like serenity settled over him. He realized he had been missing his Lagonda Rapier, the simple freedom of movement. And too, though this he only grudgingly admitted, it was pleasant to be away from Nora in her present near-frantic state.

Ahead, a cable car was lumbering up Powell Street's grade. The great box-like contraption looked rather like a railway caboose. Passengers filled the interior, while others hung precariously along the forward and rear running boards. Metal wheels clanged along the tracks. The cable of the transport's name was underground. A chain and pulley system evidently dragged the tram from below. Nora had promised that they would ride one. Fleming looked forward to the experience.

He turned west on Sutter Street. The going was slow at first as the heavy traffic made forced detours around double-parked delivery vans. As he neared a broad multilaned thoroughfare, which proved to be Van Ness Avenue, the makeup of the district changed and the street ahead cleared enough that he was able to push the Cadillac at a faster pace. He had no intention, though, of racing the auto at the speeds Nora had indulged in during their flight from the grey Dodge.

He passed through a well-kept residential neighborhood. After he had turned off Sutter onto the broader and also westward-flowing Geary Boulevard, he pulled briefly to the kerb to consult the glove box's street map. He also glanced at what he had jotted down earlier from the suite's telephone directory.

Much of San Francisco was laid out in typically American grid-like fashion, as though the city had been stamped onto its peninsula by a giant mechanical press. He quickly confirmed his bearings, then pushed onward.

Turning south, he was treated to a delightful tour of Golden Gate Park. The size and variety of the preserve was quite remarkable, something on par with even London's finest urban woodlands. There appeared to be winding footpaths all through the dense trees. Signs indicated an assortment of recreational facilities. He found himself quickly recanting his earlier categorization of San Francisco as an archetypal American city. The place had a decided charm about it, something that hinted at both a European and a bohemian character. He could understand Nora's evident infatuation with the metropolis.

When he passed the park's southern confines, his search became easier. These streets were conveniently numbered. He quickly found 29th Avenue and a few moments later the house number that had been indicated in the directory. This district was also residential but somewhat drabber than those he'd already seen.

Above, as he stepped from the car, the last streaks of blue sky were disappearing beneath the darkening bands of clouds. With what now felt like a practiced movement Fleming slipped the Beretta beneath his jacket.

He approached the stucco-faced dwelling. Its color was a weathered lime, and the small patch of lawn laid before it seemed more dandelions than grass. The house had an almost sickly aspect to it. He noted one of the numbers on the front door was hanging askew. He lifted his hand and rapped.

A querulous voice raised itself from within, but the door was not immediately opened. Fleming listened to faint odd-sounding movements. He kept sight of the curtained windows to either side of the door, bouncing ever so slightly on the balls of his feet, ready to move—and move fast—in any direction.

At last the knob turned.

"What—do you—want?"

The man looked to be well into his seventies, but his was an unhealthy, even painful-looking, old age. He stood stooped unnaturally over a pair of mismatched canes. One was several inches shorter than the other, making his posture that much more awkward. His hairless skull appeared yellow in the dimming outside light, and his face was a caved in mass of wrinkled flesh and jutting bone. He wore an unpressed checkered shirt buttoned to his wattled neck. His eyes were awash with cataracts, and the expression on his mummified features was quite inhospitable.

"Mr. Charles F. Winstead?" Fleming asked loudly and clearly, presuming this disintegrating wretch's hearing must also be in decline.

"Yes. Now, what—" the ancient man started to heave a fresh question, then gave up on the rest of his sentence and merely asked, gruffly, "*What?*"

Even though he was operating without any specific gauge, it was manifest that this wasn't the man Fleming was looking for.

"Mr. Winstead, my name is Archie Havens, and I sell insurance."

The elderly Charles F. Winstead made a hostile croaking noise as he struggled to lift one of his canes. Fleming backed smoothly away from the door as it was kicked soundly shut.

He returned to the Magic Gold Cadillac, leaving the Beretta tucked at the small of his back as he drove onward. He left the numbered avenues, crossed several districts and arrived finally at a house—this smaller but in much better repair—that lay a few streets off Portola Drive. The phone directory declared that a Chas. Winstead resided here. The truth, he learned from a Mexican housewife holding a plump infant on her hip, was that Mr. Winstead had died of cancer four months earlier.

Fleming tooled idly awhile. He'd had scant expectations about this mission and so wasn't especially disappointed in its lack of success. Surely Hoover's boys had cooperated sufficiently with Whitehall to inquire into the Charles Winsteads listed in this city's phone book. Doubtlessly the post office box from which the coded communiqués had been stemming had also been investigated. No doubt as well that whoever was using the Winstead alias had had the foresight to take security precautions. At the first sign that the post office box was compromised, the line of communication had surely been shunted elsewhere.

And what right did Fleming have in poking about in this matter? He had declined Francis Davenport's offer to participate in it on any level. He was out of the spy game, permanently. He was not, however, out of the journalism game, and his curiosity about this affair was a nagging thing.

Also, by a roundabout avenue, it seemed that Nora Blair DeYoung had entered into this affair, at least as far as Oscar Winterberg figured into it. If Fleming would not involve himself in an official capacity, he must finally admit that his personal—and increasingly acute—interest in Nora was luring him deeper into the tangle.

At that moment the dark clouds above chose to loose their rain upon the city.

Chapter 27

Nora had labored late into the evening yesterday, organizing her notes on Winterberg. She had barely glanced up from her efforts when Fleming returned from his hunt for the elusive Charles Winstead; and then it had only been to tell him in a distracted tone that Detective Casini had rung the suite. Casini had reassured her, without offering any tangible information, that leads were being scrupulously followed in the matter of the two men and the grey Dodge. Fleming wasn't holding out much hope that the case would enjoy a hasty resolution.

She also mentioned that Merlin Powell had called. The editor was polite, even meek, when speaking to Nora; but doubtlessly he would not have been so civil had Fleming picked up the telephone. He would need to talk to Powell soon, to string the man on awhile longer.

They had dined out last night but returned to their rooms relatively early. Their lovemaking had, for the first time, been somewhat awkward. Their bodies seemed incapable of finding those by-now-familiar rhythms. By mutual assent they had decided to let the situation go as a bad job and even managed to laugh at the predicament.

She had evidently slept well, but Fleming found himself suffering, in the small hours, one of his renowned headaches. He hadn't fallen properly asleep until something like four A.M. and—again, for the first time—hadn't awoke until after Nora had stirred.

Nora this morning was tense but not manic, like yesterday. Her demeanor, in fact, was more grimly resolute than anxious. She showered, then hauled her suitcase from beneath the bed and spent a determined hour choosing her wardrobe. Her comely features were set in firm lines. She studied each article of clothing with a severe critical gaze, as if each item must conform to a single overall effect.

Fleming, meanwhile, busied himself shambling about the suite. He ran his shower first piping hot, then bracingly cold, in an effort to shock himself into fullest consciousness. He shaved and ate a small breakfast, then helped himself to several cups of room service's coffee.

Though he had surrendered to Nora's inflexible insistence that this interview go through, he had been well prepared to give her an argument had she attempted to persuade him not to accompany her. On this point, though, she immediately acquiesced when he had broached the matter last night.

"Why, of course, darling Ian," she had said. "Actually I'd be grateful to have you along. As moral support."

Naturally Fleming meant to do more than bolster her spirits. They would be entering Oscar Winterberg's lair. It was possible—by a stretch of the imagination, even probable—that Winterberg knew that the two of them had visited Deborah Byrd. If Winterberg were as dangerous a man as Nora claimed, then she required protection. Fleming would act in that capacity. In fact he had taken a silent oath while shaving this morning that not a hair on her head would come to harm . . . not if he had to take the most drastic measures available to him.

Toward that end he now entered their bedroom. It was nearing noon. Nora was nodding with solemn satisfaction over the clothing articles she had strewn across the rumpled coverlet. Apparently she had successfully chosen the armor she would wear into battle today. Presently she was dressed in only a satiny pink slip.

"Nora?"

Her mouth was pressed into a hard stripe above her tapering chin as she turned. "Yes?" she asked, voice rather far-off.

Fleming stood at the foot of the bed. He crossed his arms, posture erect. He said evenly, "When we pay this call on Oscar Winterberg this afternoon, I should like you to know that I intend to be carrying that handgun of yours on my person."

He watched for her reaction, but she did nothing but blink once.

Feeling the need to fill the silence, he went on, "You admit freely that Winterberg is a menacing chap. You insist on confronting him nevertheless. Very well. You've declined to inform the police of your concerns, excluding the option of bringing them along as security. Again, very well. I accept these conditions. What I am determinedly unwilling to allow is for you to enter the man's presence without an armed escort. *I* am that escort. I shall be carrying that smart Beretta concealed on me. If difficulties arise . . . I will use it. I wish you to know these facts beforehand."

He of course might simply have borrowed the pistol without her knowledge, as he had done twice yesterday. But these circumstances were pointedly different. Yesterday's adventures had been solo efforts. Today Nora would be with him. It seemed a wise safety precaution—not to mention a judicious strategic move—to inform her that he would be armed.

Once more he waited upon her response to his firm oration. At last Nora nodded sharply.

"That's an excellent idea, Ian. I'd been planning on

carrying the piece myself. But I believe I'd be even more comforted knowing it was in the hands of a former Navy man. Yes." She nodded again, then reached into a zippered pocket of the opened suitcase on the bed. Palm up, she offered him a loaded clip. "Here. Extra shots, if you need them."

Rather taken aback by her forthright pragmatism, he pocketed the bullets. It was heartening, though, to know with certainty that she was not walking blind into this situation. If she weren't turning away from its potential dangers, she was decidedly acknowledging them. She was also no timid girl.

She made another call to New York, then set about dressing. Fleming donned his charcoal trousers, a warm black turtleneck sweater and a neutral grey sport jacket. He eschewed the vicuña coat, as its long tails might interfere if it were necessary to make a fast draw of the Beretta. He placed the spare clip in his right pants pocket. He also refilled his sterling silver cigarette case, glancing automatically at the engraving. *Eternally yours.*

His nerves felt steady, despite the poor sleep he'd had. He felt ready for whatever surprises might be in store on this visit to Oscar Winterberg. He smiled wryly and privately to himself. He had yet to actually lay eyes on the man. But it did seem that over the course of the past weeks Winterberg had been built into an almost mythological figure, a kind of diabolic fiend. A man responsible for the kidnapping and mutilation of the twelve-year-old son of a plant owner, a man behind the beatings and even murders of scab workers. Yet all Fleming knew as fact was that the man had foolishly taken a second wife. That he was passing coded information to the Russians or that he was a gangster-like character with armed thugs acting at his behest was nothing better than speculation. Today, hopefully, some truth would be learned.

Nora at last emerged from the bedroom. She was done up in attire nearly as impartial as his own. She wore a not especially flattering gingham skirt, a pearl-colored blouse and rather drab jacket. Her red ringlets were bound up severely. She was also wearing a pair of spinsterish spectacles which dampened the vibrancy of her blue eyes.

He gazed nonplussed at her a moment.

She gave him a crooked smile. "I don't wish to distract our Mr. W. with my womanly charms, Ian. That would be a cheap tactic. I want his mind on other matters."

"Very well, my dear."

It was past one o'clock. The interview was slated for one thirty at an office on Beale Street, just south of Market. Before returning to the St. Francis yesterday, Fleming had driven past the address. It was a squat, bland-looking building, two-storied. He had taken the time to note that in addition to its front entrance there was also a freight entrance in the adjacent alleyway. He had seen no one enter or leave during the few minutes he sat parked across the street. Still, his reconnaissance efforts could do no harm.

They descended in silence to the hotel's garage. Nora had stuffed her disheveled notes into her pocketbook. They climbed into the Cadillac, Fleming's senses already on alert, eyes darting into shadows, searching for any movement. He slipped the Beretta out of the glove box and into his waistband.

Nora turned the key in the ignition, letting the auto idle a moment. Her eyes behind the unflattering glasses were narrow and tense.

"Shall we?" she asked quietly.

"Let's," said Fleming.

She put the Cadillac in gear and backed them out of the parking slot.

THEIR KNOCK ON the Beale Street office's ground level door was immediately answered by a spindly lad in a pair of undyed coveralls imprinted here and there by oily palm prints. His hair was corn-silk blond, and his bright youthful features were guileless. He looked to be eighteen years old.

"Hi, folks," he chirped pleasantly. "One thirty. You're here to see the boss, that right?"

Fleming stood a close step behind and to the right of Nora. He had been balanced to clear her aside with a swipe of his left arm and draw the Beretta with his other hand. Now he made no move as she said, "Yes. Mr. Winterberg, that's correct."

"Swell," said the boy, holding the door wide and waving them within.

The entryway was a nondescript corridor of unmarked doors. The tiles underfoot were a bilious green, peeling up at the corners. Overhead, bulbs hung in tiny mesh cages, scattering dusty light. The air smelled more than faintly of machine oil.

It seemed an inauspicious citadel for the black knight of this drama to dwell, thought Fleming. Then again, perhaps this would prove to be nothing more than a fairy tale after all, one founded on suspicion, paranoia and supposition. Not that he had any intention of lowering his guard one jot.

The blond lad led them up a flight of stairs, coming out onto a similarly dreary passageway. He stepped up to another of the unlabeled doors and rapped twice, sharply.

"Boss!" he called. "Your one-thirty people are here. Ready for 'em?"

The boy hardly seemed a thug. Fleming realized he had been half expecting this building to be policed by the strong-arm types Nora seemed to believe constituted Winterberg's private army. If this blond waif was Winterberg's notion of security, though, some serious miscalculations regarding the union leader had been made. Still, Fleming remained primed for action as the office door opened.

The salt-weathered face that peeked out seemed to belong to an aging seaman. The knit watch cap atop his bushy grey hair and the anchor tattooed on one bare forearm bolstered the conjecture. He was a large man; but even glimpsing him there in the doorway's crack, Fleming judged he was not as big as the gunman who'd emerged from the rear of the grey Dodge. Eyes beneath dense white brows took note of Nora, then Fleming, then settled on the blond lad.

"Tommy," the seaman said, digging in a pocket. "Here, be a good boy an' run to the store an' git me some smokes and chewing gum. Keep a nickel fer yourself. 'Kay?"

The boy took the money eagerly, bounding nimbly past Fleming toward the stairs, calling over his shoulder, "Sure thing, Mr. Yancy! Be back in a flash!"

"C'mon inside," the seaman—Yancy—said, pulling this door wide to reveal a cluttered and disarrayed office space that looked rather like it doubled as a living quarters. Papers, boxes and furnishings were jammed side by side. There was a cot in one corner, wedged in alongside a large shabby-looking desk whose top was stacked with books, more papers, radio tubes and an eccentric assortment of curios—ceramic figurines, a cast iron model of a Napoleonic cannon, a devilishly grinning tribal mask painted a vivid scarlet and green with long black feathers fanning away from the eye holes.

"Boss is in the head," Yancy said, settling his large-boned mass onto a well-indented corner of a frayed sofa. "Be out in a minute."

Fleming heard water running behind the office's only other door, then the whoosh of a toilet flushing. He and Nora remained standing, waiting. Her posture was poised, betraying no outward hint of the tension he nonetheless sensed crackling beneath her surface. He had not, in his most fanciful expectations, imagined meeting Oscar Winterberg in a setting as decrepit as this. With some horror he realized he was going to set eyes on the man for the first time as he emerged from the water closet. It all seemed dreadfully inappropriate.

The door to the lavatory creaked open on complaining hinges. Into the office's yellow light stepped a male figure that Fleming judged to stand an inch or so above six feet. His was lean in the manner of a well-trained athlete. His shoulders were fairly broad. He wore boots, dungarees grown soft from wear and a denim work shirt with the tails hanging casually free. His hair was thick and quite dark, except where grey had streaked it. His eyes—dark, penetrating and mirthful—leapt from his ruggedly handsome features. His jaw was stippled with dark tufts of beard that had yet to actually emerge from the flesh.

He looked very much like the mental composite Fleming had once whimsically imagined for Blake Young.

Oscar Winterberg was drying his hands on an already soiled towel. He looked first to Yancy on the sofa and said, "That *verdammt* toilet needs looking at again. Have one of Ferguson's men from the plumbers' union in here tomorrow if you can." His voice was deep, shaded only slightly by a Germanic accent.

"Sure thing, boss," said Yancy, picking a *Life* magazine from the cushion beside him and opening it in his wide lap. "Your visitors are here."

Winterberg tossed the towel away carelessly behind him. It landed inside an opened cardboard box of screws and bolts. He turned his searching eyes on Nora and Fleming, his gaze intense. His lips curled into the same wry confident smile Fleming had seen in photographs of the man.

He paused only an instant to survey them, then marched deliberately forward, firm mouth smiling wider. He strode past Nora and extended a hand toward Fleming.

"Ah, Mr. Blake Young, it is a pleasure to have you here."

Fleming took the handshake automatically, which proved to be quite firm, still balancing warily on the balls of his feet. Winterberg's hand was gritty with calluses. Fleming didn't like occupying his shooting hand in this manner but knew he could draw the Beretta with his left if need be.

"Forgive the blackened nails, if you please," said Oscar Winterberg. "Tommy and I were tinkering with the engine of his Ford earlier. My wife will surely scold me to no end tonight if I do not get them clean." He punctuated this with a throaty chuckle.

Which wife? Fleming wondered, then said evenly, "Mr. Winterberg, I believe there's been some mistake."

He realized with the certainty of hindsight that this error had been inevitable. Winterberg was expecting Blake Young to interview him this afternoon. How, he wondered suddenly, did Nora imagine she could bluff her way through this appointment? Expanding on the thought, he wondered how often this predicament cropped up in her unique journalistic career. How did she conduct her renowned interviews as Blake Young when she was quite plainly of the opposite gender?

"An . . . Englander?" Winterberg asked in puzzlement, eyeing Fleming, dark brows drawing together, when Nora interposed herself.

"Mr. Winterberg," she said, "you've just shaken hands with Mr. Ian Fleming. He's my assistant. My name is Miss Nora Blair DeYoung. Blake Young, I'm very sorry to say, has been struck with a bad case of the flu. He's asked us to stand in for him. Rest assured, *he* will be writing the feature on you. I am only here to gather the necessary information. I hope this doesn't inconvenience you too terribly."

The suave smile had fallen from Winterberg's lips in rapid stages during her speech. He at last released Fleming's hand and shifted his stance to appraise Nora more closely. Fleming found he didn't especially like the man's keen gaze. He had also been careful to note any change in expression when Nora offered her name. He saw no flicker of recognition. Perhaps Deborah Byrd had mentioned nothing to her bigamist husband of their visit to her Chinatown apartment two days ago. Actually, it made perfect sense that she would not, didn't it? She meant to betray the man to the press and the world at large, after all. Why would she expose her intentions?

Perhaps, Fleming thought, Winterberg truly knew nothing about the two of them. There were only those two men—men who hadn't been proven to belong to Winterberg—in the Dodge to worry over. And it was unlikely either of those thugs had gotten any clearer look at Nora and him than he had of them.

"Influenza," Winterberg said finally. "It is a bad time of

year for the flu. Sickness in winter. I hope sincerely that Mr. Young recovers himself."

"Will you, then, allow us to conduct the scheduled interview in his stead?" Nora asked without any tremor in her voice.

The question, however, hung perilously in the air for a protracted moment. The only sound in the dilapidated office was Yancy turning the pages of his periodical, evidently oblivious to these proceedings.

Oscar Winterberg drew himself impressively erect, holding his head at something like an imperious angle.

"I see, Miss DeYoung. I admit my disappointment, however. Blake Young has done much to expose the hypocrisies and corruptions of this nation. I have admired his efforts and looked forward to meeting with him. Yet"—he leaned a degree in her direction, dark eyes drilling through the lenses of Nora's spectacles—"so beautiful a lady as you is not unwelcome company. Won't you sit?"

Fleming carefully checked his impulse to plant his palm firmly against the union leader's chest and give him a backward shove. He pointedly held out a chair for Nora himself, then cleared one beside it and sat, feeling the Beretta pressing snugly between the chair back and his spine. Winterberg paused a moment as he moved behind his cluttered desk, eyes traveling between his two visitors, then his lips twisting into what seemed a knowing smirk. At last he took his own seat and gestured rather regally, indicating that the interview could now commence.

Chapter 28

OSCAR WINTERBERG was fiddling with one of the radio tubes on his jumbled desk as he asked, "So, do you want to know if I'm a Communist, or do you want to learn my favorite color?"

Fleming frowned at the decidedly odd question. As during the interview with Deborah Byrd, he had been relegated once more to the passive role of Nora's "assistant." Of course on this occasion, with the Beretta tucked out of sight beneath his jacket, he was also her protector.

Winterberg wasn't sparing him a glance. His dark eyes were anchored on Nora, and that gaze was filled with a brand of seductive self-assurance that Fleming did not like.

"Are those the only choices of questions you're offering?" Nora returned smoothly.

The union leader shrugged innocently, at the same time a mischievous grin twisting his lips. "It seems, Miss DeYoung, that whenever I find myself being interrogated—pardon me, *interviewed*—by an associate of the American press, the questions are invariably culled from one or the other category. Those who are seeking *Sturm und Drang* ask after my political beliefs. Those looking to write something of less substance ask harmless and inoffensive questions. Which type, I wonder at, has Blake Young instructed you to ask?"

"Your English is very accomplished, Mr. Winterberg," said Nora, plainly unwilling to take the bait.

He bowed his head, as though the compliment were

embarrassingly grand. When he lifted his gaze again, he gave Nora a wolfish wink of his right eye. Fleming felt himself stiffening but reined in his reaction coolly. Evidently Nora's frumpy disguise wasn't dissuading Winterberg too effectively. The man seemed quite the libertine.

"I learned quite much of it during the war," he said. "Afterward, in England, I learned more. However, the English language of these United States is much different. Not so very formal and—stuffy, I believe is the word." He did not need to turn his eyes toward Fleming to aim that barb as he chuckled, a resonant merry noise.

Nora's titter was polite and brief. Fleming was still waiting for her to make a first move. She had come here today to destroy this man; so she had said. What, then, was she waiting for? She need only utter the name Deborah Byrd to make him crumble.

Fleming realized he hadn't asked if she'd decided finally on what strategy she intended to use in this interview. He recalled that she had been considering the tactic of withholding entirely her knowledge of Winterberg's bigamy.

"You spent the war years on the Continent then, it would seem," said Nora, craftily not making a question of it, "and moved on to England afterwards."

He nodded. "Correct. Much of the war I spent in France."

"A France occupied by the armies of the nation of your birth."

"Ah, you've concluded that I am German." Winterberg struck a wooden match against a flange of the radio tube and lit a narrow black cigarette. "As it is, you are correct again. I make no efforts to conceal that I was born in München—*ach*, Munich is your name for it. But my nation and I . . . parted ways. I saw what was happening—to my government, to my people. I would have no part of it. The fascists came, and I departed. Really, it is that simple."

Nora had removed a small writing pad and some portion of her scrawled notes from her pocketbook. She made some notation in her personal Sanskrit on the pad's top sheet.

"I've read that while you were in France during the war, you engaged in anti-Nazi activities. Guerrilla actions, to be precise."

Winterberg rocked back in his office chair, settling his booted feet on a clear corner of the desk. His eyes roved toward the ceiling. "Yes," he said eventually, breathing out a plume of dense blue smoke. "I was a partisan for a time. However, that I do not wish to discuss to depth. I do not—how is it said?—downplay my actions, for that would be to cheapen the efforts of other courageous men. Yet, if I dwell upon that segment of my history, it might be said I was glorifying myself. Again, that would be sordid."

Nora regarded him silently a long moment, some unidentified emotion arresting her features.

Winterberg's trappings of humility might or might not be genuine, Fleming judged. Either way, his modest pose was effective. Doubtlessly the press and the public swallowed it eagerly. Oscar Winterberg was not only a hero to the American worker; he had risked life and limb against the Nazi oppressors during the war and had the strength of character to be demure about his heroics. It was all rather cunning. And also, it seemed, *false*. Fleming found himself not liking this man.

"Why did you mention the word Communist at the start of this interview?" Nora asked at last.

"A genuine question at last!" Winterberg cried in exaggerated triumph. He turned his rakish stare back toward

Nora, still ignoring Fleming completely. “Communist. It is quite a powerful word in this day and age, isn’t it? Almost magical. It conjures spontaneous images of evil, of menace. Yet I am doubtful the average citizen of this marvelous nation could provide a satisfactory definition of the word.”

“Would you care to?” Nora asked evenly.

Winterberg made an airy dismissing gesture. “No. I would not. I, fräulein, am not a Communist. I am occasionally accused of being one, however. I imagine that is inevitable whenever a man makes a stand for the sacred rights of workers in this world.”

Nora made a brief scribbling on her pad. “And those workers’ rights are your chief interest.” Again she did not inflect this into a question.

“Interest?” The union leader lifted his black brows. “I am interested in transistors, Miss DeYoung.”

Fleming frowned once more. This was some sort of verbal cat and mouse they were playing. Both were evidently accomplished competitors.

“Transistors?” Nora, not disturbed by the non sequitur, merely waited.

Winterberg grinned broadly this time, his expression at once smug and leering. “Yes. Transistors. It is a device that uses semiconducting materials. It is small and durable and consumes minimal power. A fine replacement for the electron tube. Transistors interest me.”

Casually he groped a moment among the litter atop his desk. What he came up with and brandished was a small cheaply printed magazine, its cover a lurid bit of phantasmagoria depicting a clawed metal creature breathing a stream of fire at a boldly posed man in someone’s outlandish idea of a military uniform. The digest’s name was *Thrilling Wonder.*

Good Lord, thought Fleming. It was one of those juvenile Yank science fiction magazines that catered to the adolescent—and adolescent-minded—public. Did Winterberg actually waste his time on such rot?

"With transistors one day there will be robots," said Winterberg with apparent earnestness. "Great hulking mobile machines, infinitely stronger than man and invested even with rudimentary intelligence. They will be capable of taking on all those hazardous labors which have driven so many generations to early graves. And then . . . and then there will no longer be need for workers. Human beings will be free to pursue purely intellectual matters. Arts, sciences. All those efforts which will only improve the quality of existence."

Fleming nearly sputtered but held himself in silent check. As with Deborah Byrd, he had resolved not to interfere in any way in this exchange. This was Nora's purview. He would only act—and act decisively—if some physical threat should arise.

"You hope for utopia," she now said.

"I hope that one day my efforts to secure decent conditions for the world's workers will be wholly nullified by the creation of suitable mechanical replacements. You see, I strive toward that day when my own accomplishments will become meaningless."

She wrote in a brief flurry, evidently recording his words verbatim. How, Fleming wondered, she could take such statements seriously was beyond him. Was Winterberg mad or only continuing to toy with her?

Beneath the spartan military cot wedged next to the desk he saw unexpected movement and came immediately alert. However, it was merely the shape of a long-haired white cat slinking out into the office's yellow light. The feline gazed at Fleming a moment with inscrutable green eyes, then vaulted onto the desk top and settled itself quite at home in Winterberg's lap. The union leader stroked its body absently.

"In the meantime," Nora said, "before mankind achieves this utopian state, you are fighting the good fight for workers' rights."

At that instant the door behind Fleming banged sharply open. He reacted instantly, hurdling from his seat and pivoting, hand rising but not yet moving beneath his grey jacket. He saw that it was that Tommy lad in the stained coveralls who'd come barging noisily into the cluttered office. The boy seemed out of breath and came to an abrupt standstill seeing Fleming facing him in obvious readiness for a confrontation.

"Tommy, I've asked you often to knock before entering," Winterberg said mildly.

Tommy's eyes were wide, his jaw unhinged. He snapped it shut, then said, "Sorry, boss. I was just bringing Mr. Yancy his chewing gum and cigarettes." He held out a brown paper bag in the direction of the sofa.

The aging seaman reached up and took the bag. "Thanks, Tommy. You're a good kid." With another breathless apology Tommy excused himself from the room.

Fleming returned to his chair, not embarrassed by his alert physical response. He was here as Nora's protector. Perhaps it was even a good thing that Winterberg had likely now deduced that.

Winterberg continued to pet the white cat, having shown no outward response during the incident. "Your secretary seems a bit anxious, Fräulein DeYoung. Perhaps I could offer him a cup of soothing tea."

Fleming merely stared coolly.

"Mr. Fleming is my assistant, not my secretary," Nora said almost tonelessly but driving home the point firmly nevertheless. Winterberg was plainly finding amusement in these gibes. Fleming knew enough not to react overtly.

Nora and the union leader talked for some while as she continued to conduct the curious interview, in which she asked few questions, instead making statements about Winterberg's efforts and offering him leeway to comment. It was nearly as oblique a dialogue as the one she'd had with Deborah Byrd. He spoke with intense and patently sincere passion about his crusade. He enumerated the injustices inflicted upon the workingman, backing each assertion with an array of statistics. He delineated his plans, both long-term and immediate, to free the proletariat from the shackles of capitalist management. Fleming could indeed see why this man had been accused in the past of being a Communist, spouting such inflammatory rhetoric.

Winterberg's second wife's name was never uttered. Nora, it seemed, had opted not to "drop her bomb." Time ticked away on a clock next to the toilet's door.

Nora scribbled several pages of her pad full of notes. She maintained her reserve, not responding to any of the nonchalant flirtatious overtures Winterberg continued to make. It was three o'clock when she folded shut the pad and returned it to her pocketbook.

"I see our time is up," she said.

Winterberg's eyes strayed toward the clock. "So it is," he murmured rather wistfully. "I must say I'm regretful this must end."

"I don't doubt your schedule is quite full." Nora stood. Fleming rose alongside. "Mr. Blake Young would not have wanted to keep you from your important duties, and so I shall not attempt to. Thank you for your candor during this interview."

The long-haired white cat leapt petulantly from Winterberg's lap as he stood, gliding around from behind the littered desk to take her hand, bowing graciously and inevitably laying a kiss across her knuckles.

"It has been a very true pleasure," he said, his dark eyes full of impish lechery. "I do hope to see you again."

It was, Fleming realized with mild annoyance, what he himself had said to Nora at the conclusion of their first meeting in London.

"And you, Herr Fleming"—Winterberg turned, releasing Nora's hand a beat later than he should have, addressing Fleming directly for the first time in an hour and a half—"I must say you do not strike me as a journalist. You seem more the type of semi-retired military man I met so often in England after the war."

He did not offer his hand. Neither did Fleming. Instead, he met the man's penetrating gaze squarely. "If I might be permitted a question of my own . . ."

Winterberg's dark brows lifted. "Yes?"

"What *is* your favorite color?" Fleming asked, matching the mildly sardonic tone the union leader had used during much of the interview.

Winterberg's lips curled slightly. "Red," he finally said.

Yancy held the office door open for them as they exited into the shabby corridor. Winterberg—leaning casually back against the desk's edge, arms folded across his untucked denim shirt—watched them until the door was shut once more.

They descended the stairway. The visit to Winterberg's lair had been a strange one. Evidently Fleming had been mistaken about the potentiality of physical danger, but he was glad for his precautions nonetheless. He found it difficult to pin down his impression of the workers' crusader, beyond his decided dislike of his lascivious attentions toward Nora; but that, he told himself, had at least in part been merely a ploy to try to get under Fleming's skin. Fortunately Fleming was too cool-headed to have taken the bait.

They reached the ground floor corridor. The blond-haired Tommy was loitering inside the building's entrance, absorbed in the workings of a yo-yo. The string and wheel contraption spun in complex arcs and loops. The boy was quite skilled with his toy.

"Everything go okay, folks?" he asked.

"Just fine," Nora said as Tommy held the door for her. Fleming followed her out into the afternoon. Today it was only partially cloudy with no hint of yesterday's rain. The Cadillac was parked just a few car lengths down from the Beale Street entrance.

A paneled van painted military olive drab was parked immediately before the door. A stripe of rust marked the line where the undercarriage met the windowless sides of the bed. As Nora and he stepped past, the driver's side door unlatched and a large male shape extricated itself from the cab.

Fleming saw the black duster and the black fedora, then the thick lumpy features as the man turned with a grunt, straightening. He was at least as tall as Winterberg—over six feet—and seemed to carry half again his mass. He hitched to an abrupt halt as his shaded eyes fell across Fleming. Those eyes narrowed, and his squarish mouth parted on some unsaid comment.

It was a moment of mutual recognition.

Nora had gone ahead several steps. She now paused to look back curiously. "Are you coming, Ian?"

His eyes remained locked for some seconds with the gunman from the grey Dodge. Neither man made any move. Fleming had no doubt the large man was armed; there was ample room for a weapon beneath that black coat.

Fleming did not reach toward his concealed Beretta. He backed slowly away. The large man did likewise, edging toward the door they had just exited, keeping Fleming in sight. Fleming sidled to the Cadillac's passenger door. When Nora—apparently unaware of the standoff taking place—was safely inside, he too climbed into the vehicle.

The large man in the black coat and hat stood inside the office building's entrance, the door ajar, his chunky face gazing intently at the Cadillac as Nora swung into the flow of traffic and sped them off.

Chapter 29

NORA BLAIR DeYoung, quite simply, was not listening to reason.

He had told her during the drive back to the hotel of recognizing the gunman from the grey Dodge that had pursued them following the Deborah Byrd interview. The large man in black had also evidently recognized him.

"Nora, that man is indeed one of Winterberg's thugs," Fleming said sharply. "He will doubtlessly report to his master what he saw, and it shan't require the deductive genius of Sherlock Holmes for Winterberg to conclude that you and I have visited his supplemental wife—that we know his terrible secret. That makes Winterberg as dangerous as you suspected. He will seek to stop you from revealing his bigamy in the press. One can only imagine what lengths he shall go to."

Nora tossed her note-filled pocketbook onto the parlor's dining table and removed her dowdy spectacles.

"I've said all along that those goons in the Dodge were on Winterberg's leash," she said flatly. "You should have listened."

"I *have* listened," he said firmly. "What I am saying is that we must make good our escape now. We must take the next flight out, put ourselves beyond his reach. He may be a powerful man in San Francisco, even in the state of California, but I doubt his arm extends as far as New York. Besides, you have your story and your interview. You can compile the feature at your leisure—and in safer surroundings."

She shed her drab jacket and now worked to undo her tightly bound up hair, shaking out the cascading red ringlets with a mild sigh of pleasure. Her movements were unhurried, contradicting the blatant urgency of the situation.

Fleming strode deliberately across the parlor and seized her elbow, spinning her about more violently than he had intended.

"Why on earth are you being so . . . so *obstinate* about this?" he demanded.

Her limpid blue eyes, no longer camouflaged by the spectacles, bore evenly into his. "Perhaps you forget, Ian, but I'm no fainthearted schoolgirl. I've been on battlefields before."

It was quite aggravating that her manner was so contained while she was behaving so unreasonably. He did not fear danger for himself. It was purely for Nora's sake that he was urging this retreat, this total withdrawal. His need to shield her from harm was urgent.

"And you seem to be forgetting something else," she went on, unperturbed. "Yes, Winterberg now knows that we know his dirty, carefully guarded secret. And that, Ian, puts Miss Deborah Byrd at risk. Do you think it's beyond that creature to snuff out the source of his potential disgrace?"

Fleming released her elbow, his eyes widening in horror.

"Are you truly suggesting he might do harm to his own wife?"

Nora combed her fingers through her hair. "Why not? He's got another one after all."

"That's . . . abominable."

"Yes. But in his mind it might very well solve his problem. If he can no longer cover up his secret, it might seem prudent to eradicate it all together."

It was something like the thinking of Lord Dale Hemmingford, Fleming realized. His scheme to save his nephew—and himself—from scandal had been to exterminate utterly the source of the trouble. Hemmingford was willing to destroy Oscar Winterberg for the sake of preserving the family name, despite that Winterberg was almost doubtlessly innocent in the matter of the coded communiqués finding their way into Russia. Could Winterberg be as megalomaniacal as to consider eliminating Deborah Byrd to safeguard himself?

"But it's *mad*," he said. "You've already accumulated too much supporting evidence of that illegal second marriage. You've secured a confession from Deborah Byrd. Your Mr.—what is his name?—Mr. Minter has seen the marriage certificate in Reno. What earthly good could it do Winterberg to erase Miss Byrd from the scene at this late juncture?"

"Good has little to do with it, Ian." She was still regarding him levelly.

"But the man must have feelings for her," he argued. "Warped though they might be. He married her, after all."

Nora was shaking her head. "Oscar Winterberg has the romantic passions of an adolescent boy. Capricious, impulsive, subject to whimsical change. You couldn't have failed to miss the flagrant advances he made toward me during that interview. Are those the actions of a man faithful to either wife—to any woman? I don't doubt he was thoroughly swept away by the young and virginal Deborah Byrd when he first met her. And that obsession carried on long enough for him to charge headlong into an illicit second marriage. Now, however, he will be realizing the peril of his own standing. He will look to fix things. He will conclude that with Deborah Byrd physically removed from the picture there will be no proof. The press—*I*—can make accusations but will be unable to produce the only relevant witness to his bigamy. To his thinking—and warped it is—that will leave him untouchable."

It was a great deal to digest all at once. Yet Nora's argument did appear to have some basis in rationality, speculative though her analysis might be. It was certainly not worth the risk of leaving Deborah Byrd at Winterberg's mercy.

"Very well," he said, nodding, reaching for the phone on the dining table. "We shall telephone the authorities, have Miss Byrd placed under protective—"

He had lifted the heavy receiver when Nora's hand slapped onto the cradle, keeping the line deadened.

"*No.*"

"No?" He measured out his next words clearly. "You will please explain yourself, madam."

"No police, Ian. I said it before, and I say it now. I won't have them involved. If they take in Deborah Byrd, she'll be subjected to a battery of questions and the story—*my* story—will come out prematurely, before it's ready to go to press, before I've even had the chance to file it with New York. No. I won't have it."

"Then we can phone her, warn her."

"What if Winterberg has her line tapped?" Nora retorted.

"What, then, is it you're proposing be done about Miss Byrd?" he asked.

"We go rescue her ourselves," Nora said firmly.

"Have you lost your wits?" The question sounded icy

to his own ears, all the more poignant for the emotion he'd left out of it.

Her mouth tightened suddenly. Evidently her composure was now dissolving. "Fine, Ian. I'll go do it myself!" She put forward her hand angrily, palm up. "Give me my goddamn gun back!"

He forced himself not to respond to her vehemence or language. He made no move to draw the Beretta from where it still rested at the small of his back. "*No,*" it was now his turn to say emphatically.

"Then I'll go unarmed!" she said fiercely. She dropped her hand and whirled sharply away, marching into the bedroom they had been sharing and slamming the door smartly. He heard sounds of her quickly changing clothes. Also he seemed to detect her voice, muffled, doubtlessly muttering angrily to herself.

He had only a moment, he realized, before she came storming back out to go off on this foolhardy rescue mission. He might use that interval to ring the police—but it wouldn't be enough time to explain the situation, would it? By then she would be away . . . unless he could bring himself to physically restrain her here in the suite. In her present state that would likely entail sitting on her chest and clamping a hand to her mouth. The very thought was repugnant.

The rescue of Deborah Byrd was a valid objective. Any man demented enough to think he could get away with bigamy was surely capable of other heinous actions. And Winterberg, with all that blather about transistors and robots during the interview, certainly hadn't seemed the most stable of beings.

Fleming had to decide what to do. During the war quick thinking and decisive acts had been his stock in trade. He had not been out of the game so long that those instincts had wholly withered.

When the bedroom door burst back open, he was standing between Nora and the parlor door into the corridor. She had outfitted herself once again in her hiking boots, dungarees and man's flannel shirt. It seemed practical apparel to wear into combat.

Nora was heaving tight furious breaths, her shapely breasts rising and falling. Her limbs were tensed, as though she were ready to claw her way through him to the exit. Her blue eyes had taken on a cast of blood lust.

"Will you get out of my way?" she said through gritted teeth.

He regarded her for a few silent heartbeats, then said calmly, "I think it would be best if I accompanied you, Nora. It seems only fair your knight should be along if there is a damsel to be saved. Shall we?"

She held her breath in mid-pant, then emptied her lungs slowly, deliberately. A faint wisp of a smile pulled at the edge of her lips. "Let's," she answered.

Chapter 30

Nora had already proven herself an adroit driver, so Fleming was quite willing to let her have the wheel. It left him that much more at liberty to keep a watchful eye on the vicinity.

They entered Chinatown by swinging obliquely around Washington Square from the east. Nora, complying with his instructions, let him off mid-block some three and a half blocks from Deborah Byrd's humble abode. He had traded his grey sport coat for a darker one but otherwise sported the same clothes he had worn to Winterberg's office. The change of jackets, though, might mislead the casual lookout.

He leaned back in through the opened passenger window. "Park this somewhere, Nora," he said, repeating the plan he'd concocted and outlined on the circuitous drive here. "Don't circle. This monstrosity is more recognizable than either you or I." Magic Gold Cadillac indeed. "In ten minutes from now, precisely, pull up in front of the flat. I shall have Miss Byrd in tow."

"And if you don't?" She had evidently already forgiven and forgotten the heated exchange they'd had in the suite. Her eyes brimmed with concern, but he had no doubt she would perform her duties to the letter.

"Then flee," he said evenly. "Call the police when you've safely returned to the hotel." He cut her off with a short gesture as she moved to speak. "By then, Nora, it will likely be murder, and I would not rest easily knowing my death might go unavenged." He was, as the Americans would say, laying it on a bit thick; but it appeared to drive home the point. Nora nodded silently, then blew him a kiss as he stepped away from the automobile, moving into the scurrying flow of Chinatown's foot traffic.

Nearly all of the afternoon's partial cloud cover had cleared, though the day was no warmer than any since Fleming had arrived in the city. He donned his dark-lensed glasses and did his utmost not to tower above the shorter Orientals jostling about him.

He moved swiftly toward Stockton Street, keeping alert for any Caucasian figures loitering on the corners or in doorways. He of course also had a wary eye out for the large man in black. It was entirely possible he and Nora had let this mission go too long. Winterberg might well have already sent his minions to snatch his unlawfully wedded bride.

The thought of the hazards of this rescue attempt still did not faze him. He instead felt righteously satisfied that he was putting himself in harm's way as a means to prevent Nora from undertaking this errand herself. And, he had no doubt, she indeed would have marched off alone and unarmed had he not intervened.

He recalled the layout of Deborah Byrd's building clearly from their earlier visit. There was no doorman or concierge to prevent him from entering the edifice of small stacked apartments. Her flat was at the top of the third landing. The lock, he remembered, hadn't been engaged when Nora and he had called last time. Even if it were, it hadn't been a dead bolt, and there was no chain. If need be, his shoulder would suffice in opening the door.

This being Saturday she would not be performing her stenographic duties at the law offices of Armstrong and

Utley. Which, naturally, was no surety that she would be home. Yet Deborah Byrd hadn't struck him as a socializer; more a recluse, having withdrawn in guilt and fear from the world at large . . . nursing the bitter seed of Oscar Winterberg in her womb and bemoaning her own reckless actions. Yes, she would be home, surely.

Fleming dodged nimbly through traffic as he crossed to the opposite side of Stockton Street. As well as being vigilant for suspicious characters on foot, he eyed the passing cars. He had a firm picture in his mind of the grey Dodge, not to mention the olive drab van the large man in black had climbed out of on Beale Street.

The Beretta remained tucked beneath his jacket, the extra clip of ammunition jouncing against his leg inside his trouser pocket as he hurried, without appearing obvious, toward the lobby of the apartment building.

The greater danger, of course, was inside the building, not out on the street. Winterberg's thugs could be waiting around any corner of any corridor, beyond any bend of the stairwell. And, most perilous of all, they might be in her very rooms. The building, however, had no entrance but its front one. Climbing the exterior fire escape—which looked frankly quite rickety—would surely draw more attention than was prudent. He need only be shot by some fearful tenant as a cat burglar for this all to end as tragic farce.

Fleming slowed near the entrance, eyes wide and searching behind his sunglasses. He turned as nonchalantly as possible around one of the concrete pillars that held aloft the rather shabby-looking facade crowning the entryway. He quickly stripped off the glasses as he pushed through the unlatched doorway, the shadows of the inadequately lit vestibule falling over him.

He allowed himself a few seconds for his eyes to adjust, confirming that the space was indeed empty. The building had no lift, only the stairway to the left, which he now darted toward. He paused rounding the corner, carefully noting every conceivable niche where a human body might conceal itself. All potential hiding places were vacant.

He glided up the first flight, halting at the switchback to scan the overhanging balustrades of wrought iron. He crept up onto the landing, studied the adjacent corridor, then moved on to the second flight. The walls inside were a deep green. He heard caterwauling Asian voices behind some of the doors and smelled the aromas of exotic cooking. He realized with some humor that he was hungry. Ignoring his body's needs, he climbed.

At the third landing a failing bulb was flickering theatrically. Shadows winked in and out of existence. Fleming lingered several risers below the top of the steps. His right hand was beneath the tails of his jacket, the Beretta's grip against his palm, finger curled about the trigger. He had taken the safety off the pistol. One practiced snap of his arm and the gun would be drawn.

He surveyed the scene meticulously, assuring himself before he climbed another stair that the exterior corridor at least was clear. Finally he eased silently up onto the landing, facing the door of Deborah Byrd's apartment. What might wait inside he couldn't positively ascertain without entering.

Still, hedging one's bet was a gambler's prerogative.

Fleming leaned warily and placed his left ear to the wood, ignoring all the other sounds from the building. He was careful not to stand directly before the door, lest the shadows of his feet be seen in the minute gap between the wood and the floor. He strained to listen. He heard no sounds whatever from inside the flat.

He took the knob in his left hand, waited a beat and turned it slowly. He felt for the resistance of a lock. Instead, the knob clicked softly, and the door pulled half an inch toward him.

Unlocked, then. Fine.

There were still no noises from within. Hand still on the undrawn pistol, he tensed, then drew the door open quickly and smoothly—enough space for him to slide through or easily slam it shut should danger be directly beyond the threshold.

It might have been wiser to enter with the Beretta drawn. But there was at least a possibility that Deborah Byrd might be here alone, and the sight of a man entering her home with a brandished pistol could provoke any number of unfavorable responses.

The door opened almost directly onto the cramped front room. It was there he saw Deborah Byrd. She was sitting in that same armless chair she'd occupied during Nora's interview. She wore a spartan pale blue dress and had a thick leather-bound Bible spread on her lap. She didn't appear to be reading it. Instead, her large, delicately olive eyes were gazing at a desiccated flower that had evidently lain pressed between the pages. It was an orchid . . . or its lifeless remains.

Fleming shot a glance into the small empty kitchen. The door to the bedroom opposite it was shut. The air of the cheerless apartment felt charged only by the near-inert life force of this woman. No one else was here. Yet.

Her strawberry-blond-haired head rose slowly. Her long lashes scarcely shuddered when she saw him. She regarded him, no significant sign of emotion moving the young dimpled features.

"Miss Byrd," he said in his most reassuring tone, "you may recall me. I am Ian Fleming. I accompanied Miss DeYoung, the woman who talked with you the other day. I hope you'll forgive this boorish intrusion into your home, but the situation is urgent. I must ask that you come with me."

It didn't appear that anything he'd said had reached her, much as she'd offered few direct replies to Nora's inquiries. The swiftest means of prodding her, naturally, would be to physically manipulate her out the door. But, again, he couldn't guess how she might respond. He would try reason once more, though it seemed as expedient as explaining physics to a barnyard animal.

"Miss Byrd—" he started, stepping nearer.

Without change of expression Deborah Byrd folded shut her Bible and rose from the chair. She was a short girl, no more than five foot two.

"I'll need my coat," she said as though speaking in a trance.

"Where is it?"

But she was already moving past him, reaching into a closet nearby the opened front door. Fleming put himself between her and the entrance while she donned a long wool coat of unraveling brown wool. Oscar Winterberg, he judged with offhand disgust, was decidedly not keeping his second wife in style.

"We shall need to be cautious, Miss Byrd. Please remain behind me as we go downstairs. If I tell you to move or do anything, please comply without fail. This situation is"—he shied from saying "dangerous" and settled once more for—"urgent."

She was still clutching her Bible as they stepped out into the corridor. The flickering bulb again created untrustworthy shadows, but Fleming scanned the terrain with a trained eye. He reached behind with his left hand and took Deborah Byrd's wrist, tugging her forward. She came like a trusting child.

He came to the top step, looking down the flight before moving them onto the stairs. His hand was still on the Beretta. His body was still coiled, ready for action. He hoped none would be necessary.

It was slower going with her in tow, but soon they were on the vacant second landing. He was guiding her to the top of the next flight when a voice reverberated harshly from below.

"Let her go, Fleming!"

This imperative was followed immediately by the sharp blast of a pistol. The report echoed thunderously up the stairwell. Fleming had already shoved his charge out of the way against the green corridor wall.

He was suddenly flourishing the Beretta, crouching nimbly behind the wrought iron balustrade. A second shot didn't follow the first. He scooted several feet from his original position and risked a careful look downward, peeking out between the railing's metal curlicues. He saw a small flurry of movement on the ground floor, and at that instant the second shot came.

He recoiled a scant second before the flash from the muzzle. Again the clap of the gunshot was resounding. A multitude of voices raised themselves behind the apartment doors on all levels of the building, a great cacophony of Asiatic hysteria.

Fleming had glimpsed only the vaguest outline of the man. From his angle it was virtually impossible to ascertain anything usefully descriptive. He had seen a male shape in a dark coat. He'd had no chance to discern the lay of the man's features or even his rough physical dimensions. It could be the large man in black down there. It could be almost anyone else.

"Let her go, you limey son of a bitch!"

He rolled onto his elbows and slithered rapidly around toward the head of the steps. Offering only inches of himself as a target, he peered downward, his sharp eyes narrowed, the pistol at the ready. It would surely only be moments before the police were summoned to the scene. There was also the potential of one of the building's tenants interfering. To make no mention of the fact that the ten minutes he'd allotted himself were surely nearing their expiration. Nora would be waiting out front with the Cadillac.

He caught a vague blur of motion on the ground floor, a dark coat scampering across the green shadows of the walls. He fired. The Beretta's recoil didn't shake his grip, and he was ready to squeeze another shot immediately. It was a fine neat little gun, some remote part of his mind assessed.

His target was gone. He edged out a few more inches from his supine position and scanned the lobby through the curls of dissipating gun smoke. There was nothing to see.

The frantic voices of the tenants were reaching a fevered pitch. There was no alternate escape from the building. Fleming crept back from the stairway, bounded deftly to his feet and turned to find Deborah Byrd standing precisely where he'd deposited her. Her back was pressed to the wall, one hand still grasping the Bible. Her face was as hideously blank as before.

He seized her wrist again, and they dashed down the final flight. In the lobby he looked about for the bleeding body of the gunman but saw none. The ground floor was as empty as when he'd first entered. The man had fled.

The situation was now urgent indeed. He shouldered aside the front door aggressively, casting about in all directions. He kept the Beretta in his tight grip but slipped it prudently beneath the front of his jacket.

There was a small commotion on the street outside. A few dozen of Chinatown's residents were gathering at the entrance, though the shots could not have been so loud as to draw too much attention in this bustling neighborhood. They eyed Fleming curiously as he conducted Deborah Byrd hastily to the kerb. He was forced to push aside several of these bystanders before he had a clear view of the street.

The Cadillac was there. A surge of relief coursed through his veins—but had he had any reason to doubt Nora? Evidently not. How capable a woman she was. How alluring was that trait.

A smile was actually pulling at his lips as he now yanked Deborah Byrd toward the waiting auto. He jerked the passenger side door handle and was spinning the pliant form of his new ward onto the seats when he saw what was wrong.

The Cadillac's driver's door was hanging open, and no one was behind the wheel. The keys still dangled from the ignition. The engine was growling in idle.

The acuteness of the relief he had felt was nothing compared to the severity of the shock that jolted him now to his suddenly frozen marrow.

"*Nora!*" he roared. His head whipped wildly on his neck as he searched the clutter and fuss of Stockton Street.

There was nothing, not even a glimpse of her red hair. She was nowhere to be seen among the hundreds of jostling bodies and darting vehicles.

Behind the idling Cadillac traffic was beginning to pile. Car horns erupted into life, adding to the clamor suddenly filling his head. At some distance he thought he heard a siren.

With a great rush of will he slammed the passenger door and raced about to the lolling driver's side, throwing himself inside, cursing a silent stream of invective that should have turned the air blue about him. The supple seat was still warm from Nora's body.

The onlookers were crowding along the sidewalk's edge, still gazing inquisitively. The horns honked more belligerently. The sound of the siren was now clearly discernible.

Gritting his teeth tightly enough to pain his jaw, Fleming put the Cadillac in gear.

From the seat beside him Deborah Byrd asked in a docile voice, "Are you taking me to see Oscar?"

He jammed his foot on the accelerator.

Chapter 31

HE WOULD telephone the police from the St. Francis. To hell with Nora's stubbornness about leaving the authorities uninvolved. The game was now far too serious to worry overmuch about her wishes or how she would respond when she learned he'd gone against them.

Fleming made record time to the hotel. Strategically he knew he had to get Deborah Byrd to safety before ringing the police. Their suite was the only logical place. She remained as submissive as ever, her large eyes gazing blankly through the windscreen as he whipped the Cadillac through San Francisco's streets. He committed numerous traffic violations and drove at speeds Nora had reached when trying to outrun the grey Dodge.

He did not bother putting the auto into the underground garage. Rather, he screeched the Cadillac to a halt in a fortunately empty space a half block from the hotel's Powell Street entrance.

"We're going up to my rooms now, Miss Byrd. You'll be safe there."

She was holding her Bible against her ample bosom. Fleming had the Beretta tucked once more beneath his jacket. She stepped meekly from the car when he did. He scanned the street as he hurried her along. He had seen no one follow them from Stockton Street, but who knew how many henchmen Winterberg had and how many were combing the streets in search of him—and of her now. Winterberg had Nora. But Fleming had Winterberg's ancillary wife. It was like a crafty game of chess where the players each had the other's queen pinned.

They mounted the steps to the glass doors. He once more had a firm grip on her wrist. Inside the elegantly appointed lobby, which was rather crowded this Saturday afternoon, he started jostling his way forcefully toward the lifts.

Through the eddying bodies a voice suddenly hailed him. "Mr. Fleming. Mr. Fleming!"

He halted, swinging Deborah Byrd behind him, his right hand ready to slip beneath his coat, though this would be a poor locale for gunplay.

It was the clerk from the front desk, the small bespectacled man who evidently worked rather long hours. He slipped through the crowd, a slip of paper in hand.

"Sir, a message for you." His eyes passed quietly over Deborah, but whatever curiosity he might be feeling was kept professionally masked. "It was received only a moment ago. The caller insisted it was quite urgent."

The box on the form identifying the caller was blank.

"He refused to leave a name," the clerk explained, turning away toward the marble-topped front desk.

There was only the message itself. *Call this number.* The digits followed.

Fleming pocketed the slip and tugged Deborah toward the lift doors. Minutes later they were at the suite.

She seated herself wordlessly on the parlor's plush divan. Fleming snatched the phone off the dining table. Nora's pocketbook lay on the tabletop where she had left it. There came a moment of indecision. Call the police first or ring this other number? He did not panic. These were combat conditions. He would behave accordingly.

Deciding, he dialed the numbers from the message slip.

Whoever had called should be dealt with first, before bringing the police into the matter.

The far end of the line rang only once before it engaged.

"Fleming," said a voice in a vaguely French accent.

"Yes. Who is this?" His grip on the receiver was unnecessarily tight, but his tone was even. He had been more than half expecting to hear Winterberg's Germanic voice.

"I 'ave the *femme*. Your Mademoiselle DeYoung."

"And I have Deborah Byrd," he said firmly, glancing in her direction. She had the leather-bound Bible opened once more in her lap and was staring at the dead pressed orchid. She didn't seem aware of the conversation.

"So. There we 'ave it. Obviously an exchange of these women is in order. You do want her back, do you not?" The Frenchman's tone was sneering.

"I do." Images of what he would do to this miscreant if ever given the opportunity flitted through Fleming's head. He would use his bare hands.

"*Splendide.* That leaves only for arrangements to make, no?"

"What do you propose?"

"You bring your woman. I bring mine. We meet at the front of the Ferry Building. You know where this is?"

Fleming grunted an affirmative.

"Good. Six o'clock we make the trade. You bring with you no weapon, you telephone no police. Just you and the girl. Understood?"

"How can I trust you?"

"Trust me or trust me not, monsieur. It makes no difference to me. If you want Mademoiselle DeYoung, you will comply. If you care not for her *sécurité*, then do what you will. You will understand that she will die if you renege on any of these conditions. I doubt, Monsieur Fleming, that you will take a like action against Mademoiselle Byrd. Am I not correct?"

What could he say? Threatening to kill Deborah Byrd if Nora wasn't returned unharmed was wholly out of the question. This had started out as an attempt to *rescue* the woman, for God's sake. Winterberg had simply outmaneuvered him.

"I will meet your conditions," he said.

"A wise course."

"Six o'clock, in front of the Ferry Building—" Fleming started to confirm, but the line had gone dead.

THE AMERICAN MAN's ordinary appearance allowed him to blend ideally into the milling evening crowd. He'd swapped the black coat he'd worn in Chinatown for a more neutral beige one. The grey coat he'd worn when he killed that guy on Divisadero he had burned. That had been a weird episode. He would liked to have questioned that fellow with the downy blondish mustache, find out what his involvement was in this, but there had been no time. He had seen the man in Jamaica and here in San Francisco, and that was more than enough evidence to sentence him to a summary death. No sense worrying about niceties. He had also taken the precaution of swapping out his rental car. The newspapers had reported the incident, but he wasn't worried about the police. None of those passing motorists had gotten a good look at him.

He had long ago perfected the art of disappearing into any given background, and he did so now, going absolutely unnoticed.

He casually eyed Market Street's scurrying multiple lanes. Even on the weekend it apparently never slowed.

Fleming would be putting in an appearance soon. The clock on the Ferry Building's tower behind him read five of six.

Did that Brit prig have any idea how easy he was to manipulate? Probably not. Probably thought himself infallible, like so many of his snooty breed. It was a real pleasure maneuvering him around like this.

Fleming's mistake, of course, was in attaching himself to the DeYoung broad. He had allowed himself to be tempted. And now he was stuck in her web. Women were trouble. Had been since Adam had sacrificed a perfectly good rib to create the first of the species. If Fleming didn't understand that, it was his problem.

The American man was propped nonchalantly against a wall, apparently perusing a newspaper. He had told Fleming no guns; but of course he himself was packing a pistol in the shoulder holster beneath his coat. He didn't expect he'd need it. Fleming hadn't gotten anything like a clear look at him in Chinatown—not that it mattered anymore. The two shots he'd squeezed off in that apartment stairwell had been meant to miss.

It had all been a setup. So was this supposed hostage exchange.

The Cadillac turned out of traffic and parked at the foot of Market. Fleming was evidently fastidiously punctual; that was another vaguely irritating trait of the English. The American man continued to ostensibly scan his paper, while his eyes furtively studied the scene.

Fleming climbed out of the big car, then came around to the passenger door. Out stepped the Byrd girl. She was a young thing, all right, with a fine set of juicy-looking breasts. Winterberg might've shown some bad judgment in marrying this dame, but she sure was easy on the eyes.

Not that that made her any less dangerous than any other woman in the world. Hell, it made her *more* so, didn't it? Otherwise men wouldn't be forever screwing up their lives because of them.

It was more than a little amusing watching Fleming looking around at the bustling crowd, trying to look cool about it. He was probably frantic on the inside, no matter how stiff his upper lip. He held the Byrd girl close to him, a hand locked around her wrist. She was just standing there complacently, like a cow in a field. Probably didn't have too much going in the brains department. Hah. Like Winterberg had been seduced by the little tart's mind.

The American man folded his newspaper, dropping it into an ash can as he moved forward across the wide swath of sidewalk.

He allowed his normal cloak of invisibility to evaporate as he approached, eyes locked directly on Fleming. Deborah Byrd was gazing vacantly at the ground.

"Hey, Fleming," he said breezily, dropping the phony French accent. He took a cigar from his coat pocket. "Got a light?"

The Englishman was staring hard at him, his expression tensely indecipherable, pulling the girl behind him.

"Never mind," said the American man, flicking a thumbnail over the head of a wooden match and firing the pungent cigar. Blue smoke wafted upward into the twilight.

"Where is Miss DeYoung?" Fleming's question was toneless.

"Change of plans." He offered his feral-looking grin.

Fleming seemed to bite down on some curse. Behind his shoulder the Byrd girl was still studying the asphalt.

The crowds of passersby flowed around them, leaving the three of them in a cleared circle.

"What sort of change?"

"We want something else," said the plain-looking American. "We want Miss DeYoung's notes. All of them. Everything she's got on paper concerning my client."

"Client? Such a civilized appellation. You mean, of course, the man who pays you to kidnap innocent women."

"Don't get cheeky with me, Fleming. My client—"

"Oscar Winterberg," he interjected hotly.

"My *client* wants those notes. They're back at your hotel. You leave the girl"—nodding past Fleming's shoulder—"run that little errand and be back here inside the hour. You bring us those papers, and you get your precious Miss DeYoung back. If not—"

"Unacceptable."

The American rolled the cigar between his teeth. "How's that?"

"You heard me. I will not relinquish Miss Byrd to your custody. Not until you produce Miss DeYoung. Any other arrangement is thoroughly inadequate."

"You really think you're a hard piece of work, don't you, Fleming?" he sneered.

The Englishman moved suddenly forward, faster than the American would have credited him. His hand rose and slapped the cigar sharply from his mouth.

"You will listen carefully, you miserable cur!" Fleming spat tightly, though not loud enough to raise too much of a ruckus in the open crowd. "You will not play games with me. Your French confederate was correct earlier when he said I would not go so far as to harm Miss Byrd here. I find it offensive even being coerced into using her as an item of trade. However, this promise I shall gladly make. If anything untoward should befall Miss DeYoung, I will hunt Winterberg and destroy him . . . and he will not be able to hide. Rest assured on that matter."

The American man slowly rubbed his lip. The place where Fleming's slap had clipped the corner of his mouth stung. "You talk a nice fight, Fleming," he finally said. "Fine. Have it your way. Keep the slut." He nodded once more at Deborah Byrd, who seemed oblivious to her surroundings, much less the words the two men were exchanging. "Go get the papers. All of them. My client wants every scrap that's got his name on it. You bring that and the girl back here at, say, seven o'clock. The DeYoung woman will be here. We swap. Got it?"

Fleming's eyes were drilling into his. His free hand flexed, as if he wanted nothing more than to pummel the American.

"Seven o'clock," said Fleming.

The American man offered a final sneer, turned and quickly lost himself in the crowd. He was still rubbing his lip as he went. He could taste blood on his tongue. The Brit bastard would pay for that.

SEVEN O'CLOCK. FLEMING considered. It was enough time to return to the suite, gather Nora's haphazard file on Winterberg along with the notes from the interview, then reappear here with Deborah Byrd. He had been doubtful of Winterberg's trustworthiness before. Now, seeing the cheap ploy the man had attempted here, Fleming's distrust increased exponentially.

He had been quite sincere in his threat about destroying

Winterberg. As Fleming watched the plain-looking man disappear into the crowd, he saw no reason why this man too shouldn't meet an untimely end if anything happened to Nora.

Chapter 32

FLEMING KNEW that something was not proper even before he put his key to the suite door and found it already unlocked. He rechecked the corridor in both directions, finding it empty. Then he drew the Beretta, moved Deborah Byrd out of the frame of the door and shoved it wide.

He swiftly surveyed the parlor. It too was empty. Leaving the girl in the passageway, he moved stealthily first to one bedroom door, then the other. He checked the lavatories and closets, already sensing that whoever had visited the suite was gone. He drew Deborah into the parlor and closed the door.

The suite was empty . . . empty of people, but—The thought struck him suddenly that perhaps his visitor or visitors had left something else behind. A bomb sprang readily to mind. Seating Deborah on the divan, he made a second search, this one more thorough, checking corners, beneath and behind furnishings. A bomb had mass, size and couldn't be secreted just anywhere. After a few minutes he had satisfied himself that no surprise packages were waiting.

Oscar Winterberg was a rogue. He was plainly toying with Fleming. He had sent him on that fool's errand to the Ferry Building, obviously never meaning to honor his proposal to exchange hostages. *Hostages.* A dreadful word. It had innate connotations of ignominy. The taking of a hostage often entailed the involvement of an innocent. It was the same dishonorable conduct as bombing civilian populations during the war. Winterberg was plainly no stranger to taking hostages; that persistent tale of his ransoming a plant owner's son suddenly had firm credence.

Deborah Byrd was an innocent. He was decidedly uncomfortable having the young woman as his charge. It was even more disturbing knowing he had to surrender her to Winterberg in order to secure Nora's freedom. Yet that choice was entirely out of his hands . . . wasn't it? He couldn't allow harm to come to Nora. She *had* to come first.

But Winterberg wasn't playing even by the disreputable rules of this game. He had tried to dupe him into leaving Deborah in the hands of that cigar-smoking knave. Now Winterberg wanted Nora's notes. He meant to erase all the proof of his illicit second marriage, just as Nora had said. And that scheme was still just as senseless. Mr. Minter in Reno had seen the marriage license. Nora had secured a confession from Deborah Byrd. Winterberg's ugly secret was already irrevocably jeopardized. Could the union leader be so utterly unbalanced as to think he could still bury it?

Patently he was going to extreme ends to attempt to do so. And Nora's life hung precariously in the balance.

Deborah was sitting inertly on the parlor's divan, her precious Bible still in hand. He didn't wish to imagine what Winterberg intended to do with her. To think of the matter meant rationalizing sending this young woman to a decidedly uncertain fate in order to secure Nora's return. One life for another—*No.* He could not dwell on it . . . no matter that it flew in the face of every moral principle that had so far governed his existence.

He had been instructed to retrieve Nora's papers. Very

well. She had left them—where? He cast about the parlor, then recalled she had lain her note-filled pocketbook on the dining table.

The table was empty but for the telephone.

He stared, coldness seeping through his innards before he snapped back to a state of cool alert thinking. Naturally, whoever had entered the suite in their absence had taken them; and, just as evidently, the "hostage exchange" had only been a ploy to make certain he was not in the rooms at the time of the theft.

A sharp sudden pain flared outward from the bridge of his nose, wrapping snugly about his skull. He didn't wince but cursed silently. This wasn't an ideal time for one of his migraines.

At that instant the phone rang.

He seized the jangling instrument.

"Damn you, you loathsome cad!" he barked. "Damn you to *hell*—"

"Fleming?" The voice was perplexed and surprised. It was also familiar . . . an English voice.

He stifled his outburst, then ventured, "Powell?"

"Is that the manner in which one answers one's telephone in the States these days?" his editor asked drolly.

"My apologies," he said automatically. "I thought you were someone else."

"I should hope so." Merlin Powell's tone shifted. "I am not pleased with you, Fleming. I've been anticipating a call from you for some days now. You've evidently reneged on your promise to keep me informed of events. I warned you of the consequences. I must say I'm very—*very*—seriously considering taking the actions I mentioned. Your future employment with this newspaper is in grave jeopardy."

Fleming pinched his forehead. The pain was mounting. He most definitely didn't need this aggravation just now.

"Events have gotten out of hand," he said. Thoughts of his future employment seemed remarkably immaterial beside his current crisis. He didn't feel even a pang of guilt for have left his editor in the dark. What good could Powell do him from Jamaica?

"Your sole possibility of redemption, Fleming, is to explain to me, carefully and concisely, what those events are. I want to know about this hush-hush story you've supposedly been engrossed in. I want to know about Oscar Winterberg. I want—"

"Damn it, Powell," he snapped. "The *events* are these: lives are presently at risk. I have no time for distractions." At the moment he didn't give a fig what punitive measures were taken against him. In fact, he was on the verge of simply dropping the receiver back onto its cradle.

"Well," Powell said, slowly and thoughtfully now. "I presume you're being serious."

"Of course I am."

"Of course. Even your humor doesn't run to such extremes. Lives at risk, you say. Are you yourself in peril?"

"Not at this particular instant."

"Sounds dicey." Powell made a pensive humming sound. At his end of the long-distance line Fleming thought he detected the *whick-whick* of an electrical ceiling fan. If the editor was still at his office, he was putting in quite a late day. "Is there anything I might do?"

"Nothing occurs," said Fleming. "There are some thousands of miles separating us at the present."

"Quite. I can only hope you've alerted the authorities to whatever dire straits you're caught up in."

The Frenchman who rang earlier had warned him not

to contact the police, promising lethal repercussions for Nora. Even if Winterberg were cheating at this game, Fleming wouldn't risk it.

"I'm afraid not. My hands are quite tied on that matter."

"Drat it," muttered Powell. "This all sounds like the most intriguing tale—"

"Which I do not have the time to detail for you." He glanced again at Deborah Byrd. A plan was forming in his mind, beating back the discomfort of his burgeoning headache.

"Perfectly understood." Powell's earlier testiness had vanished. Evidently the man recognized the severity of the predicament and had realigned his priorities. "Come through safely, Fleming. The only words of advice I feel I can offer—not privy to the facts of the situation—are these: offense is the surest defense."

The platitude tugged a small smile from Fleming's lips. Merlin Powell was, in the end, a good man.

"Thank you. I shall contact you when I am able."

"Do that. Best of luck."

Fleming hung up.

"Miss Byrd, we are going to relocate. I will pack some items." He nearly told her to wait where she was, but it was plain she wouldn't move unless directed. At least she wasn't making a nuisance of herself.

He hurriedly retrieved his suitcase, tossing in a change of clothing, including the vicuña coat Nora had given him. In the other bedroom most of her clothes were still strewn across the rumpled bed. He snatched up a few items at random. Deborah Byrd wasn't the same size, but Nora's clothing would have to do. He didn't know how long they would be away from these rooms.

Though he had again left the Cadillac on the street, they would descend to the garage and exit there. He would not inform the front desk of his departure. Deborah came passively in tow, silent until the lift was descending. The car's uniformed attendant was a rather shriveled elderly man, evidently hard of hearing.

Deborah turned, her large olive eyes fixing on Fleming's. A spark of life seemed to have ignited there.

"I'm not insane, you know," she said softly; but for the first time the words didn't sound like they were being spoken from a trance.

"I never imagined you were, Miss Byrd," he lied. In truth, he had judged during that eerie interview Nora conducted that Winterberg's young pregnant second wife had indeed lost her senses . . . or at least was so traumatized by all that had befallen her that she had withdrawn to a state of semi-functional catalepsy. Apparently she retained some facilities.

"You're not taking me to Oscar."

"No."

She nodded, brushing wavy strawberry-blond locks behind one ear. The white gold band on her ring finger winked. "He's done something bad, hasn't he?"

"He has."

"Am I in danger?"

Fleming drew a long breath. The lift attendant showed no awareness of their conversation. "You are," he finally said. "As am I. As is a young lady very dear to me. We've been trying to protect you. Unfortunately things have taken a ruinous turn."

She nodded again. Her eyes seemed on the verge of

unfocusing, then her gaze snapped back. "He's the Devil. How can you win against the Devil?"

The lift cage slowed and stopped. As the attendant undid the gate, Fleming said firmly, "Beat him at his own game."

Chapter 33

THEY WENT to ground.

It wasn't difficult. San Francisco was a teeming city, with a population of tens of thousands. Even if this was Winterberg's home field, his eyes and ears could not be everywhere.

Fleming stole into the city's Mission District—or stole as well as one might in the behemoth of a gold Cadillac. The neighborhood wasn't as affluent as some he had seen. It seemed a place where the lower middle class dwelled. The populace seemed chiefly Irish. Pub names had the flavor of the Emerald Isle. Some storefront windows displayed hand-lettered signs in Gaelic. There were shops for secondhand furniture, busy meat markets and groceries, reduced clothing emporiums and a plethora of cheap apartments and boarding houses.

Fleming chose a rooming house several streets off the central artery of Mission Street. It was an aging Victorian pile, likely once quite ornate in its day. Now, however, its weathered brown paint was flaking away, and tar paper flapped about the loose shingles of the canted roof. He opted for this establishment since a placard in the concierge's front window declared: INDOOR PARKING AVAILABLE.

Taking Deborah Byrd by the hand, he mounted the steps and rang the bell. It was nearly a full minute before the door was opened, the discolored blind behind the glass dangling precariously from its roller. The female face that peered out was in its late fifties, hardened in a manner that robbed it of much of whatever femininity it had once possessed. A wart stood out prominently on the woman's right cheek. Age lines tugged at her thin-lipped mouth. She wore a faded purple kerchief over her rather brittle-looking hair. Her dress was cut almost elegantly but showed more signs of wear than style.

She regarded the two of them uninterestedly. Her blankness of expression wasn't the same as Deborah's customary vacuousness. This woman was merely waiting for whatever new drudgery life laid before her, too inured to care, too set in her ways to resist. Plainly she had no intention of initiating conversation.

"Mrs. O'Dwyre?" Fleming asked, taking the name from the window's placard. The headache that had threatened him only a short while ago had somehow mercifully evaporated.

"Mmmmm." By generous definition the noise might be one of affirmation.

"I desire a room for myself and my fiancée. Separate beds, if you please. We're en route to Reno, Nevada, and would like to stop off in your fair city for a few d—"

"I rent by the week. That's the minimum." Mrs. O'Dwyre's voice was tired, but the tone suggested, strongly, that she brooked no trouble, suffered no fools, and anyone who didn't like it could go elsewhere. "I get to see the color of your money before you set foot one inside."

Deborah thankfully hadn't responded negatively to his "fiancée" comment. He hunted for and produced his wallet, feeling as he did both the cigarette case and the extra clip of ammunition in his pockets. The Beretta remained at the small of his back.

Evidently the shade of his currency was just fine. Mrs.

O'Dwyre quoted the rates in the window and plucked away several bills. The money didn't matter to Fleming. He retrieved the suitcase, containing his clothing and Nora's borrowed items, from the Cadillac and followed the concierge through a dreary common room and up a groaning flight of stairs. A few sets of eyes followed them from the ground floor where a radio was playing some comedic program for the entertainment of the house's other tenants. They seemed a weathered lot, workingmen and secretary types. None appeared especially interested in the two new residents.

The room Mrs. O'Dwyre unlocked was only mildly seedy, owing more to the general deterioration of the house than any lack of effort to keep it orderly. The two narrow beds, separated by a nightstand, wore neat matching coverlets of green and royal blue. A washbasin sat atop a bureau that bore numerous nicks in its legs, as though it had been moved repeatedly from room to room over the years. A single small table, spread with an oilcloth, and two straight-backed chairs were tucked into a corner.

"We passed the bathroom at the heada the stairs. Ye'll be sharing that wit' Douglas, the Glass brothers and Mrs. Ranlett. Don't bother banging on the door if she's taking too long in there. It won't move her any faster. Breakfast is seven-thirty, lunch is noon—if you're here for it—and dinner's at six. You've missed that." The concierge's thin lips twisted into something like an expression of grudging generosity. "I'll ladle you out some stew and slice you some bread if you haven't eaten yet."

"I'm not hungry, thank you," said Fleming, depositing the suitcase on one of the beds, then glancing at Deborah Byrd who was eyeing her new surroundings vapidly. "But . . . perhaps Deborah . . . ?"

She laid her Bible on the night table between the beds. Turning, that light of brief lucidity she'd demonstrated earlier was again in her olive eyes. "I wouldn't mind a bite . . . Ian." She offered a pale but convincing smile at the secret nod he threw her on getting his name correct. "You don't mind if I eat without you?"

"Not in the least, my dear," he said smoothly, as though reciting lines in a stage play. "You recall I have to go out this evening in any event."

"Yes, of course," said Deborah. Mrs. O'Dwyre's weary eyes bounced listlessly between them. "Please apologize to Uncle Thackery that I was too tired to come."

"He'll understand."

Deborah unbuttoned her unraveling brown wool coat.

The concierge, still standing in the doorway, handed a pair of keys to Fleming. To Deborah she said, "Come downstairs in five minutes. I'll be reheating your dinner." Then she shuffled back down the corridor toward the stairs.

Fleming let out a pent-up breath. "Thank you," he said quietly and meaningfully.

Deborah nodded, unbuckling the suitcase and examining the articles he had packed for her. "These are pretty clothes. They belong to that pretty woman you were with when you came to my apartment."

"Yes," he said, feeling a poignant tug at his heart. "A very pretty woman."

"You're going out to try to help her." She held a dress up to the wan overhead light. It was white and ocher, the dress Nora had worn when he'd first seen her in Jamaica.

"I am. I don't know when I shall return. Please remain in this house until I do." He picked a few bills from his wallet, laying them on the bureau next to the porcelain wash basin. The act had the trappings of a client leaving money for a strumpet for services rendered, but that couldn't be helped. He set one of the room keys there as well. "Here. Money, if you should require it. I recommend you stay in this room as much as possible, and do not allow anyone but myself to enter. If I need to contact you by phone, I'll ask whoever answers to fetch you by the name of Mrs. Fleming. Understood? And, again, I must strongly emphasize, do not leave—"

"I'll stay inside this room," she recited. "I won't come to the phone unless they ask for Mrs. Fleming." She fixed her large eyes on him. Any moment, he knew, the glint of intelligence there might glaze over once more into her usual emptiness.

"Excellent." He turned to go.

"Mr. Fleming?"

He halted in the doorway. "Yes?"

Her full lips pursed briefly. Then she said, "Whatever you have to do to Oscar, to help that woman . . . I'll understand."

In response he simply nodded, then pulled shut their room's door and hurried downstairs.

He made arrangements—paying out a further fee—to have the Cadillac parked in the house's garage, then set out on foot. He had meant his cautioning statement earlier to Nora that the automobile was more recognizable than either of them and, thereby, a liability. Particularly with what he had in mind for tonight.

Buttoning his black coat against the rising nighttime chill and doing his best to go unnoticed among the neighborhood's somewhat coarse denizens, he walked some blocks from the rooming house. Surely Deborah Byrd would be safe there. Surely. He stopped in at a busy corner tavern to secure some coinage. Then he located a phone box. A light came on overhead as he rattled shut the doors.

The operator came on the line.

"I wish to place an overseas call, operator. I wish to reach London, England. Whitehall, specifically. Yes, I have a number."

Chapter 34

IT TOOK a great many coins, a good deal of explaining and much patience to make the call successful.

Fleming used every last lingering bit of leverage he had at Whitehall, the seat of the British Secret Service. There were those there who surely remembered him. It was, of course, a ghastly hour back in England, and Francis Davenport wasn't in his office. He spoke with a tiring string of secretaries and supervisors, dropping names liberally and laboring to communicate the urgency of his situation. At long last he was reluctantly rung through to Davenport's home.

The line rang tinnily for something just short of an eternity. Fleming rapped his knuckles repeatedly against the phone box's streaked glass as he waited. Finally the line was picked up.

Davenport's voice was hoarse with interrupted sleep, but he answered professionally. "Francis Davenport here."

"Davenport. It's Fleming. I'm in San Francisco."

The MI5 agent cleared his throat noisily, then said with some poise, "Yes, Mr. Fleming. We're aware of your location."

"I know you are." He was gripping the receiver tightly. "I came upon Stahl a few days ago."

"I believe he came upon you. He tells me you've done nothing to violate the National Securities Act. I trust this hasn't changed."

"Your trust is well placed. What I need, urgently, is to

find Stahl. Is he still in San Francisco?" Fleming fervently hoped so.

Davenport paused for an excruciating interval, then said, "Mr. Stahl is still there. He has a flight out in the morning. I ordered him to take a day or two of furlough. You can't imagine what a workhorse that man is—"

"I must contact him."

"Why?" Davenport asked, simply and directly.

This wasn't Merlin Powell to whom he was speaking. Fleming couldn't wheedle and beguile this savvy Secret Service agent. Still, the explanation would be a long one, and he had used up much precious time placing this crucial call already.

"A life is at stake," he said.

"Whose? Yours?"

"Self-preservation isn't foremost in my thoughts at the moment. There is a young lady, however, who is in immediate jeopardy."

"Would that be this DeYoung woman, the journalist, we understand you're traveling with?" Davenport asked.

"Yes."

"For what reason haven't you contacted the local authorities?"

"She's been abducted. By that Oscar Winterberg fiend you've been so keen on."

Davenport made a startled noise. "A more dangerous chap than we imagined then."

"Quite dangerous," Fleming pressed. "And ruthless. Miss DeYoung uncovered some embarrassing facts about the man, and he kidnapped her. If I bring in the police, he'll murder her. I need help—covert help. I want Stahl."

Davenport indulged in another pause before saying, "It's

as irregular a request as I can imagine, Mr. Fleming. Now, had you agreed to aid us at the start—"

"Damn it, Davenport! There's no time for this. I'll go it alone, if need be. If you're unwilling to assist, tell me directly. Miss DeYoung has uncovered a genuine scandal concerning Winterberg, just the sort of thing you wanted to annihilate his public image and bring the man down to ruin. If she is rescued, you'll have your bloody newspaper story. Now, tell me. Will you help?"

Davenport's sigh was long. Behind it Fleming could almost hear the man's thoughts, his careful mental weighing of the circumstances. It was irregular, to be sure. But Davenport was a professional agent, dedicated to his job . . . just as Fleming had once been.

"I shall ring Mr. Stahl, apprise him of the situation and instruct him to rendezvous with you. What is your immediate location?"

Relief went through Fleming's bones. He swiped at the phone box's glass, peering out at the nearby street signs. He recited the names into the receiver. As he did, he took wary note of a pair of shadowy male shapes loitering on the far corner across the vacant intersection.

"Remain there," said Davenport. "Mr. Stahl will arrive presently. You do understand, Mr. Fleming, what your involvement in this now entails? I hereby deputize you. You will place yourself under Mr. Stahl's authority. You will obey his orders. Do you accept these conditions?"

There was no time for argument. In as solemn and sincere a tone as he could manage Fleming said, "Yes. I accept."

"Very good."

A moment later Fleming returned the receiver to the

phone box's upright hook. *Under Stahl's authority.* Well, that remained to be seen. Surely Stahl knew enough about field work to act effectively, but did the man have leadership capabilities? There was no means to know.

He pushed out of the glassed booth, the interior light winking out as the accordion doors opened. The two men on the opposite corner had plainly already seen him, though they were making an effort to appear nonchalant, one propping himself against a wall, the other looking in every direction but Fleming's. He was now standing away from the phone box's bright interior. In his black jacket, black turtleneck and charcoal trousers he was something of a shadow himself. The two men looked to be wearing work clothes, heavy boots and cloth caps. They carried the vague air of ruffians about them.

Winterberg's men? He had to consider it a real possibility. Perhaps his efforts to go to ground had already failed. Perhaps the Cadillac had been so subtly tailed it had escaped his sharp attention.

He could only wait for Stahl's arrival—and wait also to see if the two men made any move. He slipped his cigarette case from his pocket and drew out a Players, keeping the case out of the glare of the nearby street lamp. This particular stretch of the Mission District appeared empty. Sounds of late suppers came from the closest houses, but no one else was on the sidewalks. There was a pub, from which issued faint music, a block and a half distant. Fleming realized belatedly he should have named it as the rendezvous site. Too late now.

Turning to Davenport had been his only option for aid. Trying to contact Hoover's boys would perhaps have been worse than telephoning the city police. That American agency, so Davenport had said, had already made clear its unwillingness to meddle with Winterberg, whose public popularity evidently made him impervious to official harassment. At least Fleming had enlisted Stahl's services. He required *someone* to abet him in tonight's planned operation.

After ten minutes of waiting, with the night's nearly English-like winter chill seeping into his joints, the two roughs stirred into action. Fleming, of course, had been alertly anticipating any movement and waited calmly.

He drew himself fully erect, turning slightly so that he could slide the Beretta free without the two men immediately seeing. He didn't wish to draw the gun, much less discharge it. That would call unwanted attention, which might include the police, the last thing he needed now.

The two men crossed the lighted pool of the corner lamp. Their caps were low over their eyes, and they moved in the same sort of shuffling swagger, not hurrying but not trying to disguise the fact they were heading directly for Fleming. Their hard faces were unshaven, lips peeled back in unpleasant grins.

" 'ey there, swell. Spare a smoke then?" The guttural voice carried shades of an Irish accent.

"As you like," said Fleming evenly. Both men drew to a halt a good six feet away. The one who hadn't spoken crossed his arms and regarded Fleming with cold appraising eyes. Fleming unpocketed the silver cigarette case once more, this time allowing it to be seen in the light. The two men both noted it covetously.

Best to simply get this over with, Fleming thought drolly.

"Here, my good fellow," he said, offering a pair of his Players. "One for your comrade as well."

"Right kind of ye," said the same man, grinning at

Fleming's accent as he stepped forward. He was a broad-shouldered creature, with noticeable scars across the knuckles of the hand that reached out to take the cigarettes. Fleming stood primed for any untoward movements, but the rough merely passed one to his fellow and wedged his into a corner of his mouth. He drew a match from a pocket of his heavy denim coat and struck it, briefly lighting coarse heavy features that didn't appear to have enjoyed the full benefits of human evolution.

Peripherally Fleming noted the still vacant surrounding streets. Now would be a fine moment for Stahl to appear.

The Irish ruffian pitched the spent match into the gutter.

"Ye wouldn't be inclined to 'elp out a mate a bit more, would ye?" Despite the ostensibly friendly tone, the question was weighted heavily with menace.

"What did you have in mind, my dear chap?" Fleming returned suavely.

The second silent man, without obvious warning, suddenly launched himself forward, arms rising. Fleming, however, had caught the subtle shift in the man's posture and had even, it seemed, sensed the man's abrupt surge of adrenaline.

The rough was as bulky a brute as his cohort, doubtlessly strong as an ox but rather unwieldy in size and slow of reflexes. Fleming hopped nimbly, not leaping away but directly toward the charging fellow. He spryly ducked beneath the man's arms and brought his knee up at full strength into the left side of his rib cage. Bones snapped beneath the man's matching denim coat, and he coughed a great pained breath, folding over. It was a simple matter to club him across the base of his skull as he overshot Fleming. The Englishman used the flat of his hand, chopping mercilessly. The rough hit the sidewalk in a slovenly heap, unable even to emit any further sounds of pain.

Fleming bounded agilely away from the injured man, wheeling to face his other adversary.

"I ask again," he said steadily. "How else may I assist you this fine evening?"

The cigarette dropped unnoticed from the first rough's slack mouth. He stood thunderstruck a moment. Then his wiser instincts were triggered. For an indecisive instant he seemed about to flee alone. Instead, he paused to hurriedly snatch up his wounded confederate whose face contorted savagely as he was forced to his feet, both meaty hands clapped tightly over his ribs.

With a stupefied shake of the first man's head they ambled away from the corner as fast as they could manage. Fleming watched their stumbling progress for a full block, where they hastily turned onto another street.

He turned in the opposite direction at the sound of a car engine. Headlamps washed their light across the asphalt as the auto swerved and drew up to the kerb. The car was a rather cramped-looking coupé, the body painted a bland inoffensive yellow. The driver's door opened as Fleming watched from the cover of a nearby building front. Stahl was wearing his dark blue suit and dark blue overcoat. His short greying hair was mildly disheveled.

"Fleming?" he called. Almost for the first time Fleming detected no hostility in that voice.

"Yes." He stepped forward.

Stahl nodded, his short figure ducking back into the auto. Fleming opened the passenger door and slid himself onto the seat. Stahl's manner was excited, his small colorless eyes lit with an unfamiliar fire. His rather stubby fingers drummed the idling coupé's steering wheel.

"It's a rescue mission then?" Davenport's aide asked, making no attempt to mask the enthusiasm in his voice.

"It is that."

"Excellent." Stahl put the auto in gear. "You'll give me directions of course. On the way we can discuss strategy. Don't fear, Fleming. We'll deliver your fair maiden." A curious and most uncharacteristic grin pulled at his normally pinched mouth. He depressed the accelerator eagerly.

Chapter 35

IT MADE a kind of sure sense, Stahl's avid response to the situation. Fleming had once postulated that the short middle-aged agent's marked hostility toward him was founded on envy, that Stahl—an aide, an MI5 pencil-pusher—coveted Fleming's much more exotic career in military intelligence.

Well, here Stahl was getting a chance at the real action, and his zeal was palpable.

Fleming asked him to pull off briefly so that he could delineate the situation before they went charging off. The grey-haired agent, with some reluctance, pulled the yellow coupé to the kerb. They were on Mission Street, slightly past the point where the broad road bent northeast, heading eventually into the South of Market area where they would find Beale Street and Winterberg's office.

Stahl cut the ignition with a sharp snap of the key. It was almost as cold in the car as outside. Fleming wished he had added an overcoat to his ensemble, but he had taken only the vicuña from the suite at the St. Francis. That coat was less inconspicuous than he wanted. It had also been Nora's gift to him. It would have seemed odd going into battle wearing it.

"Very well, Fleming," Stahl said, fingers again anxiously drumming the wheel. "Be brief, won't you. If this is as urgent as Mr. Davenport led me to believe—"

Fleming's hand shot suddenly outward, closing over the

older agent's right wrist and squeezing sharply. Stahl's fingers ceased their tapping.

"Stahl," he said evenly. "Calm yourself. We cannot, neither of us, afford to go into this with anything but cool heads. No matter what or who is at stake. Do I make myself clear?"

The ardent grin slid slowly from his somewhat crinkly features. He took a moment to draw a deep breath. When his eyes focused once more on Fleming, they were no longer darting about wildly in their sockets.

"That's better," said Fleming. "Now, let me explain. . . ."

He did so, as quickly and concisely as he could. He mapped out the Beale Street building and its vicinity. Then he proposed his plan.

"Mr. Davenport was quite insistent that I take command of this operation," Stahl said at the end.

Fleming felt his teeth clenching. He wondered at his own wisdom in enlisting this middle-aged MI5 agent as an ally.

"However," Stahl went on, his tone turning thoughtful, "whether or not you are formally my junior officer, I can see no logic in not taking your counsel. Even deferring to your more extensive experience. What I mean to say is . . . your operational plan meets my approval." His smile this time wasn't anxious but coolly sincere.

Fleming felt a quiet rush of gratitude toward the man, which he expressed simply as, "Most reasonable of you, Mr. Stahl."

Stahl moved to restart the automobile, then paused. "She means a great deal to you, doesn't she?"

Nora. Fleming blinked, finally saying, "She does. She's, frankly, like no other woman I've ever met."

The MI5 agent nodded. "Yes. I've often said the same of my wife, lo these past twenty-three years of marriage."

"I didn't know you were married."

"Why should you?" He turned the key, and the coupé revved back to life. "When we learned you were traveling in Miss DeYoung's company, we naturally did a spot of digging on her."

Fleming recalled that, in what now seemed the distant past, he had actually suspected Nora of perhaps being a member of MI5 herself.

"What did you find?" he asked, suddenly uncertain if he wanted the question answered.

"Her credentials as a journalist are spotty but evidently genuine. We suspect she writes under an assumed name, presumably for professional reasons. No matter. We were more intrigued by her police record."

Manhattan, New York, Fleming recalled. 1938. Yes, the bombing of the apartment of her former paramour. What had been his name? Marcus . . . McCune. That was it. Nora had fled when the police tried to detain her for questioning, only to be picked up and later released when she was cleared of any involvement in the matter.

When he had learned of all this from Merlin Powell, it had given Fleming pause. Nora's hotel room at the Chabrol Arms had, after all, itself been bombed. However, he had been unable to make any rational connection between the two events.

"I know something of the matter," he said rather neutrally as the coupé swung back into traffic.

"Poor man, that McCune chap," said Stahl. "A compulsive gambler evidently. Got himself into critical debt once too often with some rather unforgiving types. A sad event for your Miss DeYoung as well, to be sure. When she learned what had transpired, she apparently temporarily lost her wits. What woman wouldn't? She even fled from the police, likely panicked that those same gangsters meant to do her similar harm. All a very tragic business." He shook his head. "And now more misfortune for her. I feel a deep sympathy for her. And . . . and for you as well, Fleming."

"Thank you," he answered softly.

"Now let's go get her out of this sticky wicket." The auto accelerated down Mission Street.

THEY PULLED TO a quiet halt on First Street, two blocks parallel from Beale. This street, so Nora had once offhandedly remarked, marked the edge of the bay in San Francisco's yore. In subsequent years the land had been filled in deliberately, spreading the city's borders slightly. San Francisco, a bustling metropolis, after all had no room for expansion, jammed as it was onto the end of its peninsula. What would happen in coming decades, Fleming wondered fleetingly, as the population inevitably climbed? Would Golden Gate Park be leveled for housing? Surely not. Surely these dogged people, who had weathered that monstrous earthquake and ensuing fire, would find a way to live harmoniously with their beloved surroundings.

He jettisoned the trivial thought as Stahl cut the motor. The headlamps winked out, leaving them in relative dimness.

Stahl shifted in his seat and slid a pistol from a concealed shoulder holster beneath his dark blue overcoat. He ratcheted a round into the chamber of the .45 automatic, the sort Yank officers had carried during the war. Fleming did likewise, drawing out the Beretta and replacing the clip, lacking the two bullets he'd discharged in Deborah Byrd's apartment building, with the fresh one from his pocket.

"A Beretta?" Stahl asked, sounding somewhat puzzled.

"Yes." Fleming left the safety off and returned it beneath his jacket.

"Hardly any stopping power to those. It's a lady's handgun."

"It happens to belong to a lady," Fleming said with a touch of peevishness.

"*Hurrumph,*" said Stahl.

They stepped out of the yellow coupé. There was a fair amount of motor traffic on First Street. It was still Saturday night, after all, and the weekend bacchanalia would be in full swing; San Franciscans, so he had learned during his short stay in the city, enjoyed their revels. There were virtually no pedestrians in evidence, however. This South of Market area was devoted almost entirely to offices and warehouses, all of which were currently dormant.

"This way," Fleming said, and the two dark-clothed figures set off down Howard Street. At the following cross street—Fremont—they turned. Fleming eyed the quiescent buildings, their windows dimmed, many of their doorways gated. There were no security guards obviously present anywhere. Now that would be a disastrous turn at this stage—to run afoul of some bored sentry set to the task of policing some clothier's warehouse. Fleming was prepared to face Winterberg's cronies. That aging seaman, Yancy. The large man in black. The plain-looking fellow he'd met at the Ferry Building. Even that blond-haired Tommy lad. But he hoped fervently that no innocents came between himself and their plans to rescue Nora.

"There," Fleming said quietly, nodding toward a chink in the palisade of building fronts.

"I see it," said Stahl, noting the narrow alleyway. Two large rusting trash cans sat at the alley's mouth. Together they crossed the street toward it.

Fleming backed himself against the sooty brickwork front of an anonymous office whose darkened windows gazed blindly as he eased toward the corner. Stahl's steps behind him were almost soundless. The tension which climbed Fleming's spine was welcome; it would help keep him alert. He neared the building's edge, the fetid stench emanating from the refuse barrels filling his nostrils unpleasantly. His hand was once more beneath his coat, gripping the Beretta's butt.

He peeked a cautious eye around the corner, which was marked by a dented drainpipe. The light in the narrow alley was quite faint, just a stray scattering from Fremont Street's lamps, barely enough to pick out the mounds of rubbish littering the ground below the high enclosing walls. Above, fire escapes dangled. Fleming spent a long minute studying the terrain, both the ground level and overhead. Winterberg might have pickets on one or more of those iron outcroppings. He saw no evidence of such. Peering into the alleyway's depths, he found nothing but further debris. No human movement.

The alley ran all the way through the mid-block, to Beale Street. Near the far end was the freight entrance to Winterberg's building that he had reconnoitered earlier.

Would Nora be in that office? He had no way of knowing. He also had nowhere else to look. Winterberg certainly might be holding her at some other location, but Fleming's plan was to take the fight to him. *Offense is the surest defense.* So Merlin Powell had rightly said.

He sidled past the two malodorous trash cans into the murky alleyway, Stahl still on his heels. Once he had slipped far enough from the street for the shadows to fall fully over him, he drew the Beretta and held it at the ready. A brief glance behind showed that Stahl had imitated his action.

He was wary of his footing. The floor of the alley was littered generously with a variety of broken glass and nameless scraps of cast-off metal. He managed to move slowly and silently among the garbage. He paused on spying a foul-looking mattress wedged against the base of a colorless concrete wall. Its seams were split, seeping wads of stained cotton. Several horrendously cheap, empty wine bottles lay about the bedding. Evidently some tramp or another was using this place as a home. That gentleman of the road was, however, currently not in residence.

They crept deeper. Fleming could see the freight entrance ahead now. It was a dull slab of a metal door set several feet above the surface of the alley with a small concrete dock set before it. His senses remained critically alert.

Something crashed suddenly behind him, the sound abnormally loud to his keenly tuned ears. He whirled and saw Stahl rather contritely mouthing the word "sorry." The middle-aged agent had only kicked some stray bit of debris. Fleming froze a moment, carefully scanning the shadowy territory ahead. He still saw no signs of movement.

Satisfied, he started them forward again. They crept up watchfully on the freight entrance. Fleming stepped up onto the dock, stooping and squinting in the dimness at the large metal door. A thick hasp was held by an oversized tarnished padlock. It appeared this entrance hadn't been used in some time.

Stahl hopped up beside him, examining the lock as well. After a moment of scrutiny he nodded. He holstered his .45 and rummaged quickly through the pockets of his overcoat. He soon produced a small leather case, tugging the zipper which opened it to reveal an assortment of tiny gleaming tools, each in its own protective sheathe. He chose a fine sliver of metal whose end was irregularly toothed. This he neatly inserted into the tarnished lock, bowing at a sharp angle until his ear was nearly level with the padlock.

He worked swiftly, deftly jiggling and twisting the pick, his features set into deep creases of concentration. No more than thirty seconds later he nodded again, just as a rusty *click* came from the large padlock. Stahl slipped it out of its hasp and laid it quietly on the concrete dock.

Fleming was impressed, but there was no time for congratulations. He eyed the door once more. It was set on runners and was made to slide open to the right. He noted the grit and grime accumulated along its edges and wondered what noise it would make on being opened.

Loud or not, it was better than entering by the building's front door. He laced his fingers through the handle, gripping tightly and bracing himself. Then he gave an experimental tug. The door seemed fused in place by long neglect. Stahl wordlessly added his leverage, and together they pulled.

The metal door groaned sharply, then with a reverberating *snap* came unstuck and slid on its runners. They opened it only enough to allow them to slip through. Beyond was a space of nebulous darkness that smelled of machine oil, a rather welcome relief after the rankness of the alley.

Stahl snapped on a miniaturized torch, the beam narrow but quite powerful. He splashed this light quickly about the area which appeared to be a disused storage space. Tiered metal shelves stood empty, and thick curls of dust rolled through the light's bright shaft. Fleming studied Stahl's torch for a curious instant. It was remarkably compact for the intensity of its illumination. Apparently MI5 field agents were being better equipped than in his days of spying.

Risking the noise, they closed the freight door behind them. A casual observer from outside would likely not notice the missing padlock. Then they stood a long moment in the empty storage chamber and simply listened. The building was silent around them. Only the muffled sounds of passing traffic on Beale Street reached here. Evidently they had successfully infiltrated the office building.

They stepped down a short cement ramp to the floor level, then wended their way through the abandoned shelves. Here and there were bundles of brittle old newspapers, but otherwise the space was utterly abandoned. There was a single door opposite the freight entrance. Stahl kept the torch beam away from it as they approached, so that no one beyond it would notice the light seeping around the jamb.

Fleming took the knob in his left hand, the Beretta still in his right. He turned it slightly, finding it unlocked. Pausing to throw a nod at Stahl, who answered with a confirming nod of his own, he twisted and tugged the door inward in a single fluid motion.

He had explained as best he could the layout of the building. They were on the ground level, in the shabby corridor of peeling bilious green tiles. Overhead, the dusty bulbs in their mesh cages still burned. Stahl had pocketed his torch.

Fleming quickly oriented himself. The stairs leading to the upper floor were away to their left. The passageway lay empty before them, lined by its sealed unmarked doors. He stepped tentatively into the corridor, still listening acutely for any warning sounds.

He peered into the alcove that held the staircase, craning to look upward. This space too was empty. His heart beating heavily but steadily, he started up onto the risers, Stahl a dark noiseless shape behind him. They turned at the switchback and prowled up the remaining steps, toward the passage that held the unlabeled door to Winterberg's cluttered office.

Fleming stole a judicious glance into this corridor, as dreary as the one below. One of the overhead bulbs was out, and the passageway was that much dimmer; but it also was vacant. He eased up off the final stair, Stahl at his elbow, the short man's large .45 in hand. Fleming noted that the barrel was trembling ever so slightly. He wondered if Stahl had ever found himself in any situation similar to this. He wondered further if the man had served as an administrative assistant even during the war. Still, he had so far proven himself capable.

Pointing toward Winterberg's door, they stepped into the corridor. There appeared to be no lights on inside the office. Thoughts of Nora crashed against the walls of his head, but he didn't allow them to overwhelm him. Nora needed him at his levelheaded best tonight. He would not fail her.

At that instant came the muted whoosh of a nearby toilet flushing. Fleming pivoted sharply about just as a door creaked opened in the corridor behind them. Stahl stood slightly in his way. A tall bulky figure emerged, the tails of a black duster swirling. He was setting a black fedora back atop his large skull. He took a single step into the passage, then jerked to a halt. Eyes went wide in those lumpy features.

Stahl was already aiming his pistol. The large man in black made a garbled animal-like sound that seemed equal parts surprise, outrage and recognition. With a shocking dexterity he threw himself to the side, ducking and dropping, rolling his bulk across the peeling tiles. With a movement almost too fast and practiced to see he drew a blue-black automatic, just as Stahl fired.

The blast of the .45 was deafening. The shot caught the tip of the large man's left shoulder, passing through to ricochet noisily off the corridor walls.

Fleming dropped as well as the man in black fired. Stahl grunted, the sound strangely petulant, and tumbled. Fleming didn't spare him a glance as his finger drew on the Beretta's trigger. The flash from the barrel was followed instantaneously by the sure impact of his bullet driving home. He had been aiming for the man's chest, his heart. He knew with the utter certainty of an experienced combatant that he'd hit his mark.

The large man in black's skull dropped heavily to the floor of the passageway. His hulking body did not stir.

Fleming straightened up and spun. His ears rang painfully. Stahl was supine on his back, both hands clapped tightly to his right side between the lower part of his rib cage and his hip. His teeth were bared ferociously, and he was sucking in air shrilly. His small eyes were wide, white ringing the colorless irises. Those eyes darted upward at Fleming. Not filled with appeal, they instead burned with purpose. The wounded agent turned his head sharply, toward the door to Winterberg's office. The meaning was clear: *go ahead.*

Fleming had to act now. The gunplay obviously would have alerted whoever was in that office. Every second he waited was potentially lethal—for himself . . . and for Nora, if she were being held here.

He leapt toward the unmarked door, the smoking Beretta raised. Grimly he lifted a leg and shot his foot hard against the wood just to the side of the doorknob. Wood splintered, and the door crashed violently inward.

Chapter 36

THE DIM light of the corridor cast only a small worthless rectangle of illumination into the otherwise darkened office. At the moment he had kicked in the door, Fleming had also jumped back from the threshold, away to the right of the splintered jamb. He crouched tensely now, the pistol leveled.

"Send out the woman!" he barked. "Do that—and no one else shall come to harm!"

He realized he should have snatched Stahl's torch from him, but there had been no time, what with the terrible speed of the last minute's events. Stahl was still gasping painfully on the floor a few feet away. A small pool of blood was spreading on the peeling tiles, at the right edge of his supine body.

Fleming couldn't afford even these few precious seconds. If Nora were in that office, he had to rescue her. *Now.* No matter the consequences.

He came up nimbly from his crouch, diving low through the doorway, his left arm flailing upward to catch the light switch. He hit the floor rolling as yellow light flared from the overhead fixture. He was on his feet half a heartbeat later, coming up behind the chair Nora had sat in during Winterberg's interview.

Someone was stirring from the cot wedged alongside the desk. An arm pushed back a ragged wool blanket.

The office was otherwise unoccupied but for its customary clutter. On the desk top lay a thick scattering of papers, including a bound notebook of blue sheets, densely typeset. A bottle of inferior Scotch—certainly not blended—stood nearly drained beside an upset glass.

Fleming pointed the Beretta at the body sluggishly reviving itself beneath the wool blanket. His sights were aimed at the head as it emerged into the light. Gummy, thoroughly uncomprehending eyes blinked in discomfort.

"Flem-ink?" Oscar Winterberg asked, giving his name a final Germanic twist. He appeared to still be wearing his boots, dungarees and denim shirt from earlier in the day. He also looked quite inebriated.

"Where is she, Winterberg?" Fleming asked. Still holding the pistol leveled, he edged toward the open door of the office lavatory and took a fast peek. It was empty.

Winterberg slurred something in his native tongue. His rugged features twisted as he made serious efforts to fathom the situation.

"*Warum* . . . why a gun do you have?" the drunken union leader managed.

The impulse to stride over to the cot and club him on the skull with the Beretta's butt was nearly overwhelming. Fleming, exercising professional control of his emotions, held himself in check . . . for the moment.

"Where is the woman?" he asked again, his voice an ominous snarl.

Winterberg was still blinking as he managed to push himself up onto his elbows, one booted foot dropping carelessly to the floor.

"I . . . meant to go home for dinner," he was saying to no one. "My *frau* . . . June . . . she will displeased be—"

"Damnit, Winterberg!" Fleming nearly bellowed. "I've murdered one man tonight. If you're so keen on being the next, I assure you I will oblige!"

Winterberg's wandering eyes—red-rimmed now, not dark and penetrating—at last settled on him. His dark brows drew slowly together.

"*Was* . . . what are you talking about, Englander?"

"Nora Blair DeYoung." Fleming now did take a step nearer the cot, affording Winterberg the opportunity to gaze up into the Beretta's bore. He cocked the pistol for effect. "Where—is—she?"

If Winterberg wasn't entirely grasping the crisis, he seemed to finally understand the jeopardy it entailed. His jaw trembled slightly as it unhinged. Gone was that flawlessly self-assured manner he had demonstrated during the interview. Now, instead, he radiated fear, all the more intense since he genuinely didn't appear to comprehend what was happening.

"Fräulein DeYoung," he said, enunciating with effort. "I do not know where she is, Fleming. Why would I know? Has she gone missing? Why—"

It was plain that something was monumentally askew. Fleming had realized it the moment Winterberg poked his drunken head from beneath the cot's blanket.

The long-haired white cat slinked out of some secret nook and bounded onto the paper-littered desk top. It regarded Fleming with enigmatic green eyes, then began preening itself.

He waved Winterberg into silence. Nothing made sense. Where was Nora? Who other than Winterberg would have had her snatched out of the Cadillac on Stockton Street, in front of the apartment of Deborah Byrd—*Winterberg's illicit second wife*? Fleming teeth ground tightly together. What of that telephone call at the suite at the St. Francis, that French miscreant who'd made those crooked arrangements for the "hostage exchange"? What of that equally despicable creature—the American—who'd appeared at the Ferry Building? If those men weren't Winterberg's, who did they work for, and why should they pretend to be Winterberg's hirelings?

An impossible tangle. And somewhere in it was Nora.

"I have Deborah Byrd," he said suddenly.

The union leader's reddened eyes widened. An unsightly mix of emotions passed over his features, among them shock and anger. He tried to push himself further upright and failed.

"Deborah . . ." he whispered, investing the word with shame and brittle longing. After a long moment he sighed, deflating. "So. You know. I suppose you and your newspaper confederate mean to publish this . . . information."

"I don't give a damn about your bigamy, Winterberg. I'm holding Miss Byrd at a secure location. I meant to trade her for Nora—for Miss DeYoung." The Beretta remained aimed at Winterberg's forehead. "All bets are off now, as the Americans say. If you wish to see *either* of your wives again, you'll return Miss DeYoung to me."

"*Scheisse,* man! How can I do that? I do not know what you are speaking! Fräulein DeYoung? Do you think I have—*wie* do you say?—kidnapped her?"

Damn it! It was all perfectly catastrophic. This rescue mission had gone fantastically awry. Fleming had been prepared to face its dangers. Now, he had shot the large man in black in the corridor (not an innocent bystander, he needlessly reminded himself; *he* had shot first), and Stahl was still lying out there wounded. And what did he have to show for these efforts? Nothing but the drunken slurrings of a German expatriate bigamist.

If Winterberg had abducted Nora, why would he be here sleeping off the effects of a bottle of shoddy Scotch? Surely he would be taking a personal hand in the matter, likely overseeing Nora himself.

There was some terrible duplicity at play here.

"I should kill you on principle," Fleming said. Winterberg's jaw again trembled. The Englishman saw in his cold mind's eye the faces of other Germans . . . those former Nazis he had dispatched after the war at the Prime Minister's behest. He recalled vividly the impassivity with which he had carried out his secret orders.

He uncocked the pistol. The hammer fell dully. The white-haired feline glanced up from its painstaking grooming on the desk top.

"But I shan't," Fleming went on hollowly. "You're a sad little man, it seems. You haven't the sand to effect something like this. You surround yourself with thugs and pretend to be fighting the good fight against capitalist oppression. You see women as trophies. Your ethics are excremental. Yes, we know of Deborah Byrd. Yes, very likely the news of your foolish immorality will grace the headlines. I care nothing of these matters."

He lowered the pistol, but Winterberg made no further move off the cot, lying instead stunned and defeated. Fleming shooed the cat, who gave an indignant hiss, from the desk. He scooped up the bound blue-sheeted notebook he had noted earlier, turning it to examine the dense typescript. Winterberg emitted a kind of helpless wavering whimper.

"This, however, does interest me," Fleming continued. "Or at least it will interest parties to whom I now find myself indebted." Namely Francis Davenport and the wounded Stahl. "Did you concoct this code yourself, or is it something left over from your guerrilla days during the war?"

He flipped a few pages, noting the Sanskrit of numerals and characters. He gathered the other strewn papers from the desk. These pages were drafted in a careful hand that had obviously grown quite slovenly during the hours Winterberg had sat here, writing and drinking at a furious clip. There were some two dozen sheets, several already translated into the code that Davenport in London had referred to as being as baffling as the Nazi's wartime Enigma.

"No matter where it came from, I suppose." He folded the loose sheets into the notebook and pocketed all of it. "Whatever you've been smuggling into Mother Russia, the operation is now over. And you, Winterberg . . . or Charlie Winters or Charles Winstead, whatever pleases you . . . you are utterly finished."

It was hardly a compensatory victory. He had failed to rescue Nora—had, in fact, only widened the possibilities of her search by some measureless factor. Still, the expression of abject horror on Winterberg's rugged face, as the reality of all that had transpired sank home, was its own sweet triumph.

He backed out of the office, pausing to snap off the light, leaving the union leader to his private darkness.

Stahl was sitting up, still drawing air through his teeth. His breaths, however, had slowed somewhat. He appeared relatively centered and looked up alertly as Fleming emerged from the doorway. The middle-aged MI5 agent had a handkerchief pressed to his wound. The cloth had soaked through redly but wasn't dripping blood. The large man in black remained an inert mound further down the corridor. A corpse.

"Can you move?" Fleming asked, crouching. "Perhaps I should have an ambulance delivered here."

"Rot, Fleming." Stahl winced as he shifted to allow

Fleming to ease him gingerly upward, onto his feet. The older man threw his weight generously onto his supporting arm and shoulder, but Stahl's movements as they made slowly toward the stairway were surprisingly steady. "I shouldn't like to be here to answer for all this muddle to the local authorities."

"Nor should I," Fleming agreed, bolstering Stahl on his unwounded left side. They started down the risers. The short older agent didn't weigh much, so their progress was fairly swift. Still, it would be a long trek back to the yellow coupé.

"This is rather like being a spy, isn't it?" Stahl said, something like an ironic smile creasing his pained features. "Creeping through dark alleyways, exchanging bullets with villains . . . a bit exciting, what?"

"Indeed." They turned at the stair's switchback, heading hurriedly for the ground level.

"I saw that big chap lying dead. Tell me, did I get him?"

"You most certainly did. Fine work." Fleming's tone shifted, and he repeated with a soft heartfelt sincerity, "Fine work, Mr. Stahl." It would give him some pleasure to present the wounded MI5 agent with Winterberg's code book.

"I can't imagine how all those field agents have gotten along all these years without me," Stahl said with vast dignity. "I may have to speak to Mr. Davenport about reassignment.

But—" His small eyes clouded. "But tell me, Fleming. Where's the lady?"

"Whereabouts unknown," he answered bleakly and hastened Stahl along.

Chapter 37

FLEMING MADE his telephone calls from the brightly lit waiting area of Central Emergency, a hospital located on Grove Street in the city's Civic Center. The space was fairly crowded, a Saturday night turnout. Worried family members huddled among the ranks of uncomfortable chairs. One disheveled-looking chap, evidently as intoxicated as Winterberg, was haranguing the plump hard-faced nurse at the glassed window who was giving back as good as she received.

Stahl, before being woozily loaded onto a gurney, had supplied Fleming with the direct number through to Davenport's home. He was connected without much fuss. The phone box was wedged into an alcove in a corner of the waiting room.

Davenport answered immediately this time. Apparently he hadn't returned to bed following the previous call. "What is Mr. Stahl's condition?" he asked, concern heavy in his voice, as Fleming started to explain the night's events.

"I'm told his wound is relatively minor. No vitals punctured. The prognosis is for a full recovery."

"Thank God."

Fleming told him of the notes and code book he had appropriated from Winterberg's desk. Davenport's response was a mix of astonishment and delight.

"My word! I must say, I couldn't have asked for finer

work from an active field agent. So, it *was* our Mr. Winterberg after all. I admit I had my reservations about the matter. You're quite certain of all this?"

Fleming had tucked the bound notebook safely away in the glove box of the yellow coupé. "The facts fit. Winterberg was translating a text into code. His socialist sympathies are not in doubt. Having experience in the underground and owing to his current powerful standing, it would not have been an insurmountable feat for him to have arranged for his communiqués to be smuggled out of the States, through England and the Continent, into Russia. He must have first smuggled the code key to the Russians, then started sending his messages. As to the nature of those dispatches, I shall leave that study to the professionals."

"I'll be sending in people to see to Mr. Stahl."

"Very good," Fleming said. "We concocted a whopper to account for his bullet wound. Seems he had a difference of opinion with a pair of Irish roughs as to the ownership of his billfold."

"Smart thinking." Davenport paused, then asked with some sensitivity, "And what of Miss Nora Blair DeYoung?"

"She wasn't at the scene."

"Blast."

They spoke a moment further, then Fleming rang off, fed another coin into the slot and dialed.

"Mmmmm," Mrs. O'Dwyre answered. He asked that "Mrs. Fleming" be brought to the phone. Fleming could hear the radio playing in the background in the common room.

"Yes?" Deborah Byrd asked alertly. Evidently she hadn't yet slipped back into her normal mental lethargy. Perhaps there was hope for the young woman yet. "Mr.—Ian?"

"Yes. I wanted to make certain you were all right. No one's come to visit?"

"No one. Has anything happened to Oscar?" A tremulous note crept into her voice.

"He is unharmed. He will, of course, have to answer for his . . . indiscretions. I wish you to be prepared for that. There will be a great hullabaloo about his personal life. Your name will surface, I'm afraid. It's unavoidable."

"I reconciled myself to that some while ago. Were you able to help that woman?"

Again the question. Fleming rubbed the bridge of his nose, which was again beginning to throb. He felt nearly spent.

"Sadly not."

"I'm so sorry."

He advised her to remain at the rooming house, preferably locked in their room. He told her once more he would return when he was able.

Outside the phone box in the corner of the waiting room, a sour-faced woman wearing makeup appropriate to someone half her age was impatiently tapping her foot. Fleming leveled an icy stare at her through the glass, harsh enough to make her gulp and slink sullenly away.

He dropped another coin and dialed a number from a slip of paper in his pocket.

"Where is Miss DeYoung?" he asked as the phone was picked up at the other end.

A long pause ensued. Fleming heard breathing.

"Mademoiselle DeYoung?" sneered the Frenchman. "She is ours, monsieur. You understand, no? You did not return to our rendezvous at the Ferry—"

"The game's up, you rogue. I know you're not in the employ of Oscar Winterberg. Neither you nor your odious American confederate." He allowed a moment for that to sink home. "If you wish to bargain further with me, you'll have to do so without any of these absurd masquerades."

The Frenchman asked, "You 'ave paid a visit to Monsieur Winterberg then?"

"I have." Fleming shook away the image of the large man in black slumping dead to the floor.

"*Magnifique.* Then you 'ave performed superbly, Monsieur Fleming. I'm certain you will join me in celebrating the death of Oscar Winterberg."

Fleming's handsome features clouded.

"Monsieur Winterberg was, you will agree, a *monstre* deserving of such a fate. His death will—"

"I did not kill Winterberg," Fleming said flatly into the receiver's mouthpiece. The image of Winterberg's trembling face as Fleming pointed the pistol at his forehead now surfaced vividly. He *had* nearly pulled the trigger. And had instead uncocked the Beretta.

He heard a sharp intake of breath over the wire.

"*What?*" the voice now shouted. "You dumb limey son of a bitch, what in hell's the matter with you, huh? Can't you do anything right? You fool, you goddamned fool—" The Frenchman had vanished. This was now the voice of the American Fleming had encountered in front of the Ferry Building. Those "individuals" were one in the same.

A thread of the great web of duplicity was now unraveling itself.

"Who are you?" Fleming barked into the phone, interrupting the profane diatribe.

The American man checked his tirade. The sneer was

again in his voice as he said, "You'll never know, Fleming. I'm a wisp of smoke, and you'll never understand any of this."

"As you wish," Fleming spat, at that moment not even caring. "Then tell me . . . where is Miss DeYoung?"

A vicious peal of laughter erupted at this. "Oh, you idiot Brit bastard! Still hot for that crooked dame, are you? Don't you have an ounce of brains in that fat head of yours—"

"*Where is she?*" Fleming fairly roared, seeing heads turn in the waiting area.

"She's here with me," said the American, now maliciously smug. "And you'll never know where that is. And by the time you get it in your witless head to have the cops or the feds or whoever trace this address through the phone number, we'll both be long gone!" He laughed again, the sound hard and cruel as it jangled in Fleming's ear.

At that moment he heard a loud crash over the line, followed by a shout of surprise and anger. The phone dropped to the floor. Two voices now, raised. One . . . a woman's? Glass shattered somewhere in the background. The American was spitting fiery obscenities. The other voice—decidedly female now—screamed, high and piercing. There were the sounds of rapid blows being struck. The brutal melee continued for at least a full minute. Fleming's heart was thundering painfully in his chest.

Silence now. Then sounds of slow movement, as of someone crawling on the floor toward the dropped telephone.

"Ian . . ." A frail whisper.

"Nora?" he said in a stifled croak.

"Come . . . to me . . . please—"

"Where are you, Nora?"

In a feeble murmur she gave the address, then said nothing more.

Fleming burst from the telephone booth, bowled over the sour-faced woman who'd returned to impatiently tap her foot and hit the swinging doors of Central Emergency as fast as his feet had ever carried him.

Chapter 38

HE RACED Stahl's yellow coupé out of the Civic Center, the area clustered with imposing official-looking buildings, including one massive pillared edifice that appeared to be City Hall. He charged the auto up Market Street, appropriating lanes at will, slewing among the plodding trams, cutting off other, less reckless motorists in his efforts to cover the distance to Eureka Street as swiftly as was humanly possible.

Fleming knew he was pushing himself just as critically. He was exhausted, thoroughly enervated by this unending day. His body was on the brink of simply collapsing. But he was a driven man. He *had* to reach Nora before . . . before . . .

He swerved sharply off Market—car horns blaring ahead and behind—and onto Eureka. The street was narrow, set in what looked to be a quaintly genteel neighborhood of nicely kept houses. These Victorians wore fresh coats of paint. The trees trimming the sidewalks here and there were neatly pruned.

He gunned the coupé along the quiet empty lane, looking hurriedly at the house numbers, passing 18th Street, then 19th, then slamming on the brakes hard enough nearly to knock his forehead against the windscreen. Almost as an afterthought he turned the auto into a vacant driveway. He was at the base of yet another of San Francisco's alpine hills, this one looming toward a starlit sky muted somewhat by the general glow of the city.

Tearing the key from the ignition, Fleming vaulted from his seat. Instinct kept him from actually drawing the Beretta as he dashed toward the proper house. Curious neighbors might be snooping from nearby windows; it would do no good at this stage, he felt certain, to have the police meddling in this matter. His hand was beneath his black jacket, however, as he bounded up a short set of cement steps to the front door. His palm was moist against the pistol's grip.

It was a two-story house, peach trimmed with a creamy off-white. Shades were drawn over all its windows, but there were lights burning on the ground floor.

He laid his free hand on the doorknob, his wits gathered as he prepared himself for whatever unknown dangers waited inside.

The door was locked, but he put his shoulder to it, hearing a *snap* as he shoved. He pushed it open, holding himself off to one side, ready to draw the Beretta in a flash.

The entryway was charmingly appointed with a small lacquered table draped with white lace. A bulb burned in an ornate overhead fixture. The interior walls were painted the same creamy off-white as the trim of the exterior, with warm lavender wallpaper above the wainscoting. The hallway extended toward a kitchen. To the left was a flight of carpeted stairs. To the right was a door. It was inset with tall rectangular panes of beveled glass. The lower two had been shattered. The shards were spilled haphazardly across the finished wood floor of the vestibule. The house was silent around him.

Fleming stepped inside, balancing silently on the balls of his feet, then pulled the front door shut behind himself. He drew the pistol.

He eased along the wall, carefully avoiding the broken

glass. He reached the doorway's edge, watching alertly as the house's front parlor slid slowly into view. It too was pleasantly furnished—a velvet-cushioned settee, armchair, the carpeting a gentle blush—but those furnishings were in violent disarray. Books, the pieces of a fractured vase, a lamp shade were all scattered across the rug, which had itself been shifted out of place. Fleming peered through the door's intact upper panes, still edging nearer. There was a tidily swept hearth in one corner. Then he saw the blood, darker spatters against the soft pink of the carpet. Then he saw the splayed foot.

He yanked open the parlor door, flinging it wide so that it hit the outer wall, breaking another pane and rattling more shards across the entryway's floor. He came into the parlor with the pistol leveled.

The splayed foot belonged to a dead male. He wore a beige suit and lay on his back, body twisted awkwardly at the waist, one hand still raised at the elbow and unmoving. The weasel-like eyes in that ordinary-looking face were wide, lifeless pupils fixed on the ceiling. His neutral features were presently contorted into a rather impassioned expression of rage and shock. The American man would never again be afforded the chance to verbally express those emotions, however. A thick triangular fragment of the shattered vase was lodged deep in his throat. It had opened the carotid artery, and a vast quantity of blood had gushed from the terrible wound—and was still trickling—to pool about his head. Next to the corpse lay a fire poker, the steel implement bent slightly at its middle.

Fleming noted these details in the briefest of visual sweeps. What drew his attention so rapidly from the oozing corpse was the second body spread across the carpet a few feet beyond.

Nora. Eyes closed. Comely features locked into a terrible rictus. Unmoving. Blood seeping from her red-ringletted hair. Her wound was grotesque. Her scalp had been horridly split beneath the hair; the gash continued from her left temple, crossing her eye and cheekbone. Bone was exposed. The abutting flesh was already blackening with bruise. She was still wearing her hiking boots, dungarees and flannel shirt, which was now flecked with red. The telephone was tumbled from its stand only a foot away.

Nora . . .

The pistol fell from his fingers. He stepped forward, vertigo twirling through his skull.

He dropped to his knees. His hands rose and hovered uselessly above her desecrated face. Marred beauty, he thought, his numbed mind latching onto the phrase. *Marred beauty, marred beauty, marred—*

She was breathing!

Her nostrils flared, a bubble of thick blood forming from the left one. A muscular tic moved her right cheek. He put a hand beneath that cheek, a rush of hope piercing his heart. He must call for an ambulance!

He must have unknowingly said it aloud.

"Too late . . ." she slurred. Her right eye came fluttering open, the limpid blue hue still bright but seemingly fading. The pupil was dilated. Her crushed left remained shut. The eye slid toward him, and her mouth twitched. "Ian."

"Nora," he gasped, still cradling her wounded head in his hand. "Nora—an ambulance. Here in five minutes. We'll get you safely to hospital—"

"Too late," she repeated, firmer this time.

"You don't know what you're saying." He moved to rise.

Her hand lifted and gripped his shoulder with a surprising surge of strength.

"I've been on battlefields, Ian. I've . . . seen men die. I saw the moment of no return in their eyes. I'm past that now. No coming back . . ." Her fingers dug deeper into the flesh of his shoulder. "Don't leave me. Not for a minute. I don't have much time."

How foul it was, how unspeakably abhorrent, that he knew deep in his agonized soul that she was correct. He too had seen men die, more than he would ever care to enumerate. He had watched life's flame flicker, gutter and extinguish. It was too late for Nora. The trauma of the massive head wound was killing her as he watched. He could not prevent what was inevitable.

"Lies, Ian." Her eye was fixed on him. "All lies. How many lies I told you."

"It doesn't matter," he said softly.

"It does. I want to confess. I want to . . . leave you cleanly."

More blood was dribbling from her nose, spilling onto her lips—those lips he had kissed. He wiped them tenderly with his fingers.

"I used you," she said, drawing on rapidly diminishing reserves to speak the words. "I tried to manipulate you into killing W-Winterberg." Her chest was rising and falling laboriously.

"Why?" he whispered, wanting only to prolong her words . . . prolong these last minutes of her life.

"Winterberg murdered my father." A fading spark of rage blossomed in her remaining eye.

"Your father?" Fleming recalled, distantly, their conversation during the flight to Miami. She had told him of growing up in Oklahoma, of the father—Wilford?—who had watched over his family and later inherited a fortune from some prosperous relative, enough to send Nora to school in New York. She had claimed her father was still living.

"Lies," she repeated, seeming to glean his thoughts. "Yes, I came from the Dust Bowl and all that. I studied j-journalism. But when I went overseas as Blake Young during the war . . . my father came with me. As a soldier. He enlisted, even though he was old. Wanted to do his part." A pained facsimile of a smile trembled her bloodstained lips. "He was at D-day. The Nazis were being pushed back, but the fighting was terrible. My father's squad got separated and bivouacked at an abandoned inn—" She erupted into coughing. Fleming saw blood in her mouth. She fought through the fit, hurrying now to get her words out. "An inn. Partisans t-targeted the house. Thought Nazis were hiding there. It was Winterberg's group. They used grenades. I was near the front lines, w-writing a feature. I heard. One survivor from the inn . . . told what happened. I investigated. Just like it was a story. I uncovered the facts. I . . . I wanted Winterberg. Wanted him to pay—"

Her coughing this time was more violent. She shook beneath Fleming. Blood speckled his jacket.

"I found him years later," she went on hoarsely. "Here. San Francisco. I'd vowed vengeance." Her eyelid fluttered.

Desperate to keep her going, he prompted, "Then this Deborah Byrd business?"

"Yes. I couldn't get to Winterberg myself. Too protected. But . . . in London . . . I interviewed L-Lord D-D-D—"

"Lord Dale Hemmingford," he supplied, watching the pieces of the sickening puzzle fall together.

Nora nodded shallowly. "We'd met before. He liked me. Trusted me. I learned about the coded messages. Learned he wanted W-Winterberg too. We hatched a scheme. You"—her hand squeezed his shoulder once more, the grip urgent but weaker this time—"Hemmingford knew MI5 wanted to recruit you. So I . . . I *attached* myself to you. Dragged you into this. Wanted you to kill Winterberg for me. Knew you could accomplish it." A single tear swelled in her eye, breaking onto her cheek.

He could furnish much of what remained of the tangle. She had come to Jamaica specifically to seduce him. The bomb at the Chabrol Arms! He realized with a bitter start that *she* had arranged that, so to draw him onward to San Francisco in the capacity of her protector. Here, following Winterberg's interview, she had contrived her own abduction, so to incite him into hunting and murdering Winterberg. Only, he had spared the man.

He didn't bother glancing over his shoulder at the dead American lying next to the bent fire poker. This creature, then, had been abetting her all along. Probably had arranged the bombing in Jamaica. He had also been the gunman at Deborah Byrd's apartment building. He had certainly played the dual roles of her kidnappers, pretending to be working for Oscar Winterberg. The plot had even included stealing Nora's papers from the suite at the St. Francis, just to make Winterberg appear even more diabolical. Nora herself must have performed that "theft."

Lies. Yes, a glut of lies. All to make him the murderer of her father's killer.

"Why didn't you have your confederate simply assassinate Winterberg?" Fleming found himself asking softly.

Nora's eye flickered toward the American's body. "Jessup is his name. I met him a year ago, on a story. He . . . does dirty work. For hire. H-Hemmingford hired him, through me, to help me. But he recommended using someone . . . disposable." Her gaze returned sharply to Fleming. "He is dead?"

"Quite dead."

"Good," she said flatly.

"Why did he attack you?"

A fresh tear welled in her eye. "I attacked *him.* I . . . couldn't stand it anymore. I hated myself . . . for what I'd done. To you. Something went wrong, you see. . . . I fell in love with you, Ian. Wasn't s-s-supposed to happen. It did. I love you. I'm sorry. I'm so sorry. . . ."

Quivering he bent further, laying his cheek against hers, her breath whispering shallowly against his ear. He gathered her into his arms, feeling the dreadful limpness of her body, feeling the dwindling pulse of her oozing blood, feeling—so quickly now—the final fated ebbing. Nora's last delicate heartbeats.

Her final breath shivered from her, carrying in the frailest of whispers her parting words.

". . . eternally yours. . . ."

Chapter 39

THERE WAS a great deal of aftermath with which he had to deal before he could escape San Francisco. There were, of course, the police with their endless inquiries. Casini, the Irish-looking detective he'd met earlier, had been attached to the probe. Fleming spent long hours with the husky policeman at his precinct house, untangling the facts of the case.

The furnished house on Eureka Street had been leased by Jessup under a false name. Reginald P. Jessup had warrants for his arrest in more American states than Fleming could name. The police had been waiting to question this very slippery character about numerous criminal matters for quite some time. Casini didn't appear especially put out that he would now never be afforded the chance.

It was impossible to leave Oscar Winterberg's name entirely out of the matter. Fleming, however, was judicious with his facts. He told Casini of accompanying Nora to the city and of the interview with the union leader. He did not mention Deborah Byrd. Before ringing the police from Eureka Street he had located and pocketed all of Nora's notes. These he had subsequently mailed on anonymously to one of her New York editors. Blake Young was dead . . . but "his" final feature would see print. Winterberg would be deposed. Nora's father would be avenged, after a fashion.

Fleming said nothing of Stahl or the shootout at Winterberg's Beale Street office. If and when Winterberg was questioned in the matter, Fleming knew the union organizer would not be eager to reveal that he had armed thugs on his personal payroll. Surely the man was also terrified that his bigamy might be made public, to say nothing of the coded communiqués he had been smuggling into Russia.

Those encrypted messages, so Fleming had learned after he passed the code book on to the two MI5 agents who'd come to see to the convalescing Stahl, had been deciphered. The dispatches were, frankly, bizarre. They were, it seemed, veritable rants, full of aimless blatherings about the true socialist crusade and calling for Winterberg's Russian "brethren" to rise up and topple the facade of Communism that gripped that nation, replacing it with a genuine socialist state. Included in the messages were endless digressions about the sacred purity of workers' rights and, quite strangely indeed, tirades about robots. The fanatical diatribes of an evidently warped mind. Though the line of communication had been cut, Fleming wondered how these missives had been received in Russia.

He found out a day later when Davenport rang him at the suite to tell him Stahl was well enough to be released and flown back to England.

"Apparently the Russians were quite baffled by the messages," Davenport said. "So much so that they sent a man of their own to investigate. An agent by the name of the Scimitar. We had some inkling the man was in London. Unfortunately we only confirmed this after he'd left, evidently for Jamaica, then the States. Seems he was tailing you. Tell me, did you happen to notice a Russian agent dogging your heels these past weeks?" He went on to describe the man.

"None that I saw," Fleming said. So, the Russians too had been involved. He found himself glad he hadn't known. The affair had been complicated enough, after all.

"Well, he's the Americans' problem now. I wonder what happened to him."

Fleming had no answer.

With no other living witnesses to the matter he was free to make whatever he liked of Nora's abduction. He kept his falsehoods simple. He explained to Casini that Nora had been snatched out of the Cadillac a few hours after her interview with Winterberg on Saturday. Instead of Stockton Street, where the police might find actual witnesses, he set the scene on a deserted lane in the Mission District, saying he had stepped into some tavern or other to purchase cigarettes. Fleming, so his story went, had returned hurriedly to the St. Francis Hotel to ring the police, where the message from Jessup was waiting. Fleming then contacted the kidnapper, who named a ransom of ten thousand dollars for her safe return, warning him that Nora would be killed if the police were approached. At that moment the sounds of a violent scuffle came over the line. Following that, Nora, obviously seriously injured, came to the phone to say she had overpowered her abductor, then gave him the Eureka Street address where she was being held. By the time he reached her, she was dead.

It was a pat tidy lie. But it matched the surface facts of the situation neatly. Fleming knew the police would welcome a swift satisfying conclusion to this grisly episode. Casini certainly seemed to accept his accounting without skepticism.

"Why would Jessup decide to abduct her?" the detective mused in the stark interrogation room where he and Fleming had spent numerous hours these past few days. He understood that these repetitive interviews were standard procedure, that the police were merely satisfying themselves that he, Fleming, wasn't party to this botched kidnapping. The room's walls were as blank and characterless as the two uncomfortable straight-backed chairs and the dull metal desk separating him and Casini.

"I fear I've no idea," Fleming said, lighting a Players with his gold cigarette lighter. His eye caught Nora's inscription on the inside lid of his silver cigarette case. He snapped it shut. "Perhaps she knew the man."

Casini shrugged his broad shoulders. He scratched at the greyish stubble lining his loose jowls. "Possible. Jessup was a nasty character. Maybe they crossed paths sometime. Maybe he had a grudge against her."

"Will we ever know?" Fleming asked quietly.

Casini regarded him dismally. "Maybe. Maybe not. We'll dig into it, that's for sure. But to tell the sad truth, we'll probably never know. That's a rotten fact of police business, pal. I'm sorry."

He had fetched Deborah Byrd and the Cadillac from Mrs. O'Dwyre's rooming house. The young woman still appeared to be in possession of at least the rudiments of her faculties. He wondered if she would ever fully recover herself. He advised her to take an impromptu holiday, to leave the city for a minimum of two weeks. She agreed readily enough to the plan.

"I've got a great-aunt up in Napa."

"Fine," Fleming said. He wondered what life would be like for her as an unwed mother. They were at her austere Chinatown apartment. She was filling a suitcase. He had promised to drive her to the bus depot. "Go there. This business about Winterberg will reach the headlines any day now. After that you may find privacy a precious commodity."

"Thank you for what you did." She laid her leather-bound Bible with its pressed orchid into the suitcase and did up the straps. She was no longer wearing the white gold band on her ring finger. "Oscar . . . he has to pay for what he's done, doesn't he?"

"It's only right."

She nodded thoughtfully. "Yes. Only right." They left the apartment.

Fleming was still billeted at the suite at the St. Francis. He hadn't changed rooms. The police naturally had cautioned him not to leave the city until the investigation was concluded. He had packed Nora's remaining things, throwing in the vicuña coat as well, and delivered the items to the precinct house. Nora's next of kin had been notified. One of her brothers, he was told, was en route to San Francisco to collect her effects and make funeral arrangements. Fleming had no intention of attending those services, wherever they would eventually be held.

He moved through these days with all the animation of a ghost, not tasting his food when he remembered to eat, not awaking rested when he slept. He felt void of emotion, as though his mental circuitry had simply been unable to accommodate the potent charge and had burnt out. Even memories of Nora, which came ceaselessly and unbidden to mind, seemed vaguely unreal, as if he were recalling a character from some drama or novel. She had betrayed him. She had loved him. She had *existed;* this he knew, intellectually. But her reality had so swiftly faded, leaving only numb melancholy behind.

From the suite he telephoned Merlin Powell. In a toneless voice he related the facts. His editor was struck into stunned silence.

Eventually Powell managed, in strained tone, "Such a

tragedy, Fleming. Truly. I can't begin to express my most heartfelt—"

"I've a story to file with you," he cut in, ignoring Powell's sincere attempt at commiseration. There was presently no place in Fleming's heart for it.

"A story?"

"Yes. You expected a feature out of this, didn't you? Something for Kemsley Newspapers."

"Sod the paper, Fleming," Powell said sharply. "I never imagined myself saying this, but I think you're quite due for some off-duty time."

Fleming, sitting in the suite's parlor, closed his eyes and said bluntly, "Here's the story, Powell. Be ready to write down every word."

An interminable time later he reached the conclusion. Again Powell had lapsed into a dazed silence.

"Incredible," the editor said at last.

"In a day or so I shall require another airline ticket."

"You should have enough funds among your expenses for a return flight to Jamaica." Powell sounded puzzled. "If you're caught short, though, I will of course gladly wire—"

"I won't be returning immediately to Jamaica," Fleming once more interrupted dully.

"Where are you off to?"

"I must stop off in London briefly."

Powell didn't press for details. "I'll make the arrangements."

Fleming hung up.

Chapter 40

The antechamber was a regal, rather haughty affair. An immense oil portrait of Lord Dale Hemmingford hung upon one wall, doubtlessly to remind any sniveling supplicants of the might and grandeur of that august personage whose favor they had come to curry.

The canvas' frame was a florid gilded scrollwork. The portrait itself, very nearly life-sized, was as epic as any of the Napoleonic era. Hemmingford was posed magnificently before the dawn, the sky behind him fluttering with delicate pinks and burgeoning yellows, swept here and there by wisps of cloud. Jagged peaks rose in the background, but Hemmingford dwarfed these.

His appearance was only marginally as Fleming recalled it to be from the passing social occasion where he had met the industrialist. Hemmingford loomed above the antechamber, with Atlas-like shoulders, one elbow akimbo, the gloved fist propped against his hip. His posture was one of assured command. He was dressed in someone's conception of a general's raiment. Flamboyant epaulets crowned the broad shoulders. The blue tunic was crossed by a gold and crimson sash. Gleaming medals decorated the barrel-like chest. A sabre was hung from the opposite hip, and scarlet piping marked the trousers above a pair of glossy boots. One had the impression that this lofty figure had only recently finished conquering the world.

Hemmingford's radiant mane of white hair was a halo about his fearsome features. His solid brows rose to two points above a pair of dark cunning eyes. The creases of crow's-feet only added to those eyes' shrewd cast. The nose was an aquiline protuberance. White-flecked mutton chops filled out the imposing face. His mouth was a hard uncompromising line with only a hint of fleeting pity for any misguided souls who got in his way. His jaw was as firm as stone.

Portraiture certainly seemed to have a flattering effect on the man, Fleming mused as he counted away the minutes. Hemmingford had kept him waiting nearly half an hour past the appointment he had secured with one of the magnate's secretaries. Fleming would wait. He wouldn't be put off so easily.

In addition to the grandiose portrait, the area was appointed with stately furniture and fixtures. The antechamber, in fact, might have been lifted whole from Buckingham and dropped intact into this high street edifice that was only one of Hemmingford's headquarters. The mogul had heavy interests in banking, oil and merchant vessels. He was a powerful figure whose time was of inestimable value, and visitors were meant to stay fully aware of that at all times.

It was at least warm indoors. The slate skies of the late morning were heavy with brooding clouds. In only the two weeks or so since he'd last been here, the harsh English winter had deepened. The chill seeped mercilessly into one's bones. There had been ice on the ground this morning. The sidewalks had since been trampled into a cold unsightly slush. A westward wind raked London with frigid fingers. Fleming was wearing a grey suit and his wool greatcoat.

He sat stiffly on the red-cushioned lounge. The secretary's desk stood opposite, guarding the cathedral-like doors into Lord Hemmingford's sanctum sanctorum. The woman at the wide desk wore a starched blouse and a severe blue jacket. Her mid-thirties features seemed set in a permanent cast of frosty disdain. Her movements as she filed, stamped and shuffled about her papers were machine-like in their efficiency. Here then might be the forerunner of Winterberg's race of robotic workers. The woman hadn't once glanced in Fleming's direction after he had announced his presence and been told to take a seat.

He wondered how Nora would have handled the situation, what canny artifice she might have employed to bypass this minion and reach Hemmingford.

Thoughts like this came constantly to mind. They rolled tirelessly through his numb consciousness. He was still unable to locate his emotional bearings. It had all been the most wretched of calamities, to be sure. Nora's deceptions. Nora's death. He did not hate her. That much he knew. Analytically he even understood and accepted the motivations of her actions. He had been used, but remarkably he did not feel soiled by the experience. Nora had done what she felt, deeply, she had to do. Only two things had gone wrong with her scheme. She had fallen in love with him. And he had failed to kill Winterberg.

Oscar Winterberg was of no importance. Blake Young's shocking feature had appeared in yesterday's papers. Fleming hadn't read the article. He wasn't especially interested in the grievous backlash against the union leader that would surely follow. Winterberg was finished, just as MI5 had wanted. MI5? Hardly. Just as *Hemmingford* had wanted. Now the magnate's good name was secure, safe from the scandal that his nephew—one of the English couriers for Winterberg's nonsensical communiqués—might have fomented.

It was surprising that Hemmingford had deigned to see him at all. Fleming, after all, had been his pawn throughout this. He was no longer of use, now that the objective had been realized. Had Fleming been unable to secure this appointment, he would have settled for writing the man a letter. A face-to-face encounter, though, seemed more fitting.

An intercom buzzed on the secretary's desk. She listened briefly, then fixed Fleming with an inhumanly chilly gaze.

"Lord Hemmingford's time is considerably precious, Mr. Fleming," said the woman in a tone that bordered on reproach. "He has generously allotted you seven minutes. I suggest you do not waste any of them. Please enter."

He was already up and crossing the antechamber. The secretary thumbed a button on the underside of her desk top, and the arched office doors automatically disengaged and swung slowly wide.

He entered the office. It was a cavernous lair that made the ornate antechamber appear shabby by contrast. Hemmingford had evidently spared no expense to dress his surroundings in the richest, most majestic trappings. Across the immense sweep of immaculately white carpeting lay an array of furnishings and ornaments. Bronze and marble statues posed themselves atop baroquely carved pedestals. A Monet was hung on one wall, alongside what looked to be a Pissarro; apparently Hemmingford had an appetite for the Impressionists. The walls themselves were a gleaming oak. Everywhere one turned there was a startling new object to captivate the eyes. A suit of burnished armor stood sentry in one corner. A pair of crossed cutlasses with jeweled pommels was displayed above a massive hearth, where presently a small segment of log was crackling. The air smelled of sweet wood smoke and tobacco. The space radiated the palpable sense of power and authority one found in a courtroom or before the throne of a monarch.

Fleming paused as the high vaulted doors whispered shut on automated hinges behind him and clicked, locking. He eyed the enormous desk at the distant far end of the office, set before floor-to-ceiling damask draperies of royal purple. The leather chair behind the desk was unoccupied.

He saw movement near the hearth and strode in that direction. Lord Dale Hemmingford was seated comfortably in a plush armchair, elbows rested on the padded brass arms, a snifter held easily between his two hands. He wore a smoking jacket patterned in blue and emerald. He was gazing into the fire, evidently perfectly at ease. His lips were curled into a vaguely amused arc.

"Ah, Mr. Ian Fleming," he said, not lifting his eyes.

"Lord Hemmingford."

"Do sit, my good fellow. Warm yourself. I understand it's beastly cold out today."

A second armchair sat at an angle to the first. Fleming took the seat.

It was possible to recognize Hemmingford from the portrait in the antechamber but only with the aid of some imagination. He wore the same distinguishing mane of thick white hair and the set of rather archaic mutton chops. What that oil painting did not effectively convey, however, was the age of the man. Hemmingford, without that artist's dramatic rendering, looked to be nearing seventy, and the inevitabilities of aging were there for all to see. He sported a thick wattle beneath his chin, which now appeared to be not so firm. The crow's-feet webbing his eyes, rather than complementing his fierce gaze, seemed instead to leave those eyes brittle-looking and somewhat lost in that generally pruning face.

Fleming was puzzled a moment. Surely it would have been more theatrical for Hemmingford to have received him at that desk, at the head of this regal chamber, forcing Fleming to cross the expanse to place himself in this mogul's mighty presence.

Then he realized the effectiveness of this tactic. By receiving him so casually by the fire, Hemmingford was saying deliberately that he feared nothing from Fleming.

"You're wise to flee to the tropics," said Hemmingford, at last turning to look nonchalantly at his visitor. "Our British winters build character in a man. But once one has reached a certain age, they do little but frost one's toes."

If Hemmingford meant to use these seven minutes to engage in breezy badinage, Fleming felt no urge to oblige. He hadn't come here for verbal sparring, merely to deliver a message.

"Nora Blair DeYoung is dead," he said in the same lifeless monotone in which he'd been speaking for some days now.

The elderly Englishman took a measured sip of brandy. The cast of his eyes didn't change, but the vague smile left his lips. "I am, of course, aware of this fact."

"She was killed by a fire poker. The head trauma was lethal. Her left eye was crushed by the blow. If she'd lived, I'm told she would never have walked again."

Hemmingford smoothed a lapel of his smoking jacket. The back of his hand was heavily liver-spotted. "It's a tragic occurrence," he said with something approaching soft sincerity.

"Tragic," Fleming said dully. "It's a fine word. It exonerates all those involved. *Tragic,* one says. And one is free of the onus of thinking about her murder in realistic terms. One is released from imagining that fatal blow to her head, the savage fracturing of her skull and the untold shock to her brain and body. One needn't even give a face to her murderer. Reginald Jessup becomes a player in one of Shakespeare's dramas. He fulfills the role that snuffs out the life of our heroine. He can be loathed for his actions. One can even feel a sense of righteousness that he too has been deprived of his life. But he lacks any actuality, overwhelmed as it all is by the sweeping *tragedy* of the whole affair."

Lord Hemmingford's lips now tightened, emphasizing the surrounding crinkly flesh. "Can this possibly be what you came so far to tell me, Mr. Fleming?"

It wasn't. Fleming had digressed. It was no matter. He realized he could talk philosophically of Nora's death to this man for hours or days on end, and nothing, finally, would ever truly penetrate. Hemmingford was a lofty personage, removed from the base ethics of mortals.

Fleming reached into his greatcoat's deep inner pocket. Peripherally he saw Hemmingford stiffen just the tiniest degree. Did the man imagine he had smuggled a weapon into his inner sanctum? Surely he knew that Fleming had been singled out and searched on entering the building.

"I thought you might be curious as to the noonday headlines of Kemsley Newspapers today. It shall be on the corners and in the shops in, say, another twenty minutes. I've secured an early copy." Fleming tossed the paper onto the top of the liquor trolley parked between the armchairs.

Hemmingford did not reach for it. His brows, as solid and pointed as those in the antechamber's portrait, drew together over his eyes which each ignited now with a small hot flame.

"If you have revealed the wayward doings of my nephew, Mr. Fleming, then you have violated the National Securities Act. The matter is under the jurisdiction of Her Majesty's government. I shall see you charged with treason." His tone was quietly ominous. This surely was the voice he used to terrorize bank presidents and rival oil barons.

It was a hollow threat, but Fleming didn't contradict it. Hemmingford had known all along that the story of his nephew's subversive socialist activities might well come to light; and once the media had hold of it, there would be no squelching the news.

"It's nothing to do with your nephew," Fleming said, standing from the armchair. "I wrote a feature that concerns your involvement with one Reginald P. Jessup. How you contracted this career criminal through Miss DeYoung to uncover discrediting material on one Oscar Winterberg, a name surely familiar to the public at large by now. It is implied in the story—but not outright stated—that you, Lord Hemmingford, had reason to fear Winterberg because of the massive strides he's made in securing rights for workers. It seems you may have feared the bettering of workers' conditions, since that might ultimately diminish the profits of your empire, founded as it is on the use of labor. Jessup, however, ran afoul of some unnamed journalist in San Francisco. That journalist was also investigating Oscar Winterberg. An argument evidently ensued, and that led to mutual murder. We shall see what the public makes of your dealing with so notorious a character. Good day, Lord Hemmingford. I thank you for your seven minutes."

Hemmingford still hadn't reached for the paper as Fleming strode away from the crackling hearth. As he approached the doors, he heard the man fumbling from his armchair. The brandy snifter dropped to the white carpeting.

He didn't look back. Standing at the looming arched doors, he raised his voice in a fierce shout. "Let me out of this damned hole!"

A moment later the doors clicked and swung slowly open. He marched past the flustered secretary, buttoning up his overcoat in anticipation of the outside chill.

Chapter 41

THERE WAS fallout, to be sure. Fleming didn't remain in London to feel the brunt of it, though he was unable to get a flight out until the following early morning. He was sick to his soul of the wintry weather, the ugly shale coloring of the skies, the sting of the wind. Winter was a time of dying. He had seen more than his share of death during and after the war. In San Francisco the body count had risen steeper still. He felt glutted with death. It seemed the Grim Reaper, scythe in hand, was still dogging his footsteps, no matter that he'd renounced his old ways, that he had made vast efforts to sponge away those dreadful memories of his days as an assassin.

Fate, however, in the comely shape of Nora Blair DeYoung, had brought his past into his present. He had murdered again, and once more his basic humanity paid the toll. He did not feel proud of his deeds. He took no real delight even in Jessup's death, though on the cosmic scale that malignant man's demise was well justified. He after all had murdered Nora . . . had staved in her skull with a fire poker, a brutal killing, almost unthinkable in its savagery. Yet, knowing human nature as he did and the awful extremes that men could go to, Fleming *didn't* find it unthinkable. It was just one more item of proof that mankind possessed little that raised him above the animal kingdom.

Perhaps he didn't even possess that. What animal, for instance, could have been manipulated as Fleming had been? He had been maneuvered into nearly killing Winterberg, a man who was himself misguided and delusional to the point of pitying. Fleming had murdered one of that man's bodyguards, the large man in black. He had been forced into the act of taking a life.

Forced. It was a curious word, really. He contemplated it as the four-prop Boeing carried him away from London, away from the horrid chill, away from Lord Hemmingford. Forced. It didn't ring true. He'd had his choices surely. He had *chosen* to involve himself with Nora, to accompany her to San Francisco, to become embroiled in the whole sorry tangle of Winterberg and Davenport and Jessup and Hemmingford. To think of himself as having been forced into those actions was as cheap a bit of self-deception as Hemmingford's self-assuaging use of the word "tragedy" to blanket the reality of Nora's death.

Fleming understood, deep in his heart, that he must ultimately take responsibility for his own actions. Yet that was quite a stone to wear about one's neck. Had he not involved himself in this matter, didn't that then suggest that Nora might still be alive today?

It was a wicked, thoroughly malicious thought. His very being shrunk from it. How much easier it was to think only that Jessup had murdered her, pure and simple, with no untidy afterthoughts about the incident. And how tawdry that was of him to think in such terms, how beneath him or any man with a shred of honor.

He slept through much of the transatlantic crossing, but his sleep was hardly untroubled.

He dreamt in ghastly phantasmagoric colors and imagery. Time warped itself into almost unrecognizable designs in his subconscious. Events from disparate segments of his life bounced and slammed together and eventually melded into one grisly whole. He found himself wandering a battlefield during the Great War, a vast muddy wasteland strung with barbed wire and littered with the bleeding jigsaw pieces of men. The sky was lit with artillery fire. The air smelled—so vivid was the dream that he could actually *smell*—of damp rotting and human decay. He wore a black duster and black fedora. His steps were sluggish, though he knew he must hurry somewhere. Someone . . . someone was waiting for him. A woman, it seemed. Yes, a woman who required his aid in rescuing her father; and her father was on a similar battlefield somewhere—actually some*when* else, in some future war. It was the hideous logic of the dream in which Fleming was trapped that caused this to actually make sense.

He stumbled and reeled through the mud, each step forward increasingly difficult. He was in pain. The copper-colored sky flared all about, and shells burst thunderously. He must be cautious . . . and then he realized that he, Fleming—only his first name was Valentine, his father's name, not Ian—was destined to be struck by one of those falling projectiles. His fate was inescapable. In fact, these events had already happened, hadn't they? They were as etched in history as Valentine Fleming's name was on its headstone.

But the *woman*! He must reach her. Time was growing short for her father . . . only that man too, in his strange future war, was also already dead. Perhaps he wasn't meant to rescue the woman's father after all. Perhaps he was supposed to save her. But from what or whom?

From the Germans. No, nearly. *A* German. Winterberg . . . yes, Winterberg, part man, part robot. He had taken the woman, this woman who was of some vast consequence to Fleming, so important in fact that he was now pushing himself past all bodily limits in his attempt to reach her in time. He slogged on through the slowing mud and his mounting suffering. Each movement now lanced a fresh white-hot pain through his chest. He put a hand to himself. His left hand came away smeared liberally with blood. On his ring finger was a band of white gold.

Of course. He had been shot through the heart. How careless of him to have forgotten. It didn't matter now if that predestined shell dropped on him and scattered him into a thousand fleshy fragments. He was already dead. He'd been shot by the Englishman, the assassin, the cold-blooded killer who had ceased to be human by any definition of the word.

Fleming halted there on the middle of the battlefield. He raised his bloodied hand to the glaring sky, hearing the shrill whistle of the final descending shell and bidding a silent farewell to the woman he'd failed to rescue.

He came awake in his seat with a jolt that caused his cramped right shoulder to pop in its socket. He had been sleeping curled into an awkward position, one that was almost fetal. Luckily there was only one other passenger in his row, a dusky-skinned fellow from the Subcontinent who himself appeared to be sleeping quite soundly.

Fleming's grey suit had grown damp with sweat. It chilled against his flesh as he regained full consciousness, the intensity of the nightmare fluttering away mercifully, leaving him with only fleeting images. He had no desire to examine the lurid dream closely. It had been too rife with potent symbolism. He wondered distantly what a psychiatrist would make of it all.

Lighting a cigarette proved to be something of a chore. His hands were shaking. Eventually he managed to get his gold cigarette lighter near enough to light the Players. He drew in deep lungfuls of smoke, looking to locate the elusive center of himself. He was feeling something different now from the all-encompassing numbness that had gripped him since Nora's death. He felt . . . what? He wasn't certain. Uneasiness, surely. Even trepidation. Not the most attractive of emotions, but at least for the moment he was feeling *something*. Yet he couldn't entirely convince himself the change was for the better.

Merlin Powell had arranged for his flight from San Francisco to London. Fleming had used the remainder of his expenses for this ticket from England back to Jamaica. He hadn't sent word ahead of his arrival. Isaiah, his houseman, wouldn't know to bring to Lagonda Rapier to the airport. That was no matter; Fleming would simply hire a taxi.

Jamaica, a lush tropical gem cradled in the vivid blue-green waters of the Caribbean, came into majestic view beyond the aeroplane's windows. He scarcely spared it a glance. The uneasiness of the nightmare had already evaporated. How empty all the world seemed. Or, more to the point, how empty was he, wandering listlessly about the globe like a barely animated spirit.

Spirit or not, he had certainly made an impact on Lord Dale Hemmingford . . . for what little comfort that gave him.

The B-314 touched down, and he went through the familiar ballet of the terminal's doings. He shed his grey suit jacket and stuffed it carelessly into his suitcase. Ruth, Isaiah's sister and Fleming's laundress, could iron out the wrinkles later. The sultriness of Jamaica's atmosphere cascaded over him as he stepped outside, working its humid fingers into his pores. He knew, clinically, he should feel himself relaxing now, should be drooping into the languid ambience of his tropical paradise. Only he felt nothing beyond the academic acknowledgment that he had closed the circle of a long journey. Or nearly closed it. He had a call to pay before he returned to his house.

"Be needin' a cab, mistah?"

The Negro wore a yellow cotton shirt patterned with purple blossoms. His knee-length trousers were khaki-colored. His smile was wide and serene as he lolled nonchalantly against the bonnet of his taxi. The auto was a rather dilapidated piece of machinery, rust scoring the lower half of its once-white body, like barnacles below the water line of a boat. One of its wheel guards was missing, exposing fully a tire that had once possessed a great deal more tread.

Fleming didn't bother glancing at the other taxis loitering about the terminal's cul-de-sac. One likely was as good as the next.

"I have a fair distance to cover," he said to the smiling driver. "My house is outside of Oracabessa."

"Somet'ing of a trip, dat," the black man acknowledged breezily, apparently undaunted by the challenge.

"Will this contraption make it?"

The driver patted the roof of his shabby auto with what seemed genuine affection. "Dis be mah sweetheart, mistah. She never fail me. Tell you, she break down on da way, I only charge half price. Deal?"

It hardly seemed one, since that would leave both of them stranded somewhere on the road out of Kingston. But it was the man's devoted confidence in his rusting metal beast that settled it for Fleming. The Englishman nodded, and the driver hopped nimbly to take his bag. He held open the rear door, whose hinges squealed painfully, then shut it firmly behind when Fleming was inside. The driver had to press his body hard against the door until the lock managed to engage. The taxi's interior smelled of sweet incense, which nearly overpowered the choking scent of exhaust that rose from the undercarriage when the man performed the complex and arcane rituals evidently necessary to fire the motor. It backfired twice sharply, but Fleming didn't flinch at the gunshot-like reports.

"I've a stop to make first here in the city." Fleming recited the address. "I shall likely be only a little while there. You are to wait for me. Afterward we make our jaunt into the countryside."

"You da boss, mistah. Whatever keep da meter runnin'."

Fleming realized the driver's somewhat exaggerated patois and easygoing banter was meant for tourists, which indeed explained why the man had been dawdling for fares outside the airport. One normally didn't encounter this sort of loose, almost insolent badinage from the Negroes of the island. Fleming naturally took no offense. He had never been able to see why, in the end, the two cultures dominating Jamaica—local and European—couldn't coexist in harmony. There certainly seemed to be sufficient strife in the world without going out of one's way to cultivate it.

The busyness and clamor of Kingston's late afternoon streets washed past the taxi's windows. His driver, whatever else he might be, was an agile driver. He curved and dodged through the crowds, passing mule-drawn carts and trudging lorries, the front fender sometimes coming within inches of the enclosing buildings on narrow streets. He wasn't, Fleming noted, taking a roundabout route to their destination, so as to enlarge his fare. That demonstrated that the man took some pride in his profession—or at least that he had judged Fleming as too savvy to swindle.

Either way, the taxi—running rather smoothly after its dramatic starting—arrived in short order at the squat grey edifice of the newspaper office.

Fleming, though not especially leery of leaving his suitcase in the car, nonetheless took the precaution of pointedly scanning the driver's identification and operating number where the card hung from the rear-view mirror.

"Excellent, Daniel. I won't be particularly long."

"I wait, mistah," he said, cutting the motor and bounding out of his seat to open the rear door for Fleming. This took a bit of forceful wrestling on the driver's part.

Fleming entered the building. He was immediately met by the normal flurry and bedlam of the office. People bustled hastily among the pool of news desks, where typewriters chugged along furiously and urgent phone conversations overlapped.

In some ways this errand was minor. He could wait and see to it later. However, he felt a keen urge to tend to it now, to seal things up. This period of his life, brief as it had objectively been, would be forever marked by Nora's ghost. Fleming wanted it finished . . . as finished as it could be.

He virtually ignored the greetings thrown his way as he sidled through this chaos toward the door to Merlin Powell's office. He rapped once on the glass, then entered without waiting on a response.

Powell was rooted behind his overcrowded desk. His office was large, but the tall filing cabinets covering every wall squeezed the space into something of a rabbit warren. The overhead ceiling fan, which likely twirled its vanes year-round, was lifting the corners of stray papers on the desk top. Powell was just laying his telephone onto its cradle as Fleming entered. A look of sharp surprise crossed the editor's face. He wore a short-sleeved shirt of beige that was inevitably damp beneath the arms.

"Fleming," he said in mild wonder. "Well, this is serendipitous. I've just finished speaking to Mason Caldwell."

The newspaper's lawyer, Fleming reminded himself.

Powell half-rose from his seat in some curious effort at etiquette, gave up the effort and simply waved his visitor toward a chair. Fleming sat.

"Have you just arrived then?" Powell asked. His demeanor was odd, as though he were speaking in the hushed reverence one used when addressing the recently bereaved.

Fleming supposed he did qualify, though even now grief seemed a distant thing at best, separated from him by a dull gulf of insensibility.

"Landed twenty minutes ago," Fleming answered. His tone was nearly uninflected.

Powell appeared disturbed by his remote manner. He shuffled a few errant pages about his hopeless desk. "A pleasant flight?"

"Here is the remainder of my expenses." Fleming took the envelope from his trousers pocket. "I've included an accounting of all the monies I used."

"That should please the financial department," said his editor, taking the envelope and trying out a chuckle that only sounded hollow and false.

"What did Caldwell want?"

Powell lifted his shoulders in a shrug, shifting his bulk in his seat. "Repercussions from this Hemmingford business frankly. Nothing, however, you yourself need to worry about, I should think. Kemsley Newspapers is taking full responsibility for the feature. The fact that your story has boosted our readership to the highest it's been in months hasn't done any harm."

"Lord Hemmingford is taking action then?" Fleming asked, trying—and only marginally succeeding—to rouse some genuine interest within himself.

Powell sighed. He brushed at his brow with an already moist handkerchief. "Hemmingford's in a froth about the matter evidently. He's threatening every conceivable legal action against the paper. He's invoking the National Securities Act as if it were a wizard's incantation."

"He's no grounds to do so," Fleming observed.

"So Caldwell has pointed out. Hemmingford appears to be having the equivalent of a tantrum. I believe you've made a lifelong enemy there. Apparently he's quite eager to have your head on a pike."

"He's welcome to come try to wrest it from my shoulders."

Powell nodded. "Good fellow. That's the stuff. As I said, you've no real worries. Other London papers have naturally picked up the story. It's making for rather something of a scandal."

Once more Fleming recognized the emotions he *should* be feeling—satisfaction, the fulfillment of revenge—but still there was little beyond the dull constructs of such emotions, like blank walls enclosing empty rooms.

"Very well," he said finally, moving to rise from the hard-back chair.

"Fleming." The editor's tone was abruptly grave and forceful. Nonetheless he sounded somewhat leery as he proceeded. "Look, old boy, what's happened to you?"

"I believe you know what's happened to me, Powell." He lingered in the chair, waiting to hear the man out.

Powell nodded. "Yes. Of course I do. The terrible catastrophe of it all. I gather you and Miss DeYoung were quite close. A harrowing enough ordeal without my poking my clumsy nose into it. I'm perfectly aware of that. But"—he grunted in exasperation—"it seems unnatural, this state you're in. I respect your grieving, do believe me. But frankly, man, you more resemble the dead than the living."

The editor bit his lower lip at this last, obviously cursing himself for his indelicate phrasing. Still, it was plain the man was attempting to help.

Yet Fleming could find no words to reassure him. "The resemblance runs deeper than you know," he said stonily at last, standing, moving numbly and exiting the scurrying newspaper office.

Daniel was waiting for him with his wide tranquil smile. When the driver had him neatly caged again in the taxi's rear seat, he regarded Fleming over his shoulder.

"So now we hit da road, mistah?"

Yes, time to go home, Fleming thought emptily. He nodded to the driver.

Chapter 42

Isaiah Hines had known for some days now that something was seriously amiss with his employer. The Englishman had returned unannounced on Wednesday evening, arriving at the house by taxi. He appeared . . . worn. His normally sprightly movements, indicative of a fit body and healthy mind, were absent. He plodded dully through the front door.

Isaiah came racing from the lounge where he had been meticulously dusting the chamber's slatted wood louvres, only to find his own surprised and cheerful greeting met with, "Lay on some hot water, won't you, Isaiah." The Englishman's face was drawn, his usually keen eyes barely focusing on his surroundings. Isaiah had hastily taken the suitcase from his hand. He could think of no direct question he could suitably ask his employer, particularly since the man's manner radiated only one clear signal: leave me be.

Fleming spent something near to an hour in the bathtub, leaving Isaiah to steep in his mounting worries. Patently something untoward had occurred to the Englishman during his vacation, if vacation it had indeed been. It seemed more like he was returning now from combat or some equally grisly hardship. Yet, again, Isaiah saw no clear avenue by which he might question the man. There were traditional restrictions to observe between an employee and employer. Isaiah had been in service too long to trample these long-held customs without sufficient cause; and even if Fleming's present behavior were grounds enough, he was *still* reluctant to do so. The English so often were a withdrawn and unapproachable people anyway, though this man had seemed, during Isaiah's brief service, to be cut from some different cloth. It seemed all he could do was wait.

Eventually he emerged from the bath, looking no more refreshed than when he had entered. He drudged downstairs in his velveteen robe and made straightaway for the lounge. Isaiah appeared in the passageway.

Fleming frowned vaguely at him, not angered but seemingly perplexed, as if he'd forgotten about his houseman's presence.

"Isn't it rather past your hour?"

It was in fact past the time that Isaiah normally departed the house. Circumstances, however, had dictated that he stay at least a while longer, perhaps to further assess his employer's condition. Base curiosity wasn't his motivation. He had no intention of spreading gossip among the other local domestics who served also in foreigners' homes. Isaiah could state firmly that his interest was professional. It was his duty to see to this man's needs. Part of that was knowing and even anticipating his moods.

"Isaiah?" The Englishman was blinking at him, somewhat puzzled.

"Yes, sah," he replied, snapping to full alertness. "I wondered if you might care for dinner. Though I've had little time for preparation, I can surely serve up something to your liking. You need only name your preferences, sah."

"Food," Fleming pronounced, as though the word were only distantly familiar. "I think not. Decidedly not."

"Perhaps I can pour you a drink, sah."

"I believe I shall handle the concocting of my nightcap,

Isaiah. Really, now. It's late. Off with you." He pushed on into the lounge without a backward glance.

Isaiah went reluctantly.

Over the next days he saw only further evidence that some drastic change had taken place in his employer. The mood of the house was now perpetually grim—perhaps not even that. Didn't it seem that the Englishman was betraying *no* emotions whatever, not even sorrow or anger? It further seemed that the man wasn't masking his feelings. He seemed to have returned to Jamaica without any.

The symptoms of his mysterious condition were all equally alarming.

His appetite wasn't what it had been. He evidently cared nothing about the dinner menus Isaiah meticulously devised, accepting indifferently whatever appeared on his plate and then only nibbling sparsely at the food. He was sleeping much later than normal, sometimes until nine o'clock. He spent a good part of his afternoons swimming alone in the cove. He received no visitors and did not venture from the house. He even ignored the correspondence that had stacked up in his absence.

Isaiah remained concerned. In the short time he had been in Fleming's employ, he had developed a not entirely decorous fondness for the man, who was markedly different from most Englishmen and other foreign residents of the island for whom Isaiah had worked in the past. Fleming had always treated him with a kind of unassuming friendliness that was rare between the different colored people of the island.

He did what he could, what little his station permitted. He began arriving earlier at the house than scheduled and stayed well past the time when he was free to leave. His elder sister, Ruth, shared his worries, surmising the Englishman's aberrant state during her brief visits to gather and deliver the laundry; but there was even less that she could do.

Fleming seemed vaguely aware of his efforts, remarking again and again on the long hours Isaiah was keeping.

"You needn't stay, Isaiah," he said with a forced chuckle, a hollow imitation of the Englishman's usual good humor. "I'm quite capable of tucking myself into bed."

"Yes, sah."

Fleming did appreciate his houseman's evident concern, but it was a cold comfort at best. He devoted himself to resettling into the serene balmy rhythms of Jamaica. It wasn't an easy task. His sleep was riddled by almost continuous nightmares, all of them of the same harrowing intensity he'd experienced during his crossing of the Atlantic. Frightening images disgorged themselves from his subconscious every time he closed his eyes. Over and over he watched the large man in black collapse to that corridor floor of peeling green tiles, a bullet through his heart. He saw the lifeless faces of Jessup and Nora. Images of his father and of the Nazis Fleming had dispatched during his secret postwar operation mixed queasily, creating macabre mental narratives. Again and again he failed to rescue Nora from a gruesome variety of fates. He woke in violent starts, perspiring profusely, reaching for the Beretta that he had disposed of in San Francisco.

He wondered, rather apathetically, if he would ever recover himself. Perhaps he was destined to fall slowly into the same mental lethargy as Deborah Byrd. He imagined himself clutching the engraved silver cigarette case, as tightly as Winterberg's illicit second bride had clasped her Bible, staring off into the nebulous middle distance and murmuring inanities about Nora Blair DeYoung. That cigarette case, etched with Nora's simple but potent words, was the only tangible reminder of her that he'd kept. He hadn't wanted any other trophies.

He enjoyed his swims, the way he had seen maimed men in hospitals during the war enjoy their meals as nurses spoon-fed them into their slack mouths. It was an ordinary activity with which to break up the otherwise monotonous day. The sun felt pleasant on his face, the water good against his skin. He was again unlearning that instinct which told him that every time he stepped outdoors he must bundle himself warmly.

Things happened slowly, as they were apt to on the island.

Fleming realized he had been expecting, remotely, that moment when the full weight of his ordeal would come crashing down on him with sudden dramatic force. He imagined that the horror of Nora's betrayal and death would of a sudden pierce him to his soul, that he would cry aloud with the magnitude of it all, that his pent-up grief would finally be vented in one spectacular rush.

That, however, wasn't the way of things. Certainly not for a man who had come of age in England. Melodramatics were not merely unseemly; Fleming didn't even possess the emotional equipment to support such behavior.

It came gradually, riding on the gentle tropical waves that broke around him in the cove. Unexpectedly one day he felt first a tingling anger. This then was his resentment of Nora's ill use of him. What a Mata Hari she had been! How cunning, how calculated her every move. How skillfully she had tempted him. And how, despite the warning of his own instincts, he had fallen under her spell and very nearly done her bidding.

Eventually this anger played itself out, thinning to indistinct threads of bitterness that dissipated themselves on the Undertaker's Wind.

What followed as the days progressed was sorrow. His being became a rich loamy soil of anguish that gave perfect root to the emotions he had been denying himself for weeks now. His heart at last bled for the woman who, he could now slowly admit, had meant more to him than any other in his life.

He pictured her face and body. He replayed in his mind's eye the extraordinarily fine times they had shared. He recalled vividly their lovemaking and the tendernesses she had whispered to him. He was able to regret, painfully, the things he hadn't said to her. But this pain was necessary. He couldn't proceed with life until this business was done, fully.

He wallowed for days in this state of suffering. Isaiah's concern only grew more acute, but Fleming couldn't tell his houseman that it was all for the best. He could only outlast his sorrow.

And he did. It was a step-by-step operation, each stage more hurtful than the last. He managed even to weep, though he was quite unaccustomed to the activity and rightly took himself off to indulge in it, wandering far from the house so as not to further upset Isaiah.

It was all rather . . . cleansing. And eventually, inevitably, his mourning reached an ending of sorts. He would of course never be entirely free of the hurt and sadness, and that too was only proper. Nora deserved to be remembered. Poor tragic woman, he was finally able to think without encountering any of the caustic indictments he'd laid before Lord Hemmingford for his use of the word. Nora was gone. She had loved him. Fleming missed her. But life necessitated that he must now push onward.

So he did.

He was returning from the gleaming white sands and turquoise waters of the cove. The clement breeze brushed his swimsuit and damp body lusciously. The afternoon was bright and inevitably humid, and the air was rife with its organic tropical scents. Insects buzzed across the pathway as he picked his way toward the house. The chill of San Francisco and London was gone from his bones. His step seemed once again to possess that animated spring. He toweled his wet hair as he strolled.

Isaiah appeared on the verandah just as he mounted the steps. The tall Negro servant had a fresh beige towel in hand and wore also that nearly camouflaged look of deep worry that Fleming had grown accustomed to seeing his houseman sporting. He supposed it would be some while before Isaiah realized that he, Fleming, had recovered himself. It would take time, as all things did. Fleming, belatedly, found he was rather touched by the man's concern. It was certainly above and beyond his duties as a houseman.

"Did you have a pleasant swim, sah?"

Fleming traded his damp towel for the fresh one. "Most pleasant. This day is an especially fine one, wouldn't you say?" He offered Isaiah an easy grin.

The houseman returned him a hesitant smile. "Why, indeed it is, sah. May I bring you a refreshment?"

Fleming glanced at the cloudless azure sky. The sun was no longer directly overhead. The day was in the P.M. then.

"Sounds ripping. Something tropical, if you would." He wasn't in the mood for the bitter taste of gin.

Isaiah had spread yet another towel on one of the verandah's lounges. Fleming settled himself with a satisfied grunt onto the cushioned cradle. Yesterday he had taken a first glance at his accumulated mail without opening any of it. There had been a missive from his friend Noël Coward and one from his sister Amaryllis. This evening he would set aside time to read through his correspondence and make replies. It was high time he got on with the business of living.

"Isaiah."

The butler had already disappeared into the house. He reappeared hurriedly, bearing Fleming's cocktail. His eyes were set in an anxious cast.

Fleming chuckled. "No need to look so fearful, my dear fellow. I've merely a question for you. Tell me, Isaiah, do you play chess?"

The houseman blinked. "Why . . . I do, sah. It's a favorite pastime. Ruth and I have spent many an hour hunched over a board."

"Excellent." Fleming took the drink, reclining luxuriously on the lounge. A colorful dragonfly buzzed briefly between them. "I've a chess set about some place. Be a good chap and see if you can't locate it. That is, if you're not averse to a game."

"It would be a distinct pleasure, sah," Isaiah said, a genuine smile curling his mouth.

"Marvelous. We shall while away a bit of this winter then in a comfortable manner." Fleming lifted the beaded glass in a salute. "Chin-chin."